MW00638289

# THE VOW: BOOKS 1, 2 & 3

3

# THE VOW: BOOKS 1, 2 & 3

## THE BILLIONAIRE'S LOVE STORY

### LILY ZANTE

Copyright © 2016 Lily Zante

The Vow Books 1-3 (The Billionaire's Love Story)

Paperback Edition

All rights reserved.

No part of this publication may be copied, reproduced in any format, by any means, electronic or otherwise, without prior consent from the copyright owner and publisher of this book.

The scanning, uploading and distribution of this book through the internet or any other means without the prior written consent of the author is illegal and is punishable by law.

This is a work of fiction. All characters, names, places and events are the product of the author's imagination or used fictitiously and do not bear any resemblance to any real person, alive or dead.

ISBN: 978-1-914467-54-7

# AUTHOR'S NOTE

'The Billionaire's Love Story', is a contemporary billionaire romance serial set in New York and consisting of nine 25k-45k installments. This boxed set consists of Books 1, 2 & 3 of The Vow, the final part of the story, and the books must be read in the following order:

The Billionaire's Love Story:

The Promise (FREE)
The Gift, Book 1
The Gift, Book 2
The Gift, Book 3
The Gift, Boxed Set (Books 1, 2 & 3)
The Offer, Book 1
The Offer, Book 2
The Offer, Book 3
The Offer, Boxed Set (Books 1, 2 & 3)
The Vow, Book 1
The Vow, Book 2

The Vow, Book 3
The Vow, Boxed Set (Books 1, 2 & 3)

Reading Order:

# THE VOW, BOOK 1

**The Billionaire's Love Story (#7)**

# CHAPTER ONE

"Just half an hour with my son, please, Jean. That's all I'm asking for." He'd won his ex-wife's mother over once before and he knew she had a soft side to her.

Colt smiled at Jacob. The boy had grown big. It had been two years, maybe longer, since he'd last seen his son. For one fleeting second, he remembered the chubby toddler in his crib, when they had all lived together, when he'd still been married to Savannah.

Looking back, life hadn't sucked as much as he'd thought.

"We need to go," his ex-mother-in-law said.

"Twenty minutes?" He pleaded. "It's been a while hasn't it, son?" He put out a hand to ruffle the boy's hair and hated the way Jacob moved away from his touch as if he were a leper.

"Don't be scared, Jacob. I'm your daddy. I won't hurt you."

His ex-mother-in-law spoke. "He doesn't know you."

He gave her a hard stare. "See what happens when your daughter won't let me see my son? He can hardly bear for me to touch him."

"It's not as if you've been beating down the door to come and see him."

"Look how far she moved."

"She needed a fresh start."

"I've been trying to come for a visit but your daughter won't let me."

"I can't say I blame her," Jean said, obviously not backing down. "You didn't make much of an effort even when you were married."

He exhaled slowly, trying to remain calm. "I was going through a tough time back then. I'm not here to argue with you, Jean."

"Then why *are* you here?"

"I already told you, I was in town."

"Savannah's not here."

"No?" He feigned surprise. "That's too bad. I wanted to let her know I was here for a couple of days." He hoped to get the money and leave, especially if he was to have a chance of leading a normal life again. Without any body parts missing.

"Why don't you come by on the weekend?"

"'Fraid I can't, Jean." He shrugged and gave her his best look of disappointment. "Can you let her know that I dropped by?"

"I'll do that."

"I was hoping to buy Jacob an ice cream and maybe a comic or a toy. I saw a few stores a couple of blocks away. Are you still crazy about them Ninja Turtles, boy?" Jacob shook his head, and he hadn't yet let go of his grandma's hand.

"All I'm asking is to buy my son a small gift. Can't you find it in your heart to let me? What do you say, Jacob?" But the boy looked at him silently with big green eyes that barely blinked. "Don't be scared. I promise I'll walk by your side, and you can stay close to your grandma."

"One milkshake," Jean insisted.

"Just the one." That's all he needed.

There had been a time once when he'd wanted to try and make their marriage work, but things weren't easy, and he'd lose his temper. Didn't help that Savannah would go whining back to her parents. He was going through a bad time and she couldn't deal with it. Yet sometimes he wished he could turn back time. It didn't happen often, just lately, now that he was caught up in all this shit.

Because life—the way it was now—was completely shit. Seeing Merle and his wife and kids shook him sometimes and made him think about the life he'd let slip by. If he'd still had his job, if he was still earning regular money, if he hadn't turned to alcohol, things might have been different. He couldn't help but take it out on Savannah sometimes when the frustration mangled his self-esteem. She hadn't exactly been supportive and wasn't there for him the way a wife should have been. She was always too tired for him but had plenty of time for the kid. He'd been a douchebag sometimes, but not all the time.

Once she left him, though, it was crazy how quickly his life had spun out of control. Small mistakes had ballooned into bigger problems and now he was in shit so deep that he almost couldn't believe it.

Coming here was his one final chance to fix his life and it was all thanks to Savannah and her new lover.

Jean and Jacob walked behind him and he turned around every now and then to pass the time by making small talk. "Where is she?" he asked, wanting to hear what the old woman had to say about it.

"On a business trip."

"A business trip?" He laughed politely. *With her lover in Miami?* Now that was some kind of business trip, living the good life and servicing her boss. He had a feeling it was going to work out better this way, with Savannah not being here. The more he thought about it, the more he realized that his initial plan might not have worked. She might never have agreed to meet him, might never have given him the chance to hear his sob story. The woman was too smart to fall for anything like that—even though his story, the parts of it he chose to reveal, was true.

"That's right." Her mom was being careful. "A business trip."

"She sure sounds busy," Colt commented. "Looks to me like she's doing good." She had landed on her feet. *Or on her back.* Either way, she was doing better than he'd ever hoped.

*Screwing the billionaire.*

If he played his cards right, her good fortune would soon be his now that life had given him a chance to put things right. His prayers had been answered and with the boy as collateral, he had the perfect solution to his problems.

He looked at the boy again and still couldn't see any resemblance to himself, except for the hair color. Jacob had eyes like his mother's. His were more of a brilliant green where hers were a murkier shade. Hazel she called them, not brown like his own.

The boy caught him staring, so Colt smiled at him, and the boy almost smiled back. A tiny prick of guilt nudged at him, at what he was doing. He wouldn't hurt the boy but even so, this was as dirty as it got, holding his own son for ransom. It was as low as being a drug mule.

He hadn't had much to do with his upbringing, but blood was thicker than water, and there was a bond, even if it was weak. Now that he was with him again, he felt it more. Seeing his son reminded him of what he had missed out on and what he would never get back. Flashes of those moments stabbed at him as they walked down the street to the parade of stores nearby. "Can we call Mommy?" Jacob asked his grandma.

"Let's call her," offered Colt and called the number to his own house. "She's not answering," he sniffed. "Mommy might be busy, or in a meeting or something," he replied, giving Jean a friendly smile.

"Maybe Mr. Stone took her somewhere nice. He always takes us to nice places," Jacob said.

Colt forced a smile. "That's mighty kind of him, ain't it? It's not fair that they're having all the fun. How about we get a milkshake or an ice cream?" he asked. "I feel like I'm missing out on you growing up, Jacob. Sometimes it makes me real sad." The boy attempted a smile.

"We can't stay out too long," Jean cautioned. "Dale will be wondering where I've gone. Maybe I should call him." She reached into her bag and pulled out her cell phone.

"We won't be long, Jean," said Colt quickly. "There's no need to call him. Dale hates me and you'll only make him worry if you tell him I'm here. He'll probably charge right over and take you both home."

She put her phone back into her bag. "Okay, but hurry up."

"How about a nice chocolate ice cream?" Colt asked the boy. "This store looks like it might sell some." He was familiar with the parade of stores because he'd been hanging out around here while killing time during the day.

"Come on," he beckoned to them both and walked in. "What can I get you, Jean?" But Jacob's grandma politely declined and in the end he bought the boy a double scoop of chocolate ice cream and picked the cheapest ice pop for himself.

"How's school?" he asked, as they walked out.

"Okay."

"Just okay? Made any friends?"

"Yeah."

"Yeah? Do they have names?"

"Lenny."

"Lenny?"

"He's my best friend."

"Lenny." He turned to Jean. "He seems kind of settled in."

"He is," Jean replied. "They're both settling in just fine." She glanced at her watch again and looked as if she couldn't wait to get back home again. As if she couldn't wait to be rid of him.

He attempted to set her mind at ease. "There's a store along here that sells toys. I want to buy him a gift, then I promise I'll leave you both in peace." He pretended to look at his watch. "I didn't realize it was that time already. I'd better get back."

"All right," she replied. After a while she asked him, "What kind of work are you doing now?"

*A bit of this and a bit of that.* The truth wouldn't sit well with her, so he lied. "Trucking. I was helping a friend out part of the way, that's how I got here."

"Part of the way?"

"We drove up to Philly and then I got a ride here. It was the only chance I was going to get to come to New York. Seemed a waste to come so far and go back without seeing my boy and Savannah."

Jean wrinkled her brow. "Philly is still a couple of hours away."

"Like I said, I was close by. Closer than being ten hours away."

Jean's mouth twisted, as if she was watching what she was saying. "Helping a trucking friend doesn't sound like a consistent way to earn money."

"I keep my hands in a lot of pies, Jean," he told her stiffly. "It's tough. I never found a stable job that paid as much as my foreman job did but I'm doing the best I can."

*Crazy old cow*, he thought. She never lets up. Always

interfering, always thinking her daughter was too good for him. He turned to Jacob. "What kinds of toys are you into now?"

"Marvel superheroes," the boy mumbled. Jean had paused at the entrance to a small grocery store.

"Do you need to get something?" Colt asked.

She frowned, as if she wasn't sure whether to go in or not. "I need to pick up a few things for dinner."

"Go right on in," Colt urged her. "We'll wait."

"I won't be long. Those avocados look nice and ripe."

"You might as well get them now," Colt insisted and watched as she wandered into the store. "You still like model cars don't you, Jacob?" The kid had liked them when he was three. But the boy shook his head.

"No?" Colt asked. "What do you like?"

"Iron Man, but you don't need to get me anything. The ice cream was enough." Refusing to give in, Colt pulled out his cell phone and scrolled to some photos of his ex and the billionaire that he'd found online. "Look," he said, "Mommy sent me some pictures."

Jacob looked, then wrinkled his nose. "That's not a picture," he said. "That's from a newspaper."

"So it is," mused Colt. "I had some she sent, wait a minute." As he started to scroll through his cell phone once more, a cab turned the corner and slid down the street, coming towards them. He had a split second to decide.

*Why wait to lose Jean later?*

This was it. His only chance. He hailed it down, his heart thumping like he was on drugs. The cab slowed, and he glanced quickly at the store door, saw Jean with her back turned and walking away to another aisle. "Mommy has a surprise for you, Jacob. She's coming home early and she wanted me to bring you to the airport."

Jacob looked and made a face, his eyes dubious. He looked at the grocery store. "What about Grandma?"

"She'll come later." He opened the cab door quickly. "Come on, son."

"But Grandma said—"

*Screw Grandma.* "It's a surprise." He grabbed the boy's arm and pulled him towards the car door and in his haste to get the boy inside, Jacob dropped his ice cream. "Don't worry, I'll get you another one." He shuffled the boy into the cab and slammed the door shut. Sweat licked at the hairs on the back of his neck.

"Drive," he barked, because he had no idea what the hell he was doing.

Jacob looked out of the window, his lower lip trembling, "But Grandma—" He looked at Colt and shrank towards the car door, moving away from him.

"Don't worry about Grandma, son. I promise you Mommy wanted to surprise you. Here, speak to her yourself, if you don't believe me." He got out his phone and it seemed to settle him a little.

Once again he called his own home number. Colt shook his head. "She's still not picking up." *Stay calm,* he told himself, even though his heart rocked violently against his chest. But he knew it wouldn't be long before Jacob figured out he was lying. And he only had a small window of time before Jean raised the alarm.

"Tobias has his own airplane," said Jacob, with a touch of defiance in his voice. This lie wasn't going to last much longer.

"His own airplane?" asked Colt, swallowing hard. The fucker had his own jet, did he? In that case, thought Colt, shrewdly, why not ask for more?

Forty thousand dollars.

It would buy him a pretty good life. It was enough money to pay off Santino and disappear to a new town to start over again.

"Why would Mommy tell you to come to the airport when she's got Mr. Stone now?"

"I told her I was in town," Colt replied, the muscles around his neck cording as he fought to remain calm. "I like the sound of this Mr. Stone," he said, smiling at his son. "He sounds like a good man."

# CHAPTER TWO

She could now make the perfect avocado dip to go along with the chicken wraps for dinner tonight. Jacob loved wraps and he loved her dip even more. Jean stepped outside but her heart pitter-pattered when she didn't see her grandson.

She looked to the right and the left and then across the street. Then she continued to look again, even though her chest tightened, as if an iron fist had landed across it.

Where were they?

And then she saw the ice cream cone lying in the middle of the road. The half-melted dark ice cream bled out into a bigger circle. At that very moment, she dropped her bag of groceries. "No," she murmured, panic rising up her stomach and tearing into her throat. She rested a hand against her chest and blinked a few times, as if the scene might suddenly change and Jacob would magically reappear.

"No, oh, no," her voice caught as she struggled to breathe.

*What had Colt done with him?* She struggled to pull air into her lungs and knew that she should never have left her grandson alone with his father. Had they gone into a store? They had to be around here somewhere. Colt had said he was buying a toy for Jacob, didn't he? He wanted to spend time with his son. She'd only turned her back for a moment.

A fast-fluttering feeling whirled and whooshed around her stomach as fear turned her thighs to jelly. She reached for the wall to steady herself then, taking a few breaths, she started to walk. She rushed frantically along the row of stores, going into each store she came across, desperate to see the familiar bright yellow of Jacob's school t-shirt

"Have you seen a young boy? In a bright yellow t-shirt?" Each time she asked, they all shook their disinterested heads and she rushed out and asked the same in the next store.

Same answer.

They couldn't have gone far.

She crossed the street and rushed along the row of stores on the opposite side, clutching her grandson's coat and schoolbag in her hands, but there was no sign of him anywhere.

Confused and breathless, desperately hoping this was a dream, she walked back towards the grocery store where she had last left them. The enormity of what had happened suddenly gripped her as she felt the tears sliding down her face.

"Are these yours?" An elderly man stopped and picked up her bag of groceries. "What's wrong?" he asked, suddenly concerned.

"I need to call my husband," she croaked, struggling to breathe as her chest tightened even more.

---

"I want to go back to Grandma," cried Jacob, looking more worried by the minute. "Why didn't you wait for her?"

"Because..." He paused. "Because the cab came and we had to leave." It was clear to him that his excuse was so flimsy that a six-year-old could see right through it.

"But why didn't you wait for her?"

*Shut the hell up.*

Colt's patience was wearing thin. He didn't have time for questions and he hadn't had time to think this through. He'd acted quickly—planning wasn't something he did well and this situation was fluid. The cab arriving at that moment had been his one opportunity and he'd leapt at it.

He had been driven to desperation because of the next payment that he knew he could not meet. The thought of Santino forcing him to go on another drug run out of state had spurred him on to carrying out his risky plan. But a whining child by his side was going to give him problems.

He tried to think whether to call Savannah now or to wait a while. But Jean would have alerted her daughter by now and he had no choice but to act on it immediately.

"Where to?" The cab driver asked, staring at him suspiciously through the rearview mirror.

"This is fine," Colt replied, seeing children's swings and a field of grass. A play area. Perfect. It would give him some thinking time. He shoved a few bills at the driver and pulled Jacob out, trying to be as gentle as he could. He didn't want to risk the boy shouting out for help and screwing up his mission.

"What are we doing here?" Jacob asked, looking around. "This isn't the airport."

"Your Mom's flight doesn't get in until later." He grabbed Jacob's hand and led him over to the area where the swings were. "I missed taking you to the park when you were little." Colt put on the friendliest voice he could find. "How about we spend some time here, getting to know each other?"

"Why?"

Colt clenched his jaw. "Why not? Your Mom's flight—or should I say Mr. Stone's jet, doesn't get here for a while."

"Then we shoulda waited for Grandma."

Patience had never been a virtue of his, and he'd never had the time to spend with the boy when he'd been a crying, whimpering baby. Back then, he'd always needed his mother's breast, or his mother to soothe him and it was only later, when he was a toddler, a walking, talking, inquisitive little thing, that Colt had experienced a little more interaction with the child and found him more interesting.

But that had also been around the time that things had started to worsen. The factories in and around his hometown started to close down and a lot of his friends lost their jobs. Mortgage payments went unpaid, and a glut of foreclosures had forced many to leave the area, leaving their houses and their lives behind. At least he'd stayed and tried to make things work. Had Savannah ever considered that he didn't just up and leave when he could have? That he'd tried to find work. So what if he'd needed a couple of drinks every now and then? The pressure he'd been under, the stress of going from a regular income to nothing, was enough to drive anyone to drink.

"I don't want to go to the park! I wanna go home!"

*Shut the hell up, you little shit.*

Colt wiped his hand across his face, spreading the sweat all over it. "Calm down." He tried to damp down his irritation as he pressed his fingers along the bony ridges of his eye sockets. The last thing he needed was for the kid to blow up and have a temper tantrum. His pulse quickened knowing that he had no fixed plan and a miserable child to contend with instead. But he was in too deep now, had come too far, to send the boy back. He couldn't do that, even though he knew this was wrong. Going back home with nothing meant Santino owned him and he could no longer live like that. He needed the alternative. It wasn't fair. Things were working out fine for Savannah. She seemed to be enjoying her life. Why was he the only one suffering?

The jubilant cries of children echoed around the park and plucked him from the darkness of his thoughts. "Go play," he suggested. He needed to call his ex and make the claim, collect the money and leave Jacob someplace safe.

Easy enough.

He'd be back home by Sunday. A free man.

"I don't want to play." The boy looked back at him with hate-filled eyes. "I want to go home."

"I'm calling Mommy. Do you want to talk to her?" Jacob's eyes grew wide and he nodded.

Colt rubbed his brow, feeling suddenly restless as his stomach turned queasy. Pacing around the clump of trees, he called Savannah and felt the boy's eyes on him. Greedy thoughts suddenly besieged him. What if he asked for $50k? The billionaire would pay up, wouldn't he?

But what if he didn't?

He'd based his plan on the billionaire giving a shit about Savannah. What if he didn't? What if the man took Savannah for being nothing more than a good lay? What if he refused to pay?

Colt started to panic, then tried to banish the doubts from his mind.

Forty thousand dollars sounded reasonable.

The call went to voicemail. Angered by the outcome, he raked his hand roughly through his hair and tried to figure out what to do next.

*Damn her.*

She was ignoring his calls on purpose.

And then it dawned on him. She couldn't ignore Jacob. "Here," he said, shoving the cell phone towards the boy. "Leave a message." He knew she'd call him back in an instant once she heard Jacob's voice. Jacob took the cell and waited.

"Mommy," he looked at Colt, his face ashen. "Mommy, where are you?"

Colt listened carefully, his ears Doberman alert. "Da—ddy," the boy said the word as if it were foreign to him, "came to school and took me away and he didn't wait for Grandma. We'll see you at the airport, Mommy." Colt grabbed the cell off him and heard the boy shriek. "I wasn't finished yet!"

But Colt had already turned his back on him. "You'll call me back now, won't you?"

# CHAPTER THREE

I t was blue all around. When she looked up, the sky was a perfect blue and when she looked across, the swimming pool was an azure blue. Miami heaven. Golden sunshine poured down and the 83-degree heat made her lazy.

Every once in a while, she'd dive into the glittering blue pool and cool down. She hadn't been swimming for years and this, having a pool at her fingertips, was a luxury. Swimming was a luxury. She loved the peace and quiet of his beautiful home and the sight of Tobias sitting on the sun-lounger while she glided through the water—all of this was divine.

It hadn't been as hot every day. The weather varied, but it was still beautiful. Every day with Tobias was beautiful. Even if she had been caught in a snowstorm with him, it still would have been beautiful.

She'd been falling headlong and breathlessly, unstoppably, insanely and deeply in love with him. The feeling frightened her sometimes, and she blamed the heat for making her mind go haywire.

Now that he was quiet and working, she sat back on her

sun-lounger and thought some more about his idea. "You think I can do this?" she asked, putting her pencil down.

"Do what?" Tobias asked absentmindedly, his forehead creasing as he concentrated. She couldn't help but stare at him as he sat on the sun-lounger wearing only swim shorts and with his laptop on his thighs.

Tobias in a business suit was the height of Armani cool but now that he was almost naked, except for his swim shorts, and with that body, he was something else altogether; a sight not just for hungry eyes, but for take-me-to-bed-and-screw-my-brains-out ravenous eyes. It was no surprise that most of their time had been spent doing nothing but getting physical.

It saddened her that they would set off just after noon tomorrow so that she could surprise Jacob by picking him up after school. She'd been calling him and her parents every day but as much as she was desperate to see her son again, she knew she would be sad about saying goodbye to this love nest.

Tobias had been right. This place was paradise and she was reluctant to leave the perfect world they had created. He owned her heart now, but as insanely happy as she was, she knew it also made her vulnerable. It was strange how love could do that, how she could feel so deliriously happy and yet anxious too, wondering how long it would last. It was so new to her and it felt strange. Maybe she had to trust life and give herself time to get used to it. Just because her past had been littered with sadness didn't mean her future shared the same fate.

They had gone out for lunch earlier and spent the whole afternoon out by the pool. Tobias had already made plans for the evening. He told her he wanted to cook at home and make the most of their last night together. She knew what that meant and smiled as she stretched out. She could have happily spent another week here with him, could have happily spent her time going from his bed, to the pool, to the bathroom, and kitchen, and all the other places where he had made love to her. There hadn't even been a need to leave the house.

Making love hard and fast, and rough, then sweet and slow and gentle; she would cherish every moment and every memory they had made. She was lost in her thoughts again; easy enough to do given the company and the surroundings.

"Do what?" he asked again.

"This project, the single moms' thingy?"

He turned to her and frowned. "Only if you want to, and 'thingy' won't cut it. If you want to do this, you'll have to be committed and passionate."

"The single mom's *initiative*, then," she said clearly and loudly, enunciating each word carefully.

"I'm not making a dig at you," he replied. "I know how serious you are about your work but if you choose to do this, people will look to you for leadership. If you're vague about it, you won't send out the right message." He was giving her business tips and she was noting them well, filing them away for future reference.

"Understood," she replied, watching how his gaze had dropped to her bikini again. Warming under his gaze, she leaned over onto her side and thrust her breasts out just a little, before running a hand through her hair provocatively. She watched his Adam's apple rise, knew that look when he lifted his gaze to meet hers. She could read him like a book, and right now, his book was red-hot and steamy.

This new white number she had on was especially flattering, now that she had a slight tan. Thank goodness for the sales where she had picked up many bargains and she had been wise to think ahead. She had planned to take Jacob on a small vacation during the summer and had picked up a few bikinis, never thinking she would get to wear them so soon, or with Tobias.

"You know the hardships you've faced, Savannah. If you feel you can make things better for other women in the same situation, and you think you can make a difference, then you should do it."

"Why are you so eager for me to do this?" She was used to questioning every good thing that came into her life, but was it such a terrible thing for him to want to help her set up a charity that would help make life easier for other single moms on a low income? "You're not planning on replacing me, are you?"

"You're irreplaceable."

The charmer. Her gaze skirted over his firm body and she automatically licked her lips, wondering if she could persuade him to come inside for a short while. Not that he would need much persuading. She considered taking off her top and sunbathing topless, as she had tried to do a few times, only she hadn't quite managed it—but knew it was a great distraction tool in her arsenal of seduction tactics.

"But here's the thing," he said, bringing her mind sharply back to business. "My publicity people tell me that giving to causes helps my profile. I say bullshit. I like giving to causes because it makes me happy. I like putting a smile on those children's faces. I like making them happy. Making *them* feel happy makes *me* feel happy. It's a wonderful thing, to be able to do that." But she knew there was more to it when he hosted the Christmas evening at the toy store for the adoption centers. She understood that he needed something else to think about around that time of the year. It had been a crucial element in helping him to get over the death of his wife and their unborn son.

"You're proud of that, aren't you?" she asked softly.

He nodded and she could tell he didn't want to talk about it. "I've made some notes."

"Good," he replied, smiling. "When we get back, I can set up a meeting with a few charity organizers and we can see how this would work. Only if you want to. I won't ever force you."

"That woman who was at our table at the gala dinner, the one who made the speech."

"Brigitte Obenchain?"

She nodded. "She was so confident."

"You can be like that."

She shook her head. "I don't think so."

"Why? It takes practice to learn the speeches. She's a good front person, has good contacts, is slick and professional, but she doesn't have what you have."

"What's that?"

"You've lived it, Savannah. You've experienced the difficulties and you know exactly what you're talking about. She's just *talking* about it but she has no real frame of reference. You'll come at it from a different perspective. I could introduce you to each other, if you like. Maybe you could run your ideas by her and we could take it from there?"

"Let me think about it." She loved the way his gaze traveled over her body and she breathed in a little, hoping to tighten the stomach that had seen a good tasty salad lunch. Her cell phone rang and grabbed her attention but she made a face and ignored it when she saw Colt's name on the caller display.

*Why didn't he leave her alone?*

This was the third time he'd called in the last few days. As before, she ignored it again. The first time he'd called, she'd mentioned it to Tobias and he'd been mildly irritated by her ex's intrusion. Since then, she'd had it on a low ringer, but was always checking in case her parents or the school called.

"I need another half an hour to finish up on this," Tobias said, turning his attention back to his work.

"Half an hour?"

"Then I'm done for the day. No more work, I promise." He looked longingly at her. "Make it fifteen minutes," he said, his eyes signaling sinful pleasures ahead. She smiled as her body started to respond in anticipation.

"Fifteen minutes," she said, picking up her phone and seeing a voicemail message appear. She lay back on the lounger with her eyes closed and listened.

The sound of Jacob's voice was like a burst of sunshine yellow happiness straight to her heart. But his first word shocked her like a bucket of ice thrown over her. *Daddy?*

*'Daddy came to school and took me away and he didn't wait for Grandma. We'll see you at the airport, Mommy.'*

Her breath stuck in her chest as she bolted upright, her feet hitting the ground as she replayed the message. It had come from Colt's number.

Everything around her turned into a mirage of sounds and images.

*What was Jacob doing with Colt?*

The hairs on her neck straightened up and she whimpered as she replayed the message a third time. She stood up, shaking all over and heard Tobias by her side. "What's wrong?" But she blocked him out and called Colt.

He picked up on the first ring. "What's going on?" she asked, struggling to make the world stand still again. She felt as if she was spinning out of control, as if the ground was shifting beneath her feet.

"Got your attention, did it?" Colt said, in that slow, rough voice she had come to hate.

"What're you doing with my son?"

"In my own sweet time, sugar. In my own sweet time."

"Let me speak to him!" she shouted. Tobias had put his

hand on her arm but she shook it free and moved away. Her heart dropped lower, hitting the base of her stomach and suddenly, she felt weightless. Thoughts flew around in her mind as she struggled to make sense of his words.

*What was he doing in New York anyway?*

Where were her parents?

The pounding in her ears made her nauseous and she struggled to keep the afternoon's lunch down.

"I figured you might take notice of me if I got Jacob to call you."

"Let me speak to my son, you asshole!" she screamed, seeing only Jacob's frightened face in her mind's eye. Her son was already scared of the man and it chilled her to the bone thinking that he was with him now.

"Listen up, sugar," Colt's unnaturally quiet voice frightened her even more. She'd heard of men who wanted to get revenge on former wives and ex-girlfriends, had heard of the things they had done to spite their former lovers.

"If you want him back," Colt threatened.

*If I want him back?*

What was he talking about?

"Of course I want him back!" Her legs crumbled as she fell stumbled backwards, falling into something warm and solid. Tobias's arms.

"Calm yourself down and listen carefully."

"I'm listening." She was almost hyperventilating but she forced herself to listen, already expecting the worst as she pushed her ear closer to the phone. She thought she could make out the sound of children playing in the background.

"Please don't hurt him," she begged.

"Shut the fuck up and listen to me. I don't have a lot of time. If you do as I say, nothing will happen to him."

She gasped.

"I haven't hurt him," he said, his voice suddenly losing the aggression. "But he's a miserable little runt, ain't he? He don't want anything to do with me. You've done a good job of poisoning him against me, haven't you?" She wanted to tell him that she'd done no such thing but kept her mouth shut.

"What do you want from him, Colt? He hasn't done anything to you. If you're angry with me—"

"I wanted to spend some father and son time together," Colt said. The color drained from her face at his words and she looked up to find Tobias's gunmetal blue eyes on her. His head was tilted as if he was trying to listen in.

*Father and son time?* Her breath caught in her throat.

"You could have just asked me."

"You never answered your phone," his voice was getting louder again. "I called you enough times."

"What is it that you want, Colt?" she asked, trying to keep calm.

"Money. That's all. I'm in trouble, and this is the only way I know you will listen and help me."

*Money? He had taken Jacob for money?*

"What kind of trouble?"

"Trouble that $40k can set right."

She gasped. "Forty thousand dollars?? What have you been—"

"Don't ask questions," he barked, unsettling her further. "I want the money in my bank account in the next hour and if you do that, you'll get Jacob back."

"He's your son!" she cried out. "How could you do this?" The words stuck in her throat like a knife and all she could picture was Jacob's big green eyes filled with tears.

"No drama. I don't have a lot of time. Just get me the money."

"But I—I—I don't have that kind of money."

"Your lover does."

Tears rolled down her face. "Please, please don't do this..." She felt her chest tightening and her mouth drying up as she struggled to swallow. "It's not my money," she croaked through sobs. "I don't have it, I can't...I can't..."

"You want your son back, don't you?"

"He's your son too..."

Tobias placed his hand on her arm, trying to draw her attention. Worry had colored his face dark and twisted his features but she refused to hand over the phone. She blocked his voice out, tuning in to Colt and his demands.

"I want the money, Savannah. If I don't get it, I'll be dead within days. I know what I done is wrong. I know that after this, you won't want anything to do with me but I'm as good as dead. There ain't no other way out for me aside from this."

"Let me speak to him. I need to know he's okay."

"Did you hear me?" he roared. "Did you hear a word I said?"

"Yes, yes, I heard you but before I can help you, I need to know that Jacob is fine."

She heard him shout out. "Jacob!"

A few seconds later, she heard Jacob's mouse-like voice. "Mommy?"

She fell to the ground at the sound of it. "Honey?" Sheer relief swept over her mind and soul and she was handed a sliver of hope. "Are you okay? Has he hurt you?"

"He said we were going to the airport to get you. He pushed me into the cab, Mommy. I'm sorry we left Grandma behind."

She stifled a sob. "No, honey, it's not your fault. You didn't do anything wrong. I'm coming to get you. You be good now, okay? Promise me? Be good and do as he says, and Tobias and I, we're coming as fast as we can. I love you, Jacob, just you be strong for me for a little longer."

"Hurry, Mommy, I really miss—"

But Colt was back on the line.

"You listen to me very carefully," he snarled.

"You touch a hair on that boy's body and—"

But Tobias had pried the phone from her before she could finish.

# CHAPTER FOUR

The bastard. Tobias couldn't stand there a moment longer. He'd pieced it all together from the words he'd caught, from the way Savannah had broken into pieces in front of him.

Brookes had Jacob and he wanted money in return.

*How had she ever met up with a pig like him?*

Tobias didn't need Savannah to tell him that Brookes expected *him* to make the payment. He'd do it in a heartbeat, too. The bastard could have whatever he wanted—anything, for Jacob's safe return.

With his stomach hardened like steel, he grabbed the phone from Savannah. His lips drew back in a snarl. "What do you want, Brookes?"

"You must be the new man in her life," the lowlife snorted.

"Cut the bullshit," growled Tobias. "How much?"

"Forty thousand dollars should do it."

"I'll take care of it."

"I knew you would."

Tobias bit his teeth together as he pictured his left fist smashing into the man's face, breaking bone and spurting blood. "You harm a single hair on that child's head and I'll—"

"You'll what? I call the shots here, asshole," Colt barked back. Tobias breathed in slowly, forcing himself to calm down. He couldn't lose it, not while the man had Jacob. "Tell me where and when."

"How 'bout in an hour?"

Tobias glanced at his watch. He knew that even if they left right now, as he planned to, they wouldn't touch down in New York until after 7:00. "I'll get someone to come and make the exchange," he offered. "We won't make it back until around 7:00."

"How about that?" croaked Colt. "The two of you shacked up all the way in Miami. Kept you busy all night, did she? I hope it was worth it." Tobias's fists balled up as he tried to restrain himself.

He could have Ludwig deliver the money. Ignoring the man's jibes, Tobias continued, "Five o'clock then. I'll get the money to you but here's what I want—"

"Now you hang on a min—"

"I'm assuming you don't want the police involved, do you?" Tobias said, his voice as cold as steel. "Something tells me you would prefer to keep this between you and me."

"Yeah," the man replied. "No police or reporters or anything."

"Give me your bank details and I can get the money into your account now. Tell me where you are and I'll send someone over to get Jacob."

"Wait." The man sounded nervous, his earlier facade slipping all of a sudden. "No bank transfer. I need cash."

"Cash?" Tobias growled.

"Yeah. Yeah. Definitely cash." The man paused, making Tobias think that he was in a panic. "Cash is what I want."

"No problem," Tobias replied smoothly. From the report Ludwig had given him a few months ago, he recalled that the man was in debt. He sensed the man's desperation, even though he couldn't get his head around what he'd done to his own son. "Within the hour," Tobias told him. "You better take good care of Jacob." He warned, his concern for the young boy growing. He vowed to get him back as fast as he could.

"You're talking like he's your son."

"Maybe you should try acting like he's yours," he snapped. "Let me speak to him."

"We don't have time for—"

"Let me speak to him." Tobias thundered. A few moments later, he heard a quiet voice.

"Mommy?"

"Jacob? Hey, buddy, it's me. You hang in there for me, okay? We're coming to get you."

"When will you get here?"

"As soon as we can, Jacob. I wish we were there now. But, listen carefully, buddy—I need you to be strong, okay? You think you can do that?"

"I think so."

"Sure you can, Jacob. Like Iron Man, remember?"

"Like Iron—"

"That's enough," Colt snarled, coming back onto the line. "Tell me where to meet you."

"How well do you know the city?" Tobias asked, making a mental note to meet with Colt later and smash his face to pieces.

"Not too good, but I have a map."

"We could meet outside the Empire State Building," Tobias suggested.

"Ain't it busy around there?" Colt asked, suspiciously. "I don't trust you and you might do something stupid."

"As much as I'd like to put a bullet through your head, I wouldn't waste my life serving time for you," Tobias replied coldly. From the corner of his eyes, he saw Savannah staring at him with her pale face and sunken eyes. "What about the corner of East Thirty-Third Street and Fifth Avenue? It's around the block from the Empire State Building. There's a Wendy's close by. Outside there?"

"Wait, I need to write it down."

Tobias shook his head when he heard the man mumbling to find something to write on and a pen. When he came back on the phone, Tobias repeated the location.

"Don't forget. Forty thousand dollars and not a dollar less." He hung up and Tobias slipped the phone into his pocket just as Savannah reached out with her hand. She was shaking.

"I wanted to speak to Jacob."

"I'm sorry but he hung up." She looked like a shadow of the woman she had been up until a few moments ago.

"I've got this," he said, pulling her towards him and holding her as she crumbled against his chest, sobbing uncontrollably. He remembered what he'd promised her only yesterday; to keep her safe and from harm and he had already failed.

"You have to be strong, Savannah." He lifted her chin up and wiped away her tears. "We told Jacob to be strong but we have to be strong as well." His voice wavered because he couldn't bear for any harm to come to the boy. "He'll get the money and we'll get Jacob back."

"I don't have that kind of money."

"But I do. I'll take care of it." This was as much his problem as it was hers and he was as anxious to get Jacob back as much as she was.

"But he wants $40k."

"And I told you," he said slowly, "I'll take care of it. I care for that boy, and I want him back as much as you do."

"Thank you," she mumbled, rubbing her wet tears into her skin.

"Don't ever thank me," he replied. "Jacob is like my..." He

stopped and rubbed his hands along her arms. "I can't bear the idea of anything happening to him."

"I hate him," she hissed against his shoulder. "I never thought he could stoop this low."

"Don't waste your breath on him. Get changed while I arrange for a car to come and get us in ten minutes."

"How long will it take to get back?"

"Almost three hours."

"But you said you'd meet him within the hour."

"We won't get there in time but by the time we land, my head of security would have made the drop. Mark my words, Savannah, we'll be spending the evening with Jacob. That's all I want you to think of."

"I have to call my mom," she said. He took out his cell phone and called Ludwig.

# CHAPTER FIVE

H e ran as fast as his sixty-four-year-old legs and his chest condition would let him.

His wife's incoherent rambling and tears on the phone had raised the hairs along his back and he'd rushed out of the apartment, following the route to the school.

But Dale Page wasn't prepared for the sight of his wife in pieces.

Even from a distance, a chill sliced through his skin when he saw she was alone.

*No Jacob.*

He hadn't misheard.

Jean rushed towards him with tears streaming down her face and clutching Jacob's belongings. She was a breathless bag of nerves as she fell into his arms. For several painful seconds, she muttered and spluttered incoherently, his mind spewed out images of police tape and blood and darker life-changing horrors.

"Hey, hey," he said, stroking her hair while his lungs froze up and his body became lightweight. He knew time was of the utmost importance but he had to calm her down first.

"Tell me what happened, Jean. We need to call the police quickly."

"Colt took him," she replied, her faint voice wavering.

"Colt Brookes?"

"He said he wanted to see his son and that he was in the area and wanted to meet." He listened to his wife explain what had happened and she cried through the retelling of the incident. She was such a mess and crying so hard that a small group of people had started to form around them.

"Did you call Savannah?"

His wife shook her head. "I was so scared; I just wanted to come back to you. I didn't know what to do."

"It's all right," he said, taking a few moments to calm the ferocious beating of his heart. If there was any relief in any of this, it was that his grandson wasn't with a complete stranger. That had been Dale's first worry. The fact that he was with his father was a slight relief, only just. He had never been too fond of the man his daughter had married but he had respectfully minded his own business and then supported her when she had left him. He suspected his daughter hadn't told them everything but from the few things she had let slip, he disliked the man even more. Her moving away to a new city had been the best thing for her. Being near Brookes would have held her back. The man was selfish and controlling, but this—taking his own son—it was a new low, even for a scumbag like him.

"We need to tell Savannah."

Jean sobbed on his shoulder. "I only turned my back for a few moments, that's all. I never thought he would take Jacob. I was stupid to trust him."

"Calm down, Jeanie." Dale took his wife's hand and started to walk back towards the direction of the apartment. "Don't beat yourself up. We both know what he's like." He was desperate for answers. What did he want with the boy? Why now? It was almost as if he'd been waiting for Savannah to go away. While he soothed his wife, he called his daughter's number again and once more her line was busy. He wished she were here so he could tell her in person. Not like this, not on the phone when she was miles away.

They were almost near the apartment when his cell phone rang. "Daddy?" From the panic in her voice, he could tell she already knew.

"Ruby Red."

"Daddy, Colt's taken Jacob." She burst out crying.

"Is it Savannah?" Jean whispered. He put a finger to his lips as they crossed the street.

"I know, Ruby Red. We've been trying to call you. Did he call you? Is Jacob all right?"

"He called and said he wants money. He wants $40k in exchange for Jacob." He absorbed the information slowly, the words filtering through to his brain and made his blood boil dark red. He quashed an urge to lash out and kick the lamppost.

"Is that why he took Jacob? For money?"

"Yes." His daughter sniffled on the other end of the line.

"And Jacob?" he asked, his heart squeezing to the size of a walnut. "How is he doing? Were you able to speak to him?"

"I spoke to him and he seems fine for now, Dad. Whatever Colt is, he won't hurt Jacob," Savannah said. "He won't. I know that much."

"Jacob's a brave boy," Dale agreed. "He's sensible."

"I know." Her voice wavered, and he heard her sniffling, felt his own heart crumble in the silence that separated them, in the worry that filled that space. Dale hadn't ever trusted or warmed to Colt Brookes before and he now regarded the man so immoral as to be inhumane. Who would kidnap his own son for ransom money? A man like that didn't deserve to be a father.

"How does he expect you to come up with that kind of money?"

"He knows Tobias is wealthy."

Ah. He understood it now, why that cockroach had crawled out into the open in the first place. Somehow, Colt had found out about Savannah and her new man. If a man like Dale had been able to look Tobias Stone up online, then so could anyone else.

"We're on our way back but we won't get there for a few hours. Tobias has a plan. Can I talk to Mom please, Daddy? I need to know how Jacob was before Colt took him."

"Don't worry, Ruby Red. We'll come through this and Jacob will be fine." He handed the phone to his wife and listened as she sobbed, and recounted what had happened.

"I'm sorry," she kept on saying.

He squeezed her hand as they walked into the lobby of their apartment. The elderly concierge looked concerned to see Jean crying but Dale shook his head, choosing not to explain.

# CHAPTER SIX

The whole time they were being driven to the airport, Savannah had been on the phone with her parents. But when she hung up, she looked even more panicked than ever.

"What is it?" he asked, his brow creasing with concern.

"Jacob doesn't have his inhaler. He gave his school things to my mom." She sat back, crumpling into a heap against him.

"He'll be fine. We only have to wait an hour. Ludwig's working on it."

She wasn't convinced. "Don't you see?" she murmured, looking at him with red, spider-veined eyes, "If anything happens to him, it could be fatal."

It *would* be fatal if Jacob suffered an asthma attack and had no medication on hand. Tobias knew Savannah would focus on this, but what were the chances of that happening? There was no use in dwelling on negative things now, they needed to keep it all together. He had to take her mind away and have her focus on the positive—that they would get Jacob back before such a thing happened. "Is he prone to getting attacks?" Tobias asked. The weather was mild and Ludwig would have the boy within the hour. Colt would get what he wanted and he saw no reason for the plan not to go smoothly.

"He doesn't plan for them," she replied bitterly. "They can happen at any time, if his lungs get exacerbated."

"It's going to be all right, Savannah." He checked his phone and read the text. Ludwig had told him it was going to take a little longer to get the money in cash. Maybe an extra fifteen to thirty minutes. Meeting at five would be pushing it. Tobias also wanted to make things easier for Jacob, and he needed to call her parents to explain what he had in mind.

He turned his attention to Savannah. "Don't focus on the inhaler."

"Don't focus on it!"

"He hasn't had any problems with asthma since winter, has he?"

She shook her head.

"Then let's concentrate on getting him home and safe tonight. By the time we land, we'll all be together."

"How can you be so sure?" She turned away from him and stared out of the window. "Please don't make any more promises." She was referring to what he'd said yesterday.

"I meant what I said yesterday, but I just didn't know that your ex was capable of doing this."

She turned back to him and put her finger to his lips. "But I nearly believed you." That hurt even more. Tobias looked at her, at her sunken, red-rimmed and swollen eyes with worry lines that stretched out at the corners. The sexy woman in the white bikini had faded away.

He wanted to hold her and comfort her but there was something hard and cold about her all of a sudden. "Don't push me away because of this. I meant what I said. I *will* protect you." He would make damn sure of it, now that he knew what he was up against. He watched as the security men carried their luggage into the plane. When they returned to New York, he would ensure that she and Jacob had security at all times. "Come on," he said, "we need to board."

As they settled down into their seats, he told her. "He's asked for cash."

"That much money in cash?" Her mouth made an 'O.' "Who's taking it to him?"

"Ludwig, but it's going to take a little longer than an hour. Maybe an hour and a half, maybe two. I want it to happen as fast as possible and right now I need you to send me photos of Jacob and your parents so that I can send them to my men. I also need to speak to your parents."

"Why?"

"Jacob doesn't know Ludwig and I don't think he should make the exchange. Jacob will be even more scared when he sees another stranger. I think it would be better if one of your parents went instead."

"My mom could do it." She searched through her phone and sent him the photos he needed. "My dad hates Colt and he might say something that could make things worse. My mom would be the better choice."

"Does he carry a gun?" Tobias didn't want to risk an already nervous man getting panic-stricken. "I'll have my men watching him from a distance but I don't want him to do something unexpected at the last moment."

"Not that I'm aware of," Savannah replied. "He might do anything. I never expected this from him, but the man is full of nasty surprises."

"Thanks," he said, and sent the photos to Ludwig.

"Don't you need a photo of Colt?" she asked as she searched through her phone. "I don't actually have one. I deleted them all."

"Don't worry about it," he said quickly. She didn't need to

know that he already had a photo of her ex. "Jacob will be with him, and that will be enough." His answer seemed to satisfy her.

"I still don't understand why he wants all that money," said Savannah, a slight frown settling on her face. "What is he going to do with $40k?"

Tobias wasn't about to tell her what he'd uncovered from the updated report that Ludwig had sent while they'd been driven to the airstrip. His trusted head of security had underground contacts and ways and means of obtaining information. Tobias didn't need to know how he collated his intel but he had now learned that it was possible that Brookes had mixed with the wrong people. People he probably owed money to; people who dealt in drugs. He didn't know how far Brookes' involvement was but it might explain why he needed so much money in cash. For now, he chose not to say any of this to Savannah.

"He's being greedy and he most likely thought to ask for as much as he could," Tobias replied. Maybe the man had intentions of starting over and going someplace new.

Tobias hoped so. That plan of his would suit him well. If anything, it surprised him that Brookes hadn't asked for more. "Can you give me his number?" Tobias asked. "I need to tell him that we're meeting at 6:00—and hope it's not a problem." That would give him enough time to speak to her parents and arrange for them to be picked up and taken to the meeting point.

Tobias wasn't about to let history repeat itself. He wasn't prepared to lose two more people whom he had come to love.

# CHAPTER SEVEN

"**E**at up," Colt growled, as the boy's burger and fries lay untouched.

Stone had called to tell him he needed more time to get the money and to get the boy's grandmother to the meeting place. To kill the time, and because the kid was complaining that he was hungry, Colt had taken him to a diner a few blocks down.

Six o'clock, Stone had said. The boy's grandma would meet and give him the money in exchange for the boy. He pushed away the thoughts of what his former in-laws might now think of him. They hadn't had a particularly great relationship before and what he'd done now would be the end of it.

He watched Jacob as he sat miserably playing around with his full plate of food. "I thought you were hungry."

"I'm not no more."

With the promise of the money coming to him soon, he was no longer in as foul a mood as he had been in earlier. Out of all the shitty things he'd done, and he'd done plenty, the kid didn't deserve this. "Look, Jacob," he said, leaning forward. "You gotta eat something. We might be a little later than I had planned. I know this don't feel right—me and you sitting here and you're probably worried about your mom and your grandma but you'll see them again soon."

The boy's eyes narrowed to slits. "Why can't you just take me home?"

"Because I've arranged to meet your grandma downtown in an hour." Not that this would make sense, he had a feeling that his own son was far too clever to fall for the bullshit he'd been feeding him. "Eat a little bit."

"I'm not hungry."

"Are you always such a miserable little—" He stopped himself. *Runt.* Instead he grabbed a few fries from his son's plate. "Your mom will think I didn't feed you."

"My mom hates you."

Colt sighed and wiped the cuff of his shirt across his sweaty forehead. The kid sure hated him and he only had himself to blame. Getting out of their lives for good would be about the best thing he could do for them. "Soon as you finish those, we can go." He looked at his watch and the city map he had on him and figured he'd need to get a cab to the Empire State Building. It looked to be around twenty minutes away, and they still had time.

"Why's Grandma coming?"

"Because..." Colt stopped and chewed on a fry while he pondered. He didn't want to admit the real reason. "You ask a lot of questions for a seven-year-old."

"I'm not seven, I'm six."

Colt frowned. "Six? Yeah," he remembered. "Six."

"You told me we were going to get Mommy from the airport. You lied."

"Your mommy is coming home early. Aren't you excited about seeing her?"

"I'll be happy to see her *and* Mr. Stone." There was defiance in the boy's voice. "Mr. Stone loves Mommy."

"Is that right?" he drawled, pilfering more fries from the boy's plate.

The boy nodded. "He's the best friend she ever had and he cares about her. He cares about me too."

"I bet he does," sniped Colt, his anger rising. A man would do anything to get some pussy. *Filthy little slut,* he thought, working for someone like Stone and ending up in his bed. He hoped the man was only using her; screwing her while he had the chance. Something she'd never been too keen on doing with him once Jacob was born. "Why do you call him Tobias sometimes and Mr. Stone other times? Can't you make up your mind?"

The boy said nothing.

"Eat your cheeseburger, Jacob."

"I don't want it."

"Stubborn little thing, ain't you? Just like your mother."

"I want to be like her," the boy shot back. "It's better than being like *you.*"

Colt ground his jaw and resisted the urge to slap his hand against that little face. He knew he couldn't lay a finger on his precious cargo and he struggled to maintain a modicum of restraint. It was a relief to hear his cell phone ringing. But he almost choked on his fry when he saw who was calling him.

What the hell did Santino want? He never called unless there was a problem and there shouldn't be a problem because he still had a few days to make the next payment. That was when he intended to clear all of his debt and disappear. It was the main reason why the timing for this mission was so crucial. "Santino," he said, shifting his body to the side, away from the boy.

"Any reason why you left town?" the man asked.

"Who's lookin'?"

"Word gets out. You have a payment due."

"Not until Sunday."

"Need you to do another drop."

*No way in hell.* "Can't do it. I'm in New York but I'll make it back in time for the next payment."

Santino laughed. "You sure about that?"

Feeling brave, Colt told him, "Yeah, I'm sure."

"'Cos I'd hate for you to miss a payment."

"Screw you and screw your payments." Not with $40k coming his way. The lure of easy money made his tongue loose and he could almost feel the wad of money in his hands. Jacob stared at him across the bright red Formica table, his eyes like two big shiny marbles, his mouth open.

The line went silent for a few long, drawn-out seconds. Colt tried to still his breathing as he waited for Santino to say something. "You need discipline, Brookes, and I'm going to make sure you get it when you come back."

"Here's what's going to happen, Santino. I'll come find you when I get back and I'll have enough to pay you scumbags off forever." He'd heard of what had happened to the others, the ones who could no longer afford to pay back the debt that had been inflated to such a ridiculous amount that it would never be cleared.

Unless the sucker won the lottery.

That sort of thing wasn't going to happen to him, thanks to Tobias Stone. "You sound confident, Brookes," said Santino. "I hope for your sake you make good on your promise."

Colt knew he couldn't fuck up now. "I'll have your money and I know where to find you." He hung up, a cruel smile twisting his narrow lips. "Damn assholes," he muttered, taking a slurp of his Coke. He'd be glad to be rid of them even if the manner in which he expected to procure the money meant he would have to give up his rights to ever seeing the boy and his mother again. After this, Savannah would hate him more than she already did. She hated him anyway, but doing this was sure to seal his fate.

*Tough shit,* he thought bitterly. There wasn't much he could do about that now. He needed the money.

Damn Santino for calling him out of the blue. It had rattled his nerves further. "What are you staring at?" He barked at the boy whose huge saucer-shaped eyes were unblinking in his direction. Jacob bowed his head, his lower lip trembling.

*Pussy,* thought Colt. That's what he had for a son. A goddamn pussy. A lily-livered, miserable little runt of a child. That's what being raised by a whimpering woman did.

"Who were you talking to?" Jacob asked.

"None of your business," Colt snarled back. He stared at the uneaten burger which lay on the boy's plate. "You're not going to eat that?"

The boy shook his head. "I need to go to the restroom."

"Go on and come straight back." He picked up his son's burger because he wasn't going to waste good money. The boy had only had his milkshake. At least it was something and he couldn't complain to his grandma or his mother that he hadn't been fed. Colt stared at his watch. He had almost another hour to drag it out.

He sat back, chewing on his burger and thinking about how much his life was about to completely change. He would make the exchange, spend one night at the motel and hitchhike back to North Carolina tomorrow. It was going to take him a full day to reach home. Maybe he could stretch to taking a train or a bus this time. He'd be able to afford it now and it would be safer than getting a ride in a stranger's car carrying such a large amount of money.

Smiling, he took a chunk of the burger and chewed it slowly.

# CHAPTER EIGHT

H er eyes were closed as she listened to Tobias make plans with someone named Ludwig. Her heart filled with hope, and she prayed that she would soon have her son in her arms.

The thought of her son with Colt, a man he barely knew and a man whom he feared, made her heart ache. She couldn't imagine the terror he'd be going through. Jacob rarely spoke about his father, and the few times that he had mentioned him had been to say that he was happy they had moved away from him. It killed her to imagine the way in which that brute had wrenched him away from his grandma.

"What are you thinking?" Tobias asked, putting his cell phone away. He'd been on the phone most of the time, making arrangements. She had no idea how many men he had at his disposal, but if anyone could help her now, it would be a man like Tobias Stone. His fingers touched her cheek lightly as he sat down beside her. "I know you're scared, and you're worried but Ludwig's with your parents now and he's taking them to the meeting point. It shouldn't be too long now."

"Jacob will be so scared," she whispered. A different kind of fear than she had ever known before took hold. It was worse than what she'd felt when Colt had hit her. This was a thick and suffocating heaviness that now settled over her body and pushed her spirits to the ground.

The worry of Jacob having an attack now, with no inhaler on him, made her sick inside but she couldn't dwell on it now. Tobias was right, she had to be strong for Jacob's sake but it was easy for Tobias to tell her to focus on the positives. Jacob wasn't his son.

She felt his warm hand on hers and didn't pull her hand away.

"Why can't we put out an Amber Alert?" she asked.

"He said no police. He just wants the money, Savannah. I'm getting it to him as fast as we can. I can pull strings but I can't push it to an Amber Alert, and I don't think, even if I was lucky, it would happen fast enough. We don't want to piss Colt off. Did you ever get a restraining order against him?"

She shook her head. "I never went to the police. I was scared they would take Jacob away if they found out we had problems in our marriage, and that he hit me."

"They wouldn't have taken Jacob away from you because of that."

She shivered, hating to speak of that time out loud, hating to admit that it had happened to her. Talking about it made her seem like she'd been weak, as if she'd taken the abuse easily, without putting up a fight. In the beginning, she had, because she had nowhere else to go and because she thought she could turn things around. At that time, she thought Colt was going through a bad patch and that he would come out of it soon and they would be able to make things work again. Most of all, she wanted to believe in her family but the reality was far different than the truth. "I didn't know any better, then. I've never told anyone before, except you."

"I know." His hand entwined with hers, lifted it to his mouth and kissed it. "I won't tell a soul."

"It's shameful to tell another person that the man you married hit you. It wasn't only because of Jacob," she said, speaking in hushed tones. "I couldn't face painting a real picture of how awful my life was. I never reported it and then I moved to my parents' place and then to my aunt's in Pennsylvania, and there was never a need to talk about it because he never came looking for us. He never called us much either. He never called Jacob to wish him a happy birthday, or Merry Christmas, or anything."

"But he started calling you recently, didn't he?"

She bowed her head. "He made it sound as if he could help me with the hospital bill. Thinking about it now, he was probably trying to figure out how I could afford to live here, and how I managed to pay the bills. I'm sure of it. He must have wondered what kind of job I had." Tobias took a deep breath, and tried not to think too much about it, but there was no denying it. This had happened because of the gala dinner, because of the trip to Miami, because he had gone to Jacob's awards ceremony. Each event had been a stepping stone to the next and now Jacob had been taken. It could have been avoided if they'd kept things hushed as Savannah had tried to. This had been his doing.

"Stepping out into the public eye is what brought him to me. It's what put Jacob in danger, and I don't know how he found out my home address," said Savannah. "But I guess that if my Dad could surf the 'net and find out about you, so could Colt."

"You can't blame yourself for what happened," Tobias said gently.

"Can't I?"

His eyes narrowed. "Do you regret going away with me?"

"This might not have happened if I'd stayed back home, if I'd never gone to the gala or—"

"Don't, Savannah."

"It's true. You and I both know it's true. Colt knew I was away. He knew you and I were together. He knew how he could get to me. And when he saw you and me together on TV, he knew how to manipulate the circumstances to his advantage. He didn't care what he was going to do, or how it might affect Jacob, he saw money."

Tobias rubbed his forehead, his face unforgiving. "He would have found another way to get to you even without all of that."

"What next? What if someone decides to get to you through Jacob or me? You said yourself you only got security because you were worried for Ivy. I didn't know what you were talking about then, but I understand it now."

He looked at her sharply. "What are you saying?" But she was silent. There was nothing more to say on the matter, not yet. Not until she had her son safe and sound and in her arms. She didn't need to spell it out for Tobias but she knew for herself. If she wasn't with Tobias, would Colt have done this at all? Would Colt have ever found out about her—that she was dating a wealthy man? Would he ever have come after her?

Probably not.

# CHAPTER NINE

Thud, thud, thud. Jacob's heart made a sound like galloping horses. He'd never been to the bathroom by himself before, and he was scared. His mommy always went with him and they went to the ladies' room which was clean and nice and didn't smell like this. He wrinkled his nose and locked himself in one of the cubicles.

His daddy scared him. He didn't like him before and he sure didn't like him much now. Not with that angry face and those swear words he had been using. And he lied.

First, he lied that they were going to see Mommy at the airport. He had taken him away from Grandma and now he was telling him that Grandma was coming to get him. Jacob had a feeling that this was a lie. His daddy showing up like that right outside his school gates had scared him even more.

He rubbed his eyes as he stood in the cubicle wondering what to do next. He didn't want to go back out there. He wanted to go home. He tried to figure out what were lies and what was the truth. He wanted to believe he was going to see Mommy but it didn't make sense that Grandma was now coming for him. He knew something was wrong but he didn't know what. It was like the time that Henry Carson said mean things to him. Henry didn't always use bad words, but it was the *way* he said them that told Jacob Henry wasn't being nice, even if he pretended to be.

He had that same feeling now.

He didn't believe Daddy and he didn't like being with him.

Mommy had told him she was coming back home and Tobias had told him to be strong, like Iron Man. He liked Tobias loads and he wished that Tobias was his daddy instead.

When he heard the door open, it felt like someone had sucked the air right out of his lungs. He stopped breathing and waited, hoping that Daddy hadn't come looking for him. When nobody called out for him, he knew he was safe.

He let his breath out slowly and knew what he had to do. He waited for the other man to leave. When he heard the door open and close again, he opened the door to his cubicle and looked out. The bathroom was empty. He pretended that he was wearing Iron Man's stealth suit and that he was invisible. He quietly tiptoed out. If he walked on the other side of the tables, away from where his daddy was sitting, he could leave without anyone knowing.

---

Colt burped.

He'd finished Jacob's burger and eaten all of his fries and now the boy's plate was completely empty. What the hell was the kid doing? He looked at his watch again.

Almost five thirty.

Crap!

He'd been gone too long. Colt slid out of the booth and strode quickly towards the bathroom. Except for one man standing over the urinal, it was empty. He pushed the doors of the two cubicles wide open. Empty.

The little bastard.

He spun around and rushed out, his eagle eyes scanning around the busy diner looking for the boy. "Jacob!" A silence fell as soon as he hollered and for a few seconds everyone stared at him oddly. He could feel the veins around his neck throbbing and weaving, like tiny snakes sliding through grass. He asked the waitresses and the people sitting down, "Have you seen a small boy?" They looked at him and shook their heads.

*The little shit.* Colt's insides heaved as the burger and fries started to clamber back up his throat again. He scratched the back of his neck, stupefied at the thought that he'd lost his $40k ticket. The boy couldn't be too far.

A passing waiter stopped. "You've lost someone?" he asked. And then another waiter gathered around, and then he saw someone who looked like a manager approach him.

"What seems to be the problem?"

"No problem," he growled, and plunked down a couple of bills on the table. He fled the diner, running along the street and looking for signs of a boy in bright yellow.

# CHAPTER TEN

I t was killing him being helplessly stranded on a plane at a time like this.

Tobias couldn't sit still and anxiety clawed at his gut like a hundred army ants eating their way out of his stomach. It was a goddamn nightmare being up here where he couldn't do a goddamn thing to find Jacob.

He couldn't imagine the agony Savannah was going through. Her skin was pale and her eyes were ringed with blue-green circles. The happy smiling woman he'd made love to every day and every night had vanished.

Had they really shared those moments? The whisper-filled nights seemed like part of another world, with other people and other memories. Growing restless, he got up and walked into the bedroom, needing to talk in private. He called Ludwig.

"What's happening?"

"We're there. The men are scoping out the area and we're parked up on a street within easy view of the entrance."

"No police, no media," Tobias cautioned. "Don't go raising any suspicions or make a scene. I don't want idle passersby recording anything on their cellphones. Don't give them a reason to."

Brookes was unpredictable and Tobias didn't know what else he might have up his sleeve. Reading through the report had confirmed what Tobias already knew; that the man was a lowlife idiot but even an idiot, when desperate, was capable of doing far more dangerous things. Tobias couldn't risk anything going wrong, especially while Jacob was with him.

"Are you expecting surprises?" Ludwig asked, as if he sensed his anxiety. "This should be a straight swap."

"It should be," Tobias confirmed. "No surprises. Let Jacob's grandmother walk over with the money and come back with Jacob. You make sure you're no more than an arm's length away. You be there to walk them back to the car. Tell Jean who you are. I've shown her your photo so she knows what you look like but remember she'll be scared and hasn't seen you before. Tell her Tobias sent you and the password is Ruby Red—in case she has any doubts." He'd already spoken to Jean and told her but knew that when it came to the moment there was a good chance she would forget everything and panic.

"Understood."

"It should happen in the next fifteen minutes. Good luck." He hung up and leaned against the door, taking a moment to collect himself before he ventured back to Savannah again. She was in pieces and he already knew what that was like, to lose someone. She hadn't lost Jacob, and he was going to see to it that the boy was returned unharmed, but until that moment happened, until Savannah had him in her arms again, Tobias knew what she was going through; he had experienced that feeling of hopelessness, of surrendering to fear yet wanting to believe in a better outcome—and he would take care of her and be there for her.

It had been the longest hour of his life. Almost. He'd

experienced a loss greater than this before. His wife and son would never return. But this, even though Jacob wasn't technically his, even though he'd only known him for a short amount of time, this still hurt as much. He was determined to get the boy back unharmed.

He walked back to Savannah and found her sitting forward on her seat with her elbows on her knees and her head down. He took her hand and helped her to stand. "Hey," he said softly, and wrapped his arms around her. She was as limp as a rag doll and said nothing as her face rested against his shoulder. He only heard a soft sigh escape her lips.

"They're going to make the swap in the next fifteen minutes." He placed a hand around the back of her head, almost pinning her to him, as if he couldn't bear to let her go.

"Anytime now?" she asked, sounding hopeful.

"Our boy's coming home."

He didn't know how long they stood together like that, drawing strength, drawing energy from one another but when his cell phone rang, he was sure it would be Ludwig reporting success. "See, I told you," he said to her, his arm still around Savannah's shoulder as he answered on the first ring.

"He hasn't shown up yet."

Tobias looked at his watch. It was 6:05 p.m. Still early. "Wait it out." Jacob might have needed to go to the bathroom or something. Jacob was tired and scared, and obviously not used to being around his father.

"We're not going anywhere," came Ludwig's reply. "I wanted you to be aware."

Tobias knew instinctively, as Ludwig probably did, that a man in desperate need of money wouldn't have run late at all, unless something had gone badly wrong.

"Keep me posted." He hung up.

Savannah lifted her face to his. "What's wrong?"

For one painful moment he considered stalling. But he had to tell her. "Colt hasn't shown up yet." Her face fell. "I'm sure he's on his way. He'll come," Tobias assured her. There was no reason for the man not to show up.

---

It was loud. Louder than the beating of his heart and even louder was the strange noise in his ears. Like a waterfall. Jacob started walking quickly, away from the diner, away from the way they had come.

*Riverdale Apartments.* That was the name of the place where they lived. That's where Daddy might go look. Jacob decided to go in the opposite direction. Soon he was running and he ran for as long as he could until his breath ran out. He stopped and now he was tired and cold, and he wanted his coat.

And his grandma and grandpa.

Most of all he wanted his mommy. His arms and legs felt twitchy, like he wanted to run again, but he couldn't because he didn't have the energy. He looked behind him again.

Daddy hadn't followed him.

This time he let out a longer breath, then another and another. He made sure to wait at the crosswalk just like Mommy had always told him. He waited for the lights to change so that he could cross carefully, the way Mommy had shown him. It was a busy road but there was a gap in the traffic and even though he wanted to run across it because he wanted to get away from danger, he knew Mommy would be angry with him. So he waited.

Daddy was danger and the quicker he moved, the faster he would get away from him. Jacob knew that Daddy was going to be looking for him and when he found him, Daddy would be very angry. Jacob knew how angry he could get and he didn't want to get caught.

But he waited for the safety sign to cross. If he found someone to help him, if he told someone where he wanted to go, they might help him get back to the apartment before Daddy found him.

## CHAPTER ELEVEN

She gripped the headrest, feeling the contents of her stomach rising upwards and when her knees buckled, she gripped the headrest tighter, refusing to fall. Behind her, she heard Tobias say something to her but she blocked him out. Colt hadn't shown up and she needed to speak to him. She called his number again but it went to voicemail.

*If he wasn't picking up, it was because something had gone terribly wrong.*

"He'll come," Tobias assured her, refusing to move out of her way.

"Then why hasn't he? It doesn't feel right." Fear gnawed at her gut like a starving rat trying to claw its way out as she called him again. Tobias had gone over to the corner and was talking in whispers.

It didn't matter that she didn't hear his words, it only mattered that there had been no exchange.

No exchange meant that Jacob was still with Colt.

No exchange meant that anything could have happened.

No exchange meant that she had no idea where her son was.

Scared more than she'd ever been in her life before, she

called her dad. Tobias had told her not to call her mom in case she called at the moment of exchange and any interruption might have frightened Colt off.

"Is Mom okay, Dad?" She worried about her mom, who was right in the thick of all the action. But it would have been too risky for her dad to do it. Her dad would have said or done something to Colt. It wasn't worth taking that risk.

"She looks to be holding up."

"You still don't see Colt anywhere?" She pressed her fingernails hard into the palm of her hand, leaving moon-shaped marks. Jacob's release was a hair's width away and yet Colt was running late. No matter how much she willed it, her intuition told her that something wasn't right.

"No, Ruby Red." His voice was somber. "I'm on the opposite side of the street, and I can see your Mom and all around her, but no sign of Jacob, or *him*." Her father refused to call him by name. Her heart sunk to the base of her stomach at the news.

"He doesn't know his way around here, Dad. He might've gotten lost." Maybe he took the wrong exit, maybe he got on the wrong subway. Maybe he had a change of heart.

Maybe he didn't.

Maybe something or someone else had found him first. She had a feeling that Tobias knew more than he was telling her. Colt wasn't the most reliable of men but she knew he would have come running for the money. For forty thousand dollars, he'd have done anything.

"He could have," her father agreed, but he didn't sound too convinced. "Savannah, you keep it together, you hear me?"

"I am, Dad." *I'm trying.* She hung up to find Tobias's arms around her once more. "It's getting late," she said wearily, stepping away, needing some space and some distance. Needing to find out what he was keeping from her.

"How are your mom and dad doing?" Tobias asked. Something about the tightness around his mouth told her he had noticed her aloofness.

"They're pretending to be fine, like I am, but Colt's now half an hour late for the money and I know something's gone wrong, or..." She clasped her hand to her chest. "Something's happened to Jacob. He's had an asthma attack or..." The sobs started as the words stuck in her throat. Images of her son's sweet face, of him lying on the hospital bed when he'd had the last asthma attack, vaulted into her mind's eye.

"You don't know that."

"You don't know otherwise," she snapped. "I can feel it here," she placed a fist over her heart. "Colt wouldn't keep anyone waiting, not for this. He needs that money, why else would he demand such a thing? Why else would he take Jacob if he wasn't in trouble?" Tobias grabbed her arm gently and didn't let go. "There's something you're not telling me," she said, her eyes widening as she tried to back away.

"Don't push me away, Savannah. I won't let you do this." The small amount of hurt in his voice stabbed at her.

"My son is missing," she said, her voice hard and cold. "And if I ever find out that you kept things from me, I'll never forgive you."

He loosened his grip on her. "I know it hurts. I know what you're going through but you mustn't lose hope or assume the worst." She bit her teeth together, knowing he was right, but hurting anyway. Her body tensed under his touch as he pulled her close. She could still smell the chlorine from the pool water as his face drew close to hers. For one moment, she remembered the way she'd writhed beneath him, begging him not to stop, but pushed the thought away as fast as it came.

"Colt isn't used to traveling with a six-year-old, Savannah. Jacob might have been hungry or needed to use the bathroom.

He's probably tired after a long day at school and slower on his feet. Look how late it is."

She wanted to believe him but her mind lingered on gloomier alternatives. "Then why won't Colt pick up each time I call?" Because if it were any of the reasons that Tobias had mentioned, Colt would have answered the phone and told them he was running late. The fact that he had avoided her calls told her he was hiding something. Or buying himself more time.

"He'll call us," said Tobias with a confidence that felt out of place. It immediately aroused her suspicions. "But if you don't agree, then you tell me what to do, Savannah, and I'll do it."

She didn't know what to do. Calling the police and involving them when Colt had specifically told them not to might make him angry and put Jacob's life in even more danger. But if Jacob had had an asthma attack, he would need urgent medical treatment.

She was torn. "We'll wait a little longer," she replied, and picked up her phone to call him again.

## CHAPTER TWELVE

W here the hell was that kid? The roaring sound of traffic faded away and the swooshing whoosh of blood pounding in his ears took over as he frantically searched for his son. Half-running, half-walking, half-breathing, Colt craned his neck and peered through store windows.

He'd been looking all over the place but there was no sign of Jacob anywhere.

Sweat slicked across his hairline as he fought the urge to disappear from the surface of the Earth. Unless he found Jacob, he could not return to Santino because his life was as good as over. He had disrespected the man. Others had fared worse for lesser things. Now there was no question of him ever returning home without the money. He might as well take a leap off the Brooklyn Bridge.

But he couldn't disappear, not until he found the boy. Not only because Jacob was the answer to his problems—his winning lottery ticket—but because he was also an innocent boy and god help him if anything happened to him. Colt knew he was a lousy father but he wasn't cut from the same cloth as men like Santino and his ilk. He wasn't a complete scumbag, despite what Savannah, and her new man, and her parents, would now think.

"Jacob!" The dampness made his shirt stick to his back as he scrambled around the streets. The ragged pounding of his heart grew louder until he almost struggled to breathe.

This was bad.

*Real bad.*

It was almost six thirty. When his cell phone rang again, he cursed, fear prickling his skin and senses as Santino came to mind. He relaxed when he saw Savannah's name on the caller ID but knew he couldn't speak to her yet. Couldn't tell her what had happened. He pressed the button to send it to voicemail.

With his heart in his mouth, he set off again, pelting in and out of stores with bullet speed, running past office buildings. He desperately scanned the streets, looked in and around the crowds of tunnel-visioned people, looked over and around the angry monster traffic that roared along, heading downtown.

Maybe he'd been looking in the wrong direction? Colt turned and stared in the direction from where he had come. Maybe the boy was trying to make his way back home? He turned around and headed back towards Sunnyside.

When the cell phone went off again, he was half tempted to answer. It was Savannah and he knew she was probably freaking out because he hadn't shown up. There was no point answering when he didn't have the boy. As long as they thought Jacob was with him, Jean would be waiting with the money. She wasn't going anywhere without Jacob.

---

Jacob peered through the huge glass front of the shopping mall. It would be a good place to hide, he thought, and it would be good to get away from the streets and all those people. And away from his daddy who was probably coming for him.

The wide doors softly opened, making a swishing noise as he walked into the building. At least it was warm inside.

He looked around. Most people rushed by not noticing him. A few of them stared at him, then quickly looked away and walked past, making him feel almost invisible.

But as he walked around, he realized the mall was much bigger than it had looked from the outside and he suddenly felt very afraid. His heart was beating so fast that he thought it might explode. He wanted Mommy and as soon as he thought of her, it made him cry. Sobbing, he walked slowly, looking into stores as he shuffled along, lost and lonely.

Mommy had always told him that if he got lost, he had to run into a store and find someone who was wearing a uniform and tell them that he was lost. That's what he would do now. He walked along and looked inside a few stores. They looked busy and were full of people and he couldn't see anyone in uniform. The people around him were so big and tall, he felt they wouldn't even see him.

A big man in a coat looked down at him. "Are you lost, young man?"

*Mommy said don't talk to strangers,* Jacob reminded himself. He stared back at the man silently, then quickly rushed past him and ran up the escalators. When he turned and looked down, the man had disappeared.

He stepped off the escalator and stared at the store in front of him. It had lots of soaps and creams and pretty frilly boxes in the windows. It looked like the sort of store mommy liked going into. He thought he saw someone in uniform at the back. *This one,* he thought and started to move towards it when someone tapped him on the shoulder. He turned around.

"Hello, you sweet little thing. Where's your mommy?" Jacob

stared at the woman's wrinkly face. "Now, now," she said, looking all around then bending down so that her face was directly in front of his. "Have you been crying?" Her eyes were shiny, as if they were made of liquid and when she smiled, he saw that she had lipstick on one of her front teeth.

Jacob's body froze.

"You've lost your mommy, haven't you?" She smiled again but her smile didn't reach her eyes. Jacob didn't think she was really happy. He wanted to cry because she was standing so close to him and he couldn't see the man in uniform in the shop behind her.

"Do you have a name, sweetie?"

Jacob stared at her silently and his chest felt squashed, like it did that time Henry Carson sat on him in PE, when the teacher wasn't looking.

"You're scared, aren't you?"

He couldn't help it. His pee, warm and smelly, trickled quickly down his legs. The woman stared at the small puddle on the floor. "Sweetie," she said, standing up straight. "That's not very nice. Let's go get you cleaned up."

She held out her hand.

# CHAPTER THIRTEEN

I t was way past their meeting time, and Colt still hadn't
shown up. This was confirmation enough that something
wasn't right.

Tobias called Colt's number again but the man still didn't
pick up. He left him a message instead. "Brookes," he tried to
keep his voice mellow, to suppress the rage that simmered under
his skin. "Where the hell are you? Jean's waiting right by the
place we agreed. Your $40k is ready. Come and get it. We'll
wait all night if we have to, but know this—Jacob doesn't have
his inhaler and if anything happens to him, you don't want to
know what I will do to you." He glanced over his shoulder and
saw Savannah sitting on the floor with her back against the seat,
staring straight ahead.

Ludwig called and gave him an update. "Still no sighting,"
his man reported.

"Stay put," said Tobias. "He'll show up. He needs the
money." He walked over and sat down beside Savannah,
reaching for her hand, needing something to hold, to help
counter the shakiness in his stomach. His eyes fell on the
photo of Jacob that she held. A crack formed along his chest

as the boy's sweet smile tore at his heart. He wanted to comfort her but couldn't find the right words to offer reassurance. How could he when he no longer felt so sure himself?

Something had happened, either to Jacob or to Colt. Something that had prevented him from showing up. Could it be the people Colt was hiding from? Could they have tracked him down?

Tobias wasn't exactly sure what it was that Colt was mixed up in and he was no longer sure it was wise to play the waiting game. If the men after Colt had caught up with him then Jacob was in danger. He rubbed his hands across his forehead and tried to think carefully about his next course of action.

It didn't help that they didn't know where he was, but he knew this much: Jacob had left school and Colt had probably called from a park. Savannah had said she'd heard children in the background. He could get Ludwig's men to at least look along that stretch of land and further.

———

She couldn't bear to sit on the seats and had instead slid to the floor, her skirt falling back to her thighs as her arms rested on her knees. She'd pulled out a recent photo of him taken just after Christmas, the one she carried in her handbag. Now she gripped it like a lifeline, refusing to let it out of her fingers. Jacob's impish face smiled back at her.

Sobs gathered at the base of her throat and the pain cut deeper each moment she stared at it. She would give anything to feel his skin against her fingers, to feel the texture of his soft hair, to hug him and to hold him in her arms.

She had been relieved, knowing that Colt had him, because no matter how much of a pig the man was, he would never hurt him. But now, with him not showing up or contacting them, it was the silence that was killing her.

Tobias slid down beside her but she continued to stare at the photograph, not acknowledging him at all. When he took her hand in his, she was powerless to draw it away. "I've got my men on the streets looking along the area from the school and the park."

*Men?* She wondered. How many men? "You know something's wrong too, don't you?" she asked, knowing the answer already, that he was as worried.

"It's a backup plan, Savannah. It's getting very late. It could be a simple mistake, like he doesn't know the area." But he'd have caught a cab or the subway. He'd have found a way to get there. For $40k, Colt would have been there. It wasn't as if the Empire State Building was hard to find.

"How long before we land?"

"Not long. Less than half an hour."

"And we'll go straight there? Where my mom is?"

"Of course." He rubbed the skin along her thumb softly.

Time seemed to have stopped ever since she'd listened to Jacob's voicemail by the pool. How sharply that moment had snatched her from the bubble she'd been living in. It felt as if days had passed since that time.

The familiar ring of her cell phone made her reach for it immediately. She saw Colt's name on the caller ID and answered with a galloping heart.

"Savannah." Colt's voice, thick and mangled, sent shivers along the back of her neck. It didn't sound like him. "Jacob's gone. I can't find him anywhere."

A creepy-crawly sensation wriggled down her back. "What?" She gasped, not sure that she'd heard him right.

"He ran off and I don't know where he is."

"Ran off?" she said, letting the words sink into her skin.

"Ran off?" She slowly rose to her feet, her voice rising to a crescendo. "What do you mean HE RAN OFF?" The air stilled in her chest and her lungs froze up, like ice.

"He went to the bathroom and then he never came back."

The light dimmed as the floor fell out from beneath her. She heard a scream, like a thousand banshees flocking together, and then realized the scream was her own. "What do you mean he never came back?" Soft sobs stifled her words as the reality sank in.

"We were at a diner and he said he wanted to go to the bathroom and he never came back out."

"You let him go alone?"

"He's old enough, isn't he? I thought he'd come back. But..."

*That was the reason for the delay.* For Colt not showing up.

"When?" she screamed. It felt as though the contents of her stomach had landed on the floor.

"Maybe an hour."

"AN HOUR AGO?" she shouted, hate spewing out of her mouth and the urge to strangle the man running deep in her veins. Tobias now stood by her, his face a contortion of twisted fear and worry.

"I've looked everywhere. I'm still looking. I've gone back to your apartment, to the school and I can't see him anywhere."

"You find my boy, you worthless piece of shit!" she spat the words out as the world around her started to spin. "You find my boy."

The line went dead.

"Savannah?" Tobias's hands grabbed the sides of her face as she dropped the cell phone. "What is it? What's happened?"

"Jacob...he...he...he....he..." her chest heaved, and she started to shiver. "He ran off an hour ago and Colt can't find him."

"Jacob ran off?"

She turned away from him before he could feed her more

lies, before he could tell her that everything was going to be all right. He'd promised her that before, and he hadn't been able to protect her.

Tobias was only a man, nothing more, and what he had were only words. It didn't matter how many men he had on the streets or how much money he had to meet Colt's demands. None of that mattered now that she was faced with a new nightmare. A parent's worst fear. She saw posters of missing kids every day. She had read about the reports more times than she cared to remember.

Her son was alone on the streets of New York; a six-year-old with no one to protect him, no inhaler, nothing. He was anyone's for the taking.

## CHAPTER FOURTEEN

"Come on, sweetie," the woman with the lipstick on her teeth held out her hand. "You must feel really dirty. Let's go to the bathroom, shall we?"

Jacob shivered. He stared at her thin, scaly hands. Mommy said never to go with a stranger, even if they seemed nice and friendly. Even though the pee made his pants hot and yucky, he knew he shouldn't go with her. He didn't like her smile, or the way she looked at him.

*Find someone in a store, Jacob.*

That's what Mommy would have told him. He stepped towards her outstretched hand and then ran as fast as he could, straight into the store behind her.

"Hey!" he heard her shout out behind him but he ran all the way to the counter at the far end where a man was working. Jacob stopped in front of the counter, panting away. He wanted to tell the man that he was lost and that he wanted his mommy but his mouth was dry, like popcorn. His chest was beating like bongo drums and his icky wet pants stuck like glue to his legs.

He squirmed. "Excuse me." His lips moved and he thought he said the words but he didn't hear them out loud. "Excuse..."

The man suddenly looked down at him, smiled, and then continued with what he was doing.

"Come on, sweetie." Jacob's body froze when he heard the voice behind him.

"Excuse me," he whimpered, stepping closer and placing his hands on the counter. It was so high that it came up to his shoulders. It was hard to get the man's attention especially now that the man had turned his back to him and was on the computer.

The woman stood next to him. "Will you get a move on?" She grabbed his hand. "I don't have all day." This time her voice didn't sound as friendly as it had before. Jacob tried to move his arm away but she was holding it so tightly that he couldn't.

When she tried to pull him away again, he tried once last time and stood on tiptoes. "Excuse me." But the man didn't turn around.

"We're going. NOW!" The woman said, dragging him by the arm and pulling.

"It doesn't look to me as if he wants to go with you." A girl in a red leather jacket pulled her earplugs out and planted herself next to Jacob.

"What's it got to do with you?" the other woman asked. Smiling, she turned to Jacob once more. "Come on, sweetie." She pulled him along with her and out of the store.

# CHAPTER FIFTEEN

---

In less than thirty minutes, they would touch down on the tarmac in New York City. They sat quietly on the seats, waiting for more news.

Savannah squeezed her eyes shut, not wanting to let her mind wander to the dark places where these types of events often ended. She tried to focus on her son's face, on a safe and happy outcome, and on putting him to bed tonight.

But evil thoughts pickaxed their way into her mind. She couldn't speak or answer to Tobias's reassurances even as he held her hand and tried to provide comfort. She could tell that he was struggling too, that he'd been silent for a while, and that when he spoke, the conviction in his voice was no longer there. There was nothing he could say which would make things better for her.

She was all cried out and clutched Jacob's photo tightly. Tobias had broken the awful news to her parents, and they hadn't taken it well either.

She didn't know whether she wanted to kill her ex or make him suffer a slow and prolonged torture. Despite her attempts to think of positive things, her mind kept drifting to Jacob out on the streets, alone and scared. He would be easy prey for the many predators that roamed around, and her insides churned at the thought of the danger that lurked at every street corner, of the crazy people who harbored evil thoughts; of cars and traffic, of his lungs and asthma, of friendly liars pretending to be something they were not.

She'd told him what to do, had tried to give direction and instruction in the worst-case scenario. Would he remember? Would he have a chance?

Her heart seemed to jerk upwards and smack into the base of her throat—what if she never saw him again? A slow numbness crawled over her body, like a rolling mist off a frozen lake. It had been paralyzing every muscle in her body ever since she had heard the news. Tobias had been on the phone instantly, issuing orders, and talking to her, touching her hands, her arm, but she withdrew from the world and buried herself in her own private hell.

If she never saw her son again, she didn't want to live. Not like this. She tried to suppress the thought, tried to put a heavy lid over it, but in her mind's eye, she kept seeing Jacob walking down the wrong street, taking the wrong turn, going up to the wrong door or the wrong stranger.

"We need to set up an Amber Alert now," she cried, suddenly jolting back to life. "We need everyone to be out looking for my baby." Now while they had the window of opportunity to find him *alive*.

Tobias's features twisted, as if he was battling to find the right words. "We haven't told the police yet that Jacob is missing," Tobias reminded her. "Your ex said specifically he wanted no police or press involvement."

Her lungs constricted again and she felt as if she had to work harder to breathe again. "But Colt doesn't know where my son is."

Tobias looked at her strangely. It was that guilty look, she suddenly realized, the one he often had when he had done something he shouldn't have. "What?" she asked quietly. "What aren't you telling me?"

This time when he pressed his hand over hers, she pulled hers away, not trusting him or wanting his sugar-coated caresses. "Because your ex is mixed up with people who would happily kill him." Something hard and heavy landed inside her, as if a metal truck had just rammed into her at full speed.

"Kill him?" she asked faintly. "Who would want to kill him?" *Aside from me.*

"The people he owes money to. He has a lot of gambling debt," replied Tobias.

"What gambling debt?" In the empty gap between her question and his reply, something rankled. "And how come you know about it?"

"I had my head of security compile a report a few months ago." Her eyes grew wide in disbelief. Tobias continued, "He's racked up a huge debt and sold off most of his possessions, except for his TV and his phone."

"What report?"

He inhaled deeply. "I wanted to find out more about you, Savannah."

"Why?"

"Because I did back then, in the beginning, when I wanted to know where you lived, and what was in your past. I routinely do background checks on people and companies."

"People and companies?" She stumbled back in surprise. "So if my background had been wrong, if I'd had more negatives against me than my debt, you might never have pursued me?"

"That's not the kind of check I commissioned. I don't care about your past. I'm a good enough judge of character to know you as a person."

"You do, do you?" The bitterness in her voice cut into the air.

Her brittle tone appeared to startle him. "I ran a check on you in order to find out why you had come to me for the advance on your salary."

"Why didn't you just ask me—like a normal person would?"

He sighed and scratched his chin. "This isn't important right now. We should be thinking about Jacob," he said.

"Tell me why you conducted the background check."

He raked his hands through his hair, irritation crept across his brow. "Don't make this into anything else, Savannah," he warned. "It doesn't really matter."

"The hell it doesn't."

"I can't even remember. It couldn't have been that important. You weren't an open book back then when we first met and I needed to find out more about you."

Her mouth settled into a firm line and she didn't like his answer.

"It looks worse than it is, Savannah. You know my past, you know how difficult it is for me to trust people and to let them into my life."

"Is it trust or is it control that you need? Your need to know everything, to have everything be a certain way, makes me feel claustrophobic." She pulled her hand away when he sought it again.

"I'm not letting you fight with me, Savannah. You're angry, and you have every right to be. But right or wrong, I asked my security people to find out about you. In the process, I found out about your ex-husband. The fact remains, Savannah, the man you married has a debt of more than twenty thousand dollars."

Her mouth fell open.

"Online gambling," he said, answering her next question.

Now she felt even more wretched but her anger quickly

turned to worry. "The people who are after Colt, you think they might come after Jacob?"

"I don't know. I don't know who they are. Ludwig thinks he might have become involved in a criminal element, but that's all I know. It will take time to get more details."

She felt her body folding forwards, as if the very bones that supported her frame were starting to disintegrate.

"It's a possibility but I don't know. You tell me that you want an Amber Alert and I'll get one set up. I have the contacts to make it happen."

She'd seen the alerts for missing children on TV and knew how they ended. Never happily. It would be surreal to see Jacob's photo flash up in households everywhere showing his beaming, happy smile. But it could also put him in even more danger, thanks to that father of his. But if she didn't send out an alert and sat back and did nothing, what then?

"No alert," she said, trying to think what Jacob might have done, and where he might have gone if he was lost. "Not yet."

All she could do was pray.

---

F ear rolled over him like a tidal wave and sweat poured down his back. He had walked the entire way back to the diner, then continued walking further towards downtown. No Jacob meant no money, and no money plus disrespect meant he was in for a slow and painful death.

*Where the hell was the boy?* For the first time ever, Colt was worried, genuinely scared and shit-in-his-pants worried about his boy. The streets were busy, the people distracted, the cars growling along the streets. Nobody would take notice of a lone six-year-old boy.

Nobody except the wrong type of people.

Worry pierced through his skin like a spear. It was still light outside but within a few hours, darkness would descend and the streets would turn cold and perilous for a small child.

His chance to make a new life had started to slip slowly through his fingers. His insides felt hollow, but it was something else too. Fear for the boy. Colt didn't like this city much. He found it too busy, too noisy, too dirty, too much of everything. And if he felt like that—a grown man who could take care of himself—how would his innocent slip of a boy fare out here?

He smacked a fist into the wall of another restaurant and peered inside the greasy windows. For a moment a crack opened up in his conscience, just wide enough for concern to seep through. The boy couldn't have gone far. He had to be here somewhere.

Determined to find him, Colt set off again. His fast-paced walking soon turned into a run as he raced along the streets, his back damp, his breath bursting in and out so quickly it hurt his chest.

Savannah would never forgive him for this, but it wasn't her forgiveness he sought. For a moment, he considered going to the police station and telling them everything he knew but his fear about Santino suddenly mushroomed. And then he remembered; the child didn't share his surname and Santino wouldn't know who Jacob was. While it remained thus, the boy at least would be safe from Santino and his gang. But if he went to the police now, it might later come out that he had taken Jacob. He couldn't risk Santino ever finding out about his boy.

There was no way he could meet Santino now—not unless he wanted his balls sliced off and fed to him piece by piece. He'd heard what they'd done to the last person who disrespected them.

# CHAPTER SIXTEEN

"**W**hy didn't you tell me sooner?" Matthias asked.

"I couldn't," Tobias replied as he paced around outside. They'd landed a short while ago and his men had driven him straight to where Ludwig and Savannah's parents were waiting.

It hadn't been the ideal first meeting he'd envisioned with her parents. Savannah was with them now, in the black SUV which was parked across the street from the arranged meeting point.

Jean had been waiting across the road in vain, when he and Savannah had arrived. It was only when they'd walked over to talk to her and had explained the situation that they were able to get her to leave her post and wait in the car with her husband.

With no further news, Tobias knew the situation looked bleak. In his despair, he had called Matthias and sworn him to secrecy. He needed to know that he'd done the right thing in not alerting the police, even when it made sense to.

He'd needed to speak to someone because Savannah had shut herself away from him. He felt as if he'd lost Savannah, as if she'd slipped away from him but he understood. If he felt like this, he couldn't imagine the hell she was going through. It was a blessing that her parents were here to support her because even though he was trying to be strong, as time passed on and still no good news emerged, he felt himself caving in to the fear and delving into his past. It was cruel that a similar loss threatened his life again.

"Do you want me to come over?"

He had kept Colt's name out of it, knowing that there were undisclosed parts to Colt's story that needed to be kept out of the public domain, for Jacob's safety.

"No," he replied. There would be no point.

"How's Savannah holding up?"

"Not too good, as you would expect."

Matthias turned unusually quiet. "I'm sorry, buddy. I don't know what to say."

"There's nothing to say," Tobias replied.

"Keep me posted, and let Savannah know I'm thinking of her and her boy. If there's anything I can do..."

"Thanks." He hung up and pressed down hard on the sockets of his eyes. It hadn't even been a week since the gala dinner and yet it seemed as if a lifetime had passed between that night and this.

His well-intentioned plans of leaving the city the day after in order to avoid the media frenzy had worked but he would never have dreamed that they would soon become embroiled in a situation such as this.

He walked back to the car where Savannah sat and climbed inside. Her father looked up from the somber silence and acknowledged him. "We should go out and stretch our legs," he said to his wife. "Come on, Jean," he helped her out of the car.

Savannah looked distant again as she stared out of the window. "It's so dark out there," she said, after a while, her faint voice barely audible.

"I know." He was worried but he couldn't show her his fears. His men on the street hadn't reported anything back. He'd also sent Ludwig there since Colt wasn't about to show up and the more men who were out there looking for Jacob, the better. He wanted to be out on the streets himself, looking for the boy, but he knew Savannah would want to come along and he didn't think it would be the right thing for her to do. She would be in a state if she went. It was better him being here and keeping an eye on her.

Tobias reckoned that the ransom money would have been Colt's way of getting out of the trouble he was in. But without the boy, there was no money, and without the money, Brookes was in bad trouble. In fact, Tobias wagered, Brookes was on a one-way street to Hell and sooner or later those people would get to him.

Which was why Tobias needed to get to him first.

---

He wanted to cry but his throat was stuck. He wanted to scream but his voice had vanished. He wanted to run but his legs had stopped working. And now he was more desperate than ever for his mommy.

The memory of her smiling face made him cry again and when the woman pulled him out of the store, he was too weak to stop her.

Where was she taking him?

"Hey!" He heard a voice behind him, but the woman was holding his hand so tightly that he couldn't pull his hand out or turn around to look behind him.

"Hey, you!" This time he heard footsteps, fast, running footsteps rushing up behind him and suddenly the girl in the red jacket appeared before him.

"What do you want?" the woman snarled, squaring her shoulders. But the girl ignored her and crouched down on one knee, like Tobias sometimes did.

"You look scared," she said to Jacob. Then she sniffed and Jacob felt embarrassed because he knew she could probably smell his pee. "You don't have to be scared."

"Piss off or I'll call the police." The woman with the lipstick teeth said. The girl got up.

"Call them," she said. Jacob tried to move more towards her because he got the feeling that she didn't want to hurt him, but the other woman was still holding his hand and he was stuck by her side. "Is that your mommy?" the girl asked him. He tried to answer but even when he opened his mouth, no words would come out.

"Mind your own business," the woman warned her. She sounded really angry. Like Daddy.

"Shake or nod your head," the girl said to him softly. "Do you know that lady?"

He shook his head quickly.

"What did I tell you, bitch?" the nasty woman shouted and moved closer to the girl.

"He says he doesn't know you." The girl looked like she wasn't going to move out of the way.

"He's with me," the woman insisted.

"He's scared of you," the girl said, looking at him with a soft smile. Jacob felt as though he wanted to cry.

"Is there a problem, ma'am?" A mall security guard walked past and Jacob's heart leapfrogged with hope.

The young girl looked at the man in uniform. "I don't care if I'm wrong but I believe this boy is lost and I don't think she's his mother." She turned to the woman, "You can sue me if you want." The security guard took a step towards them and all of a sudden, the woman let go of his hand and rushed into the elevator.

The girl in the red jacket crouched on the floor and looked at Jacob. His chest felt loose and soft and he started to cry.

---

He didn't know what to do. It was approaching eight o'clock, and he'd gone around the streets but there was still no sign of his boy. Night was starting to fall and the streets were getting darker.

Colt walked along a dark alleyway cluttered with debris, and slid to the ground, wishing he were dead. Surrounded by rotting food, boxes and garbage, he knew his life was as good as over. He'd more than failed this time, he'd fucked up so big, he'd lost his own son. He pressed the palms of his hands together as his body started to shake.

No Jacob, no money, and Santino would want his blood. He would be dead within days. Shaking, and beaten down with guilt and fear, he pulled his cell phone out and called Savannah.

"I can't find him."

"Is that you, Brookes?" a man answered. In the background, he heard the sound of a car door shutting, and then the sound of moving traffic.

He guessed he was talking to Stone. "I can't find Jacob. I've looked everywhere."

"Look harder."

"What do you think I've been doing?"

"I've met some real sleazeballs in my time," Stone continued, "but you must be the biggest loser around."

"Screw you, Stone," he snarled, his hate for the man rising fast. "What would you know about my life? Things are so easy for people like you."

"Believe what you want, asshole. I would never do what you did, no matter how bad things got. My men are out on the street looking for that boy, so if you have any humanity left in you, you should do the same instead of giving up like the loser that you are."

"You didn't call the police?"

"Not yet. Savannah didn't want me to. We didn't want to put Jacob at risk, knowing that the men who'll want your blood might come after him."

*They knew about his troubles?*

"How did you—"

"I have ways and means of finding out things."

"What do you know?" Colt asked, something heavy landing in his gut.

"More than you could imagine." *He had to be bluffing*, Colt thought. There was no way he could know everything. Stone continued, "I have an idea of the kind of shit you're mixed up in, Brookes. People like me have access to more dangerous men than that. Men who will do certain things, at the right price. And as you know, money is of no concern to me. If anything happens to that boy, there is no place on Earth you'll be able to hide."

Colt coughed and slowly lifted himself up from the ground. "You wouldn't. Not someone like you."

"Try me."

# CHAPTER SEVENTEEN

The asswipe scumbag. A man like that didn't deserve to be a father, least of all to a boy like Jacob.

He slipped Savannah's cell back into his pocket and answered the call on his cell. It was Ludwig.

"Good news," he said, his voice breathless from excitement. "They've found Jacob." Tobias almost dropped the phone.

"How is he?" he asked, not daring to breathe.

"He looks shaken but he seems fine and unharmed."

"Are you sure it's him?" Tobias asked, almost unable to contain his excitement.

"Looks just like the picture you sent over. I can see him now. The police officers are talking to him and he appears to be with someone."

"With someone?" asked Tobias, lifting his head.

"A girl."

"Who?" He wondered out loud. "Where are you?" He started to walk quickly towards the black SUV.

"At the mall off Queen's Boulevard. We were searching the streets outside when a couple of police cars raced past us and we followed them inside."

Tobias's chest felt light and his hands and fingers started to tingle. "Find out which police station they're taking him to and don't let him out of your sight." In fact, he had no plans to let the boy out of his sight, or his protection, ever.

He pulled the car door wide open. "They found him!" he said, trying hard not to yell. Savannah looked up and a tiny sliver of hope flickered across her face.

"They found Jacob and he's fine." His voice was close to cracking as the relief overwhelmed him. She stared back at him and her parents, who were on either side of her, looked at him as if they were too afraid to believe him.

"Are you sure?" her father spoke first.

Tobias nodded. "I'm sure. Ludwig's there on the scene and confirmed it was Jacob. He's fine and unharmed, but he looks a little scared, as you would expect."

"Where is he?" Savannah asked, sitting forward as if she was about to take off and run out onto the street. Her eyes glistened with tears that threatened to spill.

"At the mall off Queen's Boulevard. They're taking him to the police station now."

At that, she burst out crying and fell into her father's arms. Tobias hung his head, contemplating the sense of peace that came over him as he listened to Savannah's sobs. Her mother smiled at him and all he could do was hug her—even though he didn't really know this woman, the relief they all shared was much needed.

"I want to see him," Savannah said.

He had one of his men take her parents home while another drove him and Savannah to the police station. He knew how lucky they were that this had ended happily. Even so, he was interested in finding out who the young girl with Jacob was.

"I should call Colt," she said suddenly, as the car stopped outside the mall.

"Why?" Tobias asked, his gut hardening.

"To tell him Jacob's been found."

"Not yet," said Tobias. "Let him suffer a bit longer."

---

He sat in a room where two friendly officers asked him questions. One of them was a woman who seemed nice. Jacob felt sad when the girl in the red jacket said goodbye to him. She told him that he would be safe now and that he would see his mommy soon and that the officers would make sure he got back home safely.

Jacob wanted her to come with him, even though she was a stranger and even though Mommy said not to go with strangers. The girl was nice and she made him feel safe and warm, kind of how he felt after he'd eaten a hot dog.

The police officers spoke to her for a long time as well because he could see her sitting at a desk when he looked through the window of the room he was in. Even though he was in the police station, Jacob still felt scared but not as scared as he had felt with that other woman. He told the officers what he knew, and even though he didn't want to tell them that he ran away from his daddy at the hamburger place, he knew he couldn't lie. So he told them that he ran away to get away from Daddy and that he wanted to get back to his grandma and grandpa. But he was still scared that his daddy might still show up at any time.

He wished his mommy would hurry up, and that Tobias would hurry up and that they could all go home soon. That's what Jacob wanted more than anything.

"Are you hungry, Jacob?" the nice lady officer asked. He nodded. He was *really* starving. "I'll see what I can get you," she said and got up.

"Not sure it's worth it," the other officer said. "His mom's on her way."

Jacob turned his head.

"Did you hear that, Jacob? Your mommy is on her way."

"She's coming here?"

The officer smiled at him. "She'll be here before you know it."

---

Gripping Tobias's hand, Savannah walked into the police station with her heart racing.

Everything around her was a blur as she quickly scanned the busy police station looking for Jacob. But the place was teeming with officers, as busy as worker bees, and there was no sign of her son anywhere. While Tobias spoke to an officer, the atmosphere slowly quietened until she realized that everyone was looking their way.

Soon after, they were led down a corridor and shown to a room at the end. She already saw the bright yellow of his t-shirt through the window and as soon as the police officer opened the door, she screamed at the sight of her son sitting on a big leather wing chair. A mangled sob escaped from her lips as she flew to him.

"Jacob!" She hugged him as if she would never let go of him again and held him for the longest time, loving the feel of his tiny arms around her neck and his small body against her. After a while, she forced herself to pull away enough to examine his face carefully—her frightened eyes darting around his face to check whether he had been hurt. She cupped his face, examining each pore of his skin, trying to look deeper beneath his eyes, trying to find out what had happened to him. The real scars would be invisible to the eye and she knew that she would need to keep a careful watch on him.

She had a million questions and wanted to find out about those hours when he had been alone. She needed to know everything so that she could never forget the guilt, or let go of the blame; so that she would never again make the same mistake and let him out of her sight again.

"Mommy," he said, his voice was so tired that she could barely hear him. "You came."

"As fast as I could. You're safe, honey. Oh, thank god you're safe. Did anyone hurt you?" she asked as her son clung to her with arms of steel. She was lost in the surreal thankfulness of the moment, and the peace of knowing that she was one of the lucky ones to have gotten him back.

He shook his head. "But I was scared, Mommy."

She fought back the strangled sigh that caught like a fish hook in her throat. Biting down on her teeth to stop herself from falling apart, she mustered every ounce of energy in her body. "I know, Jacob, I know you were scared but you're a strong boy, a brave boy, and we're taking you home now. I'll never leave you again."

Tobias had been silent by her side the whole time and she only became aware of his presence again when she felt his hand on her shoulder. Slowly, she got up off the floor and saw that they were alone in the room. Jacob rushed towards Tobias and threw his arms around his waist, burying his face in Tobias's stomach. Without saying a word, Tobias lifted him up, chest to chest and wrapped his arms around her son. At first Tobias didn't speak, and then she saw from the way his jaw tightened that he too was fighting to keep himself strong.

"You had us worried there, buddy."

Jacob lifted his head. "I tried to be like Iron Man."

"You did?" Tobias replied softly. Jacob nodded. "Did you run away because I said that to you?"

"I was scared of Daddy," Jacob whispered. "I wanted to look for Mommy."

"It's so great to have you back," Tobias said, giving the boy another hug. Jacob's lower lip trembled as he put his arms around Tobias's neck like a tiny little human clamp.

She watched the two of them together and a wave of relief rolled over her as the tension that had buried deep within her muscles slowly began to lift from her body.

Tobias slowly put him back down on the floor. Savannah took his hand. "Who were you with, honey?"

"There was a woman first but she wasn't nice. I was scared of her too."

"What woman?"

"The one who tried to take me with her."

She felt a ball of lead drop into her stomach and slide down. "Take you with her?" Savannah dropped to one knee and looked him straight in the face. "Where did she want to take you?"

"To the bathroom to clean up. I peed in my pants," he whispered. "I'm sorry, Mommy."

She pressed her fingers to her lips and kept them tightly closed in case the gasp that almost escaped turned into a sob. Then in a voice that was barely a whisper, "It doesn't matter."

"Then Izzy said I looked scared."

"Izzy?"

"The girl in the red jacket." Savannah stared at Tobias, who didn't seem to know any more.

"Izzy said I didn't have to go with that lady. She told the lady to stew her, but she wasn't going to let me go, 'cos she knew I was scared."

"Stew her?" asked Savannah.

"Sue her," suggested Tobias.

"A security guard came up to us and then the other woman ran off. That's when they called the police, and Izzy told me not to be scared and that you were going to come and get me." Savannah clapped a hand to her mouth as she stood up.

*Someone had tried to take him.*

The fact that the woman had run off when the security guard approached made her think there were ulterior motives. She suddenly felt sick to her stomach and turned away for a moment to compose herself.

Behind her, she heard Tobias talking and making Jacob laugh. Unlike her, he was doing all the right things, putting her son's mind at rest, not talking or dwelling on what had just happened.

She was desperate to know every detail, desperate to know the minute-by-minute account of what had happened to her son, but it was for her sake that she needed it. She hoped the police officers would have more information for her later.

For now, it was time to take her son home.

# CHAPTER EIGHTEEN

She fretted over Jacob, and even though Tobias understood her fear, this was the third time in half an hour that she had checked on him while he was asleep.

They had returned home a few hours ago to a tearful reunion between Jacob and his grandparents. After dinner, and attempting to regain a semblance of normality again, her parents and Jacob had gone to bed, leaving the two of them alone in her living room.

"He's asleep," Savannah said in a hushed voice, walking back into the room. Tobias eyed her as she sat down on the single seater, away from him.

"Just like he was the last time," Tobias remarked.

"I had to be sure." She looked anxious, as if she wasn't going to sleep tonight, for fear that something, or someone, might take Jacob again.

The moment turned quiet and awkward again. The mood was already subdued as the adrenaline that had been keeping them all going throughout the long day trickled away.

"It's natural to be worried, Savannah, especially after everything he's gone through," he said softly, wanting to put his arms around her, wanting to tell her that it would all be okay now, wanting to make good on his promise but he sensed an aloofness in her, and for now he let it go. He wanted her to know that he wasn't only here for the good times, but the darker times too.

"I want to talk to the girl in the red jacket."

"As soon as I find out more, I'll let you know." His contact in the police department would tell him everything. The man had already texted Tobias to warn him that the news had gotten out.

Savannah fingered the necklace he had given her. "I want to thank her. I owe her everything because I think..." She stared down at the floor as if she was struggling with the words. "I think she might have saved Jacob from being abducted."

"You can't know that for certain."

"But it sounds like it. You know it does."

"The police are putting together a visual based on Jacob's and the girl's descriptions. I'm certain they also have CCTV footage. It will help to track her down but I'm not sure they will be able to do much even if they find her."

"But what if that girl hadn't stepped in?"

"Don't think about that," he said, and he could see she was tired. He ought to go, but he didn't want to leave with things between them so brittle.

"I can't not think about it," she replied. "Each time I close my eyes, I think something's happened to him."

He understood her fear, but he worried about her nonetheless. He walked over to her and gave her his hand, pulling her up to a standing position. "I know you will replay the whole thing a million times over in your head but we have Jacob back now. He's home and you shouldn't waste any time thinking of the bad things that *might* have happened. They didn't. Be thankful that Jacob's back and unharmed." The alternative didn't bear thinking about.

"*Is* he unharmed?" she asked, her eyes suddenly blazing. "Colt kidnapped him for *money*. My son doesn't know why his father took him and I don't intend to ever tell him why but my son was scared enough to run away. And then he met that crazy nutjob and it scared him even more. He told me he wet his pants, that he couldn't help it. I can't stop thinking how terrified he must have been and I—I...I wasn't there for him." She buried her face in his shoulder again.

"He ran away, Savannah. He was fearless." Tobias smoothed his hand over her hair.

"He was silly to run away," she replied, lifting her head. Her water-filled eyes sparkled like clear-cut crystal.

"That was probably my fault," he said, feeling guilty and taking the blame. "I told him that he was brave, like Iron Man, and now I hate that he might have taken my words literally."

"Don't beat yourself up. He was scared of Colt, and he wanted to get away and come back home."

"You don't have to let me off that lightly, Savannah." He blamed himself regardless and so—he had a feeling—did she, but she was trying not to apportion blame.

She placed her hands on her cheeks. "If there's anyone to blame in all this, it's me."

"And why is that?"

"I got so caught up in us that I let my instincts fall to the side. I had a feeling Colt was up to something what with his phone calls and suddenly getting in touch with me after so long. He needed money. That's all it was, he was after me because he thought I had a good job and because I was making a life for myself here. He must have thought he could wrangle his way back into my life somehow. Once you and I became an item, it became easy enough for him to track me down."

"Why are you to blame?" He still didn't follow.

"Because I made it so easy for him. You coming to the

awards ceremony, me going to the gala dinner, us going away to Miami, and all the publicity that followed. If my dad could find out about you online, and Kay could do the same all the way from Hong Kong, it's not surprising that Colt found out about me. He's not the brightest of people, but he found me and he seized the perfect moment to take the most important thing in the world from me."

"I'm sorry you feel that way." Tobias flexed his fists, fearing the worse, knowing she had begun to harbor doubts about them being together. Maybe he should have taken things slower.

He had tried. They'd been together two months and he'd kept things as quiet as he could. It wasn't as if he wanted to shout it from the rooftops but he also didn't want to creep around in secret any longer. How much more time did she think she would need before it was safe enough? A man like Colt Brookes could have crept out of the woodwork in months and years to come. She was mistaken if she thought she'd ever be completely free of him.

Maybe he needed to fix things now.

Her eyes filled with tears.

"Don't," he told her, wiping her tears away with his fingers. "It's not something either of us could have foreseen."

She pulled out a tissue and blew her nose. "I'm not going to send Jacob to school tomorrow, and I was hoping to take a few days off work." He was glad to hear it because he was going to suggest it to her anyway.

"That's a good idea." It was time to tell her. "Someone already leaked the story."

"Which story?"

"Someone saw us leaving the police station and knew Jacob had gone missing."

She sank back down onto the couch and held her face in her hands. "They'll print it?"

"They can damn well print what they like." And there was no doubt that they would, all because of the gala dinner, and the new woman in his life. Interest in the two of them was high.

"I don't know how to deal with any of this," she moaned.

He sank to his knees and grabbed her wrists gently. "You don't have to deal with this alone."

"You can't fight all my battles for me, Tobias."

"I want to help you and Jacob through this."

"You have a company to run."

"Why are you pushing me away?"

"I'm not."

"You're not?" He couldn't keep it in any longer. "I love you, Savannah. I know it as easily and as automatically as taking my next breath. I love you."

Her mouth hung open, and she blinked, then blinked again. He waited for a response, a reaction even, but her words didn't come and the silence between them mushroomed like a rising soufflé. He sensed that his words had surprised her and had turned what should have been a beautiful moment into something awkward.

"I never want to see you or Jacob hurt again," he said, needing to say something so that his declaration of love didn't hang in the air. She moved her mouth.

"You..." she let out a loud breath, as if she couldn't say or didn't have the words to say anything back. "It's been a long day. We're both tired and it's getting late."

"You're right. It is late and I should go." He raised himself to his feet. "I could come by tomorrow if you want." But the slowness of her reply told him all. "Maybe it would be better for you and Jacob to spend time at home with your parents," he suggested, in the absence of her reply. How quickly things had changed between them. They would have been coming back from Miami tomorrow night and now the vacation seemed not only to have happened a long time ago, it seemed to have happened to two different people. Had it only been this afternoon that they'd both been sitting by the pool again, talking about the single moms' initiative and making plans for their last evening?

"I think that might be better. They're worried about me and Jacob. It would help set their minds at ease if we spent some time with them, especially since I've been away practically the whole week." The way she said it made him wonder if she regretted it.

"Of course," he said, even though he wanted to help her through it, helping Jacob to heal and return to normality. Whether she admitted it or not, Savannah still needed him—that's what he liked to think. He was here for her and he would always be but right now, at least, it didn't seem as if she wanted him around.

"You don't have to worry about Colt anymore. He's on the run, and the last thing he'll do is come here again."

"I wanted to see him one last time," she said.

"Why?"

"So I could slap him and ask him why."

"Do you want to see him?" asked Tobias. "Do you feel the need to meet one more time to have your say?"

*Before the bastard crawled back into the ground.* She'd called him just before they'd gone to the police station to get Jacob, to tell him that Jacob had been found. It had been a short call from what he'd heard of it. She shook her head. "I never want to see or hear from him again."

"You won't." This time he was going to make sure of it.

"You sound so sure of it," she said, rising to her feet slowly.

"I plan to have someone assigned to you both from now on."

"Assigned?" She scrunched up her face. "As in have a

security man trailing after me and Jacob?" She shook her head as if she hated the idea.

"We don't have to do that, if you don't want to." Not yet, but later on, it might have to become a way of life. Colt was an amateur, and there were far deadlier threats out there for a man with his position and wealth.

"You'd better go," she said, looking at her watch, "It's late."

———

Though it was past midnight when Tobias left, he pulled out his cell phone and made the call. He wouldn't be able to sleep until it was done.

"Brookes," he said, when the man picked up.

"Who's asking?"

"Tobias Stone."

"What do you want?"

"To meet. Now."

"It's after mid—"

"You don't have much time and from the way things have gone, you don't have a plan either."

"What's it to you?"

"I'm giving you a chance."

There was a pause before he spoke. "A chance for what?"

"To live." Another pause.

"I don't trust you," Colt said.

"And I don't trust you. I don't even like you but you don't have many options left."

"Why do you care?"

"I don't."

The man made a low noise, more like a groan and an exhale. "Where?"

"Tell me where you are," said Tobias, "and we'll come get you."

"I don't want any funny stuff," Brookes warned.

"I wasn't planning to make you laugh."

He gave Tobias the address of where he was staying.

"Be ready in ten and don't tell Savannah." Tobias hung up and called Ludwig.

# CHAPTER NINETEEN

The black SUV pulled up right outside the motel where he was waiting. Colt's muscles tensed and he wondered if he'd done the right thing. It was the dead of night and he was getting into a car with a man he didn't know, a man who clearly hated him and a man who was probably as dangerous as Santino.

Colt swallowed again.

He felt like he did with Santino, like an underling, and he didn't care for it. Panic gripped his stomach as it dawned on him that he was outnumbered, unarmed, and at their mercy. His life seemed to be full of dark moments like this, meetings with dangerous men in dark places. Yet there had been a time, not too long ago, when things had been simpler. He'd had a job at the factory, a wife and a baby on the way; beer on Friday nights with Merle and the boys, and fishing and a BBQ on weekends if they could arrange it.

It was nothing like the crap he was in now.

The window rolled down and a man shouted out to him. "Colt Brookes?" He nodded. "Get in." The front door opened and he did as the man asked. Sliding into the front seat, Colt examined the driver whose gaze was fixed firmly ahead as the SUV sped away.

"Where are we going?" he asked, glancing over his shoulder. In the moving shadows, he saw the other man sitting behind the driver's seat and even though he couldn't make out his features, he knew it was Tobias.

"Somewhere where I can kill you," answered Tobias smoothly and making Colt's breathing speed up as he realized this was it.

*It was too late to get out now.* He tried to open the door but the safety lock was on. "Let me out," he cried.

"Are you scared?" Tobias asked. "Peeing-in-your-pants scared?"

"Let me go."

"Jacob must have felt like that. A young boy, your *son*, no less, frightened for his life." Stone's voice was smooth, deadly and controlled. Men who kept their cool in situations such as this were dangerous. Stone wasn't at all the type of wealthy business man he had at first assumed. The man wasn't a sleazebag like Santino, but the two men weren't so different after all.

"I didn't hurt him. I never laid a finger on the kid."

"You didn't have to."

He shifted in his seat, looking out of the window into the opaque black of the night. "I told Savannah I was sorry. Told her I didn't mean it. I was stuck, that's all."

"I'm stuck too," replied Tobias. "I can't make up my mind whether to shoot you through the head, or to punch you to death."

Sweat trickled down the sides of Colt's face. He turned to the man who was driving. "Please let me out." But the driver stared straight ahead and ignored him completely.

A short time later, they turned into a gated rundown

development. Colt looked out of the window, desperately trying to figure out his escape plan. It looked like an industrial area and all the buildings were shrouded in darkness. There were no lights on anywhere.

"Get out." The driver parked and got out his gun. "Don't even try to run away," he warned, and pointing the gun at Colt's face, he got out. "This way," he ordered, and told Colt to come out from the driver's side. Stone was already standing outside, waiting. His eyes glinted in the light of the lamps. Colt tried to step back but the gun pressed hard into his ribs, reminding him that he was at their mercy. "I told you not to try anything stupid," the man behind him warned.

The blinds opened and a second man morphed out of the night like a dark shadow.

*He'd be dead soon.*

Adrenaline pumped beneath his chest and spread around his upper body as the man roughly pushed him inside. When the blinds closed, he glanced around and saw that he was in a poorly lit garage that reeked of gas and grease. Stone's smug and smooth face examined him.

"What do you want?" Colt asked, staring at the businessman who stood with his hands in his pockets. The man was tall and striking and he could see why his ex had fallen into this man's bed. Like Santino, he was cool and laidback, and almost as dangerous. But Stone seemed untouchable, not because of his wealth and his fancy-schmancy appearance, or whatever it was that women fell for, but there was something else, too. Santino didn't have it but this man did. Something that made Colt's eyes linger on him, unable to look away.

His heart rate started to climb when the man didn't answer right away.

Finally Stone spoke up. "What will it be?" he asked. "A bullet or a fist? You choose." Colt's breathing sped up and he blinked at the man who'd just given him a choice of how to die. He wanted to run faster than he'd ever wanted to run in his life, his limbs tingling as if fueled by a sudden burst of energy. But the blinds were down and there was no escape.

His mouth turned dry and the blood-pumping, heart-thrashing thud-a-thud-a-thud sounded in his ears.

*Was this what it felt like, in the moments before death?*

"Of course, I can choose for you, if you're unable to make up your mind."

He could smell his own sweat rolling down his back. Stone had lied about giving him a chance to live and he'd stupidly believed it. "A bullet," he said, closing his eyes and mentally preparing himself. Maybe this was better than what Santino would have in store for him.

"The easy way out," Stone remarked, walking up to him and flexing his fingers. Colt's muscles tightened as he stepped back but the gun against his side kept him pinned in place. "If it were my choice," Stone continued, balling his hands into fists one moment, then flexing his fingers the next, "I'd punch you to death for all the things you ever did to her, for the hell you put her and Jacob through, for each and every goddamn mark you left on her body and her face." Stone's voice lowered dangerously as he edged nearer and Colt tried to lean back. "You motherfucking son-of-a-bitch," he hissed. "I should kill you now. At least it would make me feel better." Colt swallowed nervously and saw the muscles twitch along the man's jaw. Suddenly, he felt the urge to take a leak. "Nothing would give me greater pleasure than to break all the bones in your face first, before I bent your fingers all the way over, one by one."

*The man was a psycho.* Colt shrank back into himself and almost gagged. He thought his insides would leak out any moment now. "A bullet, please," he begged as Stone walked away, calmly adjusting the cuffs of his jacket before slipping his hands into his pants pockets.

"Unfortunately," he replied smoothly, peering at him through narrowed eyes, "it's neither my choice, nor yours."

The hairs on the back of Colt's neck slowly stood up. "It's not?" he asked. *What game was Stone playing?*

Stone shook his head but said nothing.

"Then—then whose choice is it?"

"Jacob and Savannah's."

"Do *they* know about this?"

"No, and neither will they. But I know what they would want." Stone nodded and lowered his head for a moment. "And they wouldn't want me to kill you, or for you to die—I wouldn't get my hands dirty, of course. One of these fine gentlemen would do the deed."

Perspiration started to trickle down from his forehead. *Did he have a chance or was Stone screwing with him?*

"What would they want?"

Stone snorted. "You were lucky enough to be married to that woman for years and you still don't know what she'd want?" His nostrils flared. "You still don't know the type of woman she is? She wouldn't hurt anyone. Not even a fucked-up loser like you. Not even after what you did."

Colt's breathing turned ragged and short.

"What she would want is for you to disappear and never show your face or contact her again. That would be their choice, and I have to honor that."

Colt was suddenly hopeful. "I didn't mean to do it. I never meant to hurt Jacob. I was lookin' for him the whole time, I never told him to run aw—"

"Enough," Stone spoke quietly but Colt listened and shut up.

"I'll go. I'm going. I swear I'll never, ever contact them again."

Stone nodded at the man who'd driven them here. The man stepped forward and handed Colt a bag. "What's this?" He was too afraid to take it.

"Forty thousand dollars, and not a dollar less," Stone replied. "I bought you your freedom and I expect you to keep your side of the deal."

*Stone was still giving him the money?*

"Take it," he said.

Colt shrank back, thinking it was some kind of sick joke.

"Take it," Stone growled, taking a step towards him. "I don't know what you're running from. I could have let you crawl back into the sewers from which you came and let you go to your well-deserved fate."

"Why didn't you?" Colt asked. What was this all about anyway?

"Because Jacob doesn't deserve that kind of history. I would never want him to grow up and discover that his old man had been hacked to death because he hadn't been able to pay back the money he owed. I never want Jacob to find out why you took him in the first place."

Something thin and icy wormed its way through Colt's veins at the moment and he realized that this man loved his son more than Colt ever had.

"With one call, I can command the type of people who will track you down and kill you in your sleep. I can have people watching your every move and you won't ever know it. From time to time, I *will* have people watching your every move to make sure you keep your end of the deal." Stone leaned forward and his face was only a few inches away. "Don't ever give me a reason to have you killed. Now go."

"Go?" Colt asked, hesitating. He hadn't dared to open the bag and look inside either.

"Go before I take a good swing at you. My hands have been itchy ever since we picked you up. You have no idea how hard it's been to keep my fists from landing on your face."

Colt stepped towards the blinds which the other man opened. "Where am I?" he asked, looking out into the pitch-black wall of darkness. "It's dark. Do you have a flashlight? I don't know where I'm going."

"Neither did Jacob, you son of a bitch."

He gripped the bag tightly. "You'll never see me again," he mumbled, then fled into the darkness.

# CHAPTER TWENTY

"You don't look as if you've slept much, dear. Why don't you go back to bed?" her mother suggested, even though it was mid-morning. Savannah had been trying to but had tossed restlessly since eight, after barely four hours of sleep.

"I can't sleep."

"How late did Tobias stay?"

"Until midnight."

"He seems to care a great deal about you." Savannah sipped her coffee and wished her mother would leave her in peace. She knew her mother meant well, but this morning she needed silence so that she could go over everything that had happened. It seemed surreal for a few moments, until the terror and the chill of not knowing where her son was clawed back at her.

"Why don't you invite him over for dinner? It would be lovely to get to know him better. Your father and I didn't get much of a chance to talk to him yesterday."

"Yesterday wasn't exactly a normal day, Mom," she replied, sounding grouchier than she had intended.

"But why don't you ask him over, anyway?" Her mother poured herself a cup of coffee and joined her at the table.

Savannah put her hand to her head. She wanted to take things at her pace. There were too many things to think about, and she didn't want to answer questions about her and Tobias's relationship.

It was a delicate time, and Jacob was her priority above all else. She couldn't even begin to think about him, or work, or how she was going to deal with things, and Tobias was the least of her worries. She'd barely slept a wink, waking up every so often to make sure Jacob was still by her side. This morning when she'd looked in the mirror, a haggard, dark-ringed face stared back at her.

She peeked out of the living room windows and was relieved to see that the few photographers that had camped outside earlier had now disappeared. Another problem she didn't want to confront. More gossip, more intrusion, more cruel jibes for Jacob to deal with. She'd been hoping to keep his disappearance out of the public eye and this had been one of the reasons. Perhaps when he returned to school in a week's time, the buzz of it would have died down. Tobias had called her earlier to forewarn her about the possibility of photographers turning up at her door but he'd assured her that it would die down quickly. It had definitely been a wise decision not to go into work today.

She sat back down at the kitchen table and heard the sound of the front door closing. "Dad went out?"

"He went for his morning walk a little later than usual." Her mom poured a cup of coffee for him.

"Morning." Her father walked into the kitchen with a somber look on his face. He plunked a couple of newspapers down and grabbed his coffee. "I thought you should know, Ruby Red. It's all over the news."

"I thought it might be," she said, staring quietly at the headlines. '*Tycoon Lover's Son Found Safe and Well*'

She bristled, instantly coloring at the way she had been labeled.

*Tycoon lover?*

She skimmed the paper quickly, relieved that no mention had been made of Colt. The main article mentioned that the boy's 'estranged father' had unknowingly taken the boy for an after-school dinner and that the boy had wandered off. What irked her more was that the main point of it wasn't concern for Jacob but that he had been the son of a billionaire's single-mom lover. At the bottom was a photo of her and Tobias at the gala dinner and next to it a photo of them in Miami. The implication being that she was living the good life, while leaving her son to languish at home.

She held her head in her hands at the despair of it.

"Not much to report," her father replied, trying to put on a brave face. "It will blow over soon enough."

"I'm going to let Jacob sleep for as long as he needs," she said, sipping her coffee and savoring its bitter tang. "And I'm keeping him at home all of next week as well."

"That's wise," her father agreed.

"Will you be taking a week off too?" her mother asked.

Savannah nodded. "He's been through a traumatic experience and I want to make sure he's back to himself before he returns to school." She also felt guilty for having been away from him for the week she'd been in Miami.

Her father spoke up. "Your mother and I are worried about you, Ruby Red. I wish we could stay on a little longer and keep an eye on you both but I can't get any more time off."

"It's okay." She understood. Her mom didn't know it but she knew her dad was trying to keep some of his days set aside for her mom's surprise birthday cruise. She didn't want to jeopardize that so she decided not to tell them just yet about the woman who had tried to take Jacob away. Not only would it frighten them, but they'd try to find a way to stay here longer, and she didn't want them to put themselves out. She'd have to make do by herself.

Though a part of her was looking forward to having the apartment all to herself and it just being her and Jacob again. She needed to focus on her son and make sure he was all right. As for herself, she needed the week away from Stone Enterprises and the idle gossip at work which would follow her there. Gossip aside, she was still anxious, and the fear and worry that should have vanished once Jacob had been found, refused to leave her. The guilt of leaving her son and going away continued to fester.

"Are you sure? We could try to stay on a few more days, but—"

"No, Dad. I'll be fine. Tobias will help me through it." As she knew he would, but she wasn't so sure that it would do her any good being around him and hoping for a future when right now she wasn't sure of anything anymore.

"There's something else you should know," her father said.

Her mother interrupted. "Let her finish her cup of coffee, Dale."

Savannah looked up sharply. "What?"

"Kay called while you were in Miami."

"I hope she didn't call you while you were away. Did she?" her mother asked. "We told her not to disturb you because you were—"

"What did she say?" Savannah interrupted, finding the coffee too strong all of a sudden.

"She's coming back next month."

"For a vacation?"

"For good. She said she had a chance to cut short her year-long placement and she jumped at it." The wind went out of

Savannah's body and she slumped like a deflated doll against the chair.

"Was it next month, dear, or did she say June?" her mother asked.

"Next month."

It didn't matter anymore. She'd suddenly been given her marching orders. Of course Kay wouldn't throw her out onto the street, but her time in this apartment was now finite. So much for having the apartment during the summer while she made alternate arrangements. Now she didn't have much time.

This news was the final blow on top of everything else that had happened this week. How different things had been a few days ago when she had started to believe in a future with Tobias. They had been so good together, had been so blissfully happy. He was the other part of her and he understood her like nobody else ever had.

But ever since yesterday and Colt and Jacob and all of that, she felt as if a tiny crack had formed in the fabric of their relationship. She hoped it would pass, but this news didn't help. The hope she'd had of needing time for things to return to normal had suddenly disintegrated. She had a new and bigger worry to think about.

Her father looked concerned. "What will you do, Ruby Red?"

"I'm not sure, Dad." There were too many things to handle, too much to think about, and none of it was simple.

"We don't suppose you're ever coming back home, dear?"

"There's nothing for me to come back to, Mom, aside from you both." New York had started to feel more like home to her, all because of Tobias.

"Why don't you take some time off and spend a few weeks with us during the summer, when Jacob's school closes?"

"I might." She'd have to think quickly now that everything

was up in the air all of a sudden. She scratched the back of her neck, already overwhelmed by the life decisions she would have to make. "We'll see how it goes."

One month left.

The thought of it turned her stomach to mush. Who knew how things between her and Tobias would turn out by then?

"Will we get a chance to see him before we leave?" her mother asked.

She turned her head and frowned. "Who?"

"Your young man."

Savannah almost rolled her eyes but stopped herself in time. Her mother's newfound enthusiasm for Tobias grated on her already-frayed nerves. "He's working today. He's a busy man." No point telling them that he'd offered to come by and spend the day with her today but she had pushed him away.

"He seems to be handling the reporters well." Her father had turned the TV on. They all stared at the screen which showed Tobias walking into work and uttering a cold 'No comment' through gritted teeth when a reporter had asked him about Jacob's disappearance. "I'm getting to like him, Ruby Red," her father said, patting her on the back gently. "He seems like a keeper to me."

# CHAPTER TWENTY-ONE

"The media circus is slowly leaving town," Matthias said, walking into his office and closing the door behind him.

Tobias looked up. "It would seem that way."

"How are Savannah and Jacob doing?"

"Okay, I think."

"You *think?*"

"I haven't seen them."

"No?" Matthias seemed curious.

"Savannah's parents were leaving this weekend." As if that explained it all. "She's been busy with them. Jacob's off school this week and she's also taken a week off work."

"Back to the grind for the rest of us." Matthias rested his foot across the other knee and stretched his arms in the air. "You've had more than your share of excitement lately, buddy, but I never thought a touch of romance would have this kind of impact on your life."

Tobias looked at him curiously. "It's not the romance part of it that's causing the problem. But throw a shifty ex-husband into the mix and all sorts of hell will break loose."

"The man only wanted to spend time with his son?"

"Apparently. He said he was in town, then Grandma panicked, and Jacob got separated in all the kerfuffle. There was never much to it," answered Tobias. His contact in the police department had ensured that the story would remain the stripped-down version of events. Tobias didn't want details of Colt and his demand for ransom money to ever become public knowledge.

"No charges brought against him?"

"Not for kidnapping his own son," Tobias explained, wondering why his friend was digging again.

"Where's he now?"

"Slithered back to his hometown, I would imagine."

"And still the media managed to make something out of it," Matthias quipped. "It's all your fault, you know," he said good-naturedly. "You've only to show up at a police station and news spreads. You realize that this is because of the new interest in your love life?" He rubbed the back of his neck, and muttered, "There was always goddamn interest in you, but now that you have a beautiful young woman on your arm, people want more entertainment."

"They're not going to get any more fucking entertainment," Tobias growled. His dislike of the media was no secret, but now it was impacting Savannah and Jacob, and he felt even more protective of his privacy than ever.

His friend looked at him for a few seconds. "It's all business as usual now, is it?"

"Of course." He had been working away at full speed since the early morning, unable to sleep and trying to make up for the week he'd been in Miami. Yet his mind wasn't totally on the business, either.

"Are you all set for the trip to San Diego next week? We're meeting with Dextronics, remember?"

Tobias shook his head. He wasn't going. There were more important matters to tend to, whether Savannah wanted him to or not. "I was about to touch base with you about it later on."

Matthias sat up. "You're not going?" he asked casually. "I was under the impression that this was an important meeting. What else has come up?"

"Things I need to take care of. There's no reason why you can't handle it yourself, Matthias. You carry as much weight. There's no need for both of us to go."

"But what are you doing instead?"

"Nothing," he replied, shrugging. "I'd rather not travel right now, not with everything that's happened. I need to be around for Savannah and Jacob." Despite the fact that Savannah didn't seem to share this line of thinking. Despite the fact that she seemed to want to push him away. He knew she needed her space to deal with things alone and he understood that need for solitude but he wasn't going to allow her to bask in it or push him away for too long. He had decided to give her a few more days before he visited her one evening.

Matthias let out a whistle, and placed his hands on his head, as if he'd unveiled a rare object. "I had no idea it was that serious. It's not just a fling, is it?"

"It never was," Tobias replied.

Matthias stood up and smiled. "You leave Dextronics to me," he said, and walked towards the door then turned around. "I haven't seen you this distracted before."

"I'm not distracted, Matthias. I still have my eyes on the business. You don't need me by your side as much as you think you do. I know you're capable of making executive decisions." He smiled. "It's the reason I hired you in the first place."

"That's right," replied Matthias, giving him a wink and a grin. "That's why I'm here."

———————

"You miss Lenny?"

Jacob nodded. "So, can I go back to school tomorrow?" Savannah felt deflated that he seemed well enough to want to return. She, on the other hand, didn't want to leave the apartment.

She tried to pacify him. "Thursday's an odd day to go back to school, honey. Why don't you go back on Monday like we agreed? I'm not going to work until then and we could do some more fun stuff together."

Didn't he want to spend time with her? Since her parents had left, she and Jacob had watched TV, read together and enacted scenes that he had thought up. He'd convinced her to become Hulk to his Iron Man. She thought they were having fun and it hurt her to hear that he was eager to return to school.

She had taken Jacob to the park on Monday and nobody had stopped them. A group of moms with their children in strollers had stared at her and whispered among themselves. Savannah was certain they knew who she was, but they didn't approach her and Jacob, and other than that, nobody else had bothered them either.

She'd tried to talk to Jacob as subtly as she could, to find out more about what had happened to him during the hours that he'd been missing but he seemed to be over it and didn't want to discuss it. He'd asked her where Colt was and she told him he'd gone back home. A few times, she had been tempted to call him and had even called his number but she'd cut the line before it connected. What did she have to say to him?

Nothing.

She wished she could handle things as well as Jacob seemed to be but each time she laid her head on the pillow at night, sleep was the last thing to come to her. Instead she would be besieged by images of a faceless woman leading Jacob away and she would spend the rest of the night wide awake, while horrors floated around in her head.

She couldn't shake it off and it had left her in a place where she didn't want to connect with anyone. She'd let most of her phone calls go unanswered, aside from the one from Jacob's teacher who wanted to see how Jacob was. Kay and Lenny's mom had both called a few times and left messages asking how they were doing. She'd only texted back short replies. The only person she'd really been glad to hear from—aside from her parents who sometimes called twice a day—was Briony. But even so, she'd managed to prevent her from coming over to visit.

Maybe if she had a chance to meet with this girl named Izzy, the one who'd stepped in to save her son, it might help her to move on. She'd have to ask Tobias about the police reports and what he'd found out.

"You promise I can go back on Monday?"

"Yes."

He seemed happy with that answer and lay back down on the couch, watching TV. When the doorbell rang, she jumped, wondering who it could be then remembered it could only be Tobias. Arnold seemed to know him well enough now to send him up without buzzing her. She braced herself as she opened the door.

"I thought I would surprise you," he said, giving her a smile that almost made her melt.

"It *is* a nice surprise," she said, feeling her heart flip a little at the sight of him in his dark gray suit. Did this man never have a bad suit or bad hair day? She opened the door wider to let him in and caught a whiff of his cologne as he leaned in to kiss her on the lips. It was a light kiss, nothing deep or heavy, but enough to ignite a few happy memories.

"Tobias!" Jacob leapt up from the couch and ran towards him. "Why didn't you come before?"

"Before?" asked Tobias, scooping him up into his arms. "Before when?"

"Before now."

"I'm sorry, I should have but I've been busy," he said, stepping inside, "and I thought you needed the rest." He put Jacob back down on the floor.

"I'm all rested now and I can't wait to go back to school."

Tobias gave him a questioning look. "Already?"

"I'm bored."

"Bored? With this gorgeous woman?" Tobias reached for her waist and pulled her towards him. "How could you be bored?"

"Eww!" Jacob giggled. "You're not going to kiss her again, are you?" Savannah remembered this was the first time Jacob had seen the two of them together ever since she'd told him that she and Tobias were *together*.

"He's not going to kiss me," she said, sliding out of Tobias's embrace before he did. "Can I get you something to drink? Iced tea?" she asked, ignoring the look of surprise that flickered behind his eyes. She walked towards the kitchen and he followed her as they left Jacob engrossed in a children's TV show. He tried to grab her waist again but she moved away, out of his reach. "Briony says 'hi' and Matthias sends his wishes."

"She called me earlier. She's been calling me every day, in fact." She smiled and leaned against the countertop, crossing her arms even when Tobias walked up to her. There was a time once when she would have fallen into his embrace.

"What is it?" he asked, his face solemn.

"I'm sorry," she replied sheepishly. "This isn't right, me behaving like this. It feels funny with Jacob around."

"Is that all it is?" His searching eyes pinned her gaze in place.

And other things, everything that had happened, and Kay, but she wasn't going to tell him about that yet. She had a feeling he would try to fix things, the way he always did, and make things easy for her. She wasn't even sure what she wanted anymore. "I think I need a little time."

"Time?"

"To work things out."

He wiped a hand across his brow. "To work what out? Do you need time to get over the whole Colt saga—or because of the other day—when I told you I loved you?"

"No. No. It's not that." But she wondered all the same if it was part of it. She tried to assure him but before, she would have gotten up and moved closer to him, pressed her body against his and convinced him with her touch, not just her words.

It was a general uneasiness about many things but more than anything, it was the guilt of leaving her son and having him suffer a horrific ordeal, while she had been on vacation.

It was many things all tied together: Tobias being who he was, the fame, and the wealth and the public interest in him—the very things that had led her ex to New York. Being with Tobias wasn't just being in a relationship with a man she loved, it was stepping out into the world and letting the world look in. She wasn't ready for it, and didn't want it.

But could she get used to it? For him? Could she do it for him? Would she?

Before this had happened, she might have but now, she wasn't so sure. Even when Tobias had told her he loved her, she should have jumped for joy. Weren't those the words she'd been wanting to hear? Wasn't that the way she felt about him? She didn't fully understand it herself, why she was backing away instead of letting him take care of her, but she wasn't that kind of woman—it didn't matter who he was, because one day, he might get bored with her, and then what?

She couldn't give in to him, not yet, not like before, and so she chose to trust her instincts and right now they told her to protect herself. She couldn't do that if she made herself vulnerable again. Falling in love with Tobias made her completely vulnerable and she couldn't be vulnerable because her son needed her to be strong. Even though Jacob felt ready to return to school again, she felt that she'd let him down once and she wasn't about to do it again.

"Is this about the press coverage and the newspapers?"

"That doesn't help." She still flinched each time she thought of the *tycoon Lover* headline. "It's about a lot of things, I can't pin it down exactly. It's not you, Tobias. I swear."

"I can't control what the press reports about me, Savannah, or the way people I don't know seem to take an interest in what I do in my personal life. I try to have some control over it, I try to keep things private but it doesn't always work out like that."

"But I can."

"You can what?" he asked quickly.

"I can control what happens in my life."

"Can you?" he asked. Damn his strong jaw, and the way he looked at her. She was melting again, the way she always did with him around and forced herself to look away. Maybe this unease had come because he'd made it vocal. He'd told her he loved her, and if she told him she loved him, the future was theirs.

A woman like Kay would jump at the opportunity—and she would probably jump in her Jimmy Choos. But Savannah shied away from all of that. She had Jacob to think about and he didn't deserve to be ridiculed by children at school. *'Gold-digger'* had hurt as much as *'tycoon lover'* and she didn't want to subject her son to any more taunts.

"I keep thinking he'll be back."

"Colt?"

She nodded. "I took Jacob to the park a few days ago and I kept looking around for him. First, I kept looking for photographers and then I kept worrying that Colt would show up."

"He won't."

"How do you know?"

"Why would he? He's on the run."

She put her fingers to her lips to tell him to shush. There was no dividing wall or partition between the kitchen and the living room, and Jacob sometimes had super hearing powers, when he chose to.

"But he didn't get the money and you said he's in trouble as it is and he can't go home. He has nowhere else to go. I keep thinking he'll show up on my doorstep."

"Never."

"Never?" She folded her arms and angled her head towards him. "You seem pretty certain of that."

And when Tobias remained silent, she felt something cold and heavy settle in her stomach. "What did you do, Tobias?"

Still he said nothing.

"Did you kill him?" she whispered. "Or *pay* to have him killed?"

His face twisted. "Neither. I swear, but I wanted to. Unfortunately, he's alive, I assure you. I didn't even touch a hair on his head. You can ask Ludwig."

"What good would that do? Ludwig's on your payroll. He'd do and say anything you wanted."

He took a step towards her, and placed his hands on her arms. "I'm not the bad guy here, Savannah. You told me you wished he would leave you alone, that you never wanted to see him again." His eyes burned into her as he took her hand and even though she had the urge to pull it away, she didn't.

"And you somehow made it happen?"

He nodded.

"And how did you do that?"

"I gave him the $40k."

It was a snort, or a low laugh, or a puff of exhaled air. The sound that came from her throat was all of these things. "You paid him off?"

"Same thing."

"You gave him forty thousand dollars? Just like that?"

"In exchange for him never coming near you or Jacob again."

She clapped a hand to her forehead and sat down at the table. The weight was too much, the burden too heavy. "So now I'm beholden to you."

"I did it for me, if that makes you feel better," Tobias replied, visibly irritated.

She wanted to thank him for what he'd done, if it was true, if she could believe him.

But could she? Or was there another side to this man that she did not know? She searched for her cell phone then remembered it was lying in her bedroom.

"Call him, if you don't believe me." Tobias's voice had lost its softness. "I thought I understood you, Savannah, but I honestly don't have a clue. I don't want you to thank me but I thought this was what you wanted."

He could see right through her again and even if he didn't like to hear it, she still felt as if she owed him even more. No matter how he saw it, she was in his debt. But had Tobias not acted, what would have been the alternative? A life spent always looking over her shoulder for Colt to come back and shatter her world again? She loved this man who always protected her and did the right thing by her, but being with him had its problems. She'd almost lost her son because of it. Despite what Tobias thought, it wasn't an easy choice for her to step into his life and become a part of his world.

"I don't know *what* I want. I just want my life back."

"You have it back, don't you see?"

She said nothing, but stared at the table with her hands clasped in front of her. She wanted Tobias, needed him, and he needed her, but things were already complicated and were going to become even more so. Jacob loved him as a father, and she knew what her boy wanted deep down. She couldn't control the way things would end up, and she wasn't sure if she could lead the kind of life being with Tobias demanded.

"I get it," he said, taking out his car keys. "It's me you don't want. That's the thing you can't bring yourself to say. Telling you how I feel about you wasn't supposed to frighten you away."

She looked up at him suddenly. "I need some time. I'm not asking for us to go our separate ways. I love what we had."

"Had?"

"In Miami. I loved what we had but so much has happened."

"But you're talking about it as though it's a thing of the past."

"I need some time to get over this."

"Time away from me?"

"No," she said, shaking her head slowly. "That's not what I said."

"But it's what you meant." His voice was quiet and he had a faraway look in his eyes that made her want to tell him to stay, but she said nothing, not even when he placed a rushed kiss on top of her head. "You take care, Savannah." He walked away and she heard him telling Jacob he had to go, then they high-fived and the front door closed.

She was left alone at the kitchen table, staring at the breadcrumbs and listening to the background noise of the TV, wondering why her life had suddenly turned upside down.

"I love you," she whispered, closing her eyes and forcing herself not to run after him.

# THE VOW, BOOK 2

**The Billionaire's Love Story (#8)**

# CHAPTER ONE

W hat the fuck did she want? Tobias stared at the missed call from Naomi and shoved his cell phone into his pocket. He no longer had any business with the high-class escort and had no intention of calling her back. When the elevator doors slid apart, he stormed out.

"Good evening, sir," the elderly concierge greeted him warmly. Tobias nodded at him as he rushed past, not even stopping.

"How's Ms. Page doing?"

This time he had to stop.

"Ms. Page." The man stepped forward from behind his desk. "I'm worried about her, all that nastiness with Jacob. Is she all right?"

Tobias frowned. "Yes, she's fine." She didn't want him around, so he had to assume she was happy to deal with things in her own way. *Time.* She needed more time. Why was it always two steps forward and three steps back?

"I've been keeping an eye on her," said the concierge, his conversation preventing Tobias from reaching the main doors. "But I don't want to impose. But you say she's all right?"

"Yes," Tobias almost hissed then let out a sigh. His bad mood was not due to this man. "I'm sorry," he said. "It's been a rough day." It had been fine until he'd turned up on Savannah's doorstep. All he wanted was to be there for her, but she was pushing him away already. He sensed she was having doubts and this whole sorry mess with Colt, Jacob and the media, it had her worried. This man had nothing to do with it.

"I'm Arnold." The man held out his hand.

"Hello, Arnold," said Tobias, shaking hands quickly. "I'm Tobias."

"I know who you are," Arnold smiled back. "I saw the pictures of you both at that fancy party at the hotel. Nice-looking couple you make."

The gala night at the Waldorf Astoria. It hadn't even been that long ago.

"Thank you," Tobias muttered, still anxious to leave. He nodded at the man and made his way out.

Across the street, he saw the familiar black SUV with his security men in it and was half-tempted to tell them to stay here and keep an eye on Savannah and Jacob. She wouldn't know even if he did assign bodyguards to her. He was determined to keep her safe and knew it was the right thing to do but he also knew how goddamn pigheaded that woman could be.

Savannah was adamant about not wanting to change her life, about not wanting someone on her back. If she found out that he had gone behind her back and assigned her a bodyguard anyway—and she probably would because she wasn't an airhead—then she would give him hell for doing yet another thing 'that he wanted to because he could.'

How could he win her over and convince her that being with him was going to work out fine in the end? He couldn't, he only had to hope she figured it out for herself. It was impossible to put ideas into Savannah Page's head.

Slamming the car door as he got into his Porsche, he closed his eyes and leaned his head against the headrest. When his cell phone rang again, he half-wished it was Savannah calling him, telling him she was sorry, and to come back.

But in his eagerness, he'd answered it too soon, just after he'd noticed the name on the caller display. It wouldn't be worth the trouble if he hung up on his mother now.

"Mom." He tried to inject a tone of light-heartedness into his voice.

"At last, my son answers." His mother's cool, clipped tone fried his already-frayed nerves.

"I've been busy, Mom."

"I can see that, my darling. You've been in the news, a disappearing child, an ex-husband, a vacation in Miami and a new woman in your life. I think it's about time you came over for lunch."

"I can't, I'm busy. I've got a lot going on."

"I thought you might say that. Your father and I will be around mid-week. We'd love to meet up with you."

Tobias groaned under his breath. Maybe it wasn't too late to go to San Diego with Matthias. "I'm not sure—"

"I checked your schedule with your PA and she's booked dinner with your parents for Wednesday evening." Tobias ground his teeth together and felt like a helpless twelve-year-old again; not old enough to do his own thing, but no longer young enough to want a mother's attention.

"Have you seen the state your brother's in?"

Tobias jolted up in his seat. "Xavier? Why? What's happened?"

"He's been dumped by that Russian oligarch's daughter."

"Petra?" He hadn't even met her yet, had only heard of Xavier's infatuation with her. "I didn't think her father was an oligarch. I thought *she* was a model."

"They're all oligarchs and *all* their daughters are tall and thin enough to be models."

Tobias sighed slowly; he was used to his mother's sweeping generalizations, and completely ignored her. "She dumped him?"

"He's in pieces," Millicent stated, in a casual tone embellished by a dash of the dramatic. Tobias felt a twinge of guilt. From their last conversation, he recalled that his brother had been infatuated by this girl. Tobias had intended to meet with Xavier but he'd been so wrapped up in his own romance with Savannah, that he hadn't even called him.

"I thought it would be a good time for us all to meet for dinner," his mother continued. Xavier being there made the bitter pill easier to swallow.

"Wednesday at 8:00 at The Carlyle."

He could feel the tension along his neck and shoulders.

"Well?" his mother continued, after the lengthy silence.

"Well, what?"

"Aren't you going to tell me anything?" His mother demanded. "Or must I always get my information second-hand from TV and those trashy magazines?"

"You love those trashy magazines." He'd found them hidden beneath the copies of glossy home decor and travel magazines on the coffee table when he had last visited them. "Why don't we save it for Wednesday?"

"How long exactly has this been going on?" his mother asked, as if he was a cheating spouse.

"Are you really asking me that, Mother?" He replied testily. As far as his mother was concerned, no woman was good enough for him.

"I'm asking out of interest."

"You're asking because you're nosy."

"I'm merely concerned, my darling."

Tobias rubbed his forehead and kept his eyes closed as he listened. "Concerned about what?"

"Your ready-made family, but that's a conversation for another time."

"My *what?*" he barked, loosening his tie and frowning. He'd really didn't need this after the day he'd had.

"Your father and I are worried about you, my darling."

"Dad's fine. I think it's just you, Mom. You should be happy for me, you should be happy that I've finally found someone who makes *me* happy." Although his words didn't ring true at the moment, not with things cooling between them, and Savannah claiming to need more time and space. *Why didn't she let him in?*

"I *am* happy."

"Then make an effort and at least sound as if you are."

He heard her exhale loudly. "Are you okay, my darling? I don't want to fight with you. You sound tired and irritable, but I'm used to that. We saw the press hounding you on TV as you came into work. Don't let this wind you up."

Nothing wound him up as much as his mother did. Though it wasn't himself he was worried about. He was worried about losing Savannah. This time it mattered. He wanted her, and needed her and he wasn't used to *not* having things he wanted.

Perhaps that was the reason he hungered for her even more, because she didn't fall easily into his bed. Because she didn't take for granted that she would always be by his side. Because she didn't seem to be in total awe of his wealth.

She'd been over-the-moon grateful that he had taken her to Miami, had been blissfully happy for them to have spent time together, had fallen in love with his home and the private world they had shared—but he could see that these things didn't define who she was. He admired that, and could no longer imagine his life without Savannah and Jacob in it.

"That's okay," he replied, his thoughts a million miles away.

"You haven't listened to a word I've said, have you?" Another angry puff. "I'll see you on Wednesday. Why don't you bring your new lady along?"

"Her name's Savannah."

"That's right. Why don't you bring her?"

Tobias made a face and rolled his lips together, then, "I'll see you and Dad at dinner."

"Xavier too," his mother reminded him.

"Bye, Mom." He hung up and groaned. He loved her, but his mother drained the energy out of him sometimes and the really irritating thing was, she probably didn't even realize it.

## CHAPTER TWO

"Shall we go to the park?" Savannah walked into the living room having finished unpacking and putting away all the last remnants from her Miami vacation.

"Nah," said Jacob, lying on the floor on his belly with his hands palm-side down and his head resting on them. She watched him carefully, like an overprotective lioness.

"Shall we read?" Savannah suggested, sliding down to the floor beside him and giving his leg a loving squeeze.

He was growing taller and becoming thinner, and every last memory from his chubby toddler face had disappeared long ago. "Honey?" she asked, when he didn't reply. He shook his head, with his eyes still focused on the TV. He'd been in the living room ever since he'd had breakfast and he was still in his PJs even though it was almost noon. "We could play Marvel superheroes?" That usually did the trick.

"No, Mommy," he said in an irritable voice that was so unlike him. "I don't want to do anything."

"Sure, honey." She chewed on her lip. "Jacob," she paused, squeezing his leg gently again. "That lady who wanted you to go to the restroom with her—did you go *anywhere* with her?"

He shook his head.

"You didn't?" *Are you sure? Are you telling me everything?* "You would tell me, wouldn't you?" Doubt ate away at her core. She was desperate to believe him, and yet terrified that he was keeping something from her. Something that would rear its ugly head decades from now.

He shook his head.

"Jacob, honey. Just, please listen to me a minute. I need to know." He got up slowly, and then sat with his back against the couch, crossing his legs. "I won't blame you or get angry with you. I just need to know if you were hurt."

"I told you, Mommy. No!" His anger startled her and she wondered if maybe she needed to get him some counseling for what he had been through. The police officer had given her an information pack and it had some numbers on it.

"Like I said, Izzy showed up and then the guard came and that woman ran off."

"Okay, honey." She wrapped her arms around his shoulders and hugged his head to her bosom. "I'm sorry, Jacob. I just wanted to make sure."

"I'm hungry. Can I have some more cereal?"

---

"Thanks for coming last minute," said Savannah, shuffling her back against the wooden slats of the bench. She and Lenny's mom watched the boys playing on the monkey bars.

"I'm glad you called," Julia replied. "I would have suggested it myself, only—"

"I'm sorry I didn't pick up your calls. It's been a strange week," said Savannah, wanting to reassure her friend.

"You poor things." Julia twisted her body towards her and leaned her arm along the top of the bench. Every now and then, they would both turn their attention to the boys whose screams and laughter roared out from the play area. "How are things now?"

"My ex has gone back home. He didn't think it through, and he really only wanted to spend some time with Jacob." Savannah was careful not to divulge too much. "But Jacob doesn't really know him and so he went AWOL."

"While you and Tobias were on vacation?"

"We were due to fly back the next day."

Julia's eyes opened wide and she leaned closer. "Does he *really* have his own private jet?"

Savannah nodded.

"Do you have any vacation photos?" Julia asked, dropping her voice to a whisper. Savannah thought this was an odd request.

"No," she replied, frowning and shaking her head. It had never occurred to her to take any photos of her and Tobias together, and as for taking any of the plane? Definitely not.

"I can't believe you're dating *Tobias Stone!*" Lenny's mother looked as if she was going to explode from the excitement of the news.

"He's just a normal guy," replied Savannah, forcing a smile.

She saw him as a normal guy, but she hadn't expected him to go storming out of her apartment the way he had yesterday. She wasn't ending their relationship; at least, that wasn't what she'd said to him. She'd only told him she wanted some time to think things through. Doubts were beginning to creep in of what the future might bring, more media scrutiny and more danger. She wasn't sure she could handle it, wasn't sure she wanted to put Jacob through that but she'd kept these thoughts to herself. Still, it had surprised her when Tobias had left so abruptly and he hadn't called since then.

After spending intimate days and nights together in Miami,

she missed him more than she believed was possible. Being alone was horrible, and right now, it hurt like crazy.

"Normal? He's not normal, Savannah. He's a goddamn billionaire. Oh, my!" Julia placed a hand over her chest, her eyes turning shiny and round with amazement. "I would *so* love to swap places with you, even just for a few moments. I mean, Jerry's a wonderful guy and I'm only saying this, ya know, like hypothetically, but, sweet Jesus, sleeping with *that* guy! And living *that* life? Yes, please!"

Savannah felt her cheeks turn crimson. The sex *had* been great. More than amazing. Tobias made her shudder, made her scream and moan like she had never before. She kept her eyes focused on her bag as she relived a few of those moments.

"The houses...the things you must get to see and do and the places he must take you to. Do you know how many moms hate you at school?"

Savannah lifted her head sharply and stared back at her friend, her brows snapping together.

"Not *hate* you, as in hate hate, but, ya know, like they just want to be you for a day, or a month. We were talking about it—"

"You were *talking* about me?"

"Why are you so surprised?" asked Julia, looking surprised herself. "You've been the talk of the whole school since you brought that man to the awards ceremony. And since then, it's just gotten bigger and bigger."

"What's gotten bigger and bigger?"

"The interest in you. Right now, you two are the talk of the school again—not in a bitchy way," Julia replied quickly, "but Jacob going missing was all over the newspaper and all over the school on Monday morning. A few of us went for a coffee and someone pulled out the newspaper and ...It was just as well that you stayed away."

*Thank goodness she had,* thought Savannah. And thank goodness she'd kept Jacob at home, too. She had been thinking about it but she made her mind up to take another week off. "Who went to coffee?" Savannah asked, curious to know who was talking about her.

"A few moms from our class."

"Henry Carson's mom?"

Julia wrinkled her nose as if someone had opened the lid to the dog poop trash bin. "That woman? Hell, no. She doesn't hang around with *us*."

*Shame,* thought Savannah. She'd have wanted to know what that woman thought. Julia touched her arm. "I wouldn't worry about it. You're hot news at the moment, and I guess it sounds awful with us talking about you, but I swear it wasn't in a nasty way. We were just ...jealous...of you and *him*. And then of course someone pulled up pictures of you two on that gala dinner night. Where the hell did you get that dress from?" Julia asked, her eyes like round saucers. "You looked stunning."

"Thanks."

"We barely recognized you." Savannah shook her head and accepted the back-handed compliment graciously. That night *had* been amazing. It had made her think she could do it, she could be with Tobias, she could put up with the glare of publicity. It was worth it, just to be with him.

Even now, despite all of this, she could and would force herself to put up with it—if it meant being with him. She was in love with the man, and a love like that was hard to walk away from. A love like that was rare and she wasn't stupid. She wasn't about to let Tobias Stone walk away. But first, she had to come to peace with herself and figure out what was best for her son.

Julia scrolled through her cell phone and found some more pictures. "Look at this!" She showed her a picture of her and Tobias leaving a restaurant in Miami. "You look crazy in love together!" Savannah couldn't help but smile. These were the first pictures she'd seen of her and Tobias online. Her dad had told her that there were others.

There was no doubt in her mind that it was this online information that had led Colt to her.

But now that Julia was shoving them in her face, she had to agree, as she peered closer. She and Tobias *did* look good together. It was the way Tobias was looking at her with a smile on his face, and his eyes on her lips. It painted a picture that said more than a million words could ever say about their romance. Her heart jumped and little shockwaves of happiness darted along her nerves, leaving her with a feeling of supreme joy.

"I think they need drinks," said, Julia, pulling out a small carton of juice as the boys came bounding towards them. Jacob looked flushed and happy, and Savannah handed him a plastic water bottle.

She watched him guzzle it quickly. "You're very thirsty," she remarked as Jacob wiped his mouth with the back of his hand.

"This is where daddy took me," he said, looking around.

"Here?"

He nodded. She looked around and tried to picture it, her frightened son with Colt. This must have been where he had called her from that first time she'd heard Jacob's voicemail message, when she'd been lying on the sun-lounger near the pool, waiting for Tobias to finish his work so that they could disappear into the bedroom. Guilt pierced through her and she waited for Jacob to say something more, to open up. But instead he handed back the water bottle and both boys rushed back towards the play area.

"How do you know he won't come back?"

She turned towards Julia. "You mean my ex-husband?" She didn't know, but she had a pretty good feeling, because Tobias had told her. "He won't. I mean, he can try, but I won't ever leave Jacob alone again." She had been tempted to call Colt, just to make sure that he was still alive, as Tobias had told her he was but each time she got ready to call him, she backed away, unable to go through with it, not wanting to hear his voice again.

"What was his place in Miami like?" Julia asked, suddenly changing the topic again. "I've heard he's got holiday homes all over the world, Miami and Barbados, and Venice."

"He's got a nice place in Miami, but I don't know about the others."

"I guess you'll find out when he takes you." Julia flipped her hand lightly across her lap. "You lucky woman." Savannah could understand the interest, but there was a whole lot more that others didn't see.

"It's not always so glamorous. He has security around him a lot of the time and that's something I'm finding hard to get used to."

"Security?"

"Because any madman, or madwoman, could come up to him and do anything. It's not just the crazies out there, but what if he backed out of a business deal, or didn't follow something through, what if he pissed someone off and they wanted revenge?"

Julia looked pensive.

"And all these photos of him and us, and this interest in what we do, people we don't know looking at our private moments—it's unsettling. It's not something he likes, and I certainly don't."

"I hadn't thought of that," her friend replied.

"It's not like he's a public figure, like he's a singer or an actor. He's not even courting fame. He's a businessman."

"It must worry you, I mean, with Jacob."

"It does."

"How does Jacob get on with Tobias?"

Savannah smiled. "He adores him. Absolutely adores him."

"That's half the battle, I guess, being a single mom."

Savannah nodded, agreeing. She had never sought out Tobias Stone, but luck, providence and serendipity had brought this man into her life. They were going through a rough patch at the moment, but she was certain they could work things out. The next few months looked shaky, though. She also had to find another apartment within her budget.

Living rent-free these past few months had been a huge blessing but she wasn't sure that she would be able to survive, not in Sunnyside. The more she looked, the more she was beginning to realize that she would have to move further out but that meant she would lose Rosalee's help. The woman had been a godsend to her from the start and even this week, Rosalee had come through for her, bringing a dish or some cookies she had baked. She was like a mother to her, in a place where she had no family.

"We're hungry!" a chorus of voices bellowed out as the boys came charging back to them.

"Shall we take them for something to eat?" Lenny's mom suggested.

"Pizza!" came the unified response. Savannah was glad that she had decided to pick up the phone and arrange the playdate. She was anxious about Jacob's return to school on Monday but looking at his rosy cheeks and bright eyes, she didn't really have to worry too much. Her son looked as if he was ready to dive back into his normal routine. Though it was a pity the same couldn't be said for her. Not only was she hesitant about returning to work, dealing with her office colleagues and Tobias, she also didn't feel ready to leave the school drop-offs and pick-ups to Rosalee. Tobias said Colt had left, but what if he came back when she least expected it?

*What if $40k wasn't enough?*

"Uh," Julia's face fell. "We have karate at 6:00," she said, looking at her watch.

Lenny looked mortified. "Do I *have* to go today, Mom?"

"I've paid, and yes, you have to go today."

"But Mah-aaaaam!"

Julia looked at her and rolled her eyes. "I swear, the palpitations he gives me, sometimes I have to drag him there kicking and screaming."

"Why don't you stop it?"

"Because he will always find a reason to sit at home with his device and do nothing. We've been through soccer, baseball and judo. He's good at this and I think it's a good skill to have. He's not quitting, not until he's a black belt."

"Mom!!" Lenny looked at Jacob as if a great tragedy had befallen him and Jacob put on a sorry face in allied commiseration.

"How about we meet up tomorrow after school?" Savannah suggested. "You can come over to my place."

"Or you could come over to mine," Julia suggested. "I'll keep it simple with hot dogs or pizza, or both."

"If you're sure," replied Savannah.

"I'm sure."

# CHAPTER THREE

Laughter rippled around The Oasis—his brother's favorite watering hole. Skyscrapers, rising like majestic columns from the ground, were grandly silhouetted against the falling sun.

He'd spent the day with his mastermind group; a group of New York's most successful and wealthiest businessmen. They got together once every two months to bounce ideas off one another. While he didn't need it to guide his business decisions and plans, Tobias found that a lot of the men turned to him for business advice. He liked that and had continued to attend, and found himself enjoying the day, exchanging ideas and opinions with other wealthy businessmen.

A day of golf was followed by drinks and dinner but this evening Tobias had missed the dinner. Meeting his brother had been long overdue.

But even here in this fashionable rooftop terrace bar, the in place to be seen in if you were anyone, Tobias felt out of place. He was surrounded by easy laughter and rumbling conversation, scantily dressed beauties and the obviously moneyed clientele.

He felt he didn't belong. Or rather, he fit right in, but he didn't *want* to. The place reeked of decadence; of people wanting to display their good genes and wealth and wanting nothing more than to be seen flaunting it on a heady Saturday night in the city.

What he wanted was to be with Savannah and to get back to the life they'd started to have before Colt and that whole sorry mess had reared its ugly head.

She was always on his mind, and yet she was out of his life. He worried about her and needed to know that she and Jacob were okay but this distance she had put between them didn't make things easy.

Matthias had left for San Diego yesterday and Tobias had now decided to join him. He would fly out tomorrow. There was no reason to stay here, *just in case.* Just in case Savannah called and told him to come over, just in case she was having a bad day, just in case she needed him. He would have rushed over.

But she hadn't called.

And after their last meeting, he hadn't wanted to impose. Was it imposing to be concerned and to want to care, even if it was unwanted, even if she pushed him away? He had wrestled with these questions for days and had finally decided to go to San Diego as he had originally planned. The next month was full of business trips with a trip to Houston next month. He had been thinking of cutting back on the traveling, of letting Matthias hold the reins, but perhaps being out of town would be the thing to distract him while he waited for Savannah to come to her senses.

So when Xavier had called him and suggested that they meet for drinks, he'd jumped at the offer, feeling guilty as well that he hadn't reached out to his younger brother in the first place.

"How was billionaire golf?" Xavier asked, a slightly condescending tone lingering in his voice.

"Not bad," he replied. "You should come and find out for yourself sometime. You never know, it could help you." Tobias had tried to get his brother to attend, but so far Xavier had resisted.

Xavier made a face as if someone had retched all over him. "If I'm stuck, I'd just come and see you. Another whiskey?" he asked, looking around for a server. Tobias nodded and finished off the rest of his drink.

"So," said Xavier, taking a long drawn-out sip of his beer and putting the bottle down, "not only did I find out from Mom a few months ago that you split up with Naomi, but now I find out from the press that you're dating again? Thanks, bro, for keeping me informed."

"About that," said Tobias setting down his glass guiltily. "Things happened quickly, and besides, you've been busy with Petra."

"But this woman obviously means a lot to you—judging by the photos I'm seeing online."

When Tobias didn't reply, Xavier continued, "Is this the temp? The one who was in your office on New Year's Eve?"

Tobias angled his head, thinking back. Had Xavier seen Savannah before?

Xavier prompted him. "Brown mid-length, straight-out-of-bed hair, nice lips, nice—" he'd started to cup his hands together, as if he was holding two coconuts, then quickly dropped them. "And a good body?" he said instead.

"She's the one, but not for those reasons," Tobias replied, thinking of her body, all the same.

"This has been going on *that long* and you never said anything?"

"It was on and off."

"She's got a kid?"

"Yes."

"When did this happen?"

"Over time," replied Tobias, keeping his answers short and sweet. "I hear you and Petra split?"

"Yeah," said Xavier, looking around again. "The service in this place sucks." He clicked his fingers and caught the attention of a server. When the young man came over, Xavier ordered another round of drinks. Tobias could sense his brother's reluctance to talk.

"Mom said you were pretty cut up about it," Tobias said, trying to probe carefully and wondering at the same time why his brother would even tell their mom about his romantic problems.

The almost-empty bottle stopped at Xavier's lips and he held it there. "Mom?"

Tobias nodded.

"I never specifically said anything to her along those lines. Jeez, that woman must be telepathic," said Xavier, rubbing his hand through his thick brown hair. "Remember when we were kids and she used to say she had eyes at the back of her head and could see what we were doing without turning around?" They both laughed. Tobias remembered it well. She'd been a loving mother, was still, in her controlling, needing-to-know-everything way, and had set down firm boundaries then. Tobias wondered if she sometimes still thought of them as those little boys and not the grown men they were now.

"Why would you even tell Mom about your romantic problems?"

"I didn't, but you know how good she is at clawing things out."

"She said the two of you had split."

"We're taking a break." As if that was an explanation for it.

"She's in Croatia for a shoot. Fuck knows what she gets up to when she's on one of those. Some of the things she tells me would make your hair curl." Xavier's mouth tightened into a hard expression. "But she'll be back soon and when she is, I'll arrange for the four of us to get together," he said. "It would be good to meet your squeeze. It would be a change if we got to know this one, seeing as we didn't see much of Naomi."

"We'll see," replied Tobias. He didn't see the point in meeting Petra if she was no longer with his brother.

"Sounds kinda nasty, her kid disappearing like that. He wasn't hurt, was he?" Xavier asked.

"No," replied Tobias and leaned back in his seat as the server placed another round of drinks on the table. "Everything's okay now," he replied pensively but it was hard to tell what 'okay' was.

They had both carefully concealed their feelings from one another way back before their first kiss. Then they'd wasted more time dancing around, unsure, revealing their feelings for one another but hiding them from everyone else. He'd finally managed to convince her to let her guard down, and had taken her away and spent a few beautiful days with her, time that was intimate and private, and he'd known then that she was the one for him. But life had thrown a damn curve ball at him again and now Savannah was trying to wriggle away from him. He would be damned if he'd let her.

"Or slowly getting there," he replied.

"She seems normal," said Xavier approvingly. "Kinda nice and low maintenance, like a normal girl." He looked as if he was surprised.

"She *is* normal," insisted Tobias. *Thank goodness she was.* Then, not wanting to talk about her, he asked, "And Petra? Is she normal and nice?"

"I don't do nice girls, bro."

Tobias gave him a contemplative stare then decided against finding out exactly what he meant. Xavier continued, "She's very tempestuous, overly dramatic, and hot and fiery. I swear, sometimes she's like a volcano about to erupt. But she's a model," he said, as if that was the reason for her temperament. "Very up and down, and her schedule's hectic, which doesn't help. I swear sometimes I don't know what I've done wrong but she gets in a pissy mood for no reason. I'm still nuts about her though."

"Or maybe," replied Tobias, thinking how what he and Savannah had was so much more solid, more boring, according to Xavier, but he wouldn't change it for the world. "Maybe she just wants to be the center of attention and likes to have you walking around on eggshells."

"She's hot, like a Victoria's Secret model *hot*," Xavier insisted, completely ignoring Tobias's remark. "She's great in the sack and she's got great T&A," Xavier said, a smile spreading across his lips.

Tobias raised an eyebrow. "Is that all you see?"

"Sometimes." His brother grinned sinfully. "She's a nice person too," he said, suddenly looking serious. "She is," he insisted, when Tobias didn't look convinced. "She just happens to look amazing as well."

Tobias shook his head; his brother was concerned too much about the external things. His Ferrari, his partying lifestyle, his loft apartment in Tribeca. Tobias still wasn't sure what he did for a living but Petra seemed to fit Xavier's image of the perfect life.

"Mom's booked dinner next week," Tobias announced.

"I know. She told me. I tried to get out of it." Xavier looked as if he'd been invited to attend a funeral.

"Another family conference," mumbled Tobias ruefully. "What a shame that I'm leaving for San Diego tomorrow." He grinned at the disappointed look on his brother's face. "It was a last-minute decision and I'll be there for two weeks."

"So cancel and tell Mom, bro."

"Why don't you go and get it over with?" Tobias suggested.

"On my own?"

His brother had a point.

"Cancel it, dude," Xavier pleaded.

"You want *me* to do it?"

"She's going to be pissed."

"Don't remind me. But this is work and work comes first." Work had been his saving grace after Ivy, yet he'd been happy enough to put things on hold for Savannah.

"Is this serious?" Xavier asked, eyeing up a couple of women who had just walked in and were getting ready to sit down two tables away. "You took her to Miami and I'm thinking it sounds kind of serious."

"It is," replied Tobias. At least, *he* liked to think it was. His brother let out a slow whistle. "But things are fragile at the moment," Tobias countered. "What with everything that's happened." He looked up to find Xavier smiling at the brunette then quickly turning his attention back to him.

"Yeah, yeah, I can imagine. So things are pretty cool between you guys?"

Tobias shook his head. "No, but I guess you're too busy making eyes at that woman to hear what I said. Do you think this is wise?" he asked, nodding towards the woman.

"I'm only looking," Xavier insisted defensively. "Good to have backup."

"Backup?" Tobias asked, curious.

"Yeah, in case Petra ditches me again."

"I thought she *had* ditched you." Tobias emptied his glass, slightly disapproving of the fact that his brother appeared to live as if he were still a teenager. When Tobias had been his age, he knew he was going to spend the rest of his life with Ivy. She had been his one serious relationship. If Xavier wasn't careful, he'd end up like Matthias, in his thirties and still chasing skirts, getting bored quickly and needing newer, younger, fresher women to keep his interest. He didn't want that for his brother.

"She called last night in tears, said she missed me, said she wanted to get back with me. You watch, she'll come running back. She always does."

"She sounds like..." *Hard work*, Tobias thought. "A dramatic personality," he said, wondering how his brother put up with her. As far as he was concerned, no amount of great sex would make that relationship worth pursuing.

"Are you ever going to grow up?"

"Now you sound like my older brother."

Tobias placed his hand on Xavier's shoulder and squeezed it lightly. "That's because I am your older brother." But once again, he'd lost his brother's attention. The brunette was walking over towards them when his cell phone rang. Seeing Savannah's name on the caller display made his heart jump. He rushed to answer it.

# CHAPTER FOUR

"Hey," she said, and the sound of her voice warmed him instantly.

"This is a surprise," he said, smiling. "I thought you'd forgotten me."

"I could never forget you." Her voice was soft and husky and he could tell she was smiling from the way she spoke. "Where are you?" she asked. "It sounds busy."

"At The Oasis with Xavier." He looked up to see his brother and the brunette walking towards the bar together.

"Is that the bar you were telling me about?" She sounded disappointed.

"We're supposed to be catching up but it looks like he's ditched me in favor of some brunette he's just picked up." He sensed that he needed to explain what he was doing here. "My mom said he was devastated about the split from his girlfriend."

"The Russian model?"

"You've got a good memory." He pressed the cell phone closer to his ear, missing her and wishing she could be here, or he could be *there*. Wishing they could be anything but apart. "How's Jacob?"

"He's been fine," she said, in a way that indicated surprise. "And he's excited about going back to school on Monday."

"That's a good sign, isn't it?"

She made a noise as if she didn't quite agree. "We had a playdate after school today, with one of his best friends."

"Lenny?"

"You've got a good memory, too," she said, giggling.

"I always pay attention to everything Jacob tells me."

"I know, and I'm grateful for it. He misses you," she paused. "*I* miss you."

He liked hearing her say it. "It's good to know," he replied, watching his brother from a distance as the brunette's friend joined them at the bar. Tobias groaned in dismay.

"What is it?"

"Xavier, and a couple of females he's just picked up."

"A couple?"

"He's keeping them entertained at the bar," then, realizing what he'd said, "Not that I'm looking." There was silence at her end, prompting him to ask, "Savannah?"

"I only asked for a little time and space, Tobias."

"I know." But the way she'd said it, the way she'd pushed him away, it had sounded to him as if it was more than that. Xavier waved him over and he shook his head in irritation. "You're not jealous, are you?" he asked, laughing a little, testing the waters.

"Do I have reason to be?"

"None," he said and was about to tell her that there was only one woman for him, but refrained, lest his words made her uneasy. *Play it cool*, he told himself.

"I trust you, Tobias."

"And so you should," he replied. Her quiet tone made him wonder if he'd taken things the wrong way when they had last met. They'd both been edgy that night after bringing Jacob home and maybe they had both overreacted. He wasn't accustomed to women *not* falling all over him and had always been used to things working out in his favor—both in his business and personal life. Dealing with Savannah Page, her stubbornness and refusal to bow to him, had taught him a few things.

"Why don't you come over?" she asked. *He could.* But just then he decided to play it cool and to let her have all the distance she seemed to think she needed. He was desperate to see her again and there was nothing to stop him from going to her now but maybe he ought to drag this out a little more?

Maybe then she'd realize that what they had wasn't something good, but something great and it was worth saving.

He watched his brother about to make another stupid mistake. "Xavier's about to do something stupid," he said, frowning at the way the brunette had slipped her hand around Xavier's waist. He became even more annoyed at the way his brother seemed to encourage it.

"Like what?" Savannah asked.

"Like end up in someone's bed."

"Should I ask?"

"It's better if you don't."

"Okay." She laughed, then added, "Is the second woman making eyes at you?"

"She's trying," he admitted. "Somebody rescue me now," he said, when he caught the woman smiling at him. Savannah made a 'hmmmm' noise in response.

"Don't worry," he said, hoping to reassure her. "I belong to you."

"Don't you forget that." Her answer almost made him briefly consider showing up at her apartment in the next ten minutes.

"Why don't we meet up tomorrow night?" she suggested,

sounding eager to see him again. He had to concede that his playing-it-cool strategy seemed to be working but he hated being back at phase one, at the can-you-fit-me-in stage again. It was a world away from the closeness they had shared in Miami, before her son-of-a-bitch ex had shown up and ruined everything.

At least he had taken care of the man.

"I can't," he said, forcing himself to hold steady in his resolve. "I'm flying to San Diego tomorrow."

"I didn't think you were going?" She sounded surprised.

He hadn't intended to but she'd decided she didn't need him around, so... "We've got a lot to do. It's not just Dextronics we're seeing. Matthias has lined up a few more promising start-ups we should take a look at."

It didn't answer her question completely but he wasn't about to tell her his real reasons. Matthias had also been surprised that he'd changed his mind when only a few days ago he'd told his colleague he wasn't going. But there was no point sitting around and waiting for Savannah to summon him.

He wondered if he could squeeze in a visit to her in the morning, since he wasn't leaving until noon. Or maybe he could go to see her tonight? He could hear it in her voice that she wanted to see him, and god knows he was desperate for her. He rested his forehead in his hand, trying to do the right thing. It would be a rushed visit, and he wouldn't want to leave, but maybe leaving her alone for a few weeks would make her rethink her decision to push him away. Maybe Matthias setting up more meetings and prolonging the trip wasn't such a bad thing after all.

"Good luck with your return to work," he said.

"Actually, I've decided to take an extra week. Briony signed it off. Didn't she mention it to you?"

No, come to think of it she hadn't. But there had been a lot going on at work lately. "Not ready to go back yet?" he asked, concerned.

"I'm worried about Jacob. I'll feel better if I do the school runs during his first week back."

"Of course." He understood.

"Well, good luck with Dextronics and the rest of your meetings," she said. "If I'd have known you were going away, we could have met up today."

Everything she said pointed to the fact that she missed him. "I was busy," he told her truthfully. "I met with my mastermind group today and we had a whole day of golf and business talk."

"A whole day?" she asked, and the element of surprise in her voice wasn't lost on him. "No wonder your phone always went to voicemail when I called."

"You called?"

"A couple of times during the day."

"Sorry," he said, stretching out his shoulders, and encouraged by her words.

"We'll get together when you return," she said, sounding a little deflated.

"I'll call you," he told her, feeling the power in those three little words, sensing that something had shifted, that she was slowly becoming the eager one. Perhaps it was time to really drive that home. He was going for an extra week as well and he could tell her now or let her find out for herself. He knew what he wanted, maybe it was time for Savannah to learn it for herself?

"Have a good trip."

He hung up and watched Xavier making his way towards him with two beauties in tow. Tobias shook his head and finished off yet another shot of whiskey before getting up and greeting them with mild irritation. They grinned at him with perfect Hollywood smiles. Trust his brother to do something like that—ruin *their* evening for some female company. All Xavier needed now was for photos of him surrounded by these good-time girls to hit online, and for Petra to see them. Then there would be explosions.

No longer in the mood for hanging around, Tobias smiled at the women before Xavier had a chance to make introductions. He patted his brother on the back. "I'm making tracks."

Xavier's face fell. "You going already? You only just got here."

"You've got company," Tobias replied, lifting his eyebrow to indicate the women, "And I've got a headache." He didn't, but if he was forced to spend time with these hangers-on, he soon would.

"Don't do anything stupid," he said, giving his brother a man-hug. And without another look at the women, he walked out.

# CHAPTER FIVE

*I'll call you?*

Savannah came off the phone feeling even more dejected. Had she pushed him away completely? She had sensed iciness from him lately—it was her fault, she knew that, but she'd needed time to herself, time for Jacob, time to regroup. But Tobias was out in a bar tonight. He'd been busy the whole day, and tomorrow he was leaving for a business trip. She'd been hoping they could have spent at least one day during the weekend together.

Clearly, he'd had other plans.

So what if she'd wanted her space? She hadn't asked in order to play hard to get. She had a child to think about and he came first no matter what. It surprised her that Tobias failed to see things from her point of view.

She sat back on the couch and hugged the glossy celebrity magazine to her chest. With her curiosity piqued by the conversation with Lenny's mom, she'd bought it in order to see the photos inside of her and Tobias. Now, she tossed it to the side, next to the laptop, and wished she had something soft and fluffy to hold instead.

Or Tobias's strong, corded arms around her.

*Was he punishing her?* She had been expecting him to say that he'd been at home, or was training, or running—what she hadn't expected was for him to be at a bar, even if he was only catching up with his brother. She knew he cared about Xavier and she had sensed the protectiveness Tobias seemed to have for him. He'd often told her of his need to keep an eye out for his wayward and fun-loving brother and she admired this quality in him.

As things stood, she liked everything about him. And more than anything, she loved the way he doted on Jacob. But this recent aloofness was making her uneasy and more so because it showed her that Tobias didn't fully understand her.

For so many years now, she had been used to it being just her and Jacob, even back when she and Colt were married, and she wasn't used to having someone help her through her troubled times. Not only that, it would take time, allowing someone to become the third to their twosome. If there was any one man who deserved to, it was Tobias, but he had to understand where she was coming from.

She powered down her laptop, no longer in the mood to be looking for apartments. At times like this, when she was alone, without Jacob to distract her—especially knowing that Tobias was meeting new people, women, *two* women, to be precise— her thoughts settled on gloomier matters.

Worries about finding an apartment plagued her. More than this, she hated the idea of uprooting Jacob all over again especially when he appeared to be settling in so well at his new school. There was also childcare to think about and how to make ends meet once she started to pay rent. How could she think of her relationship when more urgent matters needed to be dealt with?

Feeling sorry for herself, she wished Tobias were here to

make it all better. He would be the first to tell her not to worry. And at the same time he'd be taking care of everything behind her back, scheming up ways of making everything okay for her. After years of fending for herself, maybe she wasn't used to being looked after, especially by a man like Tobias, who would do everything and anything he could do make her life easier.

*What a crazy thing not to be used to?* She knew there were plenty of women lining up to have what she had.

Had she gone too far this time? Tobias had been patient, and clearly he cared but he wasn't used to waiting around for women, she was certain of that. He could easily replace her if she kept him waiting too long. He'd used Naomi for specific reasons, hadn't he?

It hurt, knowing that he was getting along just fine without her. If she was to hold on to this man, if she wanted to keep him, then she had to cut loose her insecurity, give up her pigheaded stubbornness, and trust him.

She wrapped her arms around her knees and closed the screen to her laptop, not wanting to invite more misery into her evening. Knowing that she couldn't afford to live in Sunnyside had dampened her spirits long before her conversation with Tobias had completely sunk them.

# CHAPTER SIX

He left the loud, excitable chatter behind him and climbed into the empty elevator, relieved to get away. As he leaned his head against the wall, he briefly considered the idea of showing up at Savannah's apartment and surprising her.

She'd sounded down that they weren't going to be able to meet and he was also eager to see Jacob, to see how the little boy was getting along. But it was late, and Jacob would be asleep and seeing her tonight would only make it harder on him when he was in San Diego. And if they had another disagreement, well—he didn't need that.

Battling to not give in, he stepped out onto the street, thinking about the preparation for tomorrow's trip. He looked around for Morris, when he heard a voice behind him shout out his name. He turned around.

"Tobias?"

He blinked a few times. "Naomi?" She was grinning at him as if he was her long-lost lover.

"I thought it was you," she said, coming up to him and kissing him on both cheeks, obviously happy to see him again.

"Were you at The Oasis?" He was certain he hadn't seen

her there. At the same time, he remembered that she had called a few times and he had ignored her calls. He mentally prepared to get his excuses ready.

"No."

"It's good to see you again," he said, slipping her an easy smile.

"Likewise," she answered. "You look good, Tobias. I was beginning to worry about you."

"I'm sorry I didn't call back."

"I know how busy you are," she said, looking up at him through her ridiculously long eyelashes. "I called because this latest news story had me worried and I wanted to know you were okay but by all accounts," her eyes trailed slowly down his length, "you seem fine."

The way she looked at him rekindled memories of the time they'd spent together. He shrugged and smiled back uneasily.

"Do I?" he asked. He wasn't so sure that he was fine, but he could hide it well enough.

Naomi smiled at him provocatively. "You've been to The Oasis, and I can smell whiskey on you again. I'd say you seem almost fine." She knew him well. She'd had to, having seen him when he was coming out of his darker days.

"I met up with Xavier," he explained. With both hands, she clutched the straps of her overly large handbag, resting them lightly across the front of her thighs. For a few moments, she didn't say anything and instead gave him a sultry smile, her pupils dark and mesmerizing as the moment lingered with things left unsaid. He'd forgotten how small and slim she was, and how pretty too. But what he couldn't forget was that she had seen him through some rough times, and he would always be grateful, even if towards the end she had become needy, not wanting to face their separation.

"How is that charming brother of yours?"

"The same as ever," he replied, rolling his eyes.

"Leaving a trail of broken hearts in his wake?"

"Probably," he said, easing his hands into his pockets.

"You brothers have that in common," she said, lowering her head.

"Are you going somewhere? Coming from somewhere?" he asked, eager not to lead the conversation into uncharted waters.

"I was in the basement," she replied.

*In the basement?* He flinched. Her line of work already had a sleaziness associated with it and he didn't ask too many questions. When she'd been 'his,' he'd paid premium rates to make sure he didn't have to share her, but what was she doing now, he wondered? She must have read the expression on his face. "I was at The Vault. Have you ever been?"

He shook his head, relieved. Xavier had tried plenty of times to get him to go to the basement nightclub, but he'd so far managed to successfully avoid it.

"A potential client," she explained, running her hand through her hair. He couldn't help but notice that her obviously dyed blonde hair was now super straight and no longer in waves falling down her back.

"Business or pleasure, or shouldn't I ask?"

"One usually leads to the other," she replied, smiling demurely, and letting her gaze settle on his face a little too long.

"How are things?"

"Not the same since you fired me."

He looked away, fixing his gaze on a spot on the pavement. "I didn't fire you, Naomi," he replied quietly, before turning his head to her again. "It was always an arrangement."

"I know, Tobias. I understand, but a girl can always dream, can't she?" There it was again, the subtle smile but lacking the usual sure-fire strength behind it. She was almost a little weary, almost a little downbeat. "I'm looking to get out of it."

"Your line of work?"

"My glamorous line of work," she replied, moving her bag to her shoulder. She crossed her arms over the short and slinky white dress she had on. "There has to be a better and easier way of earning a living. It was good while it lasted but the girls are getting younger, and I don't have a taste for these things any more. Not since you..."

He chose to ignore that last comment, not wanting to delve deeper or take the blame. "I hope you find something you're passionate about. You can do so many things, Naomi. Don't sell yourself short."

It was all he could offer her. He had never understood why she did *this* in the first place. A woman like her, with her looks and smarts, she could train and reinvent herself; there were a thousand different things she could do. But then money wasn't an issue for him. That's what he often failed to realize. Maybe what she did paid better than most things.

"Thanks," she said, giving him a wistful gaze again. "You say the nicest things, sometimes. I wish more men were like you, Tobias. The men I meet are real nasty. I shouldn't talk about them like that but it's the truth." She stared at her open-toed stilettoes. "I always found it easier to talk to you."

He nodded but said nothing, thinking only of how uncomplicated it had been to be with her; no drama, no angst, no complications—just straightforward sex and nothing more. But despite the way things were with Savannah, he loved everything he had with her and he felt confident that it was just a matter of time before things were fine between them again.

"Some of them are old enough to be my father, or grandfather," she said quietly, as if she needed to get this off her chest. "It's vile, some of the things they want to do. You were my most normal customer."

He hadn't considered the other people she'd have slept with, or what it must have been like to sleep with someone she had no feelings for, no attachment, no desire, only the lure of dirty cash.

"You were the best one," she said, staring out at the traffic as the cars grumbled along the road. "And sex with you was out of this world." He felt uncomfortable hearing her talk about their intimate moments especially when he was looking to the future and still working out things with Savannah.

"You called me a couple of times," he said, hoping to move the conversation away from the bedroom. "I'm sorry I didn't get back to you. It's been that kind of week."

"I heard about the little boy, your girlfriend's son. I was worried and wanted to make sure things were okay."

"Thanks for your concern," he replied, taking out his cell phone. "We're trying to put it all behind us now. Savannah's keeping a close watch on Jacob."

Her smile faded slowly. "You two seem to be a hot item all over the news these days. Is she the one?"

He stared at her in silence for a few moments.

"Is she the one you let go of me for?"

"Yes."

"I can't complain, can I?" she said, clutching her bag tighter. "I had you for longer than I deserved." He found that an odd thing for her to say, but a nice thing, all the same.

"I'd better go, Naomi. You take care." He looked around and saw the Merc parked a few cars down. "Do you need a lift back?"

"No, thank you. I'm meeting friends for dinner not far from here. I always found that strange," she said, looking over his shoulder. "You looking for a cab, or getting your driver to take you back when your security men are always tailing you."

"I like to pretend that they're not there."

She nodded her head in understanding, and the corners of her lips turned up slightly. "Take care, Tobias."

# CHAPTER SEVEN

"How come we don't see Mr. Stone anymore?" Jacob asked, pulling her thoughts away from the two-bedroom rental apartments she'd been thinking about.

She still didn't feel comfortable letting Jacob sleep alone in his room and had made him share her bed, even though her parents had long gone. She would have to let her fear go soon but she wasn't ready for it yet.

"Why, Mommy?" Jacob asked her when she paused too long, trying to think of a good answer. It was his first day back at school, and the time for sleeping in was over.

"He's busy, honey."

"He's never too busy for *us*. He told me so." She paused when she heard his words. It was the kind of thing Tobias would say. He had *always* made time for her. Even with the weight of a successful company on his shoulders, this man had always put things aside for her. She ought to be grateful.

She was.

But now she felt as if she had been in the wrong. "He's away on business," she explained, sitting up in bed.

"Why didn't we go with him?"

She turned to him in surprise. "Since when do we go on business with Tobias?"

"You went to Miami with him," Jacob countered in a sullen voice.

She wasn't sure what he was getting at. "But you're back at school today."

"I didn't have to go back today, you said so."

She looked at him closely. "You told me you wanted to go back."

"You said I didn't have to, not if I didn't want to."

"You mean to say you would have preferred to go to San Diego with Tobias?"

"I want to see his plane."

"Ah. Well, maybe another time. You mustn't ask for these things, Jacob. You know that, don't you? Tobias has gone away on business. When we went to Miami, that was..." She didn't want to say 'vacation' even though she had told Jacob this. She wasn't sure why he was asking now, or why he was acting up.

"It would've been cool to hang out with him," Jacob retorted. She stood up and tied her hair up with a clip, contemplating what was going on with her son. Jacob wasn't usually given to being difficult, and some of his recent comments and behavior were starting to worry her. She wondered if it was really the plane he was eager to see, or whether he was missing Tobias. He hadn't asked many questions about Colt, and had seemed content when she'd told him that he had gone back home.

Was this a case of Jacob missing Tobias? Maybe being with Colt had made Jacob realize the real difference between the two men.

"We can see him when he returns," she replied slowly, checking her cell phone for any messages Tobias might have sent during the night. But there was nothing. He hadn't been in touch since she'd called him a few days ago when he was at the bar.

For some stupid reason, she had been half-expecting, half-wishing for a text from him but seeing nothing from him made her mood dip. And Jacob wasn't helping.

"Come on, honey," she said, making an effort to sound cheerier than she felt. "Time to get up. You've got to get ready for school." She tried to ignore the anxiety that flitted uneasily across her thoughts, and hoped that his first day back after the drama of what he'd gone through would be a pleasant one.

---

"I almost thought you'd gone missing yourself," Kay's sarcasm cut through her. "Do you know how many times I've called you lately?" She should have felt guilty for leaving her cousin's calls unanswered but right now Savannah didn't care. She was more concerned about Jacob's first day back being easy for him.

"Sorry," Savannah replied, lying on the couch with her legs stretched out. "I've been busy." She had spoken to Kay briefly last weekend while her parents had been here but she had put off returning her calls ever since. Kay's imminent arrival troubled her and was one more thing she didn't want to deal. But with Jacob at school, she'd been at a loss to keep busy and had moped around the apartment all morning. A part of her even wished *she* had returned to work. So she had taken a break from looking at apartments online and had called her cousin instead.

"I've been worried about you," her cousin protested. Savannah balked inwardly. It seemed as if everyone was worried about her. "I called your mom and dad a few days ago and they told me that Colt had shown up in town."

"He sure did." Like others, Kay knew nothing about the real story and Savannah preferred to keep it that way.

"What did he want?" Kay asked.

"To see Jacob."

"And then he went AWOL?"

"You know what Colt's like," replied Savannah, trying to put on a nonchalant air. "He got carried away and took him to the park then lost track of time. Mom panicked, as usual."

"That's all it was?"

Savannah 'uh-huhed.'

"The papers blew that out of proportion."

"They always do," Savannah replied.

"You must be glad Colt's out of the picture now."

"I am." Savannah curled her hair around her finger. "You're coming back then?" No point not talking about it. Better to get dates and facts, even if she didn't want to hear them.

"I could leave now or in August. Guess how long it took me to make my mind up?" Kay giggled. "I can't wait to get back."

"I bet." Savannah tugged at her hair. "Do you have a date in mind?" So that she could mark it on her calendar and have something concrete to work towards.

"Memorial Day weekend. I booked my flight a few days ago."

That's the date she'd been working towards. She had just over a month to find another place. Savannah took a deep breath in and let go of the lock of hair she'd been curling. "I've been looking for apartments to rent," she said quietly. "But it might take me a little longer to find something we can afford." Though looking at the prices, she'd come to the conclusion that there was nothing around here that she *could* afford and still have decent money left over for her and Jacob to survive on.

"You don't have to rush, Sav," Kay told her. "Please don't feel as if you have to move out so soon." Her cousin was being gracious and Savannah was grateful to her but she didn't want to take advantage of Kay's generosity for longer than necessary.

"Thanks, but hopefully it won't take forever, and you've been good to let me stay this long for free."

"*You've* been good," Kay replied firmly, "apartment-sitting for me. Seriously, Sav. Don't rush. I've got two rooms, and you and Jacob can share for a—OH, I GET IT!" She shrieked, as if she'd suddenly hit the jackpot. "You need your own room!"

"What?"

"With Tobias Stone coming over so regularly, and all that," she giggled again.

Savannah squirmed. "Tobias hasn't actually stayed over and we've been careful around Jacob."

"Define careful," her cousin said, and then, before Savannah had even opened her mouth, "How is Jacob taking to the new man in your life?"

"He adores Tobias."

Kay sighed loudly. "What's not to adore? So Jacob knows you're with him?"

"He knows," replied Savannah. "We had to tell him before we went to Mi—"

"MIAMI!" Kay's voice bellowed out from the phone. "How the freakin' hell *was* Miami?" she cried. "I followed you on the 'net. You looked pretty loved up, Sav."

"Miami was great," she replied, turning her mind back to the good days, the days she'd never wanted to end.

"I can't wait to meet your lover boy," Kay drawled, giving Savannah a really good reason why she had to leave as soon as possible. Not only was the expression 'lover boy' annoying to her ears, it didn't fit Tobias. But even more than that, Kay and Tobias in the same apartment, even if only for a few minutes, was a no-no. Even if Tobias wasn't around, she got the feeling that Kay would worm her way into finding out as much as she could about him, and any possible friends...or Xavier.

"Anyway," said Savannah. "Hopefully, I'll be in the process of moving out by the time you get back." But moving to where?

"Sure, Sav. You take all the time you need."

# CHAPTER EIGHT

"Something celebratory," said Matthias, as he swirled the cognac in his wine glass, then sniffed the aromas.

"At that price, I should think so," replied Tobias, feeling as if he'd eaten too much and too late and that sleep would be hard to come by.

Matthias raised his glass. "To a fruitful alliance with Dextronics and to millions in our coffers."

Tobias clinked glasses with his friend. "To a successful outcome."

"We should also toast to the fact that you showed up. I'm honored," Matthias said, raising his glass with a smile.

"So you keep saying," Tobias replied, not without a touch of irritation.

"It's true," said Matthias, settling back into the thick leather seat. It had been a worthwhile trip after all. Not that he'd expected anything to fall through. They had undertaken to invest a lot of money in Dextronics. The figures looked good and Tobias expected the business to flourish, and along with it, the investments made by his clients. The last few days had been an endless round of entertaining and drinking and eating and there had been a celebratory lunch at Dextronics' headquarters earlier. After visiting two more start-ups in the afternoon, the day had turned into a long one.

Matthias liked good food and drink and eating out. He loved the trappings of success, and Tobias had reluctantly agreed to accompany him this evening, foregoing his session at the hotel's gym.

"We're conquering the world one business at a time," Matthias said, letting out a contented sigh. "Feels good, doesn't it?"

"We've already conquered it," replied Tobias. The business side of things was running smoothly. Now it was time to concentrate on other, more personal, matters.

"What are you talking about?" Matthias asked, swirling his glass once more. "We're only just getting started. Tech stock is great but don't forget about Yanling. The Far East still has much to offer." Tobias tapped his fingers on the table but said nothing. "I thought you wanted to be the biggest and the best."

Tobias shrugged. It didn't seem to be so important any more. Matthias rolled his glass around in his hands slowly. "This is a complete change of heart. At the start of this year, you said it wasn't good enough to be one of the top ten hedge funds in the country, you wanted us to be in the top three by the end of the year. You said you wanted us to attract more investors and offer more products."

"Things change." While it would be unacceptable to him for his company to languish in the bottom ten, being number one suddenly wasn't the be all and end all for him. "I want my clients to be content," said Tobias, steepling his hands together, "and we will get there. Everything is taking place as planned. We're still looking at new offerings, looking for new business, finding new clients and investors. It's all going according to plan."

"I hope so," sniffed Matthias. "I get the impression that your mind is elsewhere lately."

Tobias stared back at him. "A lot has happened."

"Savannah and her boy?" Matthias asked.

"He's just a kid. He didn't deserve that."

"Didn't deserve what?" Matthias looked puzzled. Tobias had forgotten that his friend didn't know the complete truth behind the story. He remained silent, prompting his friend to continue. "So the kid went missing for a while, so his father wanted to spend some time with him—it all ended well, didn't it?" Matthias asked, shifting in his seat. "What's this really about, Tobias?"

"It takes getting used to," he replied carefully. "Being in a relationship."

"I can see that," Matthias replied. "But it shouldn't affect your business decisions."

Tobias snapped to attention. "I haven't compromised any business decisions. I haven't let anything slip."

"You've taken more time off," Matthias countered.

"I think I'm entitled to it, given that I work eighty- to ninety-hour weeks most of the time."

"That's not what I meant," Matthias said, his voice turning softer. "You deserve a break, hell, you deserve a break more than most people, Tobias. I'm just concerned, that's all. Sometimes it seems as if you're not thinking straight."

"Nonsense."

"This is nothing like how you were with Naomi."

"Naomi was different," Tobias replied quickly. What he had with Savannah was something new. Something unexpected. Miami had been a test. He'd wanted to see what it would be like to have her around all the time instead of having only slices of time that were never long enough—an evening after work, stolen moments on weekends and being cautious in front of Jacob. And he'd had his answer before the first day was over.

It hadn't been enough.

Even though their vacation was cut short, the time they had didn't feel like a few days, it felt like hours. And hours weren't enough.

Tobias wanted a lifetime. This was why it grated on him that the woman he adored didn't want him around.

Matthias chuckled. "No shit. Naomi *was* different. Didn't you pay her by the hour?" he asked, grinning. Tobias threw him a dirty look but remained silent. "Are you still not going to tell me where she works?" Matthias asked.

"You've got your own harem, don't you?" retorted Tobias.

"I wish there were that many," Matthias replied.

"Why would you need the services of an escort agency?"

Matthias's eyes twinkled. "Curiosity. Besides, it was good enough for you."

"She's looking to leave."

"Who, Savannah?"

"Naomi."

Matthias sat forward. "Looking to leave her profession? Or find a new pimp?" His eyes glittered with quiet mischief. "I've got a vacancy she might want," he replied, winking.

"She's looking to leave the business."

"Then I could definitely offer her something more long-term. A bit like your setup."

"No need to keep going on about it. You're beginning to sound like a broken record."

"You still remember records, old boy?" Matthias asked, looking down at his glass and refilling both of their glasses again.

"Not for me." Tobias placed a hand over his. "You might want to take it easy," he said. "I don't want you dying from liver failure."

"You'd know all about that." Matthias shot back and crossing his legs. "Those were dark days for you."

"I prefer to put them behind me."

"It appears that you have—and despite my concerns about your business mind, it's good to see you happy again."

"You shouldn't worry too much about where my mind is," Tobias told him. "I've got it all under control."

"She means a lot to you, doesn't she?" Matthias asked, his eyes boring into him. When Tobias didn't reply, a gentle smile spread along Matthias's lips. He raised his glass to his lips but before he took a sip, he asked, "Then why the hell are you here?"

# CHAPTER NINE

"So, you're okay, and Jacob's okay?" asked Briony as they sat down at a table for two that looked out onto the street.

"Jacob's fine," Savannah replied. "Kids have a capacity to bounce back from adversity in a way that we grown-ups can't." She placed her handbag on the seat next to her.

"I couldn't wait to get out of the office," said Briony, taking off her jacket and sliding it around the chair. "It's so nice to meet for lunch. Oh, and Candace says 'hi.'"

"She does?" Savannah was dubious. "When did she grow a nice bone?"

"Beats me," Briony replied. She peered closer. "How *are* you?"

"Better, thanks. Monday was hard when Jacob went back to school, and picking him up made me nervous. I half-expected Colt to jump out of nowhere at any moment."

Briony squeezed her hand gently. "It's only natural to be scared. You've been through a terrible ordeal, you and that poor boy of yours."

Savannah nodded her head in agreement. "I'm usually

better at this, I really am. I don't know why I'm falling apart for no reason."

"No reason?" Briony exclaimed. "Hon, it's not *no reason*. This is major. Your ex, your son, the scare you must have had. I don't care if your ex wanted to spend more time with his son and forgot to get him back on time. I know he wasn't a nice man, from the things you've said about him in the past. Don't try to make it sound trivial. Because it's far from it."

Savannah lowered her head. She wanted to tell Briony the truth, of what had really happened, but knew she couldn't risk it. "Kay's coming back."

Briony frowned.

"My cousin—the one who's in Hong Kong."

"I remember now," said Briony, her eyes widening. "I thought she wasn't due back until the summer?"

"She said she can't wait to leave and she arrives back a month from now." Savannah felt a pinch of sadness at the thought of it. "I've been looking for properties to rent. I might even have to change jobs and Jacob might have to change schools again."

Briony's mouth opened in a perfect circle and held there. "A new job? Why in the hell would you want to leave?"

"More money," Savannah said, making a face. Two-bedroom apartments were averaging $2,000 a month.

"More money?" Briony craned her neck forward and looked at her as if she were insane. "What about Tobias?"

"What about him?"

Briony frowned, causing a ripple of wrinkles to form across her forehead.

"Our being together doesn't depend on where I work," Savannah explained, but she knew it wouldn't help, her being somewhere else, who knew how far from where she was now. The logistics of having a relationship were difficult enough when they were working at the same place. She imagined it would be next to impossible if she worked elsewhere. Anxiety clawed at her insides at the thought that she and Tobias were in danger of quickly drifting apart.

"It's been a crappy month for you, hon. It'll get better."

"I hope so," replied Savannah. "How are things going in San Diego?" she asked, not having called Tobias since he'd left and not having heard from him either. She was still eager to find out, though.

"They've signed with Dextronics." Briony glanced at her watch. "I assume they're celebrating."

"They're coming back on the weekend, aren't they?" she asked, casually perusing the menu.

"No, they're staying another week and meeting with more clients. Didn't you know?"

*Another week?* This was news to her. "Tobias must have mentioned it, and I forgot," she said, pretending to look at the salads on the menu.

"Shall we order?" Briony seemed to be in a rush and Savannah realized it was because she only had an hour for lunch. Having been off work for a while now, she wasn't used to the fixed timing of lunches and breaks and knew it would be tough to get back into things. But returning to work might be the thing she needed in order to get out of the funk she now found herself in.

A waitress arrived and took their order. "How's Max?" Savannah asked.

"She's good." A smile fanned out across Briony's face. "She said to say 'hi' to you, too. She's doing great, overworked as usual."

"I still owe you both a meal out, when I catch my breath, to thank you for transforming me for the gala dinner."

"That seems like a long time ago," said Briony, unraveling

the napkin that had been fanned out decoratively on the table. "I don't know where the time has gone. We haven't had a chance to properly dissect that night either, but you looked like a siren in that dress."

"Thanks," Savannah sat back, and ran her finger around the tip of her glass of lemonade. "I felt like a million dollars."

"You *looked* like two million." Briony smiled at her. "And Miami? Before all this nasty business? How was it?"

"Wonderful."

"When can we expect an engagement?"

Savannah almost gagged at this. "Don't say silly things," she said, giving a dismissive snort as she picked up her glass. She wished that she'd ordered a white wine spritzer instead. The strange thing was, in Miami, when she'd had those days by the pool with Tobias by her side, and the nights, both frenzied and calm in turn, she had contemplated a future with him. She had dared to, and it had been easy to think of that as the natural progression, months and years from now. But the events that had taken place just after had taken the shine off that rosy picture.

"It's not a silly thing," retorted Briony. "I'm sure you don't think it's silly either. I'm sure the thought must have crossed your mind. I know you, hon," she said, sitting forward and patting Savannah's hand. "Men do nothing for me but even I can see how much Tobias Stone is into you. You'd have to be deaf, dumb and blind not to see it. I could tell that night at your birthday gathering for drinks. He wasn't there but you weren't really there, either."

It was annoying, but Briony had that same capacity as Tobias to see right through her. Or maybe she was just transparent in her dealings, couldn't hide her emotions to save her life and wore her heart on her sleeve? Savannah was certain she'd done her best to hide her attraction to Tobias back in the early days but clearly Briony had been watching all along.

As if reading her mind again, Briony told her, "Don't worry, nobody else knew. It's a women's thing. I picked up on it, and so, I'm sure, did Candace. It's probably why she was so nasty to you."

"Was?"

"She seemed genuinely concerned for you today," Briony told her. "I don't like that woman any more than you do, but I'm telling you, call it my feminine intuition, if you will, but when I mentioned I was meeting you for lunch, she wanted to know that you were okay."

"Why would you tell her you were meeting me?"

"I have a meeting after lunch and I needed her to organize tea and coffee."

Savannah nodded in understanding.

"And now that there's no chance in hell of her sinking her fangs into Tobias, I think she'll have to move on."

"Move on?"

"To Xavier, or Matthias or some other rich man."

"Good luck to her."

# CHAPTER TEN

The weekend passed quickly with the usual trip to the park as well as shopping for clothes. Jacob needed new pants because he seemed to have had a growth spurt lately. She picked up a few more bargains for herself. Monday arrived before she was fully ready for it.

"Welcome back!" Briony breezed in through the door to her office as if she owned it.

"Good morning," chirped Savannah, feeling happier the moment she'd walked into work. It had been an anxious morning for her again as she had dropped Jacob at the breakfast club. That wasn't so bad, leaving him at school in a safe place. The real anxiety would set in later when Rosalee went to pick him up after school.

They hugged briefly, like long-lost friends, even though they'd only met for lunch recently. "It's good to have you back, hon." Briony's dark green eyes fixed on her.

"Did you—" Savannah paused, squinting. "Have you changed something?" Briony looked different than she had a few days ago. It wasn't the style or the length of her hair. She tilted her head, getting annoyed when she couldn't put her finger on what it was.

Briony plucked at her hair. "I've added darker highlights." She announced proudly. "What do you think?"

Savannah nodded approvingly. "You don't look so much like someone off of MTV anymore."

"No?" Briony looked disappointed.

"You look more refined. Elegant, I'd say."

"Max likes it."

"Suits you." She switched on her PC and pulled out her files.

"Let's have a meeting. The glass conference room in half an hour?"

"Do we need to go there?" asked Savannah. They usually had their morning chats in here.

"I figure you—" Knock, knock. Briony turned towards the door, "and this is why I decided to go to the conference room. See you in half an hour." She smiled and left as Chloe walked in.

"Hey, Savannah," she said, smiling widely. "I heard you were coming back today. How's Jacob?"

---

B riony had been right. She'd had a steady stream of visitors throughout the morning and she was about done catching up with them all; though she hadn't seen Candace yet.

She suddenly realized that for her work colleagues, this was the first time she had seen them in a while and they had many questions. After a while, she got tired of answering the same questions about events which were so far in the past, and so much had happened since, that she felt it was someone else she was talking about. Especially when they asked about her dress and the night at the Waldorf Astoria, and the vacation to Miami.

Their obvious interest in her recent life and their wide-eyed interest in her romance left her feeling uncomfortable, especially because Tobias owned the company. She privately wondered if they were all saying something else behind her back than what they said to her face. Did they think less of her for sleeping with the boss?

It was with relief that she got her things together and made her way to meet with Briony. She had a lot of emails and to-do items to deal with, and guessed that most of the day would be spent dealing with the backlog caused by her absence. As she rushed past Tobias's office, she cast a furtive glance at his door and heard Candace call out her name.

There was no love being lost between them, and Savannah didn't want to stop, but Candace called out her name. It wasn't only a casual greeting, but more than that, it was a plea to stop, and not spoken with the usual tightness that Candace seemed to reserve for her.

Savannah turned around and saw the tall, willowy PA walking towards her. "How are you?" Candace asked, her concern suddenly making Savannah feel on edge.

"I'm happy to be back," she replied truthfully.

"It's good to have you back," Candace returned, giving her a smile she wasn't used to seeing and immediately making her suspicious.

"I heard about what happened—with your son and your ex-husband. I'm sorry."

"For what?"

"For what happened to your son."

Savannah rubbed the back of her hand. "It wasn't your fault," she said, puzzled by Candace's words. "It was a misunderstanding."

"But is he okay? Your son?" Candace asked.

"Yes, he is," Savannah replied, still surprised by Candace's over-the-top concern. "Thank you for asking."

They stood in an awkward silence and Savannah could have been mistaken for thinking that Candace was laying it on thick, but Briony had already mentioned that the woman seemed genuinely concerned about the situation.

Perhaps Candace had defied the odds and grown a sensitive side to her. "Briony's waiting," she said, by way of explaining her hasty exit and smiled and left.

As she walked into the conference room, Savannah couldn't help but think how quickly things had changed.

# CHAPTER ELEVEN

She was still in her PJs when he showed up at her door, smiling brightly, in his faded blue jeans and rumpled white shirt. At the sound of an unexpected knock on her door first thing on a Saturday morning, she'd expected it to be Kay. Not Tobias.

"Well, hey there," she said, examining him with mild surprise. She pulled the edges of her hastily found and barely worn nightgown together, as her insides started that familiar welcome dance.

"Hi," said Tobias, grinning at her.

Bra-less, and disheveled-looking, she wasn't prepared for a surprise visit from *him*. Especially after two weeks of silence.

"I didn't expect—"

"I missed you," he said, bounding through the door and grabbing her by the waist. She shrank back, feeling smelly and stale, not having brushed her teeth or showered. Even though blood pumped furiously through her body and her excitement started to build at the sight of him, her mind was more logical and cautious.

He leaned in as if he wanted to kiss her but there was no

way she could let that happen. "What's the matter?" he asked, moving back a little, with his hand still around her waist. She folded one arm across her chest and backed away, her other hand smoothing back the mane of hair which she'd roughly pinned in place with a brown tortoiseshell hair clip.

"Nothing," she said, trying not to speak too much.

He mistook her reticence for something else. "Still so cold, Savannah?" he asked, his mood quickly turning somber.

"No," she said, attempting a smile. "I wasn't expecting to see you this morning, but I'm really glad you came." She wished she'd gotten up early and had been ready to receive him properly. Just looking at him made her insides melt.

"You are?" he said, the smile returning to his lips as his hands once more skirted around her waist. "Then why aren't you letting me near you?"

"Because I've only just crawled out of bed," she replied, wanting to feel his hands and lips all over her, "and you're all— you're all—" She stared at him, even in a creased-up shirt and fresh off a plane, he was still gorgeousness personified.

"Tobias!" Jacob yelled, standing in the hallway with his head peeking out from the bedroom.

"Hey, buddy," Tobias waved, and in the next second Jacob came charging at him like an excited puppy.

"Mommy never said you were coming."

Tobias scooped him up in his arms. "That's because I didn't tell your mommy I was coming. I wanted to surprise her." *You certainly did that*, thought Savannah, wondering if she could slip away and dive into the shower. "You've grown. What have you been eating, Jacob? At this rate I won't be able to pick you up anymore." Jacob giggled as Tobias put him back on the floor.

"Mommy's been making me eat bananas. They're soft and squishy and I don't like them that much."

"Bananas? They're very good for you," he said, and then in a lower voice, turning to Savannah, "I wish your mommy would give me something soft and squishy."

"I'll take a shower," she said, not missing the devilish glint in Tobias's eyes.

"A shower?" His lips turned up at the corners and the look he gave her put ideas in her head. For a moment, the idea of him having his way with her in the bathroom, tempted her. How much she would love him to take her—but they had to think about Jacob.

"Do you think you could maybe give Jacob his breakfast?" she asked, edging away, carrying those delicious thoughts in her head.

"I think I can manage," he replied, grinning at her son.

"He'll tell you what he wants, and help yourself to coffee or whatever..."

"Yeah!" Jacob shouted. "I'll show you where we keep our cereal."

---

S he was all mussed up and looked as if she had rolled out of bed. Just the way he liked her. He only wished he could have been the one she'd rolled out of bed with.

"Are you staying the whole day?" Jacob asked, taking his bowl to the table. Tobias put the kettle on then poured out Jacob's Cheerios and milk. He wasn't sure but if early indications were anything to go by, Savannah seemed happy enough to see him. "Would you like me to?"

"Yeah!"

"Then maybe I'll stay for the whole day." He pulled out two mugs. "How does your mom have her coffee?" Tobias asked.

"She likes it hot."

He stifled his chuckle. "Sugar? Strong?"

Jacob stopped chewing. "No sugar, and in between."

"In between what?"

"Not too dark and not too milky."

"Gotcha." Tobias slipped into the chair opposite Jacob while he waited for the water to boil. "Are you glad to be back in school?"

Jacob nodded, still chewing.

"Are you settling in fine or is Henry Carson being a pain in the butt?"

Jacob giggled. "That's a naughty word."

"I'll bear that in mind. But how is the Carson kid?"

"He's been okay."

"I'll be out in five!" Savannah shouted from the hallway.

"Your coffee's nearly ready," he said, raising his voice slightly.

"How are you *really* doing, Jacob?" Tobias asked, looking at the boy's bright green eyes and long lashes, which were similar to his mother's. "Are you still feeling brave, because I can see that being brave comes naturally to you. It must have taken a lot of guts to be brave out there when you were lost."

The boy pursed his lips together. "I wasn't that brave," he whispered. "I was really scared."

"I know, buddy. But you managed to find help, and it takes real courage to remember that when you must have been very frightened. I'm so proud of you. I know your mom and your grandparents are really proud anyway, but I am too."

Jacob chewed for a few moments, and then said, "She was making me go to the bathroom to get cleaned up." Tobias nodded, clenching his stomach as he listened. "She was very scary."

"I bet she was."

"And I didn't like the way her lipstick stuck to her teeth, and

I was real glad when Izzy said it didn't look like I wanted to go with her."

Isabel Laronde. Tobias had found out from his contact in the police department. She was a nanny who happened to be out on her afternoon off. It was a shame that they had no information on the other woman. He'd have to tell Savannah.

"Izzy was real brave too," said Tobias. "It takes guts to stand up for someone you don't know, and to walk into a situation you're not sure about." The nanny had taken a huge risk, and thank goodness that she had. Otherwise...Tobias didn't want to think about what might have happened otherwise. He knew this same thing probably kept Savannah awake, and ate away at her, and he wished she would let him help her to get through this.

"She was like a superhero."

"She was," Tobias agreed. "And you're like a superhero, too, buddy."

Jacob smiled.

"Do you get scared now?"

Jacob shook his head.

"Because if you ever are, Jacob, I'd want you to tell me about it. Or your mom, but you can always tell me as well. Okay?" The boy nodded his head.

"What are you two whispering about?" asked Savannah, walking into the room as she towel-dried her hair. She wore wide linen pants and a loose white summer top that exposed plenty of skin. He took her in slowly from head to toe, his gaze settling over her almost-bare shoulders covered by inch-wide straps. It was painful to look at her knowing he couldn't put his arms around her. They had been apart for weeks and he wanted to show her how much he'd missed her. Looking at her now would only turn his balls blue again.

How was he going to get through the day with her looking like that and him not being able to do a thing about it?

# CHAPTER TWELVE

I t had ended up being another glorious day at the park with Jacob on his scooter and hot dogs for lunch. Later, they'd caught a movie followed by pizza and finally come home late in the evening.

"What were you and Jacob talking about?" she asked, finally curled up in his arms once more as they lay on the couch. She felt the vibration of his heart beat against her hand.

"I was trying to find out what happened to him that day."

She lifted her head up. "What did he say?"

"That he was scared of that woman and that the other girl stopped her from taking him to the bathroom." Tobias gently ruffled her hair. "Don't worry. I think he's going to be fine."

"I'm glad he opened up to you," she said, because he seemed to get into a mood whenever she tried to pry. "I need to know if he's worried about anything."

"I know. I want to know he's okay, too," replied Tobias.

"And I am so grateful that you do," she said, moving on top of him. She leaned in and dropped a kiss on his lips. With Jacob having gone to sleep only a short while ago, they were finally alone.

"I hate not having you around," she said, understanding now how incomplete her life was without this man in it.

His hands lingered over her bottom and squeezed gently, and she gazed at his moist lips, then dipped her head and bit his lower lip gently. At once, his hands moved easily under her loose top and his fingers trailed slowly and seductively across her skin. His was a magic touch which awakened her most primal senses and turned her to liquid heat. Now, tasting his lips and feeling his skin against hers, she was suddenly desperate for him.

"I've missed you," he said.

"Why don't you show me how much you missed me?" she murmured, dropping tiny kisses along his jaw and feeling the heat between her legs.

"We need to clear a few things up first."

"Now?" she asked, disappointed when his hands stopped moving under her blouse and he removed them, settling them over her clothes once more.

"Now," he replied, his face turning serious. "Are we good now? You've had time to yourself, was it enough or do you need more?"

A few weeks with no phone calls, no nothing, had left her more than desperate for him. And it had done the trick. "You could have called," she said, sounding like a petulant teen.

"You could you have, too."

"I've had a lot going on."

"And I wanted to be there for you."

She traced the arch of his brow with her finger, contemplating. "I know. But I'm not used to having someone care for me. It was too much, the shock of Jacob going missing, what Colt did. Jacob is my life, and it almost wrecked me that I came so close to losing him."

His hand cupped her face. "I know," he said softly. "But you aren't alone anymore. Why can't you let me in?" His gunmetal blue eyes held her captive.

"I'm trying," she replied.

"You are? Because it seems to me as if you're happy for us to drift."

"I'm sorry if that's what you think. It hasn't been an easy time."

"I know," he said softly. "But letting me share it with you might make it easier, did you ever think of it like that?"

"Tobias," she paused, trying to tell him without upsetting him. "You have to understand that letting you in doesn't mean you make my decisions for me, or that you get to do what *you* think is right for me. I understand your need to protect me and Jacob, and I also know you have the power to do anything you want, but if you pull the strings it means I've lost control of my own life. I can't live like that. Yes, I'm stubborn sometimes, and maybe I don't take anyone's advice, but I've fought to take control of my life and to make my own decisions for what's best for me and Jacob. It's who I am."

He was listening and it felt good to finally talk about all the things that had been stewing inside her. Lying on top of him and doing nothing but staring into his eyes, she felt reconnected again. And like a lucky woman, too.

"I know it bothers you, and I get that I can come across as intimidating sometimes."

"Sometimes?"

"You're not intimidated by me, are you?" he asked, surprised.

"No, not anymore."

"I'm making an effort, and I will try harder not to do things that concern you without discussing them with you first."

"Thank you."

"What else?" he asked.

"Trust," she said. "It means a lot to me. I know you've kept things from me before, for what you thought were the right reasons, but I need you to be honest with me."

"Okay," he said. "What else?"

"Make love to me," she said, dropping her head and letting her lips fall on his. He growled, low and needy, as his hands moved over her skin once more and his thumbs fumbled around the inside of her bra, tweaking and pulling and drawing out soft moans from her. Their lips smacked together and his tongue, smooth and graceful, teased her mouth, gently exploring.

"I want you now," he rasped, his breath hot and hurried against her lips and his hardness so obvious to her as she lay on top of him. He unclasped her bra and slowly started to pull her top up revealing her nakedness.

"I can't sleep." Jacob's groggy voice behind her snatched her from the heat which consumed her. "Mommy," he said, still rubbing his half-closed eyes as she turned around; the sound of his voice pouring iced water over her heated body.

She rolled off Tobias so fast that he barely had time to cover the bulge in his jeans. She turned her son around so that he faced the door and quickly folded her arm across her chest, vaguely aware that her breasts were loose and pebbled, and that her bra hung like a loose harness under her flimsy top.

"Uh—I'll read to you, honey," she said, and out of the corner of her eye saw Tobias sitting up slowly. *Poor man,* she thought, knowing he needed release.

"Can Tobias read to me?"

"Uh," she looked over her shoulder again and saw Tobias standing up, folding his hands in front of him and trying to hide the signs of his own excitement.

"Yes, I can," he said, managing to sound excited about this sudden change of plans. But she couldn't let him sit through more pain. He'd have to go and get that taken care of...

"Honey, why don't I read to you?" she suggested, walking Jacob back towards his bedroom.

"It's not a problem," said Tobias. "Let me. I want to." He squeezed her gently from behind. "Let's see how we get along," he said and walked into the room with Jacob while she quickly refastened her bra. "I've got the most boring reading voice, buddy," said Tobias sitting on the edge of the bed. "I'll send you to sleep in no time."

Closing her eyes and sitting in the chair next to the bed, she let her mind wander back to the couch and what Tobias had been doing to her. She imagined it all and found herself getting more heated by the minute, hearing his voice, knowing that he was near, and that soon he would be in her arms again.

After a short while, she opened her eyes and saw that Jacob's eyes were closed. Hope returned. Until he opened them again, as if he was fighting sleep. Whenever they thought he had dozed off, Jacob stirred and would say, "I'm listening..." in a soft, almost-asleep voice.

When, finally, almost half an hour later, he *did* nod off, Tobias closed the book. For a few moments, they watched Jacob with bated breath and when he didn't stir, they got up and tiptoed out of the bedroom.

"I don't know why he's so restless today," she whispered, closing the door. "I thought he'd be flat out after the day we've had."

"He's excited to have me back," replied Tobias smugly.

"You're probably right," she said, lingering outside her son's door.

"I should go," he whispered.

"Why?" she asked, horrified. "I'm ten times as excited to have you back."

"I noticed," he said, cupping her neck with his hand and moving her hair out of the way. She was about to lead him to her bedroom but he sank his lips into her shoulder and kissed her there, sucking her skin and sending sparks shooting into her erogenous zones.

"You should get that seen to," she moaned, her hand sliding over the bulk in his jeans. "I could take care of that for you," she whispered seductively.

"I'm looking forward to it," he said, leaning in and stealing her breath with a kiss that left her panting. His hand had slipped under her top again and now explored her stomach and breasts.

Their forced break just now speeded up their foreplay and her heated body yielded against his with an urgency that consumed her.

"Mommy!" Jacob's voice from inside the room stopped them at once.

Tobias's thumb stilled over her breast and he looked into her eyes, desperate, lustful, and disappointed, mirroring her feelings precisely. "Not again," she muttered, the heat between her legs making her reluctant to move.

"I should go," Tobias mumbled.

"Coming, honey," she said, raising her voice. Then to Tobias, "I don't know what's wrong," she said. "He's been sleeping alone for a week now and he's been fine."

"He might just be overtired," suggested Tobias, speaking like a seasoned pro. "You've often said that."

"But tonight of all nights," she groaned against his lips, their kiss turning into something suddenly hot and frantic as they fought for one last touch.

"Mommy!" Jacob opened his door.

"Hey, buddy," muttered Tobias, almost wincing.

"I can't sleep, Mommy," said Jacob in a groggy voice.

"Go back to bed, Jacob," she said, turning the light back on and hovering around the door, "I'll come and read to you again."

"Do you have to leave?" she whispered to Tobias who was starting to head towards the living room. She grabbed his arm. "He'll fall asleep at some point."

"We can get together another time, Savannah," he said, looking pained.

"You look uncomfortable," she said, feeling sorry for him.

"Spend next weekend at my place," he suggested, resting his palm against her cheek. "You and Jacob both."

"Okay," she said. She would say 'yes' to anything now if he asked her.

"When we get together next time, you'll see how much I've missed you." He leaned in and left one last searing kiss on her lips.

## CHAPTER THIRTEEN

She was at the filing cabinet, pulling out some files for Matthias when she heard the door close. She turned around to find Tobias standing in front of her, grinning. A surge of excitement raced through her body at the sight of him and in the next second, his arms wrapped around her and his lips closed over her mouth.

She was desperate to feel him again, after their cruel separation on the weekend. "I need to see you again," he murmured, as his fingertips danced around her waist. She kept her arms around his neck, wanting to stay like this but knowing that to do so would be foolish; an uneventful Monday morning at the office. It wasn't the place for the type of welcome she was desperate to give and receive.

"I couldn't sleep," she said, staring at his lips. Heated thoughts curled around her body, waking up memories from uninterrupted nights. "The penthouse?" she asked, not caring how it sounded. It was one place they hadn't been to for a while. One place where they could be completely alone.

"Save it for the weekend," Tobias whispered, tightening his

grip around her waist. "I don't want a rushed ten minutes with you." He kissed her again. "I want to take my time."

Just thinking about it made her legs weak.

"We could fly to the Hamptons, or Martha's Vineyard, or anywhere else you want to go."

"I'd rather spend most of my time in bed with you than traveling on a plane," she replied and dropped a kiss on his lips.

A swift knock at the door made them look at one another with disappointment.

"Good morning!" boomed Matthias, opening the door and standing there. They didn't have time to pull away.

A look of mild surprise lit his features. It was Savannah who first moved apart, then turned and smiled at the intruder. But she was surprised to feel Tobias's hand, firm and steady, still around her waist.

"I think our secret is out," he said to her, surprising her again by dropping a kiss to her lips. He moved away and nodded at Matthias. "We have a nine o'clock in the conference room, I believe." He left the room without another look behind him.

"I was getting out the files you need," she told Matthias, assuming that he had come for those.

"Files?" For a moment, he appeared confused. "Yes, the files. In your own time," he said. Then, "How's your son?"

"He's back at school and very happy," she replied.

Matthias nodded. "Good," he replied, smiling again. "I'm sure the break from work helped?"

"Yes," she replied. "But it's good to be back."

"It's great to have you back, Savannah. My data still needs to be cleaned," he said, reminding her of the project she had been working on.

"I know, I'm sorry, I'm a few weeks behind but I managed to make some progress in the last few days and I think I'll be back on track this week."

"I'm joking," he said, moving towards the door. "You take all the time you need, there's no real rush. Briony might think so, but you take it easy, and that's coming from me."

"Thank you,"

"It can't be easy," he said, pausing. "Dealing with all that press intrusion."

She blinked. "You mean about the disappearance?"

"That too," he replied pensively. "But I was referring to suddenly being thrust into the limelight, with that charity dinner event and your vacation. It must be exciting to see yourself suddenly in the women's magazines. Jacob must be thrilled."

She grimaced. "It's not something that excites me."

"You'll have to get used to it," he told her. "Being with a man like Tobias will change the fabric of your life."

She stood watching him, wondering what he was getting at.

"He's a changed man recently, Savannah."

"Is he?" she asked, finding it strange that someone like Matthias should make that comment.

"Is he?" Matthias laughed. "I know what he's been through, and you're good for him. But never forget that you have enormous power over him, Savannah. Use it wisely."

She was still standing for a few moments after he had left, wondering what that was all about.

---

Matthias walked back to his office, mulling things over. Seeing the two of them together like that more than explained why his boss's mind had been otherwise preoccupied. He'd sensed that something hadn't been right between Tobias and Savannah when his friend had changed plans suddenly and shown up in San Diego, but by all accounts they looked pretty close again.

She wasn't one to turn heads in the street—unlike the college graduate he'd invited for a drink, on the strength of her shapely legs. The appeal of Savannah Page was more subtle, but the more he got to know her, and the way others spoke about her —others, apart from Candace—told him she was probably good for his friend. And that was a positive thing.

"Pssst." Candace caught his attention and motioned him into her office.

"What is it?" he asked, glancing at his watch, knowing that Tobias would be waiting for him. Candace closed the door quickly. She looked agitated, running her long, skinny fingers over her dark satin blouse as if she were trying to iron out a crease.

"There's something I need to tell you," said Candace, with a worried expression.

*Now this one*, he thought, eyeing the swell of her breasts and the slim span of her waist, this one was a looker for sure. He never understood why Tobias had failed to see her appeal, even if she was his PA, and supposedly off limits. Savannah Page was just a lowly admin person but she had captured and kept his interest. It was no mean feat, especially when Tobias could have any number of women whenever he wanted. Savannah Page must be amazing in bed, he concluded.

"What's the matter?" he asked.

She chewed her bottom lip, for once seeming to be flustered.

"Be quick, I've got a meeting with Tobias," he said, his gaze taking in her appearance slowly. He wondered whether she wore an underwired bra or one of those loose numbers which would provide gentle support. She paced around, looking uneasy, an emotion which didn't come easily to this glacial ice maiden.

"I did something bad."

"Bad?" He'd like to do something bad with her, he thought wickedly, and started to imagine what she might look like topless.

"Yes," she hissed.

And when she still wasn't forthcoming, "Either tell me now or let me go to my meeting."

"I gave Savannah's ex-husband her home address."

It took a while for this information to sink in. "When? How?"

"He called a few weeks ago. He'd been trying to get hold of Savannah but she was away with Tobias—they were in Miami at the time."

"And?"

"And then," she wrung her fingers. "And then because I...I guess I was mad at her—"

"Mad at her? You mean because of Tobias?"

She gave him a frosty look, and he enjoyed her discomfort when he raised the topic again. Her obvious desire for Tobias was no secret to him. "I was mad at her and I gave him her address. He didn't know where she lived. And now I see why. They didn't split on good terms. He wanted to get to her through their son. All this talk about the boy disappearing for a short while, it wasn't just by accident. I led that man to the boy."

"You stup—"

"I didn't know he'd go and do something like that. I feel awful."

As well she should, he thought. But jealousy was an ugly monster and it could not be easily tamed. "Candace," he said softly, taking a step towards her and grabbing her wrists gently. "Calm down. Have you told anyone else?"

She shook her head. "I want to tell Savannah. I feel really bad about it."

"This has gone too far," he said, "even given the fact that you can be such a bitch sometimes."

"I know," she said.

"You keep this to yourself, do you hear me?" If Tobias found out there was no telling what he might do. "He'll fire you if he finds out. I would leave it. Everything's turned out well."

"Has it?" Candace asked him, sounding doubtful.

"Those two are crazy about one another." He let go of Candace's wrists. "Do yourself a favor, and keep this to yourself."

# CHAPTER FOURTEEN

The evening visits to Tobias's apartment were now a thing of the past because she didn't like the idea of leaving Jacob with Rosalee longer than she had to. But knowing that they would have the weekend together made not seeing him through the week more bearable.

She showed up at work expecting a normal day, but something had gone wrong during the overnight system upgrade and the IT department was scrambling to fix things. Savannah wasn't able to log on to the system first thing in the morning as she usually did but Briony had assured her that everything would be back to normal soon.

By eleven o'clock, things were no better and she was still sitting around trying to keep herself busy. Briony walked into her office once more, obviously at a loose end for things to do. "It's still not up."

"I know," replied Savannah.

"Tobias is furious."

"I can imagine," replied Savannah, "he has no patience." She had been clearing out her handbag and the contents of it were spread out on the desk.

Briony continued to hover by the door. "How was your commute into work?" she asked.

"The same as always," Savannah replied. "How was yours?" Briony seemed to be in the mood for small talk, and didn't look too eager to move from the door.

"Fine," she said. "Everything else okay?"

Savannah put her compact mirror and lipstick back into her handbag. "Yes."

"I'll leave you to it." Briony gave her a plastic smile then left. Savannah stared at the wooden door, wondering what was up with her friend but in the next second Briony marched back in with a newspaper in her hand. "I'm sorry," she said, rubbing her forehead. "But I can't keep it in." She moved Savannah's things out of the way. "If I don't tell you," she threw down the newspaper, "you're going to find out soon enough."

The muscles in Savannah's body turned rigid as she stared at the paper. The headline screamed out at her: '*EXCLUSIVE: TYCOON LOVER RISKS ALL FOR HOOKER*'

She held back a gasp as she stared at the article again, rereading the headline, while her insides imploded. It was a photo of Naomi and Tobias, standing close. *Too close*, she thought, as close as if they had been kissing, or were about to. Their body language said it all. Tobias was smiling at her and she was looking up at him as if they were star-crossed lovers.

The nausea hit Savannah's nose and throat and her morning cappuccino threatened to hurl out of her mouth. She put a hand to her lips as she read the entire article.

"Say something," Briony pleaded, but Savannah couldn't speak. Like slow-moving molten lava, the words and images slowly seeped into her soul as she put her own spin on the story unfolding before her.

"Hon?"

"When?" Savannah asked, speaking more to herself than to

Briony. She quickly scanned the article, gobbling up everything in a desperate attempt for clues that would tell her this was an old photo, taken months before they got together.

"What a ridiculous allegation to make!" Briony exclaimed, but her voice sounded far away. Savannah felt as if the walls of the office and the chair she sat on seemed to disintegrate around her.

She reread it again, this time trying to absorb the words, to make meaning of them. 'The billionaire tycoon was seen talking to his former lover, outside one of New York's most exclusive nightclubs, The Vault. Naomi Rivera revealed that she and Tobias Stone, the handsome yet troubled hedge fund owner, were intimately involved for almost two years after the death of his wife in a fatal car accident. "He was a passionate and skilled lover," she said, "and I really believed I might get my fairytale ending."

Savannah felt hollow and forced herself to continue reading. They had met a few weeks ago. *Just before his trip to San Diego? A few days after Jacob had gone missing?*

It couldn't be. Tobias wouldn't do this to her, would he? Just because she had asked for some space? Had she pushed him into Naomi's arms?

"A high-class escort?" exclaimed Briony. "Tobias will sue them to high heaven for printing this. It's libelous."

Savannah blinked a few times before lifting her gaze. "He went back to her?" she asked softly.

*No, he couldn't have. Tobias would never do that to her.*

"What do you mean he went back to her?" asked Briony, puzzled. "You can't believe everything you read, Savannah. This is all lies. Most of what they print is garbage."

"But it's all true."

"What do you mean it's all true?" Briony asked, frowning.

"She is an escort, and he paid for her." Savannah's subdued voice was barely a whisper.

"What?"

"You heard. It's all true."

"All of it?"

"All of it."

"Oh, hon," Briony gushed, sweeping her hand over Savannah's hair. Then, "You *already* knew Naomi was an escort?" Briony asked, the surprise obvious in her voice. Savannah nodded. She could see how this was the more sensational tidbit of news for her friend, how much of a shock this revelation was, but for her, it was heartbreaking.

She didn't trust the media but this was hard to dismiss when the photos stared at her in the face, and everything that was mentioned in the article was true.

*But why would Tobias keep this from her?*

Savannah opened her mouth to say something but her throat was parched, her voice paralyzed and the words didn't come so easily.

Just then a knock at the door interrupted her thoughts and Candace walked in but she stopped at the door when she saw Savannah's face. "Your stationery order," she said, holding onto the box and taking a few steps into the room until her gaze fell to the newspaper. Briony got up and took the box from her.

"Thanks," she said and closed the door when Candace left.

Savannah's thoughts raced all over the place. Was he going back to her? Paying her by the hour again? Was this the final straw? She knew that Tobias was a physical man and she worried that he had sought Naomi out for sex again.

"The press is going to go nuts over this," said Briony. "Don't worry. Tobias will take care of it."

But it wouldn't make things easier for their relationship,

thought Savannah. Tobias *was* insatiable in bed, and Naomi's claims that he'd made love to her through the night, sometimes as many as three to four times, was something she could vouch for. Miami had been that type of vacation. She knew all about Tobias's libido, and hated that this woman was revealing such intimate details to the press.

And through the veil of her own misery, she wondered what Tobias would make of it and the effect it would have on him.

# CHAPTER FIFTEEN

"Fuck knows why," Tobias barked.

Who knew why Naomi had sold her story? "I paid her enough to keep her goddamn mouth shut." The problem was, he hadn't signed an agreement with her. Back then, he'd barely cared. He had let down his guard and assumed that paying over-the-top rates for a high-class escort implied a certain level of discretion. Putting something legal in place hadn't been the number one priority and now he'd been screwed on more than one level.

Heads at that goddamn agency would roll once he got around to it.

Right now, it was all about damage limitation. His legal team had been in a flurry of activity all morning. Parker, his chief legal counsel, would deal with it but the damage had already been done.

His secret was out.

The world would discover that Tobias Stone had used the services of a high-class hooker now that this gold-digging leech had sold her exclusive story to the press.

"I'm not sure how this will play out," Parker had said. "We'll see if we can get her to retract her statement, otherwise we have no option but to throw something defamatory at her, discredit her character."

Tobias flinched at Parker's words. He didn't like the idea of besmirching her character, even though the woman deserved it. Something about it didn't feel right to him even though Naomi had pushed his reputation into the sewers.

"She's a prostitute, despite the fancy high-class label," said Parker. "Some people won't believe her but unfortunately there will be a subset who will see her as the victim. When it comes down to the hooker and the tycoon, she'll be seen as the underdog. But we can't get a hold of her," Parker declared. "It appears that she's fled the country and is incommunicado."

Maybe that was better—that she wasn't around.

"We've got this, Tobias," Parker assured him. "We can contain it."

"You'd better," warned Tobias, bashing his keyboard. At last, the goddamn system was back up again. More heads would roll in IT.

It had been a crappy day and it wasn't even noon.

He stood up and looked out of the window, wearily loosening his tie as he contemplated the fallout. He turned around and stared at the newspapers that Parker had brought to him, then pulled the chair back with such force that it fell back onto the windowed wall. The angry thud of rich leather on glass did nothing to quell his rage.

A guttural roar escaped his lips at the sound of a knock at the door. "What?" he bellowed. Matthias walked in with a paper in his hands. "Have you—"

"I know," Tobias cut in brusquely, and shook his head, refusing to take the paper from his friend. Tobias didn't need to see it all over again. But Matthias laid the newspaper on his desk anyway and the glaring headline taunted him all over again.

'EXCLUSIVE: TYCOON LOVER RISKS ALL FOR HOOKER'

It brought it all back, everything he'd read. The private details she had divulged, sparing some specifics but mentioning enough to make him see red; to make him want to put a hole through the wall.

"Have you spoken to Parker?"

"Yes," replied Tobias, wiping his hand over his face.

*Why would she do this?*

"I know she wanted to quit, but *this*? For the money? Why didn't she blackmail me instead?"

"Tell me you had something in place?" Matthias asked, his concern easy to see across his tight face.

"Not a goddamned thing."

"You can't be serious?" Matthias gaped at him in shock.

"I *am* serious."

"Her pussy obviously turned your head."

"Not now," he grumbled. Matthias's vulgarity knew no bounds. "I don't need you to patronize me now, of all times."

"I'm only trying to help, buddy," Matthias said quietly.

"Fuck, fuck, fuck." Tobias slammed his fist on the table. This was the last thing he needed. It seemed that the world had it in for him right now, just when he thought he'd found a place of happiness.

"You'll have to answer to the shareholders," said Matthias. Tobias felt his insides tense up. Matthias was right. They'd be gunning for his balls and probably asking for his resignation.

"This could affect the Dextronics deal," Matthias muttered.

"No. They need us more than we need them." Stone Enterprises had many private investors too, and most of these wealthy CEOs would overlook something like this. It wasn't as if he'd been cheating on his wife, and these men often had vices of their own. But not the general public. A small minority, the pious and righteous, would be vocal in their disdain.

"The board might not be too enamored of this story," Matthias reminded him.

"Screw the board," Tobias snarled. "I answer to the SEC and to our shareholders—up to a point. Their interest in my company is tied purely to their profit per share. It shouldn't be because of who I fuck, where I fuck, or how I fu—"

"You'll have to handle it better than that," Matthias interjected. "There's no point swearing your way out of this hole."

Tobias gave a dismissive shrug. "If the company is doing well, which it is, they should be happy," said Tobias. "It's not as if I've had sex with an underage teenager or cheated on my spouse."

Matthias placed a hand on his shoulder. "I know it's the least of your worries," he raised a placating hand up when Tobias looked at him, his eyes narrowed, his nostrils flaring. "But—in my capacity as your friend and right-hand partner—you do need to be aware of the damage this could do to the company. I know you're probably more concerned about Savannah—but Tobias, this thing could sink you if you're not careful."

Shit.

*Savannah.*

Tobias hung his head. "These last few weeks," he said, staring at Matthias but looking through him, his mind wandering, "it's as if we're not meant to be together. The obstacles and the crap we've been through."

"It's a test, Tobias. Sometimes life gives you these things to test you. She makes you happy and she'll stand by you, won't she?"

Of course she would. She knew about Naomi, it wasn't as if

he'd ever lied to her but things were shaky, and they'd only just started to build things back up again.

"Or do you think she'll take this news badly?"

"She already knows."

"Knows what?"

"That Naomi was an escort."

Matthias's eyes widened. "Savannah knew you paid for—"

Tobias nodded.

"But my business with Naomi happened before Savannah came along, and I dumped her long before Savannah and I got together."

Matthias raised an eyebrow.

"She had no problem with you using—" He cleared his throat, "Naomi's *services?*"

Tobias looked up sharply. "She's not a nun, Matthias, and she's been completely understanding most of the time."

*Most of the time*, he thought to himself. "Savannah might not have liked the idea of it, but she hasn't been judgmental, not to my mind. She knows about my past and what I've been through. If she didn't like it, she wouldn't have gotten involved with me." The woman had been his rock but even so, he wasn't sure how she would take the news now, with recent events still raw for them both. He needed to speak to her, should have done so the moment the story had broken but he'd been busy speaking to his legal people.

"She sounds like the perfect woman," Matthias mused. "Chin up, buddy. You can ride this out. Women already love you," he said with a grin. "Your latest exploits might make you even more attractive to them."

Tobias gave him a disgusted stare. "I'm not looking to gain fans and I don't give a shit about what the public thinks. It's the share price I care about. And if it dips, it will soon bounce back up again, unless we're hit with another global crisis. The fundamentals of our business haven't changed just because I paid a woman to have sex with her. It's always the market that determines things, not trivial stories such as this."

"Many wouldn't see this as a trivial story."

"I don't give a shit," snapped Tobias.

"Just calm down," Matthias said. "Let it blow over. Is that the time?" He looked at his watch. "I have a meeting with Briony and Savannah. Aren't you seeing the finance managers now?"

But Tobias was more concerned about the effect of this story on Savannah and Jacob. He glanced at his watch and decided that the meeting with the finance managers could wait. He needed to talk to Savannah first.

# CHAPTER SIXTEEN

"We can do this another time, if you want," Briony offered, as she slowly eased into the chair opposite Savannah.

"Why?" challenged Savannah. "I'm fine, really I am." She lowered her head and continued to doodle in her notebook while they waited for Matthias to join them. She'd been trying to rein it all in—the suspicious, vulture-like thoughts tried to pick her apart.

Matthias entered the room just then and moved towards the table. "The press is going berserk outside the building," he said, turning to Savannah. "We can postpone this meeting until next week."

She shook her head and in as strong a voice as she could muster, told him, "That's not necessary." She put down her pen. "Besides, I've got questions about the data." She was being professional, she thought, and carrying on, or at least giving them the semblance that all was well with her, so that inside she could drown in her misery.

"As you wish," said Matthias and sat down. "Let's get to it, then."

"What questions did you have regarding the data?" Briony asked her.

They jumped as the door flew open and Tobias barged into the room. "Sorry for interrupting," he said, staring at her as if she was the only one present. "Could you step out for a moment?"

*How dare he?* She felt belittled and annoyed by the way he'd come bounding in and had a good idea what it was about. The idea of refusing his command suddenly tempted her but she knew that it would cause an uncomfortable scene, and that she would lose because Tobias Stone always got his way.

She rose from the chair. "I'm sorry," she said to Briony and Matthias. "If you'll excuse me. This won't take long." He walked out, away from the glass conference room, where they wouldn't be seen, and she followed him, a hundred questions swirling around her brain.

"I'm sorry," he explained, "but we need to talk," and he started to walk down the hallway.

"Where are you going?"

He gave her a puzzled look. "To the penthouse, for privacy. You've heard about Naomi?"

"I think all of New York must have heard about Naomi by now." She folded her arms and stopped. "I can't walk out of a meeting and disappear to the penthouse because you demand it." The harshness of her tone, stronger than she had intended, made him stop and examine her.

"You seem upset."

"Did you expect me to embrace this news?"

For a moment, he seemed puzzled by her response. "You need to take a step back and let me explain," he said, reaching out for her arm, but she held tight, refusing to let him comfort her. "It's not what you think."

"Now is not the right time," she replied, not wanting to discuss this yet. "They're waiting for us."

"They can wait," he replied calmly, easily, as if he had every right in the world to do as he pleased.

She had intended to go see him after the meeting, to find out how he was handling the situation, to give him a chance to explain himself, to find out what sort of damage it would cause, but now her suspicions were getting the better of her. It didn't help that Tobias, who was usually so cool and unfazed, now seemed desperate to talk to her. It made her wary.

"I would consider it highly unprofessional to let your private life interfere in the way of your business." In the past, he'd always been careful to keep the two sides distinctly separate.

"You're upset with me and you haven't heard my side of the story, Savannah."

"Do you have something to hide?"

"No," he answered, taking a step towards her so that she caught a whiff of his aftershave. "I have nothing to hide. Let's go upstairs and discuss this calmly without you jumping to any conclusions. Naomi means nothing to me." She saw his throat rise as he swallowed.

"Oh, really?" she asked, gawking back at him. "Because that's not the impression I got from looking at the photos."

"I can see how you might read into them wrongly," he replied. "That's why I need to explain what happened."

"Not now, Tobias."

"You're upset about it, I can see that. Don't you want me to explain?"

When she remained silent he persisted. "Do you really not want to know or are you going to use this to push me away again?" He sounded bitter, as if he were taking it out on her, and she wasn't going to let him do that.

"There's a time and place, Tobias, and this isn't it. I can't follow you up to the penthouse in the middle of a meeting with Briony and Matthias."

"I wasn't asking for that kind of penthouse rendezvous."

Her cheeks started to burn at his words. "And now I'm left wondering if you really did see her for an hour." She didn't mean it, but his comment stung, and she wanted to bite back. She started to turn and walk away but he grabbed her arm.

"Let's not fight over this, Savannah. I don't want to keep any secrets from you and it's important to me that you hear me out."

She didn't want to fight either and leaned back against the wall, her arms still folded. She was determined not to give in and go upstairs. "Why didn't you tell me you saw her?"

"I forgot."

"You ran into your high-class escort girlfriend," she asked, the malice in her voice rising. "And you forgot to tell me?"

"Don't," he said quietly, his mouth twisting. "Don't make assumptions. I ran into her the night I saw Xavier at The Oasis."

"That must have been quite a night," she returned icily, remembering the evening when he had called her, and he and his brother had attracted the attention of two beautiful women. She hadn't seen him that night, and she now looked at him wondering if she really knew him at all.

This news about Naomi had come out of nowhere. Had it been a coincidence that things between the two of them had cooled lately? Was Naomi suddenly on the scene because he'd needed her? She liked to think what they had was special but perhaps passion had gotten in the way of loyalty and given that they hadn't had sex for weeks, was it really so hard to believe that he might use Naomi again?

Her thoughts fought for commonsense and rationality but her emotions got in the way. Knowing that he already had history with Naomi didn't help.

"What are you thinking, Savannah?" He angled his head, frowning. "I told you about the women at the bar."

"And you neglected to tell me about Naomi?"

His mouth straightened into a hard line. She'd been okay until now. Had known and hated press intrusion, knew how they manipulated things. She had trusted Tobias, but right now she felt he was anxious to tell her his side of the story and instead of calming her nerves, it only made her more uneasy. She wanted to believe him, but she didn't want to just accept his words. And now she was more troubled than ever.

"I have to get back to my meeting."

"That's more important?"

"I'm not ready to deal with this right now," she said, feeling conflicted again. She felt as if he was desperate to cover things up, and she was more determined not to be taken in by his words.

"Then at least take my advice on having one of my bodyguards watch your back. This might be blown up in the press for a few days. It would be wise for you to let my men drive you home. I'm hoping they won't come after you and that it's only my blood they want."

She thought about it. "No," she replied quickly. But then she thought of Jacob and Rosalee. "I don't know," she said, wavering in her decision. "I'll let you know how bad it is." She'd gauge it by the commute home this evening.

"Suit yourself," he replied, then turned his back to her and walked away.

# CHAPTER SEVENTEEN

"What do they want?" asked Jacob as she quickly pulled him inside the apartment lobby.

"To ask silly questions."

"What about?"

"I'm not sure," she said, hugging the warm casserole dish that Rosalee had insisted on her taking.

"Shouldn't you have listened?"

"No, honey. Sometimes those people aren't nice."

"Why?"

"Not now, Jacob. I'm tired." She couldn't face his barrage of questions.

"Can I have Lenny over this weekend?" he asked, as they walked into the apartment.

"Sure."

"Then he can come to the park with us and Tobias?"

"Uh—," she carefully placed the dish onto the kitchen table. "I'm not sure we'll be seeing Tobias this weekend."

"Why not?"

"I think he's busy, honey."

She heard a loud disappointed sigh. "But can I still have

Lenny over?"

"Yes, you can." Good old Rosalee, she thought, lifting the lid to the casserole dish. Savannah had been ready to grab Jacob and go but her kind and caring babysitter had insisted that she come in. Rosalee was obviously anxious to speak with her after having seen the morning's paper and, over a cold soda and away from Jacob's ears, the babysitter had slowly coaxed the story out of her.

Now Savannah felt as if everyone in the neighborhood was looking at her in a strange way. She felt as if there were eyes on her, but since she didn't really know anyone in the neighborhood, aside from Rosalee and Arnold, she knew she was being irrational.

All day at work, she had avoided taking calls from her parents and had ignored Kay's texts. She'd been bottling it up and it had been good to talk to Rosalee.

By late afternoon, Tobias and the call girl had become big news in the city. Office workers talked in hushed whispers but she didn't care about herself so much as she felt for Tobias.

Despite their frosty exchange earlier, and her refusal to go to the penthouse with him, Savannah felt for him. She knew that Tobias was good at putting on a brave face but she had come to know the private man underneath that hard exterior. She knew he wasn't formidable, knew that he too was made only of flesh and bone, that he too had feelings and he would be hurting. It saddened her, what they were doing to him, and she wanted to be there for him. Putting her own feelings of uncertainty aside, she'd gone to his office a few times during the afternoon as the drama unfolded but he hadn't been around.

All through the day, the press circus outside the Stone Building had been growing, like a colony of ants. She had almost considered his offer to have one of his men drive her home, and had thought about leaving work early so that she could pick

Jacob up from school. But she had decided to see the drama through, to wait it out and see what happened. Later, when she slipped out of the building, the press barely noticed her.

It was Tobias they wanted.

He'd been busy all afternoon 'with the legal department,' Briony had told her, sensing the friction between her and Tobias. And so they had managed to stay out of one another's way for the rest of the day. She hurt for him, even though she was no longer sure what to believe. She had to find out for herself.

And that meant calling Colt later on when Jacob was in bed.

---

"Savannah?" His voice sounded surprisingly light.

"Hi," she whispered. She'd walked to the furthest corner of the kitchen, and spoke quietly, not only because Jacob was asleep, but because the things she wanted to know weren't the types of things that ought to be spoken out aloud.

"Are you okay? Is Jacob?" he asked. Colt's concern took her by surprise.

"Yes, we're fine," then, because she suddenly remembered that Tobias had mentioned Colt might have been hiding from dangerous people, "Were you worried that something might have happened to us?"

"No. I know you're well protected now. Stone ain't about to let anyone hurt you or Jacob."

"What makes you say that?"

"I know," he said firmly. Then after a while, "I never expected to hear from you again. It's awful good to hear from you but why are you calling? Something wrong?"

"No," she replied. "I wanted to know if you were still alive."

*Because I can't trust what Tobias tells me.*

He gave a short, coarse laugh. "I'm alive. Just about."

"Just about?"

"Nothing you need to know about, sugar. I'm okay. Were you really worried about me?"

Now he was making her feel guilty. "I was worried. You're Jacob's father, whether you act that way or not." The phone went silent for a while.

"I know I've been a sick bastard, that stunt I tried to pull off. I'll never forgive myself for it either." More silence, then, "How is he?"

"Jacob's doing well," she replied, folding her arm across her stomach. "He seems happy to be back at school. You put him in grave danger, did you know that, Colt? He says a woman tried to take him away."

"What?"

"I've been trying to get it out of him but that's all he's saying."

"What do you mean she tried to take him away?"

"He'd wet his pants because he was so scared, and she found him and told him she'd help him get cleaned up, but another customer in the store stopped her."

He was silent for a long time.

"Colt?"

He cleared his throat. "I'm still here." He sniffled and his voice suddenly turned quiet. "Stone was right," he said, "you're both better off without me."

"Is that what he told you?"

"He said that's what you wanted, for me to never contact you again, for me to never show my face. He's right too, even though he scared the shit out of me. I thought he was going to kill me."

"He would never do that," she said nervously.

Colt snorted. "How do you know? I thought I was as good as dead. I thought he was going to punch me to death," he said quietly.

Her stomach turned. "You really thought so?"

"I ain't lying to you. The man scared me. I been mixed up with bad company for long enough to know the truth. I don't see any real difference between the crooks I was working for and the man you're sleeping with. Only difference is that Stone just wears a better suit."

"He wouldn't have killed you," she insisted, more to convince herself than anything else.

"You don't want to believe the truth, 'cos he takes you to these fancy places, shows you his fancy jet, gets you all dressed up like some doll so's he can look good with you on his arm. How well do you know him, sugar? Not as well as you think you do. If you'd seen what I seen that night when he took me to some dark, deserted building in the middle of nowhere, you'da been shitting your pants too."

Every muscle in her body tensed up and she could barely speak. "I asked for the bullet. Straight up," Colt told her. "He gave me a choice how I wanted to die and I asked to be shot."

"Because you wanted it over with quickly?"

"'Cos I didn't want him to punch me to death like he said he would."

She felt as if her chest was squeezing her ribcage. "He had a gun?"

Colt grunted. "Your man's smarter than that. He weren't going to get his hands dirty. He had a couple other guys there to do his dirty work. Look, sugar, I know you don't want to believe me, but you have to be careful. If he was a poor loser like me, I bet you wouldn't have looked at him twice. He dresses it up with his money, and it's women like you who fall for the fancy stuff."

His words battered her to silence. "I read about the hooker today," he said, releasing another cruel laugh. "Can't say I'm surprised. Men in his position screw people over all the time without worrying too much about it. I never meant to be an asshole to you, but I was weak, and I couldn't handle the way things were going. Stone doesn't have an excuse. He has all the money in the world. What problems can a man like that have? He can screw who he wants, do what he wants, and expect to get away with it. They all do, men like him. I can see why you're with him, and I don't mean this in a bad way, but don't you sometimes wonder, when he can have any woman he wants, why he would want to be with you?"

She was too shocked to reply because sometimes, when the doubts crept in, she wondered the same thing.

"I can see what you see in him, but maybe Stone and me aren't so different after all. Seems kinda strange, now that I look back on it, that he told me to get the hell away from you both and to never show my face again. Now I'm worrying about you and Jacob being with him 'cos I know the truth about him. It's a truth he doesn't want you to see. I seen the monster he really is and he doesn't want you to see that side of him. I been wanting to call you. I been wanting to know how my son was doing, been thinking of you both 'cos I know that boy means the world to you, and when I took him like that, and then I lost him, I knew how much I'd hurt you. I know he's your life, and I reckon a part of you musta died when he was missing."

She gritted her teeth together, being suddenly pulled back into those moments when she'd had no clue where Jacob was. It had been the single most terrifying moment of her life.

She gripped her hand tightly, trying to find holes in what Colt had told her. "Why did he let you go, then? If he's such a monster? Why did he give you the money?"

"He paid me off, don't you see? So that I would never show

my face again and never ask to see you or Jacob again. He said it was what you wanted. Was it, sugar?"

She tried to remember the way she felt back then. She'd hated Colt with a passion, and she never wanted to cross paths with him again. When exactly had Tobias met up with him? She'd been in a daze and preoccupied by her son back then and though she hadn't asked too many questions, she knew the men had met. Tobias hadn't hidden that from her. But she wondered if he'd only given Colt the money to make himself look better.

Maybe one day he'd hire someone to kill him anyway. She felt sure that a man like Tobias could do these things easily.

"There's more to him than meets the eye. He's dangerous. Be careful, sugar, and you keep an eye on my boy."

She swallowed. "This trouble you were in—the reason you needed the money. Is that all over with?"

"Yeah. It's over with."

"Do you have any money left over?"

"I got enough to get me through a few months. I'm starting over. I've left North Carolina and I'm making my way around, trying to see where I can set myself down and set up roots, maybe find a job and start again."

"Colt?" she said, suddenly feeling sad again, remembering the man she had fallen in love with all those years ago. "Don't change this number, okay? Jacob might want to speak to you one day." But more than that, she was afraid that one day Colt would suddenly disappear, and she would never know the reason why.

"Does he know why I took him?" Colt asked.

"No, I never told him."

"I owe you, sugar."

"Take care."

"It's you I'm worried about. You take care, Savannah."

# CHAPTER EIGHTEEN

"Drive to the basement," Tobias ordered when he saw the hordes of photographers, like crawling cockroaches, waiting outside the Stone Building eager for a sight of him.

In one day, the crowd had doubled.

Ludwig had taken on extra security to ensure none of them made it through and into the building. Tobias had also finally, without Savannah knowing, assigned one of his men to tail her on foot, since she refused obvious protection or to travel by car.

She wouldn't like it if she ever found out but she didn't know what these parasites could be like—or the cost of being in the public eye. Ludwig had some people monitoring online activity and since the Naomi story had broken yesterday, he now held even bigger appeal for some of the losers out there. The general consensus, when he'd pressed Ludwig on his online findings, had been that Naomi was much hated for selling her story, and that Tobias was seen as the victim. It came as no surprise to him that most of the hateful comments for Naomi came from women, and the hate directed at him came from men, although even those figures weren't completely reliable, in a medium where anyone could be anyone and hide behind an IP address.

He knew there were many desperate women who followed his every move online. For this reason, he'd ensured that Savannah was protected at all times and he had also assigned another man to track the babysitter when she picked Jacob up at the end of the school day.

And still he was none the wiser as to why this story had made it out. When he looked back to the last time they'd met, Naomi had given no indication that she was about to expose their past.

Had it been the lure of money that had made her greedy? He had thought they had mutual respect and understanding for one another. Did the need for revenge run that deep? She would have liked things to have turned out differently, he knew that, but he had made it clear from the start that there would be nothing permanent between them. If he'd fallen in love with her, maybe ...but he hadn't, and he'd had no problem pushing her away.

He felt more than betrayed, he felt let down by someone he thought he could rely on. The small circle of people he trusted seemed to be shrinking, and it was a sad reflection on his life that he considered a high-class escort to be one of them.

He would never understand it, never. And now he knew what it felt like, the words he often tossed carelessly at others, the ones he'd thrown at Savannah once, that everything had a price.

The newspapers had served Naomi well, had probably paid her a handsome price for the story. She had been looking for another line of work and this was her short-term ticket. He assumed that she wouldn't have to work after this.

In light of the hostility leveled towards Naomi, he was relieved that it kept Savannah's name out of immediate public attention, and even though he was hurt and disappointed by Naomi's actions, he was in a way relieved that she had left the country.

The Merc cruised slowly along the spiraling tunnel to the basement with the black SUV close behind. With the increased risk from deluded women, there was potential for the disgruntled shareholders to use Tobias to vent frustration.

There were too many crazy women wanting to jump into his bed on account of the details that Naomi had shared. This level of visibility also made him a target for other, more criminal elements looking to make a quick buck off him. He had been a high enough target for blackmail before, but until this episode died a quiet death, Ludwig recommended that Tobias be followed more closely than ever.

He climbed out of the Merc, frustrated and resentful of the current situation, and slammed the door behind him.

Candace accosted him as he headed into his office. "Wait," she said, rushing towards him. "Your mom's been calling. She did all afternoon yesterday as well."

"Thanks." He opened the door, walked in and closed the door behind him. He had more than a few missed calls from his mother but he didn't have the patience to deal with her yet. His father and Xavier had texted him to find out if he was okay. Xavier told him to contact him 'when he wanted to talk about it.'

Another knock followed and Tobias moved away from the door, irritated. "What now?" he barked, when he saw it was Candace again.

"She's booked dinner at Lafont & Moreau at The Lancaster tomorrow at 8:00."

*Fuck, no.*

"She's what?" Why in the hell had his mother booked dinner at the most exclusive restaurant in one of New York's most prestigious hotels, on one of the busiest nights of the week, and in the middle of one of the biggest shitstorms of his business career?

It was official. The woman *was* insane. "Call her back and tell her I can't make it."

"She, uh—" Candace rubbed her temple and backed away a little. "She also said it would be in your interests not to, and I quote, try to wriggle out of this one. She actually told me to say that to you..." Her voice trailed away. "I'm just passing on the message."

"Okay," he said, and closed the door. *Dinner at Lafont & Moreau?* What was the woman thinking? As angry as he was, and as tempted as he was to spite her and cancel, he knew she would continue to hound him until he gave in. He'd been able to get out of meetings with billionaire business leaders with less hassle but his mother was something else altogether. He could miss this dinner at his peril, or he could attend and get it over with.

Tobias hung his head, still clutching his briefcase and decided. He barged out of the room and into Candace's office. "I'm going home for the afternoon," he announced.

"But you have your usual Friday managers' meeting," Candace countered.

"Cancel it," ordered Tobias, gripping the handle of his briefcase tighter and pulling out his cell phone to call his trainer. The boxing ring beckoned. It was the only way to get rid of the tension that was eating away at him. Hell, yeah. A couple of bouts punching someone's lights out would help.

"Looking forward to the weekend?" Briony chirped gaily, as she walked into her office. Savannah was getting ready to clear her desk, getting ready to leave for the weekend even though it was only four o'clock and she still had a while to go before work was over.

"I'm looking forward to not seeing those vultures out there," replied Savannah, nodding toward the window as she sank down into her chair.

"Damned vipers," replied Briony, looking out of the window. "There are more today but that's to be expected, I suppose. Hopefully, some other news will break soon and you'll be forgotten."

"They're not actually hounding me," Savannah said, picking a hair off her skirt. "There were a couple last night when Jacob and I got back home, but nothing like out here."

"That's because its Tobias they're after. Sorry, hon. You're out of the limelight this time. It seems as if Miss Rivera has vanished. I wonder where the hell she's disappeared to." Briony walked back towards Savannah's desk. "Imagine," she said, placing her hands on her hips. "Imagine spilling such a story and then disappearing off the face of the Earth. Leaving everyone else in the shit."

"I bet she got a nice payoff, too," muttered Savannah.

"How's Tobias taking it?"

"I don't know," Savannah replied, picking up a pencil from her desk. "I haven't seen him since yesterday." She started to scrape at the thin layer that covered the pencil. She used to do this at school, in her younger years; peel off the paint coating the pencil when she became bored during classes. At this moment in time, she was far from bored but she was troubled. Colt's words had crawled under her skin and stayed there. Chipping away at the pencil felt therapeutic.

"You don't know?" Briony exclaimed. Then in a less dramatic voice, "Hon, what's going on? Something like this should be bringing you two together, not tearing you apart."

Savannah chipped away silently.

"You did look mad when he pulled you out of the meeting," Briony commented.

"Tobias likes to think he can do what he wants, when he wants."

Briony laughed. "That's because he can, hon."

"It doesn't mean he should though and I still can't get used to it. I don't think I'll ever get used to it." Savannah looked up. "He could just as easily shoot a man if he wanted to but it doesn't mean he should, does it?"

Briony gave her a wary look. "What's going on?"

"Nothing."

"For goodness' sake, don't let that floozy split you up."

"Like I said," replied Savannah, getting back to her pencil. "I haven't seen him since yesterday and he hasn't been around this morning. I tried his office a couple of times."

"Why didn't you just ask Candace when he'd be back?"

"Because Candace wants to be my best friend all of a

sudden." Tobias's PA had taken an interest in her well-being and Jacob's too. "I think I prefer it when Candace is bitchy. At least I can choose to ignore her."

"I told you there was something odd about her, didn't I?" said Briony. "Anyway, Tobias has gone home this afternoon."

"Gone home?" asked Savannah, her voice rising in pitch. "I thought you have a Friday managers' meeting?"

Briony shook her head. "Candace said he was all worked up when he got back and he left in a mood. I think he's had enough. It's been a terrible week for him and the media has mauled him to pieces."

"I didn't know it was that bad."

"Aren't you keeping up to date with it?"

Savannah shook her head. She didn't want to know and she was too afraid to look, but Kay had updated her enough, even from thousands of miles away. And either her parents were too embarrassed to ask her, or they didn't know. She was hoping it was the latter and that news about city billionaires wouldn't have made its way over to her hometown. As it was, she hadn't read the papers or watched the various gossip and news channels on TV because she didn't want to discover anything else they might have uncovered—truth or lies. She didn't want to read hurtful comments from people of a dubious nature saying nasty things about Tobias, or attacking her and Jacob.

"It's to his advantage that Tobias has a thick skin and doesn't care much what people think of him. But if you think about it, deep down he must be crushed, what with everyone knowing about his sexual prowess—" Briony stopped and colored as she realized what she'd said. "Sorry."

"Don't worry about it," Savannah replied, putting down the pencil. But she knew it wasn't okay. She knew that these things grated on him.

"It's strange," commented Briony. "I've met Naomi a few

times and she didn't come across as being someone malicious. I'm shocked that she would do this to him. They were together for a few years."

Even though she knew how long Tobias had been with Naomi, it still hurt her to hear it from Briony. "How much do we really know someone?" she said, trying to put on a brave face. "You could live with someone for years and think you knew them well, and then, wham! One day they do something that reveals their real side. It could happen after a few years, or a few months, or even a few hours."

"True. Who really knows? Let's hope this goes away soon, for both your sakes. Enough of this doom and gloom," said Briony. "I've got a meeting with Matthias now. I thought I was going to have an easy afternoon now that the managers' meeting is off." She got up and fluffed her hair. "Why do I get the feeling you're going to take off early today?"

Savannah joked, "Does it look that obvious?" She was concerned about Tobias and trying to push Colt's conversation out of her mind. It ripped her into two; she'd been thinking about what Colt had said and at the same time she was worried about Tobias. Did she know him, *really* know him, or had she allowed herself to get carried away?

"Tell you what, how about we go out tomorrow night? You and me, and Max, if you want? Get you out of your apartment and get some wine or champagne, or some mixed drinks down you. Shake you out of that misery," Briony suggested. Savannah sat upright in her chair. It sounded tempting. The last few weeks had been intense, and she was tired and wanted to forget the bad stuff which seemed to be surrounding her.

"It sounds like a good idea, but—"

"But," Briony gesticulated wildly, throwing her hands in the air. "Why did I not see the 'but' coming?"

"Calm down," said Savannah. "I don't want to leave Jacob alone."

"No, you don't," agreed Briony quickly. "Sorry, hon. I wasn't thinking. How about we bring the party to you? Get some takeout and bring some bottles and come to your place?"

*That would work.* "That sounds like a plan," Savannah agreed.

"I'm looking forward to it already," said Briony, walking to the door with her hips swaying. "I'll see you tomorrow at 7:00 or 8:00-ish?"

"Any time after seven sounds good." Savannah smiled as the door shut behind her.

Her cellphone vibrated and jumped around on her desk. Savannah saw the incoming number, it was one of the rental agencies probably calling her back with some more properties. For now, Savannah ignored the voicemail message icon that showed up. She would call them later. She picked up her phone and called Tobias instead, not giving herself any time to talk herself out of it. Despite the way they'd parted yesterday, despite her conversation with Colt last night, despite Naomi and her big mouth, she didn't want Tobias to hurt any more than he already did. Her feelings ran deep for this man, and for this moment at least, she refused to accept the possibility of a dark side to him.

# CHAPTER TWENTY

They had managed to get through their appetizers without spilling any blood.

Everyone was civil, polite and being way-too-nice. Nobody mentioned the huge rhinoceros that invisibly stood on top of the table. So they ate their appetizers and pretended that nothing was wrong.

Tobias was hungrier than he'd thought. The seven-mile jog he'd gone on earlier had built up an appetite which he hadn't expected, but for which he was now grateful. He'd been dreading the dinner in view of the fact that Naomi's story was still riding high. But he reasoned that if he got this over and done with, he wouldn't need to meet with his mother for another month or two.

Rationalizing it this way made the whole event more bearable.

"The food here is simply amazing, isn't it?" his mother asked, addressing nobody in particular, as she dabbed the corners of her mouth. On his left was Xavier who ensured that no glass remained empty, and to his right sat his father, which meant that Tobias sat directly opposite his mother.

"Emil has transformed this place," crowed his mother. "The man's a culinary genius and leaving Switzerland was the best thing he ever did."

"You advised him, did you?" Tobias asked, rolling his eyes at Xavier. His mother spoke of the world-famous chef as if he were in her close circle of friends.

"It's very good," his father agreed, stepping in diplomatically, the way he always did. Silence fell as the server cleared their plates. "How's business, Tobias?" His father asked.

"It could be better," Tobias replied casually, "given the recent news." Somebody had to mention it. By his side, he heard the thump of Xavier's bottle of beer hitting the table.

"And what news might that be?" his mother piped up.

"Now, Milly, you know perfectly well."

"No, Dad. It's fine," said Tobias, sliding his fingers over the clean and polished cutlery that lay waiting for the next course. The cool metal was hard and unyielding against his fingers.

His mother looked at him. "Darling, you've been through enough as it is. I don't understand why this woman would target you with such lies, and in such a humiliating way."

"They're not lies," he replied coolly. His mother calmly picked up her slender glass and sipped her olive martini. His father fidgeted with his tie and Xavier ordered another beer. They all pretended not to have heard him.

"It's all true," Tobias said, watching her reaction with interest.

"All of it?" Millicent asked, touching her lips in horror.

"All of it, I paid her by the hour, it was strictly an arrangement, she'd come over when I wanted—"

"I think we get the picture, son," his father said quietly, patting his mother's hand.

"You were going through a bad time, my darling," his

mother said, more to reassure herself, he imagined. He had to set her straight.

"I had her for a couple of years and I only dumped her around Christmas."

"I'm sure you had your reasons," his mother said. "I think I need another martini." Xavier summoned the server.

"Then help me to understand yours, Mom," said Tobias, sighing loudly.

"Understand what?"

"Why you booked dinner now of all times and *here*?"

Her eyes settled on his, observing for a few quiet seconds. "Because I had to cancel the last dinner when you conveniently disappeared on business."

"Why here?"

She leaned in. "What better place to be seen to be having dinner than Lafont & Moreau? You can have dinner with your family and show the world that you've got nothing to hide, nothing to be ashamed of. That it's business as usual as far as you're concerned and the filthy accusations haven't upset you. That your family is behind you one hundred percent. At least you didn't have to go into hiding like that disgusting woman. It's not for nothing that she's vanished." She smiled at him as if she'd just won a humanitarian award.

"And I thought you only wanted to have dinner with your sons," Tobias replied, trying to tone down the sarcasm in his voice and failing.

"They're very discreet, Tobias," his father added. "If we'd gone elsewhere, you might have had the press hounding you as we came in. Other places might have tipped them off. At least here you know you won't have that problem."

"That's strange," said Tobias, raising his glass to his lips. "I wonder why two photographers tried to take a photo when I walked in." He turned to his mother. "Do I have you to thank for that?"

Millicent patted her short bob lightly. "I might have mentioned it to someone. Don't give me those evil eyes," she said to her son. "The press uses you, Tobias, and you have to use them back."

"And what will this prove?" he asked, sweeping his hand around the table.

"One hopes it will mitigate the sleazy image painted of you by the press. There's no need to get so worked up, my darling. We mean well, your father and I. Your family loves you and when you get hurt, we get hurt." He didn't doubt that, he just didn't like the way his mother went about things.

Sometimes, he was sure his mother had bigger balls than him, and sometimes he wondered if she'd ever had a maternal fiber in her body or whether his father had been the one to get them through childhood and beyond.

"Mother," said Tobias, fighting to keep his anger from exploding. "I hired Naomi at a time when I didn't want to make small talk. At a time in my life that was so bleak, I wanted to end it."

His father cleared his throat. "We're not judging you, son. I'm sure there were reasons behind what you did but unfortunately, what's done is done. I understand this young lady is nowhere to be found but this can't be good for your business, surely?"

Millicent coughed lightly. "Loose women have no respect for a person's privacy. They have no decency, no morals. I hope you've learned your lesson, my darling."

Tobias's brows pushed together. "Learned my lesson? How do you mean?" Of all the things a mother could say, his could only give him this kind of advice.

"What she means is—" his father tried to interject.

"No, Dad. Let Mom explain. I'm intrigued."

"That you shouldn't be mixing in such circles. I don't understand why you had to...had to..." His mother paused and swallowed. "Why you needed such services."

"I hired Naomi because I didn't want all that extra stuff that went into relationships."

"You just wanted to get on with the business, right, bro?" Xavier said, patting him on his arm lightly.

"You don't have to explain, Tobias," his father said.

"But I want you to hear it," he replied. "There were times in my life back then that I wanted to end it. I couldn't see a reason for living. I didn't want to *feel*. Do you understand what that's like? To go from having Ivy and waiting for our son to be born to losing them in seconds? To go from having everything to having nothing?" He stared at the white linen tablecloth. "Matthias helped me through it."

"We tried to be there for you, son," his father said.

He nodded his head once. "You were, Dad, but you weren't there every day to get me out of bed, to clear away the whiskey bottles, to throw me into the shower. I know you did your best."

"I was there a few times," Xavier piped up.

"Listen to me, will you?" he said, his voice tight as he picked up the butter knife and tapped it on the table.

"Put that down, son," his father said, looking slightly alarmed.

Tobias slammed the knife back down. Hell, he wasn't in danger of doing something silly now, but had it not been for Matthias watching over him, he didn't know how he would have gotten through that time. "What I'm trying to tell you is that I didn't care for anyone once I lost them." He lowered his voice. "It was a long time after that, when I started to get back on my feet, that I needed something more. Not love, not intimacy, not friendship, not a relationship. I needed to *feel*. Naomi made me feel again."

"I bet she did," Xavier muttered.

"You've been through what no one should go through, son," his father said. "I only wish we could have done more for you."

"You did, Dad. You did, but there were some things I had to get through myself and maybe having someone who wasn't family, someone who was, who *is* one of my closest friends, maybe it was something that Matthias had to do. Just like I *had* to have Naomi. I didn't want to make roots, I didn't want to commit. I didn't need baggage, or emotional ties. Some days I didn't even need to talk to her."

Xavier stared at him with a wicked glint in his eyes. His mother put a napkin to her mouth.

"But what I didn't expect was that Naomi would go running to the press. I still don't understand why she did it." His fingers slid along the whiskey glass, feeling its hard surface. "I saw her that night, as I was leaving. The night we met," he said to his brother.

"That night?"

"She'd been in The Vault."

"The Vault?" his father asked, expressing concern.

"Relax, Dad. It's a basement nightclub." His mother sipped her cocktail and listened silently, her steely gray eyes on Tobias.

"We talked and it was nice to see her again. It was a normal conversation," he said, remembering it well. "She told me she wanted to leave and find something else to do."

"She's not doing her thing anymore?" Xavier sounded disappointed.

His mother gave Xavier an evil look. "Don't you go getting any ideas," she said, pointing her finger at him.

"I think the boys are old enough to know what they're doing," his father said.

"Was it all true, bro?" Xavier asked, sneakily stealing a look at their mother. "Three to four times a night? You almost beat my record."

Millicent fanned her face with a napkin.

"Boys!" their father implored.

Tobias gave his brother a rare smile and continued. "I don't know why she spilled the story. The last time we met, we spoke like friends."

"You can't be friends with a woman like that," cried Millicent.

"Maybe she's pissed that you ended it," Xavier suggested.

"Maybe she did it for the money, son," his father offered. This was what Tobias had concluded. It was always for the money.

"And what does Savannah Page make of all this?" his mother asked.

"She's dealing with it as best as she can. She already knew, so it wasn't such a huge shock." Although other things had crept up that were causing problems.

"She knew you used such a woman and she had no problem with it?" Millicent asked in a tone that suggested she'd made her own mind up about Savannah.

"She's a very understanding woman," he said slowly. "Some women are."

His mother smiled at him brightly. "I'm sure she is. When are we going to meet her?"

"When the time is right."

"But we're more than ready to meet her, aren't we, darling?" Millicent turned to her husband.

"It's not you I'm worried about," mumbled Tobias. Xavier chortled beside him.

"And is the boy all right now?" she asked, ignoring his comment. "I recall he wandered off by himself?"

Tobias nodded. "He's fine."

"So things are back to normal?"

He breathed in deeply and lied. "Yes."

"Then we look forward to seeing her, and her son, whenever you're ready, Tobias," his father said. "I can see she means a lot to you. It makes me happy to know that you've finally met someone who makes you happy again, son."

"This calls for a toast," said Xavier. "I think we need some champagne." He summoned the waiter over.

"A toast?" asked Tobias. "What the hell for?" Then, realizing, "Ah, do we have something to celebrate, something you want to share with us?" Tobias goaded him, anxious to let his parents question his brother for a change.

Xavier gave his mother his sweetest and most mischievous smile. "I must have forgotten to tell you, Mother. Petra and I are back together again. I almost brought her with me tonight, but figured you might want to keep it low-key..." he lowered his voice, "and have it be just the four of us."

Millicent grimaced as if she had suddenly developed a toothache. "It sounds like the perfect opportunity for us all to get together," his father suggested. "What a splendid idea. Maybe Savannah and Jacob would care to join us next time?"

Maybe one day, thought Tobias. But not yet. Not with the way things were. He sat back in his chair and heard the verbal battering back and forth. He heard his mother question Xavier about Petra, heard Xavier—his tongue loosened by beer—handle her cheerily, and heard his father make peace.

He wished he had spent his evening with Savannah. Had the story not broken, she would have been at his place now, staying the night, with Jacob in the room that would have been Zachary's.

# CHAPTER TWENTY-ONE

"It could simply be a dick thing," said Max, holding up a battered shrimp.

"A *dick thing*?" Strands of wiry noodles dangled from Savannah's chopsticks. "What do you mean, a *dick* thing?" She glanced at Briony for enlightenment.

"This need that you say Tobias has to control everything around him," replied Max. "If he wants sex, he's willing to pay for it—because he can, and why shouldn't he? It could simply be because he's insanely wealthy, and self-made, or because he's a man, and that's just the way they like to roll sometimes. But it was damn shortsighted of him not to put a legal agreement in place."

"That surprised me," said Briony. "He's usually careful about protecting himself."

"I'm sure the papers paid her well."

"Why is it always the men who are the billionaires?" asked Savannah, sick of discussing Naomi-gate.

"Because women aren't that ruthless or willing to claw their way over one another's back to get to the top?" suggested Briony.

"That's not true at all," said Savannah, speaking from experience. "Women can be more vicious."

Max picked up another shrimp. "I agree. Women can be just as ruthless as men."

"Look at Piranha Queen." Savannah reminded them.

"Let's not talk about Candace tonight," said Briony.

"I'd like to know how many of those billionaires had to take care of children and the laundry when they were first starting out and building their businesses," Savannah added her two cents.

"Don't forget," said Max, pointing her chopsticks at them, "a billionaire woman's most likely going to have to pay for sex because no man is going to have the balls to want to be with her. Most men can't handle a woman earning more."

"I don't know if that's entirely true," said Savannah thoughtfully. Colt had been content for her to be the breadwinner for a while.

They had successfully managed to get through two bottles of wine and were still plowing their way through cartons of Chinese takeout. The topic still revolved around Tobias and the 'relationship problem'—something that Briony had brought up early on. But now that the wine was flowing, Savannah no longer seemed to mind that they were dissecting her relationship.

While she didn't want to hog the conversation and have it be centered around her and Tobias all the time, it did her good to discuss these things with her friends. It was something she couldn't bring up with Lenny's mom, because Julia seemed to be infatuated with Tobias. Savannah didn't have this same problem with Briony and Max.

"Why is it that in this day and age we still have those stereotypes? Tarzan and Jane don't only exist in the jungle. Why is it that Tobias is the king and you two," Max pointed her chopsticks at them again, "are running around after him like minions?"

"I don't run around after him," Briony protested.

"Neither do I."

"You're a special case," Max told her, finishing off her wine. "You're in an elevated position because you're sleeping with him—or at least we hope you will be soon once we figure out what the problem is."

"Which one of you two has that role?" asked Savannah, intrigued. Because the two of them weren't the stereotypical lesbian couple either. Max was the more glamorous of the two, with her ash blonde hair falling below her shoulders and her sharp fashion sense. And even though Briony's hair was short, it was more pixyish, than boyish. They were both very feminine. Secretly, Savannah wondered who wore the pants in this relationship, and hedged her bets with Max.

"We don't conform to those stereotypes," replied Briony. "Do we?" she asked, turning to Max.

"We don't have the dick problem, if that's what you're asking" Max replied, grinning.

"I don't think any healthy relationships these days conform to those outdated stereotypes," said Savannah.

"No?" asked Briony, snapping a shrimp cracker into two. "So life with Colt was sweet, was it?" Savannah picked up her wine glass, realized it was empty and walked over to the fridge to get another bottle.

"That was different," she said, uncorking the bottle of wine. She was keen to avoid talking about life with Colt. Her conversation with him still played out in her head and it had kept her awake many nights. She'd been forced to re-examine some of the times she'd had with Tobias. She had seen him when he was quietly seething, like the time he thought she'd taken a client's file. There was also that other time when he had completely lost it, when he'd mistakenly assumed she was blackmailing him for money. It had shocked her then, and it still did, thinking about it. But for Colt to warn her to be careful, for Colt to be intimidated by the man and to ask to be shot— that was something else. And it bothered her.

"If I were into men," said Max, slowly, gripping her wine glass, "and if a man like Tobias Stone showed an interest in me, I'd be dying to get between his sheets. It's not just those killer Armani suits he wears either, or his build, or the way his eyes pierce into you—"

Briony cleared her throat loudly. "Is there something you need to tell me?" she asked. "Your soliloquy and thinly veiled attraction for my boss is beginning to scare me. You're not tempted to the dark side, are you?"

Max leaned forward and kissed her on the lips. "Darling, I left the dark side in '98. I always had an idea I was into women, but my mom managed to convince me otherwise for most of my teen years. There's no going back for me." Briony looked more relaxed.

"So, if you already knew about the call girl, why are you so mad at him?" Max asked, turning the topic back to her.

"Because I'm not sure I know him that well."

"A week in Miami with no kid in tow and just the two of you? Darling, if you didn't get to know him well then, there's no hope for you," drawled Max. "What are you looking for?"

"It's what he's hiding."

"What makes you think he's hiding something?"

She couldn't divulge what she was really thinking. "He does things, without explanation, because he can."

"He's a billionaire, darling. Sure he can."

"I don't understand why the two of you haven't been able to work this out," said Briony. "Because, hon, the two of you just work so well together. I remember that quiet, hard-working single mom who started back in December."

"I'm still the same hard-working single mom," Savannah objected.

"Yeah, but look at you," said Briony, waving her hand at Savannah.

"What?" asked Savannah, looking down at her dress. It was a strappy sundress in turquoise and white checkers. And it had been a bargain buy.

"You look different, you dress different, you seem happier, or you did before all this recent stuff happened."

"You and Tobias worked," Max said, picking out another shrimp with her chopsticks. "Why can't you fix this? It can't be easy for him to go through this recent press storm without you."

The doorbell rang just then, preventing her from making another excuse why she couldn't trust him.

"Who else did you invite?" Briony asked.

"A foursome?" cooed Max, pouring out more fried rice onto her plate. Savannah left them and answered the door. Even as she opened it, she had an idea who it might be.

"Hey," said Tobias, just as an outburst of laughter carried over from the kitchen. He leaned against the doorframe, his hands in his pockets, his smoldering eyes looking her over. Her heart began to thump. Three glasses of pinot grigio and a belly full of Chinese food would have ordinarily put a smile on her face but seeing Tobias looking devilish in his white dress shirt and blazer over black jeans, and she was ready to forget everything Colt had said. All she wanted was to reach over and kiss him.

"Hey," she replied, keeping her hand on the door.

"You've got company?" he stated flatly.

"Max and Briony are over," she said, letting her hand drop to her side as she stood barefoot, unsure whether to ask him in or not. "This is a surprise," she said, trying hard not to look at his lips for too long, and wondering at the same time what had made him show up here unannounced.

"I was passing by," he told her.

*From where?* She wondered. "We're having Chinese, would you like to join us?" She watched his gaze dip to the hollow of her neck, a place she knew he liked to kiss her and she wondered if he was thinking the same thing. Instinctively, her fingers moved to it, found the necklace she always wore—the one he'd given her with the two entwined rings—and she realized he might only have been admiring that instead.

"I've just been to dinner," he replied, his lips curling up slightly.

"Oh," she replied and wondered where, and with whom. Another burst of laughter emanated from the kitchen.

"I'll leave you to it," he said, standing straight, and taking a small step back. "It sounds as though they're having a good time."

"Three bottles of wine does that," she replied, her mind sifting through the possibilities of what his evening had been like.

"Won't that noise wake Jacob up?" he asked.

"He's completely out of it. I made sure of it. We spent the day at Bryant Park and he rode his bike all afternoon."

"Bryant Park?" he asked. "Why didn't you ask me along?"

"It was a playdate with Lenny and his mom."

He nodded his head. "I met my parents and Xavier for dinner," he said. "My mother arranged it and I couldn't get out of it."

"That's not a nice thing to say about your mother."

"You haven't met my mother."

"I'd hate Jacob to say that to his...friend about me." She'd almost said 'girlfriend.'

"Jacob would never say that about you, you're nothing like my mother. I still love mine, but she's an acquired taste, as I've already told you." She nodded, remembering what he'd told her in Miami.

Feeling relieved to hear who had kept him company during dinner, she tried again. "Are you sure you don't want to come in?"

He shook his head. "I didn't know you had company. I was hoping we could talk," he said, "about the way things have been since the story broke. About the way things have been since a lot of things have happened. Seems like we take one step forward and three steps back."

She was falling for his words, for his looks, for that face, for those bedroom eyes. If her friends hadn't been here, she'd have let him in, and with Jacob sound asleep, not having woken once through their noisy laughter, she knew the night would be golden.

*There's more to him than meets the eye. He's dangerous. Be careful.* Colt's words came back to haunt her. In her mind, she tried to reconcile this heart-stoppingly gorgeous man with the person Colt had described.

How easy it was to forget all his vices. And her son loved him. How could she not fall for it all?

"Maybe another time, Tobias." It was hard to say it, but she had to try to be strong. Not duped as easily.

"Another time," he said, taking another step back, but he still seemed reluctant to move away completely. He suddenly moved closer, one step was all it took, and she was unprepared when he lifted his hand to her face and caressed her cheek gently. Goosebumps sprang up all over her skin, and she shivered at the scent of his cologne, and from his touch. And just as she was getting used to the feel of him, he moved forward and dropped a gentle kiss on her lips. It was so sudden, so unexpected that it both shocked and excited her.

She was even more shocked when he didn't follow it up properly but backed away instead and stared at her, as if he was examining her response, or assessing the level of risk.

And then he kissed her properly. His mouth covered hers and thought disappeared, logic fell apart, and her resolve melted. All she could do was fall into his hard-as-steel chest and stay there, kissing him with abandon. It had been weeks, goddamn it, since they'd been intimate and now her body was on fire wanting him desperately. His fingers closed around her waist and he pulled her body so that it was flush against his. He smelled divine, and even though in her head she knew she had to tread carefully, her body was already in his bed.

"You might be more comfortable doing that lying down," Max suggested. Savannah pulled away from him reluctantly, her lips wet, her body heated. She turned to see her friends standing awkwardly behind her.

"We only came to check who it was," Briony explained, "it suddenly went so quiet..." before giving Tobias a weak "Hey."

"Ladies," he said, taking in the three of them with a cool glance, and slipping them a smile. The embarrassment was left to Savannah. So much for everything she'd said to them before.

"It might be better if we left," suggested Max suddenly.

"On the contrary, it seems I'm the one who interrupted," replied Tobias. "I was leaving anyway. We'll catch up another time," he said, looking at Savannah.

*Another time?* Her body was on fire now, she wasn't sure she'd last until tomorrow. The possibility of Sunday sex suddenly tempted her.

"Aren't you going to Texas?" Briony asked.

"Tomorrow," he replied, "but I'm back next weekend."

*Next weekend?* Every inch of her body craved for his touch, and knowing he would be out of town made it even worse.

"Enjoy the rest of your evening, ladies."

There was an awkward moment when he looked at her, as if he wasn't sure whether he should give her a goodbye kiss or not.

"We need more wine," she heard Max say as her two friends wandered away. She was doing it already, thinking of being with him and knowing she could not until she unraveled who he really was. Knowing she wouldn't see him for a few days made her head and her resolve stronger.

"It's good to know you've missed me," he said, smiling and tracing his finger gently down her bare arm, as if there was no problem in the world at all. As if she knew nothing about the man who'd threatened her ex with a bullet.

"We need to talk, Tobias."

"I know, that's why I came over. And because I miss you."

"And I miss the sex," she said, because it was uppermost in her mind, because with the pinot grigio, her filter was no longer there, and because she didn't want to admit that she missed him too.

"Well, I miss *you*, Savannah," he said, a flash of anger hardening his face instantly. It told her that she'd hit him where it had hurt. "Goodnight," he said in a flat voice and walked away.

# CHAPTER TWENTY-TWO

The humidity in Houston made wearing a tie unbearable. If it wasn't for these meetings upon meetings, he would have happily walked around in a t-shirt and shorts.

"See you at the bar later?" Matthias asked as they walked into the hotel lobby. The chill from the AC cooled him instantly.

"I was hoping to hit the gym first."

"So hit the gym first," Matthias said, punching the buttons as they climbed inside the elevator.

"Yeah," Tobias replied, taking his tie off. "I'll meet you around 8:30." It would give him time to shower, check a few emails and make some phone calls.

Savannah hadn't called him since he'd flown out and it was beginning to more than irritate him. Their unresolved issues were beginning to interfere with his thinking.

"How's Savannah doing?" Matthias asked.

"She's getting on with it." *Whatever it was she was getting on with.*

"All this messy business with Naomi can't have helped."

"Who knows?" said Tobias, wiping the sweat from his forehead. He needed a shower before he went to the gym.

"That doesn't sound too promising," Matthias remarked. "No wonder you seem edgy lately. Don't let that Naomi nonsense bother you."

It wasn't Naomi who bothered him.

Matthias continued. "I admit, we were lucky that nobody mentioned it."

"Wouldn't have mattered much if they had," Tobias countered. It wasn't as big a deal here as it was back home. Tobias knew that money talked and as far as business meetings went, he was still respected because not only was he wealthy, he was pretty damn shrewd and smart, too. And in business, it was results and return on investment that mattered the most.

"You'll get over it," Matthias said, as they stepped out of the elevator. Tobias thought he was over it too, as much as it was possible to get over the feelings of betrayal with someone he'd been intimate with. She was a call girl, but still, he knew she had cared for him. That she had chosen to expose him out of an act of revenge disappointed him.

"Nothing I can do about it."

"If it's any consolation, Candace says there have been fewer people outside the building lately."

"It was about time they got lost," Tobias muttered in annoyance.

"Parker hasn't convinced you to do an interview?"

"He's tried," he replied grinding his jaw. They walked along the carpeted hallway to their rooms. "I've never commented on my private life before and I have no wish to do so now."

"By the way, that was a brilliant idea, having dinner in The Lancaster Hotel with your family."

"It was my mother's idea," replied Tobias drily.

"You should get her to do your PR," laughed Matthias. "I haven't seen Millicent in a while, how is she?"

"As opinionated as ever."

Matthias chortled, then turning somber, he asked, "This can't be easy on you and Savannah?"

"We're taking time out. Time and space," Tobias replied, echoing Savannah's words.

"Sometimes that's what you need, to clear your head," his friend declared as he got out his keycard. They stood briefly at the doors to their rooms which were directly opposite one another. "I find nothing clears my head as well as a bottle of bourbon."

"I think you'll find that it empties it." Tobias replied. "I'll see you later," he said, and entered his room. The first thing he did was turn up the AC unit.

He showered then tended to his emails and phone calls. Only one thing remained before he went to the gym. Shaking his head, more out of irritation than anything else, Tobias called Savannah's cell phone and when that went to voicemail, he called her landline. The anger that was starting to build quickly melted away at the sound of Jacob's voice.

"Hey, buddy," he said, his mood suddenly lifted.

"Hey, Mr. Stone. I mean Tobias. Are you still Tobias?"

Tobias laughed. "Last I looked in the mirror I was. What do you mean?"

"Mom said I had to call you Mr. Stone before you made her your girlfriend, and then I started calling you Tobias. And now I'm not so sure anymore. We don't see you."

"That's because I've been very busy, Jacob." The boy obviously knew that something was wrong between him and Savannah. "I'm sorry I didn't make an effort to come and see you but things have been hectic at work. As it happens, I'm calling you from Texas."

"You are?"

"I am. So you see, I'm not even in New York right now, and I couldn't even come over to see you if I wanted to."

"*Do* you want to?"

"Sure, I want to, Jacob. I'm always ready to see you. Don't you ever think I'm not."

"Did you and my mom have a fight?"

"No-ooo," he said slowly, dragging the word out. "What makes you think we did?"

"'Cos we don't see you anymore, and Mom doesn't talk about you, and she doesn't look as happy as she used to, and ..."

"Hey, buddy," he said. "Your mommy's just worried about you, and there have been other things that have been going on nothing to do with your mommy, or me or anything about us— but sometimes stuff happens. Just like you have people at school not being nice, I get that too and just like it makes you unhappy, it makes me unhappy too, and then," he knew he was stretching the truth here, but the boy didn't need to know the details, "it also makes your mom sad. But I'm coming back this weekend, and we're going out, you tell your mom that," he said, suddenly making plans for them all. He'd suffer the consequences of taking charge and commandeering her weekend without her knowledge later.

"Really?" asked Jacob, sounding happier.

"Really."

"If you want to talk to Mom, you can't because she's taking a long bath."

"Is she now?" asked Tobias, picturing Savannah naked and wishing he was beside her. Best not to go there. She'd left him with a raging hard-on that night he'd shown up when her friends were over. If they hadn't been there, he knew how that night would have ended, and he had a feeling she'd have broken her rule of not having him stay the night while Jacob was in the other room. That was a first that had to be broken at some point.

"How's school?" he asked, dragging his thoughts out of the bathwater.

"'Sgood."

"It's good?" he asked, listening out for potential problems that might be brewing. "Are the children being nice to you?"

"Kinda."

"Kind of?" Tobias cocked his ear, listening intently.

"Can I ask you something?" Jacob lowered his voice.

"Anything."

"I wanted to ask Mom, but she'll only get mad."

"You can ask me and I promise I won't get mad."

"Is my mom a hooker?"

In that moment, Tobias forgot to breathe. "A what?" he asked, remembering his promise.

Jacob whispered. "A hooker. Is my mommy a hooker? Henry Carson said you were dating a hooker before and she cost a lot of money and now you found another one."

Tobias bit his teeth together. *Henry Fucking Carson.* He balled his hand into a fist so tight that the skin across his knuckles stretched taut. He wanted to slam it into the wall but knew that Jacob was waiting on his words of wisdom.

"No, buddy. Your mommy is not." He couldn't bring himself to say the word.

"Does it mean something bad?" Jacob asked.

"It depends."

"What does it mean?"

How in the world was he going to explain this? And more than that, how was he going to live with the knowledge that Jacob knew he had used the services of such a woman? He was stumped knowing he couldn't answer the question without coming across as a total douchebag. "A hooker is a...a...a woman who dates someone for money."

"Like a gold-digger?"

Tobias scrubbed his forehead and suppressed an anguished sigh. "You could say that, yes," he replied, with great difficulty. "But it's not exactly that either."

"Henry said a hooker was a woman who did dirty things."

"Uh—" Tobias put his hand to his forehead and held it there.

"Like get muddy?" Jacob continued.

"Uh—" Tobias sat down on the bed and contemplated the mini bar. He was tempted to break his rule of not drinking in the room. "I—" For once he was at a complete loss for words. His heart crashed when it dawned on him that the boy had been holding it in all week.

"So is Mommy one?"

"No," Tobias replied firmly. "Your mom is not."

"But Henry Carson said she was and that's why you were dating her."

"I don't think you should listen to—or believe—a single thing that comes out of Henry Carson's mouth, Jacob," he said, baring his teeth. "That boy is a nasty, little—" *Brat.* He took in a deep breath. "Boy...he's a nasty boy and he's being mean to you because he's jealous."

"Of what?"

"Of you."

"But why? And how do you know?"

"I just know," replied Tobias, just as he knew that he wasn't doing a good job of explaining. He wondered what Savannah would say. "The boy is so god—" he stopped himself, squeezed his eyes shut and tried to breathe out slowly. "That boy is so mean and hateful towards you because you have a mommy who thinks you're the most precious thing in the world, and a father who... who cares for you as well. And I already love you to bits, buddy."

Jacob didn't say anything.

"Jacob?"

"Yeah."

"You are loved so much, and I bet that kid can't stand it."

"Okay," said Jacob, sounding unconvinced.

"How about when I get back, I pick you up from school in my brother's Ferrari?" It would annoy the heck out of Savannah but he would explain it to her later. Some things could only be resolved by blatant in-your-face boasting.

"Can we?"

"Sure, we can. Does that sound good, buddy?"

"Yeah!" The joy in the boy's voice made Tobias smile again. "And maybe we can go out to the park or grab a hot dog and you can tell me all the things you're scared to tell your mom?"

"Promise you will, Mr. Stone?"

"That's a promise."

"I gotta go," Jacob whispered quickly. "Don't tell my mommy I told you."

"I won't," he promised.

"I think she's coming out now. And she usually has some green stuff on her face so I don't think she can talk to you yet."

"That's okay, buddy. You take care. One more thing, Jacob," he said, standing up and raking a hand through his damp hair. "I'm not Mr. Stone. You call me Tobias."

# CHAPTER TWENTY-THREE

They'd been in a round of meetings all morning but Tobias was distracted, and he sensed his colleague knew. "You can't be hungover," Matthias commented, as they were driven back to the hotel for a brief refresher before heading back out to the rodeo, courtesy of one of their clients.

"I'm not." Tobias wasn't in the mood for more steak and beers, let alone sitting and watching a man being thrown off a bucking horse.

Whatever this was, this fidgety, unsettling feeling that put his nerves on edge, he didn't like it. What he also didn't like was that he'd let Jacob down, that the poor boy had been keeping this information all to himself, unable or unwilling to tell Savannah. He'd been waiting for Tobias, and Tobias hadn't gone to see him.

"If you're still worried about the Naomi story," began Matthias.

"I'm not," said Tobias, with a wave of his hand. What concerned him more was the effect it had had on those around him.

As they walked into the lobby, Tobias started to head

towards the elevator. "I thought we were going to have a beer first?" Matthias called after him. Without turning his head, Tobias waved and disappeared into the elevator. He'd become increasingly desperate to talk to Savannah as the morning wore on and he had barely walked into his room when his phone rang.

It was her.

*This should be interesting*, he thought, having worked himself up into a ball of slowly simmering rage.

"You hired security for me even when I told you not to?"

He slammed the door shut and ripped off his tie. *That's why she'd called him?* "That's right. I did."

"Did you not understand me when I told you I didn't want anyone tailing me?"

"I heard you," he said, wiping his hand across his face and staring out at the pool from his window. "I chose not to listen."

"There you go again—"

*Blah, blah, blah.* He couldn't take it anymore. "I care about you and that means being worried about you—"

"But I told—"

"Listen to me," he said in a tone that was quiet and deadly, one that he often reserved for negotiations that weren't going his way. It immediately silenced her, as he knew it would. "Let me have my say. I need you to hear me out."

He took her silence for agreement. "I love you, Savannah. I don't know what that means in your world, but in mine it means caring for someone, it means worrying about them when you're not with them, it means having their back when you're not around to protect them, it means not being able to think of anything else but that person, even when that person pushes you away. I love you, it's really that simple. I gave you your space, I stayed away, I kept my distance. I did everything you asked because I understood that the love and concern you have for your son is always the number-one priority for you, and rightly so. I was happy to slink into the shadows but this latest thing, you pushing me away again and me not knowing why— this irritates the hell out of me. It can't be because of Naomi, can it?" He didn't even give her a chance to reply. "You knew about that arrangement. Or do you think I went back to her? Is that it?"

"I wish it were that simple."

"It can be that simple. What's the real problem?"

"I don't think I really know you."

"Not again," he moaned. He thought they had covered that already. "We spent a week in Miami, no interruptions, and you still think you don't know me?"

"You're like two different people sometimes."

"I can't be the same man all the time, Savannah," he sighed. "I can't be to you what I am to ...to...Yanling or the Dextronics executives. There are two sides to me. But you should know the private me by now. That's who I am to you. No bullshit, no defenses, no guard."

"I'm not sure which man I'm falling in love with."

"I'm the same man."

She breathed out loudly, and he understood her exasperation but he felt they were going around in circles getting nowhere.

"You scare me."

"When?" When had he scared her? But she didn't give him an answer. "I would never hurt you, Savannah. And I would never intentionally try to frighten you."

"And yet you manage to," she said softly.

"How?" he asked, getting angry. "And when?" He was still none the wiser as to what she meant. "I don't know how else to prove it to you, the way I feel about you," he said, feeling suddenly weary. Talking to her had made him more confused than ever. "It's as if you can't help but push any chance of happiness away."

"That's not true," she said quickly. "I agree, I might have been cautious when I first met you but you have to realize that I had my reasons. When I first met you, I wasn't sure, but I took a chance on you anyway."

"And what made you take a chance on me?" he asked softly.

"You were my lifeline, Tobias. I didn't think I deserved anyone like you. But now, now I'm not so sure."

"Why the fuck not?"

"Must you swear?"

"Must you drive me insane?" He sensed that there was something more going on, something else that fueled her fears; something she was keeping from him. "We need to talk," he said finally, "but not over the phone." Not like this. She sounded mad enough already and they were just getting more worked up.

"I guess we do," she said, and the way she said it suddenly made him wary.

"What is it?" he asked, his voice losing the sharp edge. "Is Jacob all right?"

"He's fine, I think."

"What do you mean, you think?"

"He came home with a bruise on his cheek the other day. He said he fell and hit it on the ground at playtime." Tobias had an idea where that might have come from.

"There's a lot going on for us both," she said, her voice dropping to a whisper. "Maybe we should just...just..."

"Say it," he said, his gut heating at the thought of her next words.

"Maybe we should just take some time out."

"We're already taking time out."

"No, I meant..."

"Break up, you mean?" Something cold snaked its way inside his stomach. "Are you bailing on me, Savannah?"

"I'm moving out," she revealed. The line went silent as he tried to figure out how the hell it had come to this all of a sudden.

"You're moving out? Going back to North Carolina?" he asked, thinking the worst.

"My cousin's back in a few weeks and I'm looking for an apartment." She sounded as if the fight had gone out of her.

His shoulders relaxed a little. This wasn't *that* bad. She wasn't breaking up. But he wondered how long she'd kept this news from him.

"I think it might make sense to look for a new job, somewhere in the suburbs. I might need Jacob to change schools again. I don't know. I don't know what to do or think lately." She sounded deflated, and he understood why she had pushed him away.

"Don't do anything," he said, wishing he could be there to put his arms around her. "I'll be back on the weekend, and we can talk then." He was going to fix this too, and to hell with the consequences.

"I have to go," she said. "It's lunchtime."

"Bye." He turned up the air conditioner, feeling the heat suddenly became oppressive. Staring out at the pool again, he was tempted to dive right in, to cool down, not only his body but his mind. But seeing the group of scantily clad women in bikinis lounging around the pool made him change his mind.

It would be his bad luck to be photographed with them and for the lies to be printed and circulated in the papers.

And all he wanted was a goddamn swim.

# CHAPTER TWENTY-FOUR

"What do you mean you're leaving?" Matthias fixed him with a pointed stare. "We've got dinner with the executives from Sygon tonight."

"You can handle it," replied Tobias, snapping his briefcase shut. This morning's meeting had gone well and all that was left now was entertaining and socializing to seal the deal. "It's only dinner. I'm sure you'll handle it."

"It's dinner in the hope of getting to know them better," returned Matthias, glaring at him with displeasure. "You ought to be there."

"The executives like us," said Tobias. "Dinner tonight and a day playing golf tomorrow isn't going to make an inch of difference. They'll sign."

"You *need* to be here," insisted Matthias. "You can't simply vanish."

"I can do what I like," Tobias replied smoothly.

"You can't jeopardize this deal. You *need* to attend," said Matthias, grabbing hold of his arm as Tobias made to move away.

"I can't."

"I don't understand," exclaimed Matthias, raising a hand to his head. "You would never have let anything get in the way of a deal before," said Matthias, letting go of him. "What's gotten into you all of a sudden?"

"Nothing," replied Tobias. Except that different priorities beckoned.

"You do realize that this is completely unprofessional of you?"

"I have things to do," Tobias muttered, slipping his pen back into the pocket of his blazer. He'd taken care of the business side of things, and had no desire to stay until the weekend, being wined and dined and golfed to death. "You're better at all the entertaining, Matthias," he said. "And I have matters to tend to."

"What matters?" Matthias asked testily. "Business related? Matters that will affect our bottom line, or *other* matters?"

"*Everything* affects our bottom line," answered Tobias. He was in no mood to debate his personal business with Matthias.

"At least have dinner with us all and then fly back," Matthias protested. "This won't put you in a good light, especially with the recent stories in the papers. We need to let them know that they are important to us."

Tobias grabbed a hold of his briefcase, anxious to get away. "I'm flying back *now*." He patted his friend on the back. It was nonnegotiable. "Show them a good time," he said, and walked out the door.

---

"What are you up to this weekend?" Briony asked, sitting comfortably in Savannah's office and showing no inclination to leave.

"A playdate with Jacob's best friend, Lenny, and his mom."

Savannah was clock-watching. It was approaching 4:00, and she was hoping to leave early today. She'd taken a shorter lunch break to make sure she was up to date with everything.

"Another playdate?" Briony asked. "Your son has a better social life than you do."

"That's very true."

"How about you come over to our place tomorrow evening? I'm assuming you're free since you don't go anywhere—and because Tobias is still out of town; not that it would make much difference where he was." She muttered the last part sarcastically, then gave Savannah a plastic smile.

"We'll sort things out when he gets back," said Savannah testily.

"I feel as if it's all my fault, telling you about the bodyguards. You really didn't notice them?"

She shook her head. She was usually fretting over Jacob, or rushing to get to school, or to work or to Rosalee's, and talking to Jacob, so looking around to see if someone was tailing her would never have crossed her mind. But Briony had noticed the black SUV parked around the corner from the apartment last week when they had visited. She'd casually mentioned it to Savannah.

"He's only looking out for you," said Briony, taking Tobias's side, probably because she felt guilty for telling Savannah in the first place. "You should feel lucky that someone like him cares so much about you."

"Whatever," replied Savannah. It didn't feel like that from her viewpoint.

"Pleeee-ease make up with him. I feel responsible for getting in the way of a beautiful love story."

Savannah snorted in reply. "Love stories end sadly."

"This one had better not," said Briony, lifting her eyebrow. "I want to go to a wedding in the Hamptons."

"You live in the world of celebrity drama," replied

Savannah, picking off what looked like a dried-up piece of a Cheerio from her skirt.

"You belong to that world now," said Briony, squinting at her. "Anyhoo, Max still wants updates on you both. Are you free tomorrow?"

She nodded. Her social calendar was almost always empty.

"Great," said Briony, her smile looking more genuine. "Come to our place and we'll have dinner and catch up."

Savannah looked unsure and wondered if she could leave Jacob with Rosalee that evening. Knowing Tobias had his bodyguards watching her gave her a sense of safety and she no longer felt as vulnerable, not that Colt would ever come back and pull a stunt like that again.

"Bring Jacob," Briony said, second-guessing her dilemma.

"Are you sure?"

"Yes, I'm sure. We only saw him for a little while last time, and he's kind of cute. He might even be the first child I don't mind having around."

"Thanks." She stared at Briony's face, which all of a sudden seemed fixated at a point behind her. Briony looked puzzled.

"What is it?" Savannah asked, turning around to look, just as Tobias walked in.

"Ladies," he said, acknowledging them both swiftly.

*What was he doing here?* He wasn't supposed to be back until the weekend.

"I didn't expect to see you until Monday," remarked Briony, sounding just as surprised.

"Matthias is still in Houston," he explained, looking at her. "I had things to tend to. I'm sorry to interrupt—"

"We've finished," said Briony, gathering her file and pen with record speed.

"We have?" asked Savannah, and watched as her friend made her way to the door within seconds.

"We are *so* done," said Briony sweetly. "Have a good weekend, you two," she said, over her shoulder, and winked at Savannah behind Tobias's back.

Savannah's leg started to twitch, and she smoothed her hand over her knee to keep it steady. "Another meeting commandeered by Tobias the Great," said Savannah, wondering why her heart rate was starting to speed up.

"Come upstairs," said Tobias, then, "Please. We need to clear the air." She stared back, narrowing her eyes as she got up and followed him out. The awkward silence continued in the elevator all the way to the penthouse door.

"What's going on?" he asked, as soon as they were inside. She looked across the room, at the huge windows and the golden May sunshine that streamed through them. Then she lifted her gaze to him, as he stood facing her with his hands in his pockets.

"Why are you back early?" she asked, ignoring his pointed question.

"To see you."

She almost laughed out loud. "Didn't you have some golfing event to attend?"

"I did," he said, taking a step towards her, "but *this* was more important. Shall we?" He motioned for her to move towards the sectional sofa pit.

One look at the orange and green brocade cushions brought back heated memories of their first time together. She shook her head. It was safer to stand where she was, by the door, for an easy exit, in case she needed to flee because she was all too aware that of this man's ability to melt her panties in seconds. She folded her arms. "Should I be honored that you came back for me?"

"Take it any which way you want," he said calmly. "I just need you to tell me why you're giving up on us."

"Giving up?" she asked, surprised that he hadn't danced

around the subject or made small talk, or asked about Jacob, or anything else but dove straight into it. He took another step towards her and she instinctively backed away. A few more steps like this and she'd have her back against the wall.

"Giving up," he murmured, his lips set in a hard line. "You've been distant, and trying to get away, and yet I know you can't quite keep away. Your kisses tell me one thing but your words say something else. Your head's telling you one thing, but your feelings..." The back of his index finger grazed her lips then moved gently down her chin, beneath her jaw and down her neck, sending sparks and shivers along every part he touched. She swallowed, standing paralyzed by his forward action and was unable to tell him to stop. His eyes bore into hers as his finger trailed lower, keeping her frozen while a fire lit inside her. "Your feelings," he murmured, "tell you otherwise."

The breath hitched in her throat as he traced over her breast, then her stomach and stopped just below her belly button and she tried to remember what he had been saying.

He'd done it again; started that subtle foreplay thing he was so good at. Seducing her with words and touch, except that this wasn't supposed to be about foreplay, or sex, or ...what was it that Colt had warned her about?

She flinched, snapping out of the spell and coming to her senses. "Don't try to seduce me," she said, and hoped she sounded as if she meant it. "I know all your tricks."

"My tricks?" he asked, the pupils of his eyes large and black. Heat licked the insides of her legs and she tried to block out where her thoughts were taking her.

"What tricks, Savannah?"

This time he backed away, and she tried to control her breathing. "You're doing it again," she said. "Seducing me, but it only makes me wonder if you're hiding something from me. I see your dark side and then I see the tender one. It's black and white, like night and day, like sun and moon."

He looked puzzled. "Is this about the security men I assigned to you? Because I went against your express wishes?" His eyebrow lifted and he peered at her. "Dangerous people don't send advance warnings when they want to hurt you. They don't ask your permission when they want to abduct you. They just *do*. I've lost my family once before and I won't let that happen again. I promised to protect you once, but I wasn't fast enough or sharp enough and I failed. But I will *never* make that mistake again."

His words left her breathless, and the slow-burning anger she detected in his voice left her almost too afraid to challenge him. "If it's not about the bodyguards, then what else?" he demanded, encroaching further into her private space. She moved back, hitting the back of her high-heeled stilettoes against the baseboard. He had her pinned against the wall without laying a finger on her.

She tried to summon every ounce of her courage she had in order to remain strong. After all, wasn't this the way he usually played his games? Wasn't this what he thrived on? Scaring the wits out of people so that they wouldn't challenge him?

"You almost killed Colt," she said.

A flicker of surprise flashed across his eyes before he controlled it quickly, and his expression hardened again. "I wanted to," he said slowly, "but I didn't. I didn't touch him."

She didn't like his vague answer. "When did you see him?"

"That night we got Jacob back. I thought I already told you."

"You never told me it was that night," she answered, examining his eyes and wondering if he was hiding something.

"I thought I did," he replied calmly, his brow furrowing. "I told you that I paid him off, that I gave him the money."

"He said he was scared of you, that he wanted you to shoot him." Her voice balanced on the edge of fear and anger, until anger won out. She carefully leveled her accusation at him. "For a man like Colt to tell me he was scared of you," her voice started to rise in pitch, "it makes me wonder what kind of man you really are and what else you've done that you haven't told me about."

"I haven't done anything," he said, looking completely unruffled. "And you should already know about the kind of man I am."

"That's what I'm trying to figure out."

"Did he call you?"

"*I* called *him*. He said you told him not to ever contact me again." Her chest lifted and fell quickly as her breathing sped up. "Why, Tobias? Why would you say that to him? He's the father of my child."

"Because you told me you wanted him out of your life."

"But I said that after he'd taken Jacob and put his life in danger. I was in shock."

"And now?" he asked, scowling. "What's changed that's made you think otherwise? Have you forgiven him? Have you forgotten the danger he put Jacob in?"

"You don't have the right to control my life. You don't have the right to put a gun to my ex-husband's head," she protested. She saw the way he struggled for composure, saw the way the veins along his temple throbbed and the way his jaw set hard. It was as if he was trying to stop himself from exploding.

"I didn't put a gun to his head. I didn't lay a finger on him. Did I want to? Hell, yes. I wanted to smash his face into tiny pieces. I want to pound him so hard that blood would stream down his shirt. I wanted to kill him. But it's not what I do. It's not who I am. I had two other men there who could have easily killed him. I have men who can do these things and more, Savannah. And should I ever need them—if my family or my loved ones are ever in danger—I would use them without hesitation. A man in my position needs more than the NYPD to fall back on. But I haven't had to resort to such tactics yet. I wanted your ex to smell fear the way Jacob must have when he was alone and scared. I wanted your ex," he stabbed a finger towards her, "the *father* of your son, to go through what he put your son through. I wanted him to shit in his pants. But I held back. I didn't so much as scratch him." His eyes blazed with fury. "If you're looking for a man who'd die for you, Savannah, I would—in a heartbeat, I'd do it. But I'm also the type of man who would kill for you and I'd do it without blinking, if I had to. So maybe you need to decide what type of man you want to be with, because that's the type of man I am."

Blood rushed through her veins and made her dizzy—it was fear, and trepidation, and something else. Heated thoughts rose from deep within her. Rose and curled seductively around her, making her skin tingle, and her pulse rocket, turning her mind to mush and speeding her heartbeat to an insane pace.

"What else?" he demanded, stealing her thoughts and forcing her to look at him. She swallowed again, struggled to locate her tongue and wet her mouth and speak.

"What else has been bothering you? What else is making you push me away?"

"Naomi," she said, daring to ask him. "Why now? Why did that story crawl out of the woodwork now?"

"I've been asking myself the same thing," he answered, sounding more annoyed suddenly than when she'd questioned him about Colt. "I get it," he said, letting out a gruff, false laugh. "You think we had something that night, don't you? You think there was more to it than what the newspapers showed you?"

He scratched his chin. "Let me see now," he said, the laughter suddenly giving way to a quieter voice, the one that made her wary. He rubbed his thumb over her bottom lip and she almost moaned at the touch.

"Maybe you think I fucked her behind your back that night," he said, whispering close into her ear. His hot breath against her earlobe made her shiver. Arrows of electricity skidded along her skin and ignited the fire between her legs. She could barely breathe, could barely maintain her composure as she stared at him. His thumb traced around her lips, then settled over her lower lip once more, moving along it gently, teasing her, playing with her emotions and tempting her. She was almost desperate to suck it, to taste him, to get close to him. To have any part of him that she could.

"Naomi stopped meaning anything to me the moment I saw you at the toy store," he said calmly, his words setting off a tailspin of conflicted emotions within her. "I didn't know it then, and if I had never seen you again, I would never have known it ever. But from the moment you walked into my office, I've felt something for you that I couldn't even explain to myself." He spoke softly now, making her brain short-circuit and her skin prickle with desire.

"You see, Savannah, for me, being with you isn't only about the sex. It's not all purely physical. It goes a lot deeper than that. It's who you *are*, it's the way you make me *feel*, it's the things you make me want *to do*. It's *all* of it. You make me a better person. I've made love to you, sometimes for hours, sometimes through the night, and it's not just about making love slowly either but the other kind, too—fucking you hard, losing my mind when I'm inside you because that's what you do to me, because with you I can't hold back. And if you must know, all this to-ing and fro-ing, this can't-make-my-mind-up, this not knowing where you want to take this, it's driving me insane. Matthias is mad at me because I left suddenly but the truth is, it was eating me up, the thought of you leaving me. If you want to leave me because you don't feel anything for me, then go. I won't stand in your way. But don't leave me because you believe the lies. What Colt said was true, but it's also true that I never laid a finger on him. And Naomi meant nothing from the moment I saw you. That's the truth, and that's what you need to know."

She was panting almost, her mouth hanging open as she swallowed up every word he said.

"What do you choose to believe, Savannah?"

She could barely get her words out.

"Who, Savannah? Me or Colt?"

"You," she murmured slowly.

"Are you sure about that? There'll be other headlines, other lies, other stories that will crawl out. I can tell you what's true and what isn't, but ultimately what you choose to believe is up to you."

She thought about it, thought back to the moments he'd been there for her, and for Jacob, and all the things he'd ever done for her. "I believe you," she whispered. Because everything he'd ever done for her told her she had no reason not to believe him. She'd learned a long time ago that actions always won out over words.

The corners of his mouth moved upwards a little, not enough to form a full smile, but enough to give her hope. She blinked, breathing quickly because the racing blood and adrenaline mixed together inside her and turned her body electric. Words disappeared and heated emotions encircled her.

"Where do we go from here, Savannah?" he asked, his gunmetal blue eyes darkening.

"I want you," she said softly, knowing she had to have him right now.

"You want me?"

She nodded.

"Are you sure about that?"

"Yes."

"Was there anything else?" he asked, his eyes shiny, dark and hooded with desire. "Think carefully, Savannah, before you accuse me of seducing you again." But that was the problem, she *couldn't* think. He had corroborated everything that Colt had told her. There might be more questions, more points she wanted to clear further down the line but for now, all she wanted was him inside her.

"Nothing else," she murmured, her gaze fixed upon his lips. "I want you now, I want you here."

His lips curled up some more and his eyes glistened. "Then we want the same thing, for once. Right now, all I want to do is fu—"

She kissed him then, crushed her lips down against his because in that moment she didn't need further proof of his feelings. In a flash, his hard body pressed into hers and her body sang with joy. He kissed her lips, her chin, her jaw, her neck, and she could only murmur with gratitude when his hips rolled against hers. His lips brushed over hers, his breath so close that she was breathing it in.

He kissed her deeply once more and her hands clawed along his body, her fingers desperate to feel his skin, clutching aimlessly around his collar. It wasn't enough, and she ran her hands along his chest feverishly, then slid them across his bottom, wanting more of him, all of him, and all at once.

His hungry hands clawed at her clothes while his lips nipped and sucked at the exposed flesh of her neck and shoulders. There were too many buttons, too many restrictions, and she could tell he ached for the same release. There was no time to waste taking clothes off, such was their hunger and desire to feel. They moaned and sighed, and his hands felt up all her curves and groped her breasts. He was like a hungry wolf and as desperate as she was.

At last his fumbling fingers found their way under her skirt and she almost buckled when he tore off her panties then lifted her leg, running his fingers gently over her wetness, making her moan at the memory of his touch there. She dug her hands into his shoulders when he lifted her leg higher and she curled it around his hip, arching her back as his lips sucked and teased her mouth, the way he always did. A low throaty growl escaped his lips. "I want you," he rasped.

She wasted no words and frantically peeled down his zipper, freeing him quickly and running her tongue across her lips as she closed her fingers around him, feeling, stroking. He was rock hard and engorged, and ready for her.

With his hand on her thigh, he thrust into her roughly. She wasn't fully slick but the friction was sweet release. She cried out into his mouth, and again and again each time he slammed into her, his pace frenetic as their animalistic groans pierced the air. Heat and lust pooled into one raucous, rumbling melody. She dug her nails deeper into his shoulders, holding on for support as he pounded her relentlessly, each thrust building on the one before. She closed her eyes and sighed, shuddering each time he rammed into her. Shockwaves began to ripple through her body as time slowed down and she fell into him, became part of him.

---

Sinking into her at last and burying himself in her heat, the tightness that had paralyzed his body slowly uncoiled.

She moaned and groaned and he pounded until she whimpered and melted in his arms.

Later, they had ended up in bed, not caring that it was still office hours, that they were still in the penthouse, or that it was a Friday, not caring what Briony or Candace thought. Not caring about anything but being content to lie together once more.

She wrapped her arm around him, hugging him, her lips kissing the bare skin of his chest.

He was complete.

This had been missing from his life and now that he had it all back, he could sleep peacefully. He let out a long, contented sigh, feeling ready to drift off, feeling comfortable and sated in a way he hadn't when they had been apart. He was already starting to realize that he couldn't live without her and this recent distance between them had only confirmed it.

"I'm sorry," she murmured, "for all the —"

"It's okay," he said, running his fingers through her thick tresses. "You had your reasons." She suddenly rolled on top of him, her legs outside his, her breasts dangling suggestively onto his chest.

"Stay with me tonight," she implored, lust glittering in her eyes.

"Stay over?"

She nodded, dipping her head down and leaving a gentle kiss on his chest. "I want to fall asleep in your arms again."

He wanted that too. "What about Jacob?"

"He's missed you so much," she murmured. "It would make his weekend if you surprised him by showing up tonight."

"I've missed my little buddy," he said. "But you'll have to keep your voice down. No more of those noises you make."

"You'll have to behave."

"I can't, when I'm with you," he said, eyeing her breasts and beginning to stir again. "When do you have to vacate your apartment?" he asked, needing to know his timeframe.

"As soon as I've found a place to rent. Kay told me not to rush, but I'm seeing some more properties tomorrow."

*Tomorrow?* He'd find plenty to keep her busy tomorrow, he decided. She wouldn't have to look for an apartment, or a new job, or send Jacob to a new school.

Maybe they would have brunch at the new place Xavier had told him about and then spend the rest of the day at the park. Grab a late lunch wherever Jacob wanted, followed by dinner at The Lancaster again. Dressing up and going out, making an appearance—as a family.

He would gladly give the press the middle finger. Maybe this time *he* would tip off the press and let his mother see the photos in her Sunday newspapers. He'd give Naomi's story the middle finger, too, for all it had tried to do, to tear him down, and apart. He shook those thoughts away, preferring not to dwell on the whys of her motives.

For a moment, he thought of telling Savannah about the Carson kid but decided it would be better to speak to Jacob first, to not betray his trust.

"Tomorrow," he said, knowing he had other alternatives in mind for her. He smoothed his hands along her back, and settled them against her bare buttocks, making her squirm and clench them as she ground her hips into him. "But not until the afternoon."

She giggled as if knowing what that meant. "Jacob gets up early," she said.

It didn't matter what plans she had made regarding the properties. He already had an idea but it might take some convincing, a little talking and explaining to get around that stubborn streak of hers. A whole lot of loving too, to get back to where they were before.

"I'd love to stay over tonight," he said, bringing his hand up to reach for her breast. She bent down and gave him a sloppy kiss. A kiss that told him they were going to be all right. "And then you and Jacob can come home with me on

Saturday, the way we'd planned it before." Before all hell had broken loose.

"It's a deal," she replied, melting into his lips and sinking into him.

Tomorrow.

# THE VOW, BOOK 3

**The Billionaire's Love Story (#9)**

# CHAPTER ONE

"How's Henry Carson?" Tobias asked, gearing himself up to pay the school a visit and have that obnoxious child dealt with. Jacob shrugged and looked at the menu. "Jacob?" This didn't look too good. "Has he been mean to you again?"

"No."

"Because if he was, you would tell me, wouldn't you?"

Jacob nodded. "He doesn't play with me."

"That's a good thing, isn't it?" The less contact Jacob had with that child, the better.

"He's having a birthday party and he didn't invite me." Shoot. Tobias felt his shoulders tighten.

"Did you want to go?" He made a face as if he'd smelled something disgusting. "I wouldn't want to go to Henry Carson's party."

Jacob squealed, almost laughing. "But Henry wouldn't invite you! He doesn't even know you."

"I guess that makes me a very lucky man," replied Tobias, grinning. At least the boy was smiling again.

"But Lenny's going and so is everyone else."

Tobias inhaled deeply. The kid was playing *that* game, was he?

"I wish I could have a party and not invite him," Jacob mumbled, his face downcast. Tobias tried to think of something to say to make him feel better but Jacob asked, "When are you going to pick me up in your Ferrari?"

"That's a good question." Tobias was reminded of the promise he'd made. "It's not my Ferrari, it's my brother's."

"Don't you have one?"

Tobias shook his head.

"Why not?"

"I only need one car," he explained. He could have had a fleet of the most expensive cars in the world but he didn't see the need to own more than one car, and even then he didn't drive it much. Many of his businessmen friends owned strings of cars and jets and homes. Tobias owned homes, because property appreciated over time and also because Ivy had loved to travel. She loved to escape and take him away from the chaos of his business life.

In the early days he'd worked ridiculous hours, and getting away had been the only way they'd been able to spend quality time together. So he had purchased homes in the places they visited regularly.

He'd been recently thinking about buying another home. A family home in New York. A new place where he could make new memories. He found Jacob observing him silently as he became lost in his own thoughts.

"I can pick you up whenever you want, buddy."

"Mommy said I shouldn't keep pestering you because you're always busy—"

"I'm never too busy for you."

Jacob smiled.

"Let me check my schedule and I'll get back to you, though

my schedule isn't the problem." He really *did* want to show up at the school gates, not to show off, but to see the Carson kid. "The thing is, Jacob, I don't think your mom would approve."

The boy looked disheartened and winced. "She won't like it," he said, in a miserable voice. "She already said she didn't want me to show off in front of anyone at school just because you were our friend."

"Your mommy is very wise."

This seemed to cheer Jacob up and his infectious smile made Tobias grin because he loved seeing this kid happy. It was a long way away from the curious yet timid little boy he'd seen at the toy store around Christmas time; from the child that Candace had dragged into his office when she'd found him sitting under Savannah's desk, trying to hide.

"It's a man thing," said Tobias, explaining. "Men like to act first and think later. Your mommy's right. It's not the right way of dealing with things, but I don't think that kid is being fair to you, and so I consider it a good tactic—showing off, I mean. I could have a talk with him." *Or would that be going too far?* Jacob shook his head immediately. "Maybe not," Tobias said. This parenting thing was new to him and for now, he was content to sit back and watch how Savannah dealt with things. Not that he was a parent, *yet,* but he loved the boy as if were his own. "I don't think your mom would like it if I did that either. We'll figure something out, buddy. The more we do *this,* sitting and talking about things, man to man, I'm sure we'll figure out a way of getting even with Henry Carson."

Jacob looked a little happier.

Tobias knew Savannah was worried about Jacob, and they had both been keeping an eye on him, looking out for any signs of the effects that the ordeal with Colt might have had on him. There was also the time he'd been with the woman who had tried to befriend him. Tobias's contact in the police department hadn't come up with any more information on the woman, but he did have details about the girl who had stepped in and prevented her from taking Jacob.

"Man to man?" asked Jacob solemnly, mirroring Tobias in the way he clasped his hands together on the table, looking suitably serious.

"Man to man," said Tobias. "Look, buddy, if ever there's something you can't tell your mom, you must tell me because I don't want you to worry by yourself. It doesn't matter how busy you think I am. Okay?"

"Okay."

"Are you hungry?" Tobias asked, picking up the menu. "Your mom should have been here by now."

Jacob shook his head. "I can wait," he said. "I like this."

"It's pretty cool, isn't it?" Tobias looked around at the large, light-filled café that was in the Museum Mile and next to Central Park. They sat inside because the tables outside were full, and also because inside was an enclosed space, one that was easy for his bodyguards to watch over and especially these days when he found himself being even more cautious each time he had Jacob or Savannah with him.

"I mean this," said Jacob, with his hands in his lap. "Spending the weekend with you."

Tobias smiled and leaned over the table. "Me too, buddy. I can't think of a better way to spend my weekend either." He winked at the boy. He wasn't used to spending his weekends like this, with Savannah all night, and then both of them around the next day. He wasn't running, or boxing with his trainer as much, and that wasn't a bad thing either.

He liked this. He liked it a *lot*.

To step out from that place of loneliness when his weekends had been empty—and going to the office on Saturday had been an appealing option—to spending time like *this* was quite some turnaround.

But being the kind of man he was, it wasn't enough. Tobias wanted the whole thing. All of this, all of the time and forever. And he was going to make it happen. When Savannah had insisted on seeing the rental properties today, he'd seen it as a chance to spend time with Jacob, especially since she seemed anxious to want to go alone. She'd called a short time ago telling him she would meet him here at The Bluebell.

Despite his best attempts to keep her in bed all morning—an impossibility, he later learned, with Jacob getting up at the crack of dawn—he hadn't been able to convince her to move her appointments to next weekend. After thinking things over, he had concluded that it would be in his best interests to let this play out. To pretend it didn't bother him, her looking for a place to rent when he had an apartment that was huge, and when he wanted her to move in with him.

But he couldn't throw this at her. She'd only dig her stubborn and independent heels right in to prove a point. He had to let her find out for herself. Rents were high, and she was going to be in for a nasty shock.

But he was working on getting his cards all lined up so that he was ready with an alternative. She would soon realize how high rents were and that living and working in New York with a child, on her wages, would be difficult. And maybe then she might consider moving in with him, if he figured out a way to get her to. Her cousin returning sooner than expected had caused upheaval in all their lives but as always, Tobias saw the opportunity in it.

"Do you think Mommy found a place?"

"I don't know, buddy. We'll find out soon."

Jacob didn't look too happy about it.

"Don't you want to move?" Tobias asked, curious to know the boy's take on things, though he had a fairly good idea.

"I don't want to change schools but Mommy said I might have to."

"She did, huh?"

"She said she might have to change jobs as well."

"She did?" He pretended this was news to him. "Your mommy talks to you about all the decisions she's making, doesn't she?"

"She says we have to decide together but I really don't want to change schools. Lenny is my bestest friend in the whole world and I don't think Mommy wants to change jobs either but she says sometimes you don't have a choice." Tobias's heart lurched to listen to this child who was wise and sensible beyond his years. Jacob was almost too grown-up for a six-year-old, but Tobias knew he'd had to become that child because his mother had needed him to.

"I think your mommy is trying to do the right thing even though it might not be the easiest thing, Jacob." And yet she had him, Tobias Stone and he would do anything for her but she didn't always let him help her. He was always there for her and he always would be but she seemed to be taking her sweet time getting used to the idea.

Most of the women he came into contact with wanted to be taken care of. He knew from Xavier's experiences that women wanted to be wined and dined, and here he was, ready to give Savannah the world, but she was only taking it one piece at a time.

And then only after a million questions.

Sometimes it was painful to watch her make her moves, two forward, three back. He had to let her get comfortable. That was why he hadn't yet posed the obvious solution to her current problem, the so-in-your-face-it-was-blindingly-obvious answer: that moving in with him would solve everything for her.

He was biding his time.

"But if she changes jobs then you won't see her anymore." It was a question dressed as a statement.

"There's that," Tobias answered, turning his head to look out of the window as a yellow cab pulled up outside.

"Do you like having my mom around?" Jacob asked, clutching his Iron Man figurine which went with him everywhere.

"I love having *you and* your mom around," Tobias told him truthfully, making the boy smile again.

"I know she likes having you around."

"That's good to know," replied Tobias.

"Mommy's here!" cried Jacob, seeing Savannah getting out of the cab. Tobias waited to find out how her morning with the realtor had gone.

# CHAPTER TWO

Savannah calculated that she would have roughly three hundred dollars a month left over after she had paid the rent, made her monthly payment to the company for the hospital bill, and accounted for other outgoing expenses, except for food. Three hundred dollars a month for food, travel fare, anything that Jacob needed, and anything left over would go towards savings.

She scrubbed her brow as she did the mental math—she'd wouldn't have much left over at the end.

Looking after Kay's apartment had worked out so well for her but now, having to carve out a large chunk of her salary for rent was going to hurt big time. She would be back next weekend, which was Memorial Day weekend.

With a sinking heart, she pondered her choices as the cab cruised along the streets. The apartment she had just seen was the most affordable but it was small, and had one bedroom, and was further away from where she was now. The neighborhood wasn't that great, but it meant she and Jacob could stay put— Jacob at his current school and her at Stone Enterprises, and she could still get Rosalee to help with childcare.

The realtor had told her that the apartment would be snapped up quickly and she had to make her mind up this weekend. Of course, it only had one bedroom and she would have to share with Jacob, but she didn't have a choice. And it had a pull-out sofa in the living room for when Tobias wanted to stay over. It wasn't *that* bad of a deal.

She felt almost pushed into making a decision. There might be a better place if she continued to look around but she was running out of time. She was going to have to take it.

The second apartment had two rooms and was simply *not* affordable. At six hundred dollars a month extra, she hadn't even bothered to look at it. She didn't need the second bedroom that badly.

She sighed and stared vacantly out of the window. Perhaps it was time to look further out; to move out into the suburbs, to uproot and start over. She shuddered. The idea was as palatable as a bowl of cold soup.

The cab dropped her off right outside The Bluebell, a new café that Tobias had told her about. She stepped inside and looked around the room full of tables, searching and scanning until she finally found her boys in the corner towards the back. Walking towards them, she saw Tobias listening intently to Jacob and all she could see was the back of her son's head.

"Hey, champ," she said, ruffling Jacob's soft hair as she walked past.

"Mommy!"

She sat down next to Tobias. "That was quick," he commented, his gaze questioning as she leaned in and kissed him, forgetting, for a second, that Jacob was there. When she turned to face him, her son was grinning from ear to ear. Last night had been the first time Tobias had stayed over, and she felt the timing was right. Jacob hadn't said anything.

"Did you find a place, Mommy?"

"I'm not sure," she said, placing her bag on her lap. "I only saw one place."

"What happened with the other one?" Tobias asked.

"I'm going to pass on that," she said, preferring not to give her reasons. "Haven't you ordered yet?"

"We were talking," announced Jacob proudly. "Man to man."

*What did that mean?* She looked at Tobias. "We were catching up on school life," he replied, easing her worry. "And we wanted to wait for you." She breathed easier. Having Tobias around meant that she no longer felt like a single mom because he seemed to have taken on responsibility for Jacob. It was nothing set in stone but it was the thing that mattered, like now, she'd been able to go off alone to look at apartments knowing that Jacob would be fine with Tobias. There were only three people she could have relied on for that before—her parents and Rosalee, but she had seen it and experienced it with her own eyes, that Tobias loved her son and the feeling was mutual.

"That's sweet but you shouldn't have," she said, picking up the menu. "You boys must be starving."

"I'm really hungry now," said Jacob.

"We'll order then," said Tobias. "Take a look and tell me what you would like." Savannah sat back and watched her son. He'd been spoiled since yesterday evening and had been on a high from the moment Tobias had stepped into the apartment. He'd been even more excited to learn that Tobias was staying for a sleepover.

Their first Friday night together had consisted of a movie night complete with pizza, popcorn and donuts. Afternoon sex in the penthouse had left her famished and she'd dug right in to the carb fest. She had been worried that, like last time, Jacob wouldn't fall asleep easily but after two movies back to back, he'd been snoring softly on the couch and Tobias had carried him to his room.

And then the night had belonged to her and Tobias. It was the first time since they had rushed back from Miami that she and Tobias had fallen asleep in one another's arms; though sleep had been secondary.

"What was the first apartment like?" Tobias asked her, bringing her back to the present and the clattering of cutlery on plates and people chattering.

"Good," she replied. She got the feeling that Tobias wasn't happy about her looking, and she knew he most definitely would not be too happy once he found out where this apartment was and that she was going to take it. To her relief, he didn't ask anything more.

"Henry Carson's having a party and he hasn't invited Jacob."

"Oh, honey," she said, leaning forward with concern. The idea of her son being excluded stabbed her like a knife to her chest. "Don't worry. You wouldn't have wanted to go to his party, would you?"

"That's what I said. In fact," said Tobias, looking at Jacob, "That's a brilliant idea!"

"What idea?" Savannah asked.

"We could throw a party just to exclude him."

"My birthday's in November," Jacob replied quietly.

"And why don't we have a party anyway?" Tobias insisted. "It's been years since I had a party." Tobias suddenly got a crazy look in his eyes.

"You're not being serious, are you?" she asked, for a moment unsure.

"Then I could invite everyone except Henry?" Jacob asked. Savannah stared at them both as they exchanged knowing smiles.

"Except," said Tobias, "I'd ask you *to* invite him."

"You want me to invite him?" Jacob asked, looking confused.

"We're not really having this party," Savannah whispered to him, and stared at the menu, preferring to let these two continue with their preposterous scheme. "I don't want to hear any more about your crazy idea." She dismissed his idea completely but the knowing glance exchanged between Jacob and Tobias didn't go unnoticed by her.

"I was hoping to pick Jacob up from school next week," said Tobias, winking at Jacob. She intercepted the wink. *What had the two of them been cooking up in her absence?*

"What's going on?"

"Nothing," replied Tobias. "Can I?"

She remembered. "Pick him up in Xavier's Ferrari?" She looked at him disapprovingly. "I don't think so." Then to Jacob, "Honey, I've told you before, showing off isn't the way to deal with people like Henry Carson. It's better to ignore them."

"Unless he says or does something to you," muttered Tobias, "and then," he looked at her, "I'm going directly to the principal."

"He hasn't said or done anything to you lately, has he?" she asked.

"I think excluding him from a party where the whole class has been invited is pretty mean," countered Tobias.

"There's nothing you can do about that."

"This is pretty," said Savannah, staring at the low-hanging Venetian glass lamps when the server scurried away with their orders. She looked around the pale yellow and bright white interior. "Have you been here before?"

Tobias shook his head. "Xavier recommended it."

"Xavier has good taste."

"He probably needs a morning-after breakfast hangout," Tobias replied.

"Is he still with Petra?"

"The answer to that question could change in the next hour," commented Tobias drily.

"Still up and down?"

"I'm sure there's plenty of that going on as well."

She couldn't help but hide her laugh.

"What are we going to do after brunch?" she asked.

"Can we go to the park?"

They looked at Jacob. "Sure," said Tobias. "Then later tonight I thought we'd all go out to dinner."

"For pizza?" asked Jacob.

"Max and Briony invited us over for dinner," she said, suddenly remembering.

"Tonight?" Tobias looked disappointed.

"Can't it be just the three of us again, like yesterday?" pleaded Jacob. She looked at Tobias, who seemed to be waiting for her answer. As much as she loved her friends, the idea of being with Tobias the whole weekend was infinitely more appealing.

"We can always go out to dinner another time," Tobias agreed.

"And we could always visit Max and Briony another time," she said, agreeing.

"Can we have movie night again?" asked Jacob.

"Actually," she said, eager to see his reaction. "We're having a sleepover at Tobias's place tonight." Tobias squeezed her thigh under the table, making her grin. For sure, a night in with her boys, and having Tobias to herself for the second night in a row was definitely unbeatable.

Jacob's eyes grew wide. "We are?" Then he looked at Tobias. "Really?"

Tobias assured him. "Really."

"Are we going to stay there when Kay comes back?" he asked, happily getting carried away.

"Honey, it's only for tonight." She was embarrassed that he'd asked such a thing. And in that moment, she decided. "I think I'm going to take it."

"Take what?" Tobias asked, his smile disappearing.

"The place I saw earlier." She watched Jacob's reaction. "It's not in Sunnyside but it's not too far either and it means we can both stay where we are and you can still go to school with Lenny."

"Are you sure?" Tobias asked.

"I think so."

# CHAPTER THREE

J acob was beyond excited. Savannah had never seen him like this before and she didn't want him to get too carried away once he saw it.

She had warned him too, just before they'd left The Bluebell, while Tobias had gone outside to take an important business call. She'd instructed Jacob to be on his best behavior and not get carried away when he saw Tobias's apartment.

However, as was to be expected, Jacob was completely blown away. "This....is....AWESOME!" he shrieked, his eyes round like porcelain saucers. But the way his eyes bugged out and the way his mouth hung open as he gawked at the floor-to-ceiling windows, she knew she'd failed. She could hardly blame him. She recalled her own feelings the first time she'd come here. The place had taken her breath away but she'd managed to hide her exuberance.

Now she watched her son looking around eagerly, his eyes fixating on the floor-to-ceiling windows, and the large expanse of space, and then the glass staircase. "There's upstairs too?" Jacob asked, as if he was standing in the biggest place on Earth. He was itching to look around, even though he straightened up stiff as a rod when she gave him a stern look hoping it would remind him to calm down.

Even so, she knew what he was thinking when he looked at her. 'We're staying *here* tonight?'

"Make yourself at home, Jacob, and look around all you want. Nothing is off limits here. Come here, buddy," he took Jacob's hand and led him to the room next to the study. Savannah smiled. *Her son would love this.* Tobias opened the door. "You can play all you want in here."

For a moment, Jacob hesitated, hovering around the entrance, staring at the different stations. "You like it, honey?" she asked, standing behind him at looking at the room that was a child's dream. Tobias told her he didn't use it much, but she could see that it would hold her son captive with its foosball and pinball machines, the gaming stations with the latest models, and the arcade games.

"Go on," Tobias said, giving Jacob a gentle push. "This is all yours to play with, buddy. Now go and have some fun." But he didn't, not at first. He turned around and gave Tobias the biggest hug instead. And then he walked over to the Xbox.

"You've made his day," whispered Savannah, as he took her hand and they left. He led her towards the glass staircase and she was about to pick up the two small overnight bags that she and Jacob had brought along, but Tobias had turned suddenly quiet, and so she followed him.

Tobias stood outside the room next to the master bedroom. The room they didn't go into much. "I wasn't sure if he might want to sleep in here," he said, pushing open the door to what would have been Zachary's room. It was still how she remembered it from last time, empty except for the vinyl stickers on one wall.

"It doesn't have any furniture in it and so I—I mean," Tobias stammered.

"It's all right," she said, squeezing his hand. "You don't have to explain. Jacob can have the guest room. It's really not a big deal." This room held special memories, sad memories and a reminder of all he had lost. She didn't want Tobias to feel he had to do something to make Jacob happy. She leaned towards him and whispered, "I know what this room means to you."

He let go of her hand and walked towards the wall which had stickers of cars and planes. "I was going to get everything he needed, a bed and a dresser—"

"You don't have to," she whispered. "It's only one night."

"Actually," he said, clearing his throat, "I was hoping we'd have more sleepovers." He turned to her. "We don't have to dance around anymore, Savannah, and now that Jacob knows..."

"You're right," she said, putting her arms around his waist, wanting to soothe his hurt away. "No more dancing around."

"No more of these one-night-a-week dates at my place while you worry about Jacob being up late with Rosalee."

"No more of those either."

"I want you around all the time, Savannah, and Jacob too. He's not an accessory, he's part of what we have." She could have kissed, him, would have, except for the sound of Jacob's high-pitched squeal interrupting them.

"AWE-SOME!" he shrieked with excitement. "Can I sleep here tonight?"

"Uh—no, you don't," Savannah said, pulling out of Tobias's embrace.

"Would you like to?" Tobias asked. But Jacob looked at her sheepishly and she knew it was because he'd heard the cautionary note in her voice.

"No, it's okay," he said, putting his hands behind his back and shifting from foot to foot. "I can sleep somewhere else."

Tobias walked towards him. "You like this room, don't you?" Jacob remained silent. "What do you think of these?"

"They're neat," he admitted in a hesitant voice, and looked up at them. "I like the red sports car."

"That's my favorite, too," replied Tobias. "I'll get this room organized so that you can sleep here tonight, buddy."

"Really?" She could see that her son had difficulty in suppressing his excitement.

"Really," replied Tobias and before she could utter another word, Tobias headed towards the door, reaching for her hand as he moved past her. He put his finger to her lips and walked her out of the room, leaving Jacob to stare at the stickers.

"You don't have to do this," she said again.

"But I want to, so make me happy and let me get it ready for Jacob. Please," he begged. "This isn't about control, or me wanting to have things my way. This is a sleepover. It's only a sleepover, it doesn't mean I have designs for anything else."

"I understand," she said softly.

"It's been empty for so long, it needs to be used. It's only been me here all these years and I'm excited that you're both staying over. So please, allow me to be happy."

She couldn't argue with that.

CHAPTER FOUR

—————

"I'm back!"

Memorial Day weekend had arrived with a bang. Kay had landed.

"She's back." Savannah stopped packing her overnight bag at the sound of her cousin's voice and rushed towards the hallway with Jacob in tow.

"Jacob!" Kay cried out and came at him with her arms outstretched. "You've grown *so* tall." Jacob grinned at her proudly.

"Mommy's been feeding me bananas."

"It's working," said Kay, looking him up and down. Savannah walked over and hugged her tightly.

"Look at you!" shrieked Kay, examining Savannah like a hawk. She dropped the large suitcase she was pulling as well as her oversized handbag. A couple of celebrity magazines fell out as it tipped on its side.

"Look at you," replied Savannah, staring at her glamorous cousin.

"Say nothing about this dirty blonde concoction," said Kay, grabbing a handful of her above shoulder-length hair. "I need to see Craig as soon as I've unpacked. Get me some blonde back. But look at you!"

"What?" asked Savannah.

"You look *so* different."

"Not *that* different."

"Yes, *that* different," Kay insisted. "You're looking freakin' good, Sav! Better than you did when I left. Oh my god, I *love* your hair," she squealed, touching Savannah's bangs. "Are those highlights?"

"Yes," replied Savannah, self-conscious. "I wanted a change."

"You know what they say," smirked Kay, "new man, new hairdo. So, where the hell is that gorgeous stud of yours?"

"Over there," said Jacob, pointing behind her to where Tobias now stood. Kay looked mortified as she glanced over her shoulder. Tobias had just walked out into the hallway, wearing a white t-shirt and jeans. His hair was damp, and he looked freshly showered and super sexy. Savannah already knew the effect he would have on her cousin.

"I'm Tobias," he said, holding out his hand.

"You have wet hair," Kay murmured dreamily.

"Tobias has a sleepover on Friday nights," Jacob told her.

"A sleepover," Kay's voice was one octave short of seductive. She gaped at Tobias unblinking, not all there.

"It's good to meet you," said Tobias, extricating his hand from her grip.

"I'm Kay," she said, looking slightly shell-shocked.

"I know," he replied, "I've heard a lot about you."

"You have?" she asked, a little too eagerly.

"Is this all your luggage?" Tobias asked, pointing to her bags.

"I've got two suitcases downstairs."

"I'll get them for you," he offered.

"Oh, you don't have—" She watched him slip his shoes on, seemingly mesmerized.

"Can I come with you?" Jacob asked.

"Sure, buddy," said Tobias and turning to Kay with his eyes sparkling, he added, "It's not a problem," and disappeared.

"Thank you," Kay murmured to the door when Tobias and Jacob had left. "I could eat him up now and still never be satisfied."

Savannah laughed. "Come on," she said, "Let me get you something to drink. Or are you hungry?"

"I'm hungry for something and it isn't food," Kay replied, shrugging out of her long cardigan. She tossed it onto the couch then followed Savannah into the kitchen. "I can't believe that Tobias Stone is downstairs in the lobby bringing up *my* luggage. This has got to be a dream." She sank into one of the chairs. "No," she moaned, propping her face up with her hands. "A dream would be if he was still single."

"Sorry to disappoint you but he's very much taken."

"He's so goddamn freakin' hot." Kay fanned her face. "He stayed over last night?"

Savannah nodded, trying to hold back her smile.

"I'm getting giddy just thinking of waking up next to someone like him," Kay said dreamily.

"He's taken," Savannah reminded her.

"I said someone *like* him, not him. How the hell did you manage it, Sav?"

Savannah rolled her shoulders. "It kind of fell into place."

"Why does that kind of thing never happen to me?"

"Weren't you seeing someone out there?" Savannah couldn't keep track, but Kay always seemed to have someone on the go.

"Nothing worth talking about," replied Kay, looking around

the kitchen. "This place is spotless. Is Rosalee still helping you out?"

"She helps with childcare but I do all the cleaning."

"It's nice and clean and lived in," said Kay. "Thanks, Sav. I didn't want to come back to a place that was musty and dusty, and you took good care of it."

"Thanks for letting me stay," replied Savannah. "It's been great." But being in this apartment had also spoiled her. Now, all the places she looked at seemed undesirable in comparison. "I thought I'd found a place last week," said Savannah. Kay raised an eyebrow. "But it wasn't ideal." Just as she'd thought, when she told Tobias about it, he managed to convince her it was a lousy deal and that she should hold out for something better.

Kay twirled a lock of her hair in her fingers. "You don't have to move out, Sav. I'm happy for you to stay here for as long as you want."

"I know, you keep offering and it's very kind of you but I need to get a place of my own."

"Don't rush. You can still stay here rent-free for as long as you want. Rent-free," she said, examining the ends of her hair. "Think about it."

"You're only saying that because of Tobias."

"I'm not!" Kay protested loudly. Then, probing, "He really sleeps over on Friday nights?"

Before Savannah could reply, the buzzer sounded at that very moment and she walked over to answer the door. Tobias hauled in two suitcases. She heard Kay behind her. "You brought them up in one trip?" she asked as she ogled his biceps shamelessly. It was as if she hadn't seen the male species for years.

"I had my helper," replied Tobias, giving Jacob a wink as he wheeled in her suitcase.

"That's a lot of luggage," said Savannah.

"I was there for almost a year," Kay reminded her.

"Can we go now?" asked Jacob. Her son seemed anxious to get going.

"You're deserting me?" asked Kay, her smile fading fast.

"We're having a sleepover at Tobias's," chirped Jacob.

"You are?" Kay looked even more dismayed. "But it's Memorial Day weekend, I was hoping we'd get to spend some time together."

"You're welcome to join us," said Savannah, seeing her cousin's face dip with disappointment. She felt as if she had no other option but to ask her. "We're seeing my friends Max and Briony tonight," Savannah said, "but how about tomorrow or Monday?"

"I've planned something," said Tobias.

"It's a surprise," said Jacob. "But I don't know what it is. Tobias won't tell me." He'd mentioned he had plans for something but she had no clue as to what he had in mind.

"Thinking about it, I'm going to be severely jetlagged." Kay picked up her handbag. "I think I'll stay home and try to get settled back in. You guys have a good time."

"Call me if you change your mind," said Savannah, kissing her goodbye. "I've changed the sheets and emptied the dressers in your room so you can put all your clothes away."

"You didn't need to do that, Sav," Kay replied, giving Jacob a hug. "I can live out of suitcases for a while. Don't go rushing to find a new apartment, either. I'm looking forward to us living together for a while."

"Unfortunately, she's on a mission to move out," Tobias said, grinning.

"Don't do it," Kay begged. "Think of all the fun we'll have."

# CHAPTER FIVE

H e could get used to this—having Savannah in his home, not only for one night but for the whole weekend and longer. With it being the Memorial Day weekend, he'd managed to convince her to stay until Tuesday, the day they returned to work.

He suspected that Kay's return might have made Savannah hurry to find a place but his worry was that she would take the first available apartment. As it was he'd convinced her not to take the one-bedroom apartment she'd seen last week. It had been easy enough to convince her against it because the place didn't have a lot going for it. He hoped she found a few more duds until he got his act together.

In the meantime, having them both staying at his place gave him an idea of how things might be. Of what a family life could be like and it soon became something he needed to attain. Yet this wasn't a business deal that he could ruthlessly muscle in on. He was dealing with Savannah, and emotions, and feelings and a future, and he had to slowly convince her and win her over.

The more he assessed the situation, the more he came to the

conclusion, as far as he was concerned, Kay's return was not a huge wrench. In fact, it was the catalyst he needed.

A few days ago, they'd gone to Max and Briony's. Savannah had somehow persuaded him to come along even though he'd initially insisted on staying behind. He sensed it was more of a girls' night in and he didn't want to get in the way until Jacob pleaded with him to come. Briony had become one of Savannah's closest friends and it was about time he got to know her outside of the office, and not just as an employee.

As things turned out, he had a great time. The next day, he surprised them by taking them on a helicopter ride over the city. Savannah had almost had a heart attack when he'd told her he'd be flying it. She only got in because she didn't want Jacob to go without her, and she couldn't stop him from going. He was more excited than she'd ever seen him.

Tobias stood in front of the mirror thinking of how future weekends might be and wishing he didn't have to return to work today. He could have done with a few more days off to spend together. It got him thinking about Miami and planning a longer vacation there soon. And the idea of throwing a party still stayed with him. He wondered if he could have a final small party here, for their closest friends and family, before things changed.

His head was filled with all these ideas and more, as he ran the blade smoothly over his face, sweeping away the white foam, and feeling the stubble melt away. Behind him, Savannah was in the shower. He could get used to this; this easy intimacy they shared, him shaving, her taking a shower. He watched her through the mirror and stared at her under the showerhead with the water streaming over her body and washing away the sweat and signs of another hot and sleepless night. Misty condensation slowly built up and hid her naked body but even so, he felt a stirring lower down. The thought of work slipped away as he raced to finish shaving so that he could get under the shower with her. But his hopes deflated like a blown-up balloon let loose when she stepped out a few moments later with a huge, fluffy white towel hugging her.

"Hey," she said, drying her hair with a towel, her bare shoulders slightly damp and dewy, leading his thoughts astray.

"Hey," he said, turning around and patting his face dry. "I was hoping to join you in there and see if we could make more steam."

Surprise danced in her eyes. "You're insatiable."

"You're irresistible."

"We have work today."

"We can make time," he said, opening the towel around his hips and showing her evidence of his excitement.

She stole a glance at his hardness in disbelief. "Again?"

"You have that effect on me," he said, covering himself up again and securing the towel in place. He walked towards her and placed a firm hand on her butt, claiming it because he had every intention of finding a release.

"Jacob will be up soon," she said, wriggling and trying to dry her hair while he felt her up.

"When I last checked on him, I could have sworn he was snoring."

"You checked on him?"

"Yes." He'd checked on him, finding strange comfort that the nursery had come back to life again. The new furniture and Jacob sleeping in there helped turn old memories into new ones. "The excitement of the helicopter ride must have been too much for him. He'll have a few things to tell Henry Carson."

"That was very thoughtful of you. Thank you." She stopped drying herself and laid her palm flat against his chest, pushing away the idea of getting ready for work. He stiffened to her touch.

"Is that why we went?" she asked, moving away a little and

opening her towel. She teased him with a peek of her naked body as she dried her arms and shoulders.

"No." *Not entirely.*

"You don't need to impress Jacob just for Henry Carson's sake."

"I'm not." He didn't really want to have parenting conversation right now, not when he was getting harder with every passing second.

"I know that boy has been a—"

"A little shit to Jacob." He'd told her about the 'hooker' conversation.

"But showing off is not the way to handle things, Tobias."

"I know, but Jacob came to me with his troubles," he reminded her.

"Yes, he did," she acknowledged. "And I'm grateful that you listen to him, just as I'm grateful that he's comfortable confiding in you. He looks up to you, Tobias."

"I don't intend to let him down. I know you worry about him, Savannah, but he's going to be fine."

"I still wish we'd found that woman," she said. Her obsession with both women, the one who'd tried to take Jacob, and the one who had saved him, was beginning to worry him.

"She's gone, Savannah. They haven't been able to trace her and I don't think they will be able to. I think you need to let it go."

"But what about the girl? You said you were going to try to get her contact details."

"I meant to tell you, I have her details. Do you still want to meet her?"

"Of course!" She rubbed the towel along her stomach, making him even more hot and horny.

"I'll try to arrange something," he said.

"Thank you, it would mean a lot to me." She secured her towel firmly in place then dropped a kiss on his chest.

"I thought you said we had to go to work?"

She pressed her hand along his jawline. "You're all nice and smooth," she murmured. He pulled her towards him and put his arms around her.

"Oh, my goodness," she squealed, "You *are* happy to see me this morning, aren't you?" She pressed her hips into him.

"If you hadn't insisted on changing my surprise treat, we'd have been in Miami now," he said, dropping the towel and moving her damp hair back from her face. *Miami.* A four- or five-day break in Miami would have been a welcome break from the crap they had both been through lately.

"It would have been a rushed trip," she replied defensively, as she secured her arms around his neck.

"It would have been a well-deserved trip," he said, bending down and brushing his lips along her collarbone. She was the scent of lemon and honeysuckle. "We could have taken a few days off and we'd still be there now."

"Aaah," she purred. "I'll never forget our time there."

"You're thinking about it now, aren't you?" he breathed, slowly tracing his finger along her shoulder to her elbow and kissing her neck. "You're wondering if we have enough time," he said, as a faint sigh escaped her lips.

"Only because you're making me think of it," she answered, speaking in a tone that reminded him of the pool and the bedroom and all the places they'd made love in on that trip. He felt they'd been robbed of their time there, and he was eager to return. Where he had once thrived on the cutthroat business world and living life at a frenetic pace, he now longed to escape and disappear to a place that was cut off from the rest of the world.

"We could go for a few weeks when Jacob finishes school for summer."

"Would you get time off?"

"I can do what I want," he said, pulling away slowly.

"I know," she said. "But you've been so busy lately."

"I've had things to take care off." A few deals to sign off on and a few more to break off. "I need to get away, Savannah." He needed those days by the pool, and the hot, sweaty summer nights lying beside her.

"Then we should do it. Jacob would love it there." Her voice trailed off as he kissed her below her ear, moving his finger slowly back up to her shoulder, then down again, then up. He was hungry for her, addicted to the smell of her, desperate for the feel of her and he had no intention of getting ready for work just yet.

"And he'll get to fly on the plane," Tobias said, his voice seductive, and low as he nuzzled her neck. "He's been wanting to do that ever since—"

"Ever since he found out you had a private plane." She moaned softly. "We need to get ready for work, Tobias."

"In time," he said, taking her earlobe between his teeth and nipping gently. Her hands settled around his neck. She was yielding.

"Jacob doesn't need to be dazzled by such things."

Tobias pulled back reluctantly once more. "I don't do it to dazzle him, Savannah. I'm not showing off to him."

"I know," she said quickly. "But flying to Miami for a few days, and in your private plane? I don't want these things to go to Jacob's head."

"He's not that kind of boy."

"He's still a child, Tobias. These things aren't normal for most of us."

"But he'll have to get used to them." He threw that out

there, seeing if she would take the bait, waiting for her response, but instead she held the towel even more firmly in place.

"I love that you want to make him happy, but Jacob is already happy just being around you. He doesn't need all the frills." She leaned up and kissed him. "Thank you for a lovely weekend but if I don't move now, I'm going to be late to drop him to breakfast club."

"Morris will take us."

"I can't keep on using Mor—"

"Yes, you can," he insisted, keeping his hands firmly around her waist. "It's a no-brainer, Savannah." He stared at her and wondered why she insisted on making her life so difficult when he could so easily take all her troubles away. "I've already told you that you have Morris at your disposal."

She didn't say anything.

He wanted to suggest getting a housekeeper to help out as well. Someone who would cook meals and help with laundry. His current housekeeper already did that for him but Savannah was still adamant not to leave her dirty clothes at his place. They only stayed over for a few nights a week, if that, and this was only a new and recent development in their relationship. For now, he decided to let her do as she wanted. It was another issue he didn't want to rock the boat on.

"I don't want to take what you have for granted."

"What I have is yours." He wanted to hear what she'd make of that.

"It's really generous of you but—"

"You can go on doing things the way you usually do, rushing around, getting stressed, trying to get ready and have Jacob be ready and jump on the subway to get to school and then jump back on it to get to work, but why would you do all this when there is a simpler solution? Morris will drive you there, and then drive you to work. Simple. Besides," he brushed his lips along her neck again and inhaled her newly showered scent. "Jacob's still asleep, and I'm not done with you yet."

"You're not?" she asked, looking up at him seductively.

"No," he growled softly. "I'm not in the mood for work."

"No?" she asked, a smile dancing on her lips. He noted that her fingers trembled over the towel she tried to keep in place. He pulled her hand away and then opened the towel, almost salivating at the sight of her naked as the wet towel dropped to the floor. His body was already tight, his muscles tensing and twitching, and aching for release. Memories of her moaning last night seared into his brain and heat licked his body.

There was something primal about being so close to her, of having the smell and taste of her so intimately, that it drove him wild. The more she mewled and bucked, the more he wanted to explore and taste, to draw out more of those noises from her, to make her shudder harder. Her coming apart like that always tipped him over the edge and now that he was rock hard once more, his desire made him want to unravel her all over again. To not have his fill of her now would only frustrate him and he'd be thinking about it for the rest of the day. He couldn't wait that long.

"Need me to do something about that?" she asked, opening his towel and stroking him gently, turning the tables and taking charge.

"No," he murmured, caressing her breast, tweaking it to a peak. "I need to taste you first." What he wanted was to slam into her and explode, but more than that he wanted to prolong the pain and ecstasy of his excitement even more. He walked her back a few steps and seated her on the edge of the bathtub before sinking to his knees, his intentions sinful. Her body was hot to touch as he slowly pried her legs apart.

"Tobias…" she murmured, trying to bring her legs back together.

"Let me," he begged, slowly pulling her knees apart again, wider this time, leaving her fully exposed and open. His brain short-circuited at the sight of her and a strangled moan fell from his lips.

"We don't have time—"

"We have all the time," he breathed, his voice throaty and low, his hands sliding along her inner thighs. Blood pounded in his ears and a stirring, sharp and lustful and burning through him, tensed to a peak at the sight of her arousal, glistening and ready. His hands moved closer between her legs and she purred his name slowly as his fingers probed and thrummed, and his thumbs slid over her wetness relentlessly.

She moaned, arching her back, convulsing and shuddering, before he'd barely begun.


L ater that morning, Tobias strode into his office, smiling. Even the sight of Matthias hovering around Candace's office wasn't enough to wipe the smile from his face.

"Are you on part-time hours these days?" Matthias barked, glancing at his watch in exaggeration.

"You're lucky I came in at all," replied Tobias, walking past him unperturbed.

"The Sygon deal hasn't been completed. They seem to be taking their time to sign," Matthias said, following him into the office.

"I saw the email exchange."

"You don't seem particularly bothered by it."

"I'm concerned," replied Tobias, opening his briefcase and taking out his belongings.

"You'll need more than an email to fix this. It might have helped if you'd stayed for a game of golf."

Tobias snorted. "Are they sulking? Is that what you're

telling me? If that's all it would have taken to get them to sign, I'm not so sure I want their business."

"You dismiss things too easily," Matthias warned.

"I'm not being dismissive," Tobias countered, "I'm merely pointing out my concerns."

Matthias moved closer towards the desk. "Don't mind me for saying this—"

"Then don't say it."

"We needed this deal."

"Not as much as they did," Tobias answered. Nonetheless he would call their CEO later and get a better handle on their concerns. If it was something as fickle as them not feeling appreciated, then to hell with them. There were plenty of other more eager firms willing to sign up instead.

"You have to tread carefully, Tobias. We can't afford to let too many deals fall apart, otherwise our goal of getting to the top isn't going to happen."

"It'll happen. There are plenty of other companies ready to sign with us. Relax."

"You're starting to relax too much," Matthias countered.

He didn't bother to reply and instead looked at the morning's paperwork that Candace had placed on his desk.

"This isn't the time to be taking things easy," Matthias said. "We're barely recovering from the effects of the Naomi story."

"What effects?" Tobias asked. "If Sygon chose not to sign because of that publicity, then it's on them."

"No, Tobias, it's on you."

He laughed. "Because I didn't play a few rounds of golf or have a few beers?" Matthias looked him in the eye, looking none too pleased.

"It's the smallest of things that makes the difference. You taught me that. It's a shame that all of a sudden you've started to ignore the advice that helped you to get to where you are today."

"You need to calm down, Matthias. If we lose this deal, we lose it."

"You're losing your killer instinct. You can't even fucking see it," muttered Matthias, wiping his hand over his face.

Tobias huffed out a breath, disliking the tone of his friend's voice. "Careful, Matthias," he warned. "I understand your concerns and I will address them later. Memorial Day weekend has delayed things but that's to be expected. I'm sure I'm not the only one who took things easy this weekend."

"How was yours?" Matthias asked, his voice softening just as quickly.

"It was good."

"Good?"

"I took them for a helicopter ride."

"You're still trying to impress her?"

"I've never needed to impress her."

"She's down to earth, I can see that. I can see why you feel safe around her. She's nothing like a trophy wife." Tobias didn't know what to make of his words. Matthias moved towards the door. "If she has a sister, you be sure to let me know because I'm about done with money-grubbing nymphos."

"The solution is simple," Tobias told him, eyeing him carefully. "Don't go looking for them."

# CHAPTER SIX

She could get used to mornings like this, if she allowed herself to. If she threw away those crazy notions about finding an apartment that wasn't perfect but which would 'do.'

While it was good of Kay to tell her that she could stay as long as she wanted, Savannah knew it would be crowded with the three of them and she needed her own space. Tobias didn't sleep over on Fridays anymore and she had quickly grown accustomed to staying at his place more.

This Memorial Day weekend, staying longer than one night had given her a taste of normal life with him. Heat crept along her cheeks as she rekindled the memories from this morning.

It hadn't mattered that they were supposed to be getting ready to go to work, or that she was supposed to be waking Jacob up. She hadn't quite made it to getting her underwear on because he'd had other ideas, and timekeeping had flown out of the window.

It hadn't mattered at all when he'd made her sit back on the edge of the bathtub; when he got on his knees and planted his face there, between her legs.

It hadn't mattered when he'd made her come so quickly, she

hadn't been ready for it. She'd never had a man take such pleasure in indulging her like that before. "Relax," he'd told her, then, "Let go."

And she had.

It had been a precarious situation, balancing on the edge knowing that Jacob was asleep, but that he might wake up at any moment. Knowing that in the quiet time, the stolen pleasures of the morning were theirs. Tobias took her to heaven and kept her there while she bucked and her body became limp, melting at the feel of his tongue on her. He had left her a quivering, shaking mess of nerves and flesh, unable to speak until the blood rushing through her body slowed down. And then, as soon as she'd regained her breath, he turned her around, pushed her down on all fours and rammed straight into her, not even giving her time to come down from her high. She cursed out loud, unable to hold back as he filled her completely, pleasuring her so exquisitely and so deeply that her inner world shattered. Explosions rocked through her as he rode her relentlessly and her body jerked uncontrollably as waves of pleasure rippled through her.

She could get used to mornings like this. Mornings, and nights and evenings, and all days like this.

"Why are you grinning?" Briony asked. Savannah looked up in surprise. She hadn't even heard her come into the room. "You can't be that happy to be back at work." Her friend sank into an empty chair.

"What's wrong?" For Savannah could see that something was.

"Max wants a puppy."

"That's so sweet," Savannah cooed. "Jacob would *love* a puppy." But she toned down her exuberance when she quickly realized that Briony didn't look so keen on the idea. "I take it that you don't want a puppy?"

"I don't want to look after *any* pet," said Briony, crossing her legs and turning her body to the side. "Then we'd have to get someone to look after it when we go on vacation."

"You can get dog sitters."

"I like to be able to get up and go. If I want to go skiing, I want to be able to book a flight, book a hotel, and leave. I thought that was what Max wanted."

"Is this about wanting a puppy, or is there something else?"

"I'm not sure. I'm hoping it's only a phase and that it'll soon blow over, but what worries me is that Max doesn't have phases. She knows her own mind, in which case I don't know why she didn't say anything before. Anyway, I don't want to talk about it. It'll only depress me. How was your weekend?" she asked, not giving Savannah a chance to probe further.

"It was good," replied Savannah. "Thanks for having us over. We really enjoyed it."

"Tobias is very relaxed outside of work, isn't he?" said Briony. "Or is that the effect you have on him?"

Savannah smiled but said nothing.

"I forgot he was Tobias Stone that evening," continued Briony. "He seemed like a normal guy."

"Everyone says that," replied Savannah, shaking her head. "He *is* a normal guy."

"He isn't, hon," Briony argued. "I don't mean that in a bad way either, but Tobias Stone is one of the wealthiest men in the world. He can never be normal."

"You can say what you want," Savannah replied, disliking Briony's response. "He's a normal guy, and he hurts and laughs and feels like the rest of us."

Briony shrugged as if she couldn't be bothered to dispute this any longer. "How's the apartment hunting working out?"

"It's not really."

"There's a surprise."

"What do you mean?"

"You're practically living with a billionaire, I don't get why you need to find a place to stay. Why don't you just move in with him?"

"I can't. Even if he asked me, I wouldn't consider it. We're not ready." Except that they were, at least, she felt that *she* was but she was being very cautious, questioning every move, wondering if she was doing the right thing. These sleepovers had quickly become a regular thing, and Jacob looked forward to each weekend. If there ever came a time that her relationship was over, it wouldn't only be her heart she'd have to put back together, she'd have to take care of Jacob's too. Right now, things with Tobias were more than she could ever have dreamed of, and being with him was as natural as breathing, but she knew all too well that sometimes the dream died; as it had with her and Colt. She'd been bitten once before, but this time, if it happened again, it would be much harder to get over because this time it really was love. She questioned whether being with Colt had ever been.

"What do you mean you're not ready?"

"We're not," insisted Savannah, squirming in her seat. "And I wouldn't accept it on principle." It seemed she still had the capacity to say one thing while feeling an entirely different thing altogether.

"On principle?"

"We haven't been together that long."

"You've been together since Christmas. You don't consider that long enough? What are you waiting for, hon? A certificate? A 'two years in a relationship' badge of approval before you think he's the perfect one?" Briony used air quotes for emphasis.

Savannah exhaled loudly. "I think it would be better if we each had our own place. We're taking things slowly," Savannah replied defensively.

"Are you sure about that?" asked Briony, her eyebrows lifting. "Because you both looked very much together as a couple on the weekend. I see the way he looks at you, Sav. Don't you see any of that?"

Savannah frowned. "He's intense, for sure," she said, dismissing Briony's analysis. "I thought I'd found a suitable place last week but Tobias managed to talk me out of it."

"He did, did he?" Savannah wasn't sure if she detected a hint of sarcasm in her friend's voice.

"It was a one-bedroom apartment and further away from work."

"And you needed convincing not to take it?" Briony's brows almost met when she scrunched up her face. "Why would you have even considered it?"

"I don't want to hang around and inconvenience Kay. I'm sure she's being polite and even if she says I can stay as long as I want, she doesn't mean it. I know I wouldn't want anyone to stay on if the roles were reversed. You want your own space in the end, don't you?"

"I bet Jacob loves his sleepovers."

"Jacob would move in with Tobias in a heartbeat."

"At least your son is sensible," said Briony. "Why don't you get him to take on a puppy and I can get Max to visit?"

"Don't go putting that idea in his head," Savannah implored. She was sure Tobias would let him have one. Tobias would let her and Jacob do anything they wanted. Their life now was so different. She was still on a tight budget when it came to looking at rent, but her life now was nothing like the misery she had escaped.

"How's it working out with your cousin?"

"We haven't actually stayed at the apartment since she landed on the weekend."

Briony leaned forward, her brows lifting. "You're still at

Tobias's?" She sat back and grinned. "So *that's* why you were smiling when I walked in. You've spent three nights with Tobias Stone. Hell, Sav, I'd say you've almost moved in!"

Savannah tried not to let her smile slip. "We're going home tonight."

"I'm sure you are."

"He flew the helicopter and took us all over New York," said Savannah. "You should have seen Jacob's face." She recalled the look of pure delight on Jacob's face when Tobias took them up to the helipad on the rooftop of his apartment.

"Oh, my, how the other half live," Briony replied, half-sneering.

"That's what I'm afraid of."

"A great life?"

"Getting used to it."

Briony dismissed her comment with a quick wave of her hand. "Enjoy it while you have it," she said, "but I do believe he's fallen under your spell. Tobias looks like a changed man. He *smiles* a lot more. Haven't you noticed?"

Savannah bit her lip. She had noticed.

"I suppose we have you to thank for that," said Briony.

"We...we're good together," said Savannah, thinking of the man she was in love with. "He's...he..." She struggled to express what it was that she felt in her heart, what it was that he had done for her. That she'd been broken when she'd met him, that up until the moment they got together, she'd spent more time trying to hold herself together for Jacob's sake. That being with Tobias had healed her, had let the hurt bleed out and made a new space—one she had filled with love and happier moments. "He's..."

"The One. I know," said Briony, air-quoting again. "It's so plainly obvious for everyone to see."

Savannah winced. "I love him. I love this man with all of my heart and I'm enjoying it while I can."

"He's not going to let you walk away, hon."

"I don't plan on walking away."

"Good, because I still want to go to a wedding in the Hamptons."

---

# CHAPTER SEVEN

The next few weeks flew by quickly as Savannah adjusted to living with Kay, and Kay adjusted to life back in New York.

They'd spent another weekend at Tobias's since the Memorial Day weekend, but on the third weekend, after taking note of the little comments that Kay had dropped, Savannah made the difficult decision to spend a whole weekend with Kay.

It didn't go down too well with Jacob.

"It's not fair! *And* he doesn't come over any more." The disappointment on her son's face was plain to see.

"Honey, Tobias doesn't come over because there's nowhere for him to sleep." Not with her and Jacob sharing a room. "But as soon as we find a new place, Tobias promises he'll come over for his Friday night sleepovers." He hadn't stayed over since Kay had arrived.

"We can have fun here instead," Kay told him, doing her best to convince him.

"But I like staying with Tobias."

"Jacob," Savannah used her be-careful-what-you-say-or-do voice. "We haven't seen Kay for a long time."

"We see her every day!" Jacob replied, a little too vehemently for Savannah's liking.

Savannah didn't like his insolent tone. "But we haven't spent any quality time with her," she cautioned, giving her cousin a brief glance and a wince. She turned back to her son and saw his unhappy, tight little face; saw his lips twist in an effort to stop himself from saying something.

She was therefore all the more surprised when a defeated "Okay," crept out from his lips instead.

"How about we go to the movies tomorrow, Jacob?" Kay asked. "Just you and me? There are a lot of new ones out this summer with those funny characters you like."

"Superheroes," muttered Jacob, rolling his eyes.

"Please let me take him," Kay implored, turning to Savannah. "I haven't seen him for so long and I think it would be fun for the two of us to spend some time together."

"I'm sure he'd love that," said Savannah. And it would give her some time to herself.

"Would you like that?" Kay asked Jacob. "We can spend the day together and I'll buy you something."

"You don't have to buy me anything," Jacob replied politely. "I've got enough toys. Can I go play now?"

"Don't you want to watch a movie with us?" It was what they did on a Friday night when Tobias was over. Jacob shook his head.

"Go play then," said Savannah and watched him disappear into his bedroom.

"Your son is adorable," Kay remarked.

"I know." Despite his sullen behavior just now, he was a relatively easygoing kid. "I couldn't put up with an obnoxious child."

They cleared up the dinner dishes. "Thanks for spending

the weekend with me," Kay said. "It feels as if we've barely been able to catch up."

"That's not been my fault," said Savannah. "You've been working late the whole time. They didn't even give you a settling back period."

Kay didn't get home until late in the evenings so that when Savannah returned from work, after having picked Jacob up from Rosalee's place, they had the apartment to themselves. Kay got back after eight mostly and then it felt different. Savannah was certain it was probably also awkward for Kay, despite her firm insistence that she and Jacob could stay for as long as they wanted. Everything seemed more cramped. The kitchen seemed smaller, the living room seemed smaller, and they had to wait to use the bathroom. By the time she returned home, Kay was often tired and quiet and flopped in front of the TV with her dinner on her lap. Mindful of her cousin needing her own space, Savannah often went to bed early but talking to Tobias on her cell also became difficult with Jacob asleep in the bedroom, and Kay in the living room.

She hadn't seen much of Tobias at work these past few weeks either. He'd been busy during the day in meetings and had worked late almost every night. She sensed that a few deals lately hadn't panned out and even Matthias looked like a grizzly bear stomping around the office.

"I have to work late," moaned Kay. "That's how it is with banks. They suck the life right out of you."

"But end-of-year bonuses must help sweeten that for you," said Savannah, wiping down the countertops.

"I need *some* incentive for losing out on a love life." Kay paused with a dirty glass in her hand. "We're not all as lucky as you." She placed the glass in the dishwasher.

"I guess luck did have something to do with it." Savannah mused, thinking about the first time she saw Tobias.

"And it was just my luck to be sent to Hong Kong while you ended up here."

"Didn't you enjoy working in Hong Kong?"

"It was an experience, and I'm glad I went but I'm really glad to be back."

"You made lots of friends out there, didn't you?" *Lots of men friends*, Savannah remembered.

"I had to do *something* to keep busy. I was lonely, Sav, and I didn't want to talk about work all the time."

"I remember," replied Savannah. "What happened to 'dessert,'" she asked, recalling Kay's Christmas dinner dating event. *Good-Time Kay.*

Kay frowned, and mouthed the name as if she was trying to remember. "Oh, *him*..." Her eyes widened. "He was good, for a while. But..." She shrugged and said no more.

"You must have left a trail of broken hearts behind you."

Kay shook her head. "I had a lot of fun, but it was never anything serious. Nothing for me to cry about."

Savannah smiled. "I meant them, not you."

"Who knows?" Kay shrugged and ran her hands through her newly highlighted, overdone blonde hair. Savannah preferred the more natural dirty mousy-brown tone she'd had when she arrived.

"I make it a rule to leave before they wake up, and I've never met anyone I wanted to wake up with." She flicked TV channels and settled on a celebrity gossip channel. "What's it like going from having *no* sex to *lots* of it?" Kay asked, shameless in her curiosity.

*Unbelievable*, thought Savannah, marveling at how much her life had changed and everything in it, including the sex. Kay leaned forward. "Tell me everything," she said, her eyes glinting with curiosity.

There was so much that Savannah could have told her but

she didn't want her romance with Tobias to be the subject of other people's conversations. "What can I say?" replied Savannah, choosing her words carefully.

"Start from the beginning."

"You already know how we met."

"You're not going to tell me a thing, are you?" Kay examined her fingernails and sighed. "I'm surprised he's so nice in person. He's often so stern-looking in most photos."

"He's been through a tough time," Savannah replied, feeling defensive. "He's misunderstood."

The corners of Kay's mouth turned up. "I'm sure you enjoyed getting to understand this deeply wounded man. It's not too difficult when he has a body and a wallet like that."

"Have you caught up with all your friends here?" asked Savannah, directing the conversation away from Tobias.

"I've met a few for lunch since I got back," Kay replied. "Which reminds me—I must come and meet you for lunch one day. I've never been inside the Stone Building."

"We could do that," replied Savannah, understanding perfectly well why her cousin had insisted on coming to meet *her*.

"Here's an even better idea," said Kay, sitting up. "Why don't we have a dinner party or something? Or go out together one evening?"

"We?"

"You, me, Tobias, his friends, my friends."

"I don't know your friends."

"And I don't know Tobias. You and I barely get to see one another and I'd like to get to know him better, especially since you seem to be so serious about him." Savannah was about to open her mouth and say that her weekends were sacrosanct and that enlarging her circle of friends wasn't a priority for her. Spending time with Tobias was, and she already had her friends, Briony and Max. Outside of that, there wasn't much time for any other socializing.

"That sounds like a good idea," she replied, instead. She felt as if she had no choice but to comply. Kay had been good to her and she could hardly pretend she didn't exist.

Her cousin's face brightened. "How about this weekend?"

"It's too short notice," replied Savannah.

"What about the weekend after?" Kay seemed anxious to the point of being desperate and it was beginning to niggle Savannah.

It was obvious to her that Tobias was the draw. She tested her theory. "We could try next weekend," she suggested, half-heartedly. "But I think Tobias might be away on business." He'd mentioned something about going to Seattle but she wasn't sure when exactly. For now it served as a good excuse.

"There's no point getting together without him!" Kay exclaimed.

"He's very busy most of the time," explained Savannah.

"I'd much rather wait until we can all fix a date," said Kay, distracted by an A-list actress stepping onto the red carpet. "Do you think she's had her boobs done?"

"No idea."

They both examined the woman's cleavage in concentrated silence until Kay said, "I think I also need to visit my mom," as if it was more of an afterthought.

"Aunt Sylvie would like that," Savannah agreed. She was fond of her aunt with whom she and Jacob had lived before she came to New York.

Savannah's thoughts drifted to Tobias and once more she wished he were here. On a Friday night, they'd be curled up on the sofa, the three of them, and by ten, Jacob had usually fallen asleep, leaving both of them to share a bottle of wine and to talk.

Tobias seemed softer these days, more at ease with life and

not as intense as when she'd first met him. Others had noticed too. As for herself, she felt less anxious these days, more secure, happier, and more laidback. Life was no longer an ordeal to be endured, but something to be savored and each day to be welcomed and enjoyed.

"I need to hit the sack," said Kay and began to yawn.

"I thought we were going to catch up?" asked Savannah, surprised.

"Sorry, do you mind?" Kay yawned again. "It's all caught up with me, getting into the rat race again. I feel as if I've been back months, not a few weeks."

Savannah smiled and understood. "You go to bed then."

"We could go out tomorrow night, if you want," Savannah suggested, intending to make the most of her weekend with Kay and wondering if Rosalee would be free to babysit.

"I'm taking Jacob out all day and I think when I get back, I'll want to veg at home. Maybe we can order some food in and catch up properly."

"Sure," said Savannah.

Kay slowly got up and stretched. "Sorry, Sav," she said. "I can barely keep my eyes open. What are your plans tomorrow?"

"I'm going to look at a few apartments."

"Awwww," Kay made a face. "Please don't move out so quickly."

Savannah smiled. "It might not be so soon," she replied, trying to reassure Kay. "You should see some of the places I've seen."

The apartment tomorrow was a two-bedroom place out in the suburbs, over an hour's commute from work and this would present its own set of problems. But with Jacob's school getting out for summer in a few weeks' time, the school run was the least of her problems.

# CHAPTER EIGHT

"I can make arrangements for you to see both properties, Mr. Stone."

Tobias smiled to himself. Giles De Freitas would do anything for him. But then, of course, the commission on a multi-million-dollar property would put a gold-plated smile on the realtor's face.

Tobias had been looking at the brochures and personal footage of properties the realtor had earmarked for him based on Tobias's preferences. A family home, near the Fifth and Madison Avenue areas, and with no limit on price.

Now almost a month since he'd first contacted the luxury realty agency, Tobias examined his shortlist. Only two properties stood out. Huge and imposing and reeking of incalculable wealth, one of them rose eight stories high, the other was three sprawling townhouses which he intended to combine into one family home.

A home he wanted to fill with love and new memories, and more children, if Savannah agreed. It depended on what she wanted, though, and he was still trying to slowly unravel it. Priced at around the $50 million mark, this would be his biggest personal purchase yet and before he took this step, he needed to run it by the two people he intended to make a part of his future.

"I'll get back to you," Tobias told him.

"Always at your service, sir. Any time, on weekends, at any time of—"

"I'll let you know," said Tobias sternly. The man's spineless desire to please was beginning to grate on his nerves. He could see Matthias hovering around his open door, waiting to see him. "I'll call you."

"Yes, sir, and—"

Tobias hung up and summoned Matthias into his office.

"I spoke to Yanling earlier," said Matthias, walking in. "We need to schedule a conference call next week."

"Not yet," Tobias said, closing the glossy brochures and sliding a file on top to cover them.

"Not yet?" Matthias growled. "But we gave them three months. We need to give them a decision now that the time is almost up."

"I'm well aware of it," replied Tobias. And he'd been keeping a close eye on Yanling's businesses, which seemed to be slowing down in growth, exactly as Tobias had predicted. Luckily, those same senior managers who had sided with Matthias the last time were now coming around to Tobias's point of view.

"He's coming over for business next month and he wants to meet. I'm hoping we'll have reached a decision by then."

This was the last thing Tobias wanted to hear.

"Stall him."

"Stall him? Tobias, we've been keeping the poor guy waiting for months."

"The outcome doesn't look favorable," replied Tobias. "And at the moment, we have other lucrative business deals on the table. Aren't you tied up with Henderson Associates at the moment?"

"I'm going to see them next month," Matthias offered. "But Yanling is planning on visiting in the next six weeks and it would be rude if we didn't meet with him. He was good to me when I was over there."

"There's no point meeting him if we're not going to do business with him anymore."

"That's not something we've agreed on yet," Matthias argued.

"I know," said Tobias calmly. "And we'll revisit that again with management and the board, but I'm in no hurry to do so at the moment. I'll get Candace to schedule a meeting once I return from Seattle."

A new Seattle-based startup had caught his attention and Tobias had been speaking with them for the past few weeks, trying to understand the fundamentals of their business. He was eager to meet with the CEO in person before he decided to proceed further.

"Any more on the Sygon deal?"

"They're contesting a few points in the contract," Tobias told him. "I'm listening to their concerns."

"Why the hell didn't they say anything to me?"

"It depends how hard you tried to listen to them."

"At least I was there, which is more than can be said for you," Matthias retorted.

Tobias had had enough. "What's bothering you?" Matthias had been grouchy lately and he'd been meaning to get to the bottom of it. "We can discuss it here or over a few drinks."

"I need a goddamn vacation, is what I need," Matthias growled.

"What's happened to you lately?" Tobias tried to make a joke out of it. "Complications in your harem?"

"If it were only that simple." Matthias rubbed the back of his neck. "Doesn't it worry you? Sygon and Yanling and everything else that's gone wrong?"

"It's business," Tobias replied. "These things happen. They're called peaks and valleys."

"No shit," Matthias said, falling into the empty chair with a sigh. "How can you still be so upbeat about everything?"

Tobias smiled.

"Christ," said his friend, his right eyebrow shooting up. "Look at you, Tobias. You've turned into a lovesick puppy dog."

"The fuck I have," Tobias snapped with a smile. "I still have the edge, except that I'm nicer for it."

"I noticed you and Savannah coming into work a couple of times. What's going on? Are you cohabiting now?"

"We have an arrangement," replied Tobias, though this weekend, things would be different. For some reason, Savannah felt guilty about leaving her cousin alone for another weekend and had decided to spend it with Kay, much to his dismay. He wasn't looking forward to an empty weekend, and it made him realize that he needed to speed things along.

"An arrangement? Isn't that what you had with Naomi?"

Tobias cut him an icy stare. "Sorry," said Matthias, shifting uncomfortably in his chair. "I shouldn't mention her name."

"Don't."

"But seriously, Tobias, are you living together?" Matthias asked.

Tobias looked away from his computer screen. "Not that it's any business of yours, but...no." *Not yet.*

Matthias grinned as he rose slowly from his chair. "It's only a matter of time, I expect. I'd ask you if you wanted to go for a drink," he said, "seeing that it's the end of the week, but I suppose you're busy."

*Matthias was asking him to go out for a drink?* "It sounds

like real trouble at the harem," Tobias joked, "if you have no date on a Friday night." He wasn't busy, for a change and he wasn't looking forward to returning to a silent apartment. "I could do with a drink," he said. It had been a while since he and Matthias had gone out on a purely social level.

"It'll take you about an hour and fifteen at the most," the realtor had told her. An hour and fifteen minutes to get to the Stone Building, assuming she still worked there. It might not be *that* bad.

"But as you can see, it's a beautiful apartment in a lovely neighborhood and the schools around here are excellent. You need to decide quickly, Ms. Page, I have a lot of interest in this property so you need to let me know as soon as possible." She was sure he'd said the same thing to her about that other place.

She thought about the conversation earlier. The price wasn't bad either. The only bad thing about it was the distance, but she couldn't have it all, could she? She had to make the best choices for them both.

She finished reading to Jacob and had read for longer today because she felt especially guilty. Earlier, he'd gone with Kay begrudgingly and it had taken some persuading to get him out of the door with a smile. Even the lure of a movie didn't help to lift his spirits.

Savannah's heart had ached because what he wanted cost nothing: a weekend with Tobias, but she'd put her foot down and insisted he go with Kay. In the end, she promised that they would stay for a few extra days at Tobias's next weekend and it seemed to do the trick.

It was with that same feeling of guilt that she'd gone looking for apartments and this two-bedroom one cheered her up immensely. Its white walls and wooden floors made the rooms look especially spacious. If only it was as near to work as Kay's apartment was.

Now, as Jacob lay in bed, on the verge of sleep, she contemplated discussing it with him, thinking it was only fair to tell him but she didn't have the heart. Not yet.

"You've been a good boy, Jacob. Thanks for going with Kay today. She really enjoyed watching the movie."

"No, she didn't. She kept checking her cell phone for messages."

"Oh." Savannah was at a loss for what to say. "It'll be better next weekend when we stay at Tobias's until Monday morning."

"Why can't we stay there all the time?" Jacob asked.

"Honey," she said, drawing out a breath. She wished her son didn't always pin her with such a penetrating gaze, especially when she had no good answer for such a seemingly simple question. "Because we have to find our own place."

"But why?"

"Because we do, Jacob." His big, innocent eyes burned into her soul, and she couldn't hide her thoughts or give him a good answer, at least not one that would satisfy him.

"Tobias loves us coming over, Mommy."

"He enjoys our company," she said, not pandering to her son's emotional blackmail.

"He said he looks forward to every weekend now. He told me so."

"He told you?"

"He said it brightens his day when you and me are over and he forgets about work."

"Is that what he said?"

"He did, Mommy, I promise." She could tell from the urgency in his voice, and because her son seldom lied, that Jacob was telling the truth.

"You like talking to him, don't you?"

He nodded. "I love Tobias, Mommy. Why can't we live with him all the time?"

She squeezed her eyes shut and gritted her teeth together. "Because we just can't. Everyone needs their own space, even Kay."

"But Kay doesn't love you like Tobias does."

She felt a knot in her throat, unable to speak.

"And he loves me too. When I'm around Tobias, I feel safe. That's love, isn't it, Mommy?"

She scratched behind her ear. "I guess it is." And because she didn't know what else to say, she said, "Kay's waiting. I should go spend some time with her." She bent down and kissed Jacob on his forehead. "Goodnight, honey."

"'Nite, Mommy."

She closed the door and walked back into the living room, looking forward to her glass of wine. Kay was nowhere to be seen but she had refilled both their wine glasses. Savannah picked hers up. Holding the chilled glass felt like she had a layer of wet ice on her fingers. She took a soothing sip and sank onto the couch, waiting.

"Now?" She heard Kay's voice as she walked into the living room. "I don't—" She gave Savannah a guarded look. "I'm not sure," she said, sounding anxious. "Let me think about it and I'll call you back." She hung up.

*This didn't sound too promising.* Savannah flicked through

the channels and pretended to remain calm. She had an inkling what this might lead to.

"That was Dean," said Kay.

Savannah blinked. "Dean?" She blinked. The name sounded familiar. "Your ex?"

Kay chewed on her finger, looking uncomfortable. "Yup."

"What did he want?"

"He—uh," Kay examined her finger. "He said he wanted to take me out for dinner."

"Now?"

"Now."

"But you've just eaten."

Kay winced. "He said we could go for cocktails."

"And?" Savannah knew exactly how this booty call was going to end, just as she knew from the pained expression on her cousin's face how difficult it was for Kay to tell her. She had put aside her precious weekend to make time for her cousin who was now running off to see her ex. Savannah wasn't about to let Kay off without a bucket full of guilt. "You obviously want to go."

"I'm not sure," replied Kay.

"I think you are sure, I think you're waiting for me to tell you it's okay. You look as if you want to go."

"We have stuff to sort out." Kay bit her lip and looked even more anxious. "No," she said, with pronounced determination. "I'm not going to see him. It would be shitty of me because you've given up your weekend with Tobias to spend time with me." Kay picked up her cell phone. "I'll tell him I can't."

"And why so late on a Saturday night?" Savannah asked. "Didn't he think to call you earlier?" It sounded to her as if he'd gone down his list of numbers and Kay's was next on the list. Kay looked at her with embarrassment.

"He called a couple of times during the week, but I never got around to calling him back because I've been so busy."

"Are you sure you need to see him? If you've broken up—he dumped you, remember—then why do you need to meet?" She knew it was cruel to remind her cousin of this but still, someone had to knock some sense into that ditzy head of hers. Kay was a genius with numbers, but really stupid when it came to men.

"We never really talked about it, and then I left."

*There's nothing to talk about! He dumped you.*

"I want closure, Sav."

Closure with clothes off, Savannah guessed, if she knew Kay. It seemed that Kay had already made her mind up. Savannah knew it would be better to step in and stop her from making another stupid mistake but Kay never listened anyway. She might even accuse her of interfering. Was it worth the headache? Kay looked as if she'd already made up her mind. Besides, having the apartment to herself for the entire evening was more appealing.

"Then go," said Savannah. "We can do Sunday brunch tomorrow." She didn't want Kay to think that she was that mad at her, even though she was. She figured her cousin would need her wits about her and a strong mind if she was going to meet Dean.

"Are you sure you don't mind?" Kay asked, blissfully unaware.

Jacob asleep, no Kay, a glass of wine, and time to think about the apartment she'd seen earlier now that she had some quiet time. "Go," Savannah told her, "but don't do anything stupid. Don't let him walk all over you or entice you back to bed."

"Thanks, Sav," Kay promised, her eyes shining like Cinderella's when she'd been told she could go to the ball. "I have to get ready," she said, and rushed out.

. . .

S he finished her glass of wine and had poured the wine from Kay's full glass into hers. Kay had left a short while ago, wearing sexy sandals and a cocktail dress that just about covered her butt. It was not an outfit that indicated much in the way of conversation, as much as it screamed 'I'm available.'

Savannah called Tobias again and this time he answered.

"Hey," he said, sounding tired. "I was about to call you. I was in the shower."

She groaned, picturing him. "I wish I was in there with you."

"Don't go getting me all excited," he said in a husky voice, and she imagined being there beside him, doing nothing but getting him all excited and enjoying every moment of it.

She longed for him. "I miss you."

"I miss you," he repeated back to her.

"I love you." He turned silent then. She blinked. "Are you still there?" *Did you hear me?*

"It took you a while to tell me, huh?" he said finally. Of course she loved him, but it had taken this weekend and not being with him for her to know it as fundamentally as she did now.

"I miss you, Tobias and I love you and I—"

Oh, dear God, she was starting to ramble.

It had been a mistake to call him when the wine was going to her head. It seemed that her most defining moments and her most important decisions were only made once wine made her brave enough to follow through.

"What is it?" he asked, sounding concerned. "You sound down, Savannah."

"I tell you I love you and you think I sound down?"

He laughed. "That's not what I meant. I can tell from your voice that something isn't right. I know your moods." He was absolutely right. He did. He knew everything about her and he always said and did the right things by her. Her heart swelled with happiness.

"Nothing's wrong," she said, feeling grateful for him. "I'm home alone and my cousin is meeting up with her ex and I miss you. I wanted to hear your voice."

He laughed softly. "I thought she wanted to spend quality time with you?"

"That's what I thought."

"Want me to come and get you?"

She sighed. *If only.* "Jacob's sleeping and I'd rather not disturb him." Even though her son would probably not be too concerned about being woken up if he knew he was going to Tobias's place.

Tobias groaned with disappointment.

"Why don't you come over?" she asked. But she knew that it would be ten times as hard to let him go if he came to her tonight.

"Is this a booty call?" he asked. "Because I'm happy to oblige."

"I wish," she said, sipping her wine and thinking steamy thoughts all the same.

"I could come over, but knowing our luck, your cousin would probably come home early and we'd barely have had a chance to make out on the couch."

"She'd probably watch," said Savannah.

"God, no."

"We can talk," she said, putting down her glass and making herself comfortable on the couch. "I've got all night."

"Can we talk dirty later?" he asked, and she could imagine him grinning.

"Honey, we can do whatever you want," she said suggestively.

"If you're going to talk like *that*," said Tobias, "I might have to come over and give you a good seeing to."

She giggled and stretched out her legs. "You've been very busy lately," she said. "What's going on?"

"A lot of things," he replied, sighing. "There's a lot going on with the markets, a lot of negative market sentiment, a lot of uncertainty, and a few deals aren't quite working out as well as we envisioned. Everything's going wrong all at once."

"It can feel like that sometimes," Savannah agreed, having experienced this same phenomenon many times in her life.

"It's nothing that can't be resolved with time," Tobias assured her. "What about you? You don't sound so cheerful yourself. Tell me what's up."

"It's nothing," she said wearily. "I don't have your problems or the weight of the company on my shoulders. I don't know how you handle it all."

"It's all I know," he replied. "It doesn't always feel like a weight, except lately."

"Lately?"

"Lately, I'd rather spend time with you instead of being at the office until 9:00 or 10:00. I'm going to Seattle in a few weeks' time and I'd rather not. That's when it feels like a weight. I don't like being away from you and that's something new for me to get used to."

She was touched, and ran her fingers over his necklace, a reminder of him. "Think of the nice-to-see-you-again sex I'll be sure to greet you with on your return."

"Sold," he said. "When you put it that way, it sounds like an incentive for going away." He paused a while before asking, "Is it becoming awkward staying with your cousin?"

"Not awkward so much. More like cramped," she explained. "And I am annoyed, if I'm being honest. I gave up seeing you this weekend because I felt sorry for her. Jacob was *so* unhappy about it, and now I feel bad for him and she's gone off to see her ex. I can't believe it."

"She sounds desperately lonely."

"I think she is."

"I'm going to throw that party," he said.

"You're *still* thinking about it?"

"I'm serious."

"You?" She laughed. Tobias was the last person she imagined wanting to throw a party.

"Yes, me," he answered, sounding irritated. "It's been at the back of my mind ever since Henry Carson didn't invite Jacob to his."

"And you really want to have a party so that you can snub Henry Carson? How old are you, Tobias?"

"You can laugh, but it's been a while since I last had a party."

"I'll believe that when it happens." She smiled at the idea of it.

"You're going to help put it together," he said, "Well, mostly Candace, and she can delegate to a party planner we've used in the past." *We?* Did he mean him and Ivy? For some reason, talk about his past made her uneasy.

"Okay," she said. She'd deal with it if anything got off the ground. "I had a look at a couple of apartments earlier."

"Uh-huh."

"I think I've found a place."

"Uh-huh."

"But it's in a nice neighborhood and it's affordable and it's got two bedrooms," she said, talking fast, before he could make an objection.

"Where?"

"Middletown."

"Middletown? Are you sure? That would be a much longer

commute than you currently have," he said slowly, stating the obvious. "Do you really want Jacob to have such a long trip to school? Do you want a long commute to work?"

"I think we would most likely have to move but—" She hesitated, wondering how he had taken the news. "Jacob will be getting out for summer soon and I think it would be the perfect time to try to see if I could manage it without uprooting us both."

"Uh-huh."

"Actually, that reminds me. I need to look at summer day camps for him to go to." She chewed her lip. "I also need to get going with the single moms' initiative. I could do with affordable childcare myself."

"How about I get Candace to schedule a meeting with Brigitte Obenchain?" he suggested. "You might even be able to get this thing off the ground this summer."

"Maybe," she replied, secretly doubting that she could. "It would be good to meet with her and find out what the whole process entails."

"I'll get the ball rolling. About that apartment," he said, sounding anxious. "Are you seriously thinking of taking it?"

"I know it's not ideal but it's a big apartment and we'll have a bedroom each, *and* I can afford it. I'm trying to take everything into consideration."

"Are you?"

"What do you mean?"

"You'll just have a longer commute. Is that really the best alternative for you?"

"I'm not going to find the perfect place, something has to give."

"Or you could move in with me," he suggested. "You could live here and it would all be so simple."

She blinked, then stuttered. "But...but..."

"But what?" There was a pause, before he said, "You could move in temporarily, Savannah, if that would make it more palatable a deal for you, but it would solve two of your most urgent problems. You get to leave your cousin's apartment immediately and you don't have to move until you find the right place, at the right price, in the right location." He paused, waiting for her response.

"I'm not sure," she said, hesitating.

"I'm asking you for me, Savannah, because I'm being selfish. I don't want you to go work someplace else, and I know Jacob doesn't want to change schools. I don't think you want him to either."

He was talking sense, of course he was, but... "Thank you," she managed to say. Her heart thumped wildly in her chest, and she wasn't sure why. "But we really couldn't."

"Why not?"

She made a whooshing noise, as if air whistled out of her mouth. "Well, it ...it..."

"It what?" he pressed. "I have the space, as you can see. Think about it, for Jacob's sake. He loves his school. Why would you want to put him through the trauma of starting at a new school? And you have good perks and benefits at the company, why would you want to move?"

"You don't have to sell Stone Enterprises to me," she said defensively. "I already know how lucky I am."

"It seems plain enough to me," he said. "You either move out in a rush and take the first affordable apartment and compromise on everything else, or you stay with your cousin for the next few months, possibly even a year—"

"It's not going to take a year to find a place." *It wouldn't, would it?*

"Or you can stay with me. We all get to be happy."

"I don't know," she murmured, but it would be so easy, and

so doable. *Why not take what he offered for now?* "Let me think about it."

"You *still* need to think about it?"

She did. She had to make sure it would work. She knew it would. But still. "It sounds too easy."

"Most things often are, if you take the emotion out of them," he told her. "But you take all the time you need."

She picked up her wine glass, and had a feeling it wouldn't take that long.

# CHAPTER TEN

I t took a few hours for Savannah to make up her mind, after sitting through an hour of Kay's story about how her evening with Dean had gone. Rather terribly, as it turned out.

The following weekend, she moved out.

"I can't believe you're leaving me," said Kay rather dramatically. She stood in the living room with watery eyes.

Savannah was surprised. "You're not going to cry, are you?"

One suitcase and a couple of bags lay near the door. "Only these?" Tobias asked, picking the suitcase easily in one hand and reaching down for the other two bags.

"Yes," said Savannah. "But I can get those." She stepped forward to grab the two smaller bags.

"I've got them," he said, refusing to let her take them. He'd been smiling like a kid on Christmas Day ever since she'd accepted his offer to move in, and had insisted on helping her to move out early on Saturday morning.

"I'm going to miss having you both around," said Kay, miserably.

"This isn't goodbye," Savannah insisted, as she threw her arms around Kay.

"Isn't it?"

"I'm not emigrating," said Savannah. "I'm a twenty-, thirty-minute ride away, for now." She was about to tell her that she could visit whenever she wanted but decided against it, fearing that Kay would take that literally and show up on Tobias's doorstep all the time.

"For now?" Kay peered at her in disbelief. "I don't think you'll be moving again."

"I *am* going to move again," Savannah protested. "This is only temporary." They'd been dating for, what—almost six months? No way was she ready to live with Tobias based on six months of a very up-and-down relationship.

Despite what everyone thought, and Briony had been no better in her analysis of this situation, Savannah knew that she and Tobias weren't ready to make any long-term decisions. Nor did she want to rock the boat by asking him where they were heading. She didn't need anything more from him above what she already had—his love and support.

She didn't need anything but *him*. She had survived up until she had met him, and now—now life was no longer about surviving. If anything, she was more than content to sail along on the boat and enjoy the view for now because she had everything she wanted, love, happiness, security, safety. What more was there?

"I'm going to miss you," said Kay.

"I'm going to miss you," replied Savannah, overcome by a flash of guilt that she really wasn't *that* sad. She wasn't even sure that she would miss Kay *that* much.

"Can we meet up once a week, at least? Even if we go out for something to eat and catch up?"

Savannah tried not to wince. "You're behaving as if you're as far away as Hong Kong. Of course we can still meet up."

Only, she wasn't sure she could do it every week. "Let me get settled in and we'll arrange something."

Kay smiled weakly. "Look at you, Sav," she said, folding her arms. "Look how quickly and how *much* your life has changed. You're with *Tobias Stone*. You were working for him one minute, then dating him the next, and now you're living together."

"We're not living together. It's only temporary."

"It looks pretty rosy to me," replied Kay, feeling rather sorry for herself. Savannah had heard how the meeting with Dean had ended badly and as she had suspected, he hadn't wanted to meet in order to talk. Not that Kay had helped, showing up dressed like *that*. But she'd come home early, hadn't given him anything except a piece of her mind. "Don't forget, I'm still waiting for you to hook me up with his brother."

Unfortunately Tobias walked in at that moment and an eerie silence fell. "You want to meet Xavier?" he asked.

"As in a few of us getting together, that's what you meant, isn't it?" Savannah suggested, sensing her cousin's embarrassment.

"Uh—" Kay was at a loss for words.

"You see," said Tobias, throwing his arm around Savannah's shoulder and pulling her close. "Everyone wants a party, it seems."

"A party?" Kay asked, batting her lashes at him. "For what? The Fourth of July?"

"No," replied Tobias. "A party just for the sake of it, because —why not?" Kay gave him her most charming smile.

"I like the way you think," she purred.

"And I'd purposely have it the week after," he said to Savannah.

"Hold that thought," Kay said, rushing to answer the phone.

Tobias turned to Savannah. "Any reason why she wants to meet Xavier?"

"Why do you think?"

Tobias suppressed a smile. "I know he's my brother, but even I would hesitate to put him forward as a potential date. Do you think she and Xavier would get along?"

"I don't even want to go there," said Savannah. "Isn't he still with Petra?"

"It depends what day of the week it is."

"Then he doesn't sound like the sort of man I should be hooking my cousin up with."

"Exactly."

"It's your mom," said Kay, coming back into the living room. She made a face as she covered the phone piece with her hand. "I forgot to tell you she called yesterday and I think I might have accidentally let it slip that you were moving out."

"Accidentally let it slip?" She'd told Kay not to mention to her parents that she was moving in with Tobias. Not yet. It had happened quickly and she wanted to get settled in first. And moving in with Tobias, with any man, would have them worried.

"Haven't you told them yet?" Tobias whispered.

Savannah shook her head and grabbed the phone. "Hey, Mom."

"We heard you and Jacob were moving, dear. Is it true?"

"We're about to leave now. Sorry, Mom, I was going to tell you once it was all done."

"You've already moved?" Her mom didn't sound too happy.

She sighed heavily, hearing the note of disapproval in her mother's voice. "Yes, Mom. We're about to go now."

"But where are you going?"

"I'm..." She considered keeping it vague, and then decided to come clean. "I'm moving in with Tobias." She bit her lip and squeezed her eyes shut, imagining the reaction at the other end. "But it's only temporary," she said.

"With Tobias Stone?" Her mother's worried voice clearly signaled her concern. "Are you sure you're doing the right thing?"

Savannah moved into the kitchen. "Yes, Mom. Tobias kindly offered and it's only until I find the perfect apartment. I've been looking, Mom," she said, getting ready to launch into full explanation mode, "and it's not easy. Rent here is sky high."

"We've found out some things."

"Like what?"

"About the escort. Is it true?"

"Mom!" It was the last thing Savannah expected to hear.

"We read the whole thing, dear. He was with that woman for years."

"Mom, not now, please."

"Your father and I really liked him but now we're not so sure. We're very worried about you."

Her parents seemed to always worry about her. "Don't be, Mom. I promise you it's nothing like that."

"Nothing like what? Your father and I have been reading up on him. He's had a very bad time of things. Do you really need to complicate your life further?"

"Mom, stop." Savannah rubbed her forehead, trying to find a suitable point at which she could end the conversation.

"Are you sure you really know him?"

"Yes, Mom. I wouldn't do this, otherwise."

"Your father is concerned. I am too, but you know how worried he gets."

"You don't have to worry, Mom. I promise you. Tobias isn't like that."

"But is it true?"

She sighed. What else could she say? "It's true but a lot of things have happened that you don't know about."

"That's what he's told you, has he?"

She bit her tongue. "I believe him."

"We were afraid you might."

"Mom, please. Trust me."

"What about Jacob? What kind of an influence will this man be on your son?" In the background, she could hear Tobias and Jacob talking.

"Mom, please. I'll call you later."

"Your father wants a word."

"Not now, Mom!" She really couldn't handle speaking to her father, even though he would have been the easier of the two to have this conversation with. "We're literally about to walk out of the apartment." The way her mom spoke, Savannah knew they already thought the worst of Tobias. "I have to go but I will call you later."

"Everything all right?" Tobias asked when she walked back into the living room.

She shrugged.

"They sounded worried about something."

"I'd rather not talk about it."

"Okay." She was relieved when he didn't press her further. "Ready?" he asked.

"Where's Jacob?"

"Gone to check under his bed, again, to make sure he hasn't left anything behind."

"Are you ready?" Tobias asked her.

She had her mother's conversation circling around in her thoughts, and forced it into the deepest corners of her mind. "I'm ready," she said. "We're moving twenty minutes away," she told Kay, giving her another big hug. "And we have technology, and phones, and messaging, and FaceTime, and a million ways of keeping in touch."

"We could just as easily meet for drinks or dinner," Kay suggested.

Savannah nodded.

"So I could come and meet you for lunch next week?"

"Yes."

Kay was instantly vibrant again. "I'll arrange lunch next week. I'll come to the Stone Building and meet you."

"All clear," cried Jacob, with Iron Man in his hand. "Can we go now?" he asked, excited.

"Yes, buddy," replied Tobias, grinning.

"You're finally leaving?" Arnold said, giving her a doleful look. Tobias had gone outside to the car, leaving her and Jacob to say their goodbyes to the friendly concierge.

"Don't say it like that, Arnold," said Savannah, realizing now that despite what she had thought earlier, she *did* have roots, that leaving this apartment wasn't going to be as easy as she had at first thought. It had been home to her for almost a year.

Luckily, she wasn't going to have to say goodbye to Rosalee. She still needed her babysitter's help over the summer and she would continue to see her regularly. Otherwise, Savannah feared, she would have been in a flood of tears by now. But the way Arnold looked at her, as if she'd abandoned him, almost had her eyes filling up.

"I'm going to miss you, Ms. Page, and young Jacob," he said, staring at them both sorrowfully.

"I'll be back," she said, putting on a cheerful face. She had been all right until this moment. Even saying goodbye to Kay hadn't been as hard. For as long as she'd known him, Arnold and his gap-toothed smile had cheered her up, no matter what kind of a day she'd had. But looking at his mournful face now reminded her that this was a change in her life. She and Jacob always had time to stop and talk to him, to see how his day had been, and a warm and comfortable friendship had sprung up between them.

"You won't be here every day," he said, looking unconvinced. "But I know this is a good thing for you and that's why I'm happy for you, even though it's a sad day for me."

"It's only temporary," she said, ruffling Jacob's hair as he waited patiently by her side.

"We'll come back and see you, Arnold," Jacob promised.

"I hope so, Jacob," he said. "Don't forget about me, will you?" He nodded his head towards the large glass windows, outside Tobias's bodyguards hovered around the black SUV talking to Tobias. "You're moving to a different world now."

"I'm still the same Savannah Page," she insisted. "And we *will* be back to see you."

# CHAPTER ELEVEN

"Where are you?" Tobias muttered under his breath as he contemplated the empty glass conference room. He glanced at his watch.

It was 9:15 a.m.

It was mildly irritating that Matthias had gone and scheduled the conference call with Yanling anyway, but now that he had rushed back from inspecting one of the properties he was interested in, it appeared he'd cut that visit short for nothing.

Surely the call can't have been over with already? He was only a little late. He strode to Matthias's office. The door was ajar anyway and he didn't bother to knock

"What happened with the call?" Tobias asked, walking in.

"The Sygon deal collapsed." Matthias eyed him warily. "The email came early this morning."

"Fuck." Tobias scrubbed his hand through his hair. "And the call with Yanling?" he asked. "What happened?"

Matthias glared at him. "You were late."

"For fuck's sake, Matthias," he barked. "It's only 9:16 and I've just come from the conference room."

"The call was at 9:00. It's late evening over there and he got tired of waiting for you. We purposely scheduled a time that would be convenient for *you*."

"But I asked you not to schedule anything until I returned from Seattle."

"It was one conference call, Tobias. You expect me to keep him waiting for a month? It's me he's hounding, not you."

"Why are you so uptight?" Tobias asked him.

"Why are you not?" Matthias shot back. "You used to do a better job of separating your personal life from your business life. You might want to reconsider that in light of the Sygon deal collapsing. Yanling didn't like to be kept waiting so he left."

Tobias shook his head. It didn't surprise him when it came to Yanling. That man had an ego the size of China.

Becker Schwartz had often remarked on how to determine a man's worth—it wasn't by the size of his wealth, it was by how he treated others. Tobias had been guilty of being stern and a difficult boss, but he'd never been pompous, had never looked down upon others.

Most of his peers were the same, polite and gracious—men with balls of steel, no less—but men with manners. In such company, the few rude ones stood out and were easy enough to avoid. Yanling was such a man.

He wasn't too interested in what Yanling had to say and he had no intention of signing the deal. As far as he was concerned, he had no intention of pursuing their alliance any further. As if the Far East troubles weren't enough, there was chaos in Europe.

Yet the Sygon decision surprised him. Perhaps he had been a little too unfocused with regards to them. Perhaps he would arrange another meeting on his return from Seattle.

Despite what Matthias believed, he had his eyes on most things and his analysts kept him fully briefed and up to date. He kept a close watch on the markets and knew exactly what was happening at any given time. Schwartz had often admired Tobias's uncanny ability to predict ahead of the curve. Tobias watched the markets like a hawk but he knew that emotions played a huge part in market sentiment. Right now was a tricky time and he wasn't going to put his company on the line.

"I keep my personal life separate."

"Is that so?" replied Matthias, glaring at him. "And what business does our company have with Giles De Freitas?"

That item of news could only have come from Candace.

"Are you looking for a new place to live? Or were you looking to buy something for Savannah?"

It wasn't only the tone of Matthias's voice, it was the deeply personal question he'd aimed at Tobias like a missile that pissed him off. "Do you have a hotline to my PA?" he asked, trying to keep his anger in check while he made a note to speak to Candace. He hadn't told her that his meeting with De Freitas at 7:00 a.m. this morning was confidential, but still, it made him uneasy knowing that Candace seemed to offer up his whereabouts so easily, or that Matthias seemed to be keeping track of his movements closely. "Is there a reason you seem to know my daily schedule so well?"

Matthias loosened up. "No," he said, wiping his brow. "When you didn't show up, I got Candace to see where you were. I'm sorry, it's none of my business, and I shouldn't have said what I did, but," his features softened, "it seems to me that everything we're doing isn't going to according to plan."

"That's business for you. It's like the stock market, up and down, that's the only constant."

"Don't worry about the Yanling deal. It can wait," Matthias told him. "I'm going to be busy with the Henderson account and see if I can get some new business in. Things have been tough lately, haven't they?"

*No,* thought Tobias to himself. Business had been tough, with the markets tumbling in London, and Europe in a shambles. But life otherwise was beautiful. Savannah and Jacob were living with him, he'd seen the properties he'd been interested in, and he was going to throw that party regardless.

Life was beautiful.

# CHAPTER TWELVE

"So, are you throwing this party for Jacob or for my cousin who's desperate to meet a billionaire? I should let you know that she'd happily settle for a millionaire."

"Then she's sure to meet someone," Tobias replied. "A few of my friends from the mastermind group are coming and they're all millionaires *at least*. Though some of them are on their second or third marriage."

Savannah grinned. "I don't think she's too concerned about the divorce rate." She paused for a while, then asked, "Am I bad-mouthing her too much?"

Tobias shook his head. "Having had the pleasure of meeting your cousin, I agree 100 percent."

"You're sure there's nobody else you'd expressly like to invite?"

"Aside from Briony, Max, Rosalee and Kay, no."

"Relax, Savannah. This isn't going to be a huge gala dinner-style event, just an informal get together with people we know. Family and friends."

He'd already spoken to Candace and gotten her to hire a reputable party planner. And between them, he and Savannah had just finished finalizing their guest list. "Don't forget to give Jacob's list to Candace. The invitations have to go out this week. She's dealing with them and handling all the RSVPs."

"Anything for me to do?"

He didn't want to load her with too much to do, especially since he'd be away soon, and she had enough on her plate with Jacob. And he'd arranged with her to meet Brigitte Obenchain in a few weeks. Somehow, the party idea had taken seed and now it had a life of its own. He saw the event as the springboard, a milestone, a getting together. An event which was more than just for the hell of it. "It's a small affair, Savannah, and I'm not going overboard. There's nothing much to do, unless you want to change the menu for the canapes and the drinks list."

"What you decided was fine," she said quickly. "If you leave it to me, we'll be having hot dogs and fries."

"Nothing wrong with hot dogs and fries," he replied.

"My parents definitely won't be able to come. I asked them a few days ago but it's fine. I'm sure they'll have plenty of other chances to visit."

"That's a shame," he said. "I could have used this opportunity to impress them." She had told him about their concerns about her moving in with him.

"It's going to take a lot more than a party invitation to sweeten them up," she told him, walking into the master bathroom. He followed her in to continue the conversation. This first week of their living together had been smooth and seamless, and it felt as if it had always been like this, so much so that he couldn't remember too much of how it had been before.

"They still have doubts about me?"

She laughed. "After Colt, they're super critical of any man I meet."

"How many have you met?"

She turned demurely. "Nobody," she said. "There's been nobody but you."

"And there'll be no one else either," he said.

"No," she replied, opening the lid to her face cream. She would do this every night, dot cream around her face and neck then wipe it off and then massage some more cream on. Then she would return to the bedroom, smelling sweet and flowery, her face flushed and glowing, and wearing a too-sexy-for-bed silk negligee which instantly filled his mind with arousing, erotic thoughts. Was it any wonder he could barely resist her?

"What's wrong with Matthias? He seems to be tense lately."

Even others had noticed. "He was annoyed with me because I was late for a conference call this morning."

"But you left really early."

"I had an appointment. I had some properties to view."

"Oh."

"Some residential properties."

"Uh-huh," she said.

"I thought it was about time that I upgraded."

She turned around and hovered by the entrance to the master bathroom "Upgraded?"

"To a bigger place."

"A bigger place? What's wrong with this? It's huge and it's beautiful."

"Then you should see the properties I've looked at, 20,000 square feet, ten bathrooms, eight bedrooms."

Her mouth fell open. "Is this a residence for the Stones? With your parents and Xavier?"

*Yes. A Stones' residence.*

"For investment purposes," he said, seeing that he had obviously shocked her. "I'll have to show you and Jacob." He walked out and headed for bed. "As for Matthias, don't worry about him. He can get like that at times. He can be prone to mood swings."

"It's not just you then," Savannah said, smiling at him.

"I don't have mood swings, do I?" he asked, checking his cell phone for messages before he climbed into bed.

"I thought you did, when I first met you. You were someone I tried to avoid running into."

"Really?"

"Really."

"And now?"

"And now...well, I think I've tamed you."

"You've done something to me, that's for sure," he said, putting his cell phone on the bedside table.

"Am I doing something to you now?" she asked, her lips breaking out into a mischievous smile as she turned and faced him.

"Why don't you come over here and find out?"

"I will," she promised, opening the dresser drawer and getting out her packet of pills. "Is it his personal life, do you think? The reason for Matthias's moods?"

"I'm unclear on his status, except that he has women, and doesn't want to be tied down." He didn't want to talk about Matthias too much and continued to watch as she swallowed a pill and took a sip of water.

"Do you have to take those?" he asked.

"They're my birth control pills."

He knew what they were. "I know." She seemed surprised, and looked as if she was about to say something but didn't.

"But what if you didn't take them?"

"If I didn't take them then...I have to take them every day..." She didn't answer his question but slid her hand over her neck, even though she had already rubbed her cream in.

"I know how they work, Savannah," he said. "Come over

here for a second," he said, and their eyes locked as she walked over to him and sat by the bed instead of slipping in beside him.

How to put it delicately, how to say it, what he felt deep down, that she was the one for him? "Do you ever think about having another baby?" Because he had been. He'd been thinking about a lot of things.

"Another baby?" Furrows lined her smooth forehead. "I haven't ever considered another baby."

"I never thought I would again, either, but you've made me challenge a lot of my assumptions and lately I've been thinking about it." He took her hand in his. "Being with you makes me think about it." She threw him a curious glance but remained silent.

"It's just a thought," he said softly. "I'm putting it out there for you to think about...in case you ever did want to ...you know..." He felt a jumpiness in his joints, a sudden restlessness. "In case you might ever consider wanting to have another baby. With me."

She scrutinized his face carefully.

"Savannah?"

"You want to have a baby?" she asked, her voice lowering to a whisper. The words floated between them like an opportunity to be grabbed or dismissed. "Until now, I'd never even considered something like this."

"Something like this?" he asked, curious to discover her take on things. On their relationship.

"Having a relationship again, being with someone. I never dared to think I could find that kind of happiness with anyone—having something good, something solid, something I've never had before—let alone think about having another child. A second child has never been on my radar, ever."

"It's fine if you don't, but do you sometimes wonder whether Jacob might like siblings?" His hand, with hers in it, fell to her lap. "I know it's the early days of our relationship." He had to say that because that was how she referred to their relationship, as if she needed a certificate or a certain amount of time to have passed before she could allow herself to believe that this was something more, that he wasn't going anywhere, that this wasn't a temporary arrangement.

But he had to tread carefully because he didn't want to scare her off, or have her think he was orchestrating things. Coming from the past she'd had, he could understand that, yet he knew what he wanted and the future he was beginning to envision for them looked enticing.

"You've left that past behind you, Savannah, and you're not living that life anymore. Out of something good, something solid, we can build something *more*." He threw his words out there and watched her absorb them.

She frowned and creases formed on her newly cleansed face. "But a baby is a huge responsibility." He knew there would be a 'but,' just as he understood that it was her way of dealing with things, that to come from the type of life she had had, anything good was masked in something that might later turn out not so good. He had come to understand that her 'buts' were her way of preparing herself, of pushing away the good things before they had a chance to take root because whenever life had been good, the bad had come not long after.

She stood up, then stepped back. "I don't know," she said, "It's too much to think about all at once."

"I'm sorry," he said, reaching out for her and she stepped closer. "I didn't mean to throw it at you all at once. It's just that..." Having her living alongside him made him want it all now. His arm coasted around the curve of her waist, gliding over the silky satin of her slip. He hugged her closer still and buried his face into her stomach, dropping a kiss on the fabric. He felt her fingers running softly through his head.

"You're a busy man, Tobias." Another objection. He tried to unravel the question behind those words.

"I will always make time for my family," he said, looking up at her.

"But your business is so demanding, and you have all sorts of pressures, going away on business, being away late nights."

*She was worried about that?*

"I'm a family man, not a player. I'm not my brother, or Matthias, or Colt," he told her solemnly. She stared at him as if she wasn't sure she believed him.

"And how would a baby fit into everything? My work, and Jacob, and the school runs? Which reminds me," she said, suddenly looking concerned. "I've got to pay for his summer day camp. He needs to return a form tomorrow so that he can go to the summer camp near his school, otherwise I'm going to be in trouble." She tried to pull away.

"Trouble? Why?"

"Childcare. No school means I've got to find a way of keeping him occupied."

"I'll remind you tomorrow," he said, pulling her towards him again.

"I'm seeing Brigitte next week," she said. "I could do with affordable childcare for summer." She grinned, but he didn't find it so amusing. He hated that she still struggled and scrimped, when he could give her the world. If only she'd let him.

"I'm in Seattle," he reminded her, "but you'll be fine. You only need to run your ideas by her and get some fundraising tips from her."

"But if I did manage to get that off the ground, how would I juggle that on top of everything else and a new baby?" She still didn't seem to comprehend that he could take all of her worries away, that dealing with children would never be an issue because he would get her a nanny, and money would never be a problem. But if she was expressing concerns, it meant that she was starting to think about it. It meant she hadn't dismissed the idea outright. It meant she might want the same thing he did.

"The same way it did before, when you had Jacob, and ran a house, and you were the breadwinner when your husband lost his job. You've done it before and you can do it again only this time you'll have all the help you need—and you'll have me." He hugged her closer, until her thighs were pressed against the mattress. He kissed her stomach again. "Just think about it," he said, dropping another kiss there, then moving his hands slowly over the curves of her outline. "It doesn't matter if you don't want to, Savannah. I understand that it's your choice, and I would be fine with that. And we have Jacob, so it's all fine." But just in case she might have been thinking where he wanted to take this, he needed to let her know.

"It's all so new," she said, squeezing his hand gently. "So much to think about."

"I know," he answered, reaching up and tracing his finger over her silk-draped breast, "but there's no rush." Her nipple sprung to attention under his touch and made his heart beat faster. After the kind of days he had been having at work lately, and Matthias walking around like a bear that had been attacked, coming home to this woman was his salvation. "I love having you in my life, Savannah."

His thumbs circled around her peaks and her voice turned softer. "I love being in it," she said, her voice barely a whisper.

The thought of being away from her for the whole week made him pull her even closer to him. His lips traced over the satin as he kissed her stomach through the soft material.

"I'll think about it," she promised him, her fingers gently tugging at his hair. She stepped back and pulled down the straps of her satin slip. "Move over," she said, as the flimsy material rippled off her body and collected in a soft heap at her feet.

His gaze slowly traveled across her body, naked except for her panties. "Take them off," he said, his voice husky, his fingers desperate to touch. She peeled them down, her eyes never once leaving his, then slid into bed, straddling him with her knees hugging his hips and her mouth sinking onto his.

# CHAPTER THIRTEEN

"I've ordered all the canapes and drinks," Candace told her. "Was there anything you wanted to change?"

"No," Savannah felt strange sitting in Candace's office talking about the party.

"You must be so excited!"

"Actually, I haven't had much time to think about it," confessed Savannah.

"Their parties were legendary, I mean—well, back in the day," Candace's voice petered off and she looked away quickly.

"Don't worry about it," said Savannah. For the past few months, Candace had thawed out and lost her iciness. If Savannah didn't know any better, she might have even thought that Candace was looking to become friends. "I've heard about the parties Tobias and Ivy used to have. I never really imagined him to be the partying type."

"It was before my time," Candace said. "I don't think they were wild events or anything, but just that they were both good hosts. Let's face it, if you were invited to a billionaire's party, would you decline?"

Savannah wasn't sure what she'd do. "It depends on who it was, and how well I knew them."

"I'd go," replied Candace, her eyes twinkling. "If I'd been invited, I'd definitely go. Who knows when you'd ever get such an opportunity again?"

"An opportunity for what?"

"To see how they live, what they eat and drink, how they party! To be inside a billionaire's home and walk around in it."

Savannah grinned, warming to Candace a little and thinking how alike she was to Kay.

"You must be living the dream now?" Candace said, admiration dripping from her voice.

"Uh—" Savannah didn't know how to respond even though this seemed to be the number one question most people asked her.

"It must be a different world."

Savannah wrung her hands together. It was a different world, it was truly the stuff of celebrity dreams, but the real difference for her, if she was being honest with herself, was being with a man as solid, and as steadfast, and as wonderful as Tobias. For her, it wasn't about the billionaire, it was about the man he was. To her, that was priceless. "It is," replied Savannah, seeing that Candace was waiting for her reply. "Are you coming?"

"I am most definitely coming," Candace replied with an enthusiasm that was never on display. "The party planner will oversee everything on the day and make sure the whole event is running well. I just have to show up and make sure she's doing *her* job well. It's one of the perks of being Tobias's PA."

"I bet it is," replied Savannah.

# CHAPTER FOURTEEN

With Tobias thousands of miles away in Seattle, Savannah felt on her own again, like a single parent once more. She missed talking to him, missed having him to discuss the day's news with, and this week especially, there seemed to be more to deal with.

The party arrangements seemed to be moving along smoothly despite her paltry contribution. She was secretly relieved that Candace had everything in hand.

She'd spent the last two days working on her notes for her meeting with Brigitte, not sure quite what to expect. By the time the day of her meeting arrived, she'd begun to lose hope and instead started to consider that her proposal was just a waste of time and effort.

She couldn't wait to get the meeting over and done with.

"But where's your plan?" Brigitte Obenchain's elegant outstretched hands, palms facing up, taunted Savannah.

"Well," said Savannah, shifting uncomfortably in her chair, "These are only my initial ideas." She tried hard not to shrink into her chair. She waved her hand over the neat-looking sheets of paper she'd placed on the desk and really wished that Tobias had been here with her instead of in Seattle. Tobias's little pep talk before she'd arrived had helped.

"You'll be fine," he'd told her.

As it turned out, Brigitte wasn't fine with her at all and had been less than friendly to Savannah from the moment she'd arrived.

"I had hoped that our meeting today would be a springboard for a discussion," replied Savannah, her spirits flagging. "I really just wanted to find out about your fundraising efforts and how you would go about it for something like this." Brigitte removed her burgundy designer reading glasses, which, Savannah noticed, were the color of her lipstick.

"But you don't need to fundraise," she exclaimed. "Not with someone like Tobias behind you. He could easily set up a number of such places." She peered at Savannah like an angry hawk, making her squirm in her seat.

"I—uh—well, Tobias thought it might be something we want to do, as you know he already has the Christmas—"

"So none of this is your idea?" Brigitte asked. "Do you mean to tell me that you're doing this because it's something your boyfriend suggested?"

"No," replied Savannah, secretly wondering the same thing herself. It had seemed like a good idea at the time, when Tobias had asked her what she'd do if money wasn't an issue, and when they'd been talking about the Christmas party he threw for the city's adoption centers. But did she really have the time or inclination to want to do something like this? It all seemed very noble and altruistic, setting up an affordable childcare center for single moms, but how the hell was she even going to get this off the ground? How could she, when she already had a nine-to-five job, a child, and now Tobias was hinting that he wanted to have a baby.

She'd been mulling over his words ever since, and slowly,

once the shock of it had passed, the more she thought about it, the more she realized that it wasn't such an impossibility any more, that having a baby with this man might be a wonderful thing for them all, Jacob included.

"It would be another way for Tobias to broaden his charitable causes. He gets so much out of hosting the party at the toy store for the children during Christmas, he wanted to know what I would do if I had the chance. It was very much *my* idea," she gave Brigitte a pointed look.

"Wouldn't you be happier lunching, or whatever it is you do?"

"Excuse me?" Savannah sat up, feeling as if she'd been punched in the face.

"I don't mean to be nasty," said Brigitte, picking up her glasses and bending them at the hinges.

"You just were. In fact, you were downright condescending."

Brigitte fluttered her lashes. "No, no, no," she said, smiling. "But, let's be honest here, Savannah, setting up a charity to make vacation childcare affordable for single moms on low income is a worthy gesture, and I'm sure there might be a few moms who could benefit from it, but why make your life difficult? It takes a lot of work running such a place. Getting it started in the first place is going to be an almighty hurdle, and then organizing events in order to raise money—let's be frank, I don't know why Tobias doesn't go ahead and write you a check. What do you know about low-income moms?"

"Because I was one once," replied Savannah indignantly, picking her papers up. She told her story to Brigitte of how she had struggled during the summer last year, when she had arrived in New York, looking for work. She'd only found short-term temporary contracts then, but each time she did, it had been Rosalee who had helped out with taking care of Jacob. The week Rosalee had gone to see her family, Savannah had to turn a contract down because she couldn't afford to pay for anyone to look after Jacob. She knew about desperate times; she knew what it felt like to be torn between the need to work and needing someone to take care of her child. She knew exactly what it was she would want to have in a daycare that would help out single moms.

Brigitte pushed her glasses on again. "Such a rags-to-riches story," she breathed, looking at Savannah with renewed interest. She steepled her fingers and remained pensive for a few moments. "How did you do it?"

"Do what?"

"Trap the most eligible bachelor in the world."

Anger scorched her face. "I didn't trap him," Savannah shot back, deciding in that instant that she was done with this woman. She started to gather her things together.

"What are you doing?" Brigitte cried.

"What I should have done five minutes after I arrived here," said Savannah slipping her pieces of paper in her leather folder. "Something tells me your attitude might have been different had Tobias been around." This woman had been a total bitch to her from the moment Savannah had walked into her oak-paneled office.

The woman's alabaster face turned a deep shade of crimson. "I was surprised when his PA informed me that you would be coming alone."

"I bet you were," Savannah sneered, her lips curling up at the corners as she battled through her feeling of humiliation. "Because if Tobias had been here, you might have even worn your contact lenses, then? Revealed more cleavage? Pretended that I was invisible even though I'd have sat next to him?"

Brigitte was wide-eyed like a deer as Savannah launched into her tirade. "Was that why you agreed to meet with me?"

asked Savannah, standing up. "Because you assumed you'd have his attention?" She was almost quaking in her shoes. She had been slow to realize it at first but she was becoming familiar with this reaction to her from other women. Jealous women, who hated her because she had what they wanted. "I am fully aware that sleeping with Tobias Stone will no doubt open many doors for me." Brigitte's mouth fell open. "This wouldn't be a problem if I were a gold-digger," said Savannah, "but thankfully I'm not. And, now that I think about it, it was Tobias who suggested that I meet with you in the first place. The fact is, I don't need to rely on your expertise because I have other contacts who would *kill* to be associated with a venture such as this. Imagine, Stone Enterprises endorsing it, Tobias Stone backing it—it can't fail, it won't fail. Imagine the publicity and goodwill, imagine partnering with such a worthy cause. Too bad you lost out."

The woman sat speechless.

While she didn't have any other contacts lined up, Savannah had met others at the gala dinner and Tobias had many contacts. She realized that this really couldn't fail—nothing would fail if Tobias was behind it. Meeting this condescending bitch today had served only to fuel her desire to see it through.

"There's no need to rush off like that," said Brigitte, quickly retracting her words. "Run me through it again, now that I know you have a real passion for this."

"You're obviously worried that I'll tell Tobias," said Savannah, feeling victorious all of a sudden, "And you'd be damn right too. I'll be sure to tell him *exactly* how this went down." She leaned over and stared directly into Brigitte's wide-open eyes. "It's an advantage of sleeping with the boss."

She didn't look back as she strutted out of the office, with her head held high and her heart racing. Savannah decided she didn't have time for this sort of nonsense anymore. It was past seven o'clock and it was time to go home to her son.

---

S avannah sat in the Merc staring out of the window. It took a while before her mind calmed down enough for her to check her phone for messages.

This was a fact of life. To be universally hated by women wherever she went. It was the price she had to pay for being with Tobias.

She turned to catch Morris looking away quickly. He'd been watching her, but he was always the epitome of discretion and never spoke unless spoken to. She smiled at him in the rearview mirror but he wasn't looking in her direction. His eyes were on the road and he remained as quiet and as unobtrusive as ever.

Here she was being chauffeur-driven home, driving past Tiffany & Co. on her right and going home to an apartment on the Upper East Side. She didn't have to worry about Jacob, not only because Rosalee was babysitting him, but because she knew security guards patrolled outside the apartment.

She was protected, loved and taken care of.

It was hard to believe sometimes how much her world had changed and many people, she assumed, had a hard time comprehending her rags-to-riches story. That wasn't quite her story, but to many, that was what they saw and it was what they wanted to believe. It was why they hated her before they even had the chance to get to know her.

She didn't care anymore about what people thought. She could live with their jealousy and hatred because any price was worth paying to be with the man she loved.

It was working out beautifully, and she was embarrassed to say that she'd become used to this life. While she was living with him, she'd become used to being driven to school in order to drop Jacob off, and then being driven to work. Tobias had insisted on it.

Jacob's summer break had begun, and she still had Rosalee pick Jacob up from his summer camp at the end of the day. On days such as today, when she knew she would be late, Morris would pick Rosalee and Jacob up and bring them to Tobias's apartment. There was no more worrying about how Rosalee got back home either, because Morris would see to it. And if Morris wasn't available, then one of Ludwig's men would take her back.

Savannah smiled in spite of the way her meeting had gone, because she was grateful and happy for everything that had happened in her life. She was still smiling when she walked into Tobias's apartment.

But one look at Jacob's and Rosalee's grim faces as they looked up at her from the couch made the hairs on the back of her neck crawl to standing. Another woman sat on the adjacent couch and turned to look at her. It was a face that Savannah instantly recognized from the tabloids.

Tobias's mother.

# CHAPTER FIFTEEN

M illicent Stone was the last person Savannah had expected to see and after the crappy day she'd had, she was the last person Savannah *wanted* to see.

"Hello, my dear," said Millicent, rising from the couch gracefully. Her cool gray eyes appeared to examine Savannah slowly from top to bottom. Savannah instinctively smoothed down her hair.

"Mrs. Stone," she said, offering her hand. "So nice to meet you at last." Tobias's mother was thin and well groomed, with no plump or cuddly curves, unlike her mother. A handshake seemed appropriate but to her surprise, Millicent offered her outstretched arms.

"Nonsense," she said, enclosing Savannah in a forced hug. "Let's drop the formality. Call me Millicent."

Over the woman's shoulder, Savannah saw Rosalee's unsmiling face and she gave her babysitter an apologetic roll of her eyes. Then, not wanting to keep Rosalee longer than was necessary, she excused herself politely while she saw Rosalee to the door. Jacob came bounding over to say goodbye, partly, she suspected, in an effort to escape. Savannah called Morris to let

him know that her babysitter was on her way down and ready to
be dropped back home.

"A late day at the office?" Millicent asked, when she
returned with Jacob in tow.

"Yes," Savannah replied. Then, turning to her son, "How
was your day, honey?"

"'Sgood," replied Jacob, a little shyly and she realized it was
because Millicent was there.

"Why don't you go play for a little while," she told him,
"before I put you to bed." She hoped her instruction would be
enough of a hint to Millicent to keep her visit short. Jacob ran
off, leaving the two women alone.

"Can I get you something to drink?" Savannah asked. "Iced
tea or soda?"

"Thank you but no," replied Millicent. "I'm meeting friends
for a late dinner and I ought to save myself for that."

*She wouldn't be staying too long, then.*

"Sit down, my dear," Millicent instructed, and Savannah
found herself doing just that. To her dismay, Millicent sat
beside her, on the same couch but at a respectable distance.

"I think it's high time we got to know one another. I keep
telling that son of mine to bring you over but he seems to be too
busy these days."

"Tobias is away in Seattle," Savannah explained.

"So I discovered," Millicent replied. "Your housekeeper
told me."

"Rosalee isn't my housekeeper," said Savannah, her eyes
drawn to the powder blue ring of pearls around Millicent's
neck. Matching earrings, too. She couldn't help but admire the
woman's elegance and composure. Tobias's mother was
groomed to perfection, in a cream two-piece skirt and jacket
with not a single hair in her silver-gray bob out of place. It was
such a contrast to her own mother who was more at home in

loose pants and a blouse. Slacks, if she really wanted to make an effort.

"She's not?" Millicent asked.

"She watches Jacob when I need her."

"But she's your cousin's housekeeper, I understand." Her reply took Savannah back. She couldn't see Rosalee volunteering that information readily. "That's right."

"And your cousin has now returned?"

"Which you obviously know." Savannah smiled, even though she felt slightly unnerved by Millicent's interrogation skills. She could see a small part of Tobias in her. Maybe it was the forehead, or the way she seemed to coolly observe Savannah, looking at her with the same intensity that Tobias often did.

"I'm sorry you've missed him," she said again, feeling that they had already run out of conversation. "Tobias will be back on Friday." *In case you wanted to come back then.*

"That's quite all right," replied Millicent, sitting all prim and proper and folding one leg elegantly over the other. "I was more interested in meeting you." She looked entirely at ease.

Unlike Savannah.

"Here we are," said Savannah, smiling as best as she could and wondering what to talk about next.

"This must be a welcome change for you, I would imagine," Millicent said, looking around the spacious living room.

"It's only temporary."

"Temporary?"

"I'm looking for an apartment. Something affordable for me and Jacob."

"And you couldn't find anything," Millicent murmured, then smiled. "I imagine the search must have slowed down so as to be practically nonexistent."

Savannah was starting to hate that smile. "I'm still looking, Millicent," she replied, humiliated at the implication Tobias's mother was making. Though she hadn't looked lately. "I think it might be better if you came back when Tobias returns."

"Nonsense," Millicent retorted. "I'm here now and I'm delighted to meet you. I must admit I've been rather curious about you. We've heard so much about you, which is strange in itself because Tobias rarely speaks about the women he sees."

This surprised Savannah because she couldn't imagine Tobias telling his mother anything, going by the way he often spoke about her.

"The tabloids are talking about wedding bells," Millicent continued. "Should I be prepared for an announcement at this party he's suddenly decided to throw?"

"I wouldn't know."

Millicent stared at her, as if Savannah was hiding something. "As for the tabloids, they like to speculate about a lot of things," Savannah replied, finding it difficult to sit still. She fought the urge to get up and pace around the room but knew that to do so would invite Millicent to examine her more closely, and Savannah didn't relish the thought of being examined too closely by Millicent Stone. "I wouldn't believe everything they say."

"They're often right. I don't believe there's any smoke without fire, do you?" She fixed her gaze on Savannah again, making her fidgety.

"I've seen plenty of smoke without fire," returned Savannah.

"Have you? I'm not so sure I agree. What about the escort?" Millicent shivered in disgust. "I even met her on one occasion. We ran into them outside Nobu." She looked away horrified, as if Naomi was doing a striptease in front of her now. "They weren't wrong about that, were they?"

Savannah bit her teeth together. "That's something you might want to bring up with Tobias," she replied. "It's not something for me to comment on."

Millicent touched her string of pearls. "Ellery and I were shocked to read about it. We had no idea." She composed herself quickly and turned to Savannah. "It must have come as a complete shock to you, I imagine?"

"On the contrary," replied Savannah. "Tobias had already told me about Naomi very early on. When that story broke, it only made us closer."

"I'm sure it's not too much of a stretch for you to feel closer to my son. I expect Tobias is a great catch for any woman lucky enough to have him. But any relationship has to be balanced."

"I'm not sure what you mean, Millicent, and respectfully, what Tobias and I have should not concern you." The woman narrowed her eyes at her and Savannah couldn't fathom the expression on her face.

*Was that a warning?* Millicent angled her head as if considering matters. "His father and I don't want him to make a mistake."

"I don't consider myself to be his *mistake*, but I'll bear that in mind."

"I don't want to get off to a wrong start, Savannah."

"Then don't make offensive remarks."

"I was merely being upfront. You seem clever and you've obviously made inroads where many have failed in the past."

This after Brigitte was too much to take in the space of one evening. Savannah had had enough. "You appear not to like me, Mrs. Stone, and it seems you've come here knowing Tobias would be away. What was your intention?" she asked. "Did you hope to warn me off?"

"That's ridiculous."

"I love your son, and that's about all I'm willing to say to you on the matter."

Millicent's face was hard and emotionless. "Tobias is a prize catch and as his mother, I want to make sure he's not getting himself into a situation that isn't good for him."

"That isn't up to you."

"That may be," replied Millicent, "but it doesn't mean I won't do my best to protect him. You have a son, you know what it's like. I don't want to see him get hurt again."

"Then you must be mistaken for thinking I would want to hurt him."

Millicent sniffed and got up. "I have a dinner date," she said, completely off topic. "And I must leave. We'll meet again at the party, no doubt."

"No doubt we will."

# CHAPTER SIXTEEN

Had life been this difficult before, or had she simply become used to having Tobias around? Last night, she badly missed Tobias. It would have helped to have discussed her ordeals with Brigitte and his mother.

As it was, she didn't tell him a thing when they spoke on the phone later after Jacob had gone to bed. It wouldn't be fair to complain to him when he was so far away and he sounded so busy and worn out. She couldn't wait for him to get back.

Lunch with Briony the next day was a good second alternative, and when her friend suggested they go to Battery Park, it seemed like the perfect escape. But before she could tell her friend what had happened, Briony got in there first.

"She's feeling broody," mumbled Briony.

Savannah lifted her head, immediately discarding the conversation with Millicent that she'd been thinking about. "Who?" she asked, surprised. "Max?"

"Yes, Max," her friend replied sullenly. "Of all the things in the world, she wants a *child.*" She looked away, staring at the Statue of Liberty in the distance. "All of a sudden, a puppy seems more attractive."

"A child? You mean as in...as in a *baby?*" Savannah asked, unsure how these things worked in same-sex couples.

"She says she feels motherly and has been for a while now and she couldn't keep it locked away any longer."

"Huh." Savannah was still trying to process the idea of the fashionable and high-flying Max as a mother.

"I know," said Briony, biting into her apple. "It's hard to wrap your head around it. Imagine how I feel." Briony chewed slowly. "This is the last thing I thought I'd be dealing with."

"Obviously, you're not for it, then?"

"Obviously, clearly, most definitely, absolutely *not*, but I love her, and I'll give her anything she wants." Savannah listened, knowing what that was like. She pondered how ironic their situations were. Tobias's talk of wanting a baby made her heart jump each time she thought of it. A slow warmth radiated through her, a feeling of belonging, of taking root, of a solid and stable future beckoning, and one that heralded new beginnings. That's what his talk of wanting a baby with her had done—it had made her think about all this and more.

Even though they hadn't discussed it since, and she had continued to take her pills, Tobias's wish had planted a seed in her mind, and she now found herself wondering what it would be like to have another baby—with him.

It would be so different than how it had been when she'd gotten pregnant with Jacob. No fighting, or tears, or feelings of utter despair this time.

She was starting to believe that this wasn't a short-term romance any more. Tobias made her feel as if she was 'the one' and her initial fears—that he would soon move on, that with women everywhere eyeing him as if he was a prized stud, his sights could easily wander and that she'd be history—those fears slowly dissolved like aspirin in water.

In the beginning, she'd been wary, taking each step slowly,

trying not to imagine a future she wasn't sure she would ever have. But lately, everything he said or did indicated that he wanted her by his side for the long haul.

She knew what he meant to her, and she dared to imagine a future with him by her side, but it was harder to figure out what his intentions for her might be. The damage Colt had done had made her hard and she had learned to insulate herself well, so that she was prepared, in case the life she sometimes dreamed of didn't materialize and the life she was afraid of did. She'd been living in her self-preservation mode just fine until Tobias Stone had come along and shattered all her assumptions about life and what was possible.

With each passing day, she realized that she could no longer imagine a life without him, and everything else, all the negative points of being with him—the media intrusion, an exposed life, his *mother*—all of that, she would have to learn to deal with.

"I'm so glad we came out for lunch," said Briony.

"Me too," replied Savannah. They sat on a park bench in Battery Park, and Ellis Island and the Statue of Liberty stared back at them. The Brooklyn Bridge stood tall and proud in the skyline and vendors selling food and souvenirs, and drawing caricature paintings, enticed the tourists to part with their money.

"I didn't want kids, never have and those maternal instincts of hers would have remained buried had it not been for you."

"Me?" asked Savannah, surprised.

"I blame you for this." Briony narrowed her eyes and looked at her. "It's all Jacob's fault. Max adores him. I keep telling her that Jacob is an exception, that not all kids are as well-behaved."

"Thank you," said Savannah, smiling. Her son was the center of her universe, except that her universe had now shifted, and she had room for Tobias, and more.

"What am I going to do?" Briony wailed, gesticulating

wildly with the half-eaten apple still in her hand. Savannah scrunched up her empty sandwich box.

"Would it be so bad?" she asked, softly.

"It would change everything."

"Do you really not want kids at all? Because if you don't, then it would be wrong to do this just because you want to make Max happy."

"I've never wanted them," replied Briony, staring down at her lap. "But Max has always been good with kids. I never realized it before. I projected my ideal of not wanting children in *my* life onto her. I thought ours was going to be a lifetime of skiing vacations, and cruises, and exploring Europe and South America and Africa. Of going on treks and adventures unencumbered by whining, crying kids."

"They grow up," Savannah told her. *They grow up so fast, you'll want to hit the pause button.* "They mostly only cry when they're babies, and if they want something."

"I don't have anything to give!" Briony hung her head, looking as if her world had ended. "And the headache doesn't stop then, does it? At least that's what my mother continues to tell me, even now. She says she's always worried about me. She made me feel as if I was a burden to her and she made me think that her life had stopped because I'd come along and ruined all her plans."

"Moms sometimes say things they don't mean when things get on top of them," said Savannah, gently pressing her hand on Briony's arm for comfort.

"I can't imagine you ever saying something like that to Jacob, and goodness knows you've been through enough miserable situations in your life."

Savannah tried her best to offer comfort. "She might not have meant it in that way. Perhaps your mom was just worried about things, maybe she was worried about your sexuality and she believed that things might be tougher for you than others. Maybe she was trying to protect you." Briony shook her head, as if she didn't believe her.

"I know you're trying to help, but you haven't met my mom. I would imagine that mothers never stop worrying about their children but her worries are more to do with the shame of who I am than anything else."

She was right. A mother didn't. Her own mother had told her as much. Her parents worried about her when she'd met Colt, they worried about her when she had Jacob, then they worried even more when her marriage had failed. Goodness knows how much they had worried about her when she left home and ventured out to the Big Apple with a son in tow, and with her being a single mom at that.

From the moment she'd given birth to him, she'd worried about Jacob all her life. When he was a baby, she worried whether he'd had enough milk, whether she'd weaned him too early, or dressed him in too many layers. She worried that he might be too hot, too cold, too tired, too bored. When he'd been a toddler, she worried if the arguments between her and Colt would affect him. When she returned to work, she worried about not spending enough time with him, and when she left her hometown, she worried if she was doing the right thing by him, or whether having a bad father was worse than having no father at all. When she arrived in New York, she worried about his new school and his new friends, and worried whether he would fit in, and when that passed, she worried about his asthma.

And these days there wasn't much to worry about at all, but she worried anyway. She worried that he was starting to feel too comfortable, and that he was getting too attached to living with Tobias and she worried about how hard it would be to leave. She worried about Henry Carson, and worried about him leaving school, starting over and above all, she constantly worried if she was doing the right thing.

*Stay here as long as you want, until you find the perfect place.* Tobias's words echoed around her. The problem was, she *had* found the perfect place—and it was by his side. With each passing day, she became more accustomed to living with him, so much so that she'd stopped looking for new apartments for a while.

Everything was on stable ground and living with him just fit. It was more than perfect. And now he wanted a baby. She touched her stomach each time she thought about it. Knew that perhaps it was time to completely let go of the fear, of her habit of not quite allowing herself to believe that something this good, a man this wonderful, could belong to her.

"Why are you grinning?" asked Briony. "It's not funny. I really don't want the responsibility of a child on my shoulders. I'm selfish and I like doing things for me." She placed her hand on her chest, her brows inching together. "I like Broadway shows, and the opera, and I like wine-tasting evenings. If I want dim sum at 3:00 a.m. I know where to go. If I want to ski in Colorado, I can book a flight and take off right now, work leave notwithstanding. If we had a child to worry about, we would be bound. We'd be restricted and we couldn't do *any* of those things."

"You get a heap of good things in return," Savannah pointed out.

"But I don't even know how to change a diaper!" Briony stared at Savannah again, "And don't you tell me you can teach me these things. Making sushi at home is something I would choose to learn, learning how to change a diaper is *not*."

"She's really serious about this? About wanting a baby?" Savannah wondered how the other part of the baby-making equation would work out.

"We haven't discussed the finer details, because we end up having an argument. She's not sure herself, and I can't tell if we're talking about adopting a child or the need to go to sperm banks and find a prime specimen. Jesus," said Briony, wiping her forehead in disgust. "I thought I was done with sperm forever."

Savannah suppressed an untimely giggle. "You're scared because you think it's going to be bad," she said. "I get that you never intended to have children in your life, but if sticking to that means you and Max might go your separate ways, then you have to weigh up what you want against what it means to lose her. But also remember that children are with you for life and you can't return them if you get fed up or no longer want them."

"I know." Briony gave a half-shrug. "I've tried to reach a compromise." She leaned forward on the bench, craning her neck as she closed her eyes and let her face soak up the sunshine. "I told her we could get a Chihuahua." She opened her eyes and grinned at Savannah, and they both burst out laughing but she sobered up quickly. "She wasn't too happy with that and I was in the dog house for a few hours." She laughed at her own joke. "Dog house, get it?" Savannah smiled back, but imagined how awkward the situation was. How potentially threatening such an issue could be to their relationship which to her had always looked so solid. Briony turned suddenly serious. "I don't want to lose her, hon."

"You won't," Savannah said, putting her arm around Briony and hugging her. "You two are crazy about one another, and you can figure this out. If she means the world to you, you'll find a way."

Luckily, she and Tobias didn't have that problem.

"How are things with you?" Briony asked. "How did your meeting go with that woman, Brigitte what's-her-name?"

Savannah groaned. She wasn't in the mood to talk about Brigitte Obenchain. "Not very well. I don't think she likes me."

"I wonder why," Briony replied sarcastically. "You have to expect that, hon. I already told you. Women are a jealous breed, so are men, but women hold onto it for longer."

"She doesn't like me and I kind of stormed out, told her I'd find other like-minded people."

"You did?" Briony looked pleased.

"I told her that sleeping with Tobias had its advantages, and I'd be sure to tell him how unhelpful she was."

Briony clapped her hands together. "You're finally getting all territorial over him, aren't you, hon?"

Savannah shrugged.

"Why are you doing this thing anyway? Why would you want to open a vacation childcare center? I don't even know what that is," said Briony. "Though judging how my life could go, I might have a need for one later."

"If I could have had access to affordable childcare during the summer breaks, it would have taken a lot of stress off me."

"Kids have summer camp, don't they?"

"And they cost a lot. Sometimes it's not even worth working because you have to pay so much just to have your child looked after. I might as well stay at home for summer and look after him myself."

"So you figured on setting something like this up?"

"We were talking about Tobias's Christmas charity and he asked me what I would do if money wasn't an issue. I know something like that would have helped me. Mind you, it was after the gala dinner, when I'd met all these people who were raising funds for some great charities, and it was while Tobias and I were in Miami and I think I got slightly carried away."

"Sun, sea and sex. I bet it was easy to get carried away," muttered Briony.

Savannah blushed, because it had been all of those things, in heavy doses. "I'm not so sure I can really pull this off."

"You sure it wasn't Tobias's idea?"

"No! It was mine. Why?"

"You'll have to find something to do when he knocks you up and puts that ring on your finger." Savannah colored, and turned away, not liking the way Briony phrased her thoughts.

"Something I said, hon?" said Briony, when Savannah didn't respond right away.

"I know that's what you think," Savannah said slowly, staring at the Statue of Liberty in the distance. "And whether those are his intentions or not, I don't know. But I *can* tell you that Tobias is a very cautious man. He doesn't rush into anything. Every move he makes is calculated. He thinks five steps ahead of everyone. We haven't known each other that long." She turned to her friend. "And do you know something?" she said, realizing it for herself in that instant. "I've lived my life from paycheck to paycheck, from one scary moment to the next, unplanned, and not knowing what I was going to do next. I've had to be reactive rather than proactive because I didn't have the money, or strength to make the decisions that needed to be made. And Tobias, being exactly the type of man he is, isn't such a bad thing. For the first time ever, I'm not living out of fear. And if he's thinking ahead, and putting things into place, I find it comforting. I think of myself as lucky to have met someone like him. Do you know how scary life is when you don't even know if you'll be able to make rent next month? When you have to make groceries stretch an extra week because you don't get paid until the end of the month? I've been there, and I never want to be there again."

They sat in subdued silence for a moment. "I'd better head back," said Savannah. "Candace had a few things she wanted to go over about the party."

"We're looking forward to it," said Briony. "I'd bet a thousand dollars there's going to be an announcement."

"Why don't you just give me that thousand dollars?" suggested Savannah, picking up her trash as she stood up.

"You wait and see," Briony told her.

# CHAPTER SEVENTEEN

"I like coming here," Jacob announced. Tobias had arrived late last night and this morning they were back at The Bluebell for Saturday brunch.

"I like it too," Tobias agreed. "It's getting to be quite a tradition with us, isn't it?"

"What's a tradition?"

"It's like when you follow something, or when you do something with a group of people and you do it many times. Like at Christmas, when Santa leaves the presents under your tree, and you all get up the next day and open them together. That's a tradition. That's what it's like, when you pass things down."

"Down where?"

"Down from my parents to me, and then," he paused. "And then maybe I could, *we* could," he looked at Savannah, "we could pass it down to you, whatever the tradition was."

"So coming to this place is a tradition?"

"No," he replied, "but coming here the day *after* I return from a business trip seems to be."

"Did you go in your private plane?"

"Yes."

"Where?"

"To Seattle, then Houston, then back home."

Coming home to these two made all the lonely days, the power deals and hard negotiations worthwhile. Jacob had been asleep when he'd arrived back late last night and Savannah had waited up for him. They'd talked for a while, catching up on each other's week, but he'd fallen asleep soon after and there had been no time yet for a proper welcome.

"You're going to fly in that plane soon," Tobias told him. "When we to go Miami, after the party."

"I can come this time?"

"You know you can, Jacob," Savannah exclaimed. "No summer day camp for three weeks."

His eyes sparkled. "Three whole weeks?"

"It's going to be great, you wait and see," Tobias told him. "How's school been, buddy?" But Jacob paused before answering.

"Jacob?" Savannah asked.

"'Sbeen good," he replied, but Tobias could see through it.

"Just good?"

"Jacob Samuel Page," said Savannah. Yeah, he was going to have to do something about changing that surname too. Jacob Samuel Stone had a nice ring to it.

"What's up, buddy?" he asked, as the server came over to take their order.

"Hey, Mr. Stone." Tobias jerked his head up and glared. "Hey, guys," he said, overly familiar and cheesy. "Do you all know what you're having this morning?"

"Not yet, could we have a few moments?" Tobias replied.

"Sure," he replied, and then "Were you looking at properties in the Upper East Side?" he asked.

Tobias looked at the man with a mixture of surprise and suspicions. "You're here to take my order."

"Yes, sir. But would you care to comment anyway?"

"Comment on what?" Tobias snarled. What did it take to even have breakfast in peace? He could see his bodyguards rushing towards him. "Jacob, buddy. What are you having?" Tobias asked, ignoring the reporter, because he knew for certain that this man was an imposter.

Jacob sank lower in his seat, his expression somber. "Hey," said Tobias, reaching for his arm gently. "Sit up, buddy. Don't be scared. It's okay." In the next moment, his bodyguards had each grabbed the server's arms and dragged him towards the door. He didn't go easily or quietly and a commotion ensued. Diners turned and stared.

"What do you think you're doing?" the imposter cried but Tobias's men were cold, like robots. They threw him out and stood over him, preventing him from re-entering the café. A slow murmur spread around the café, and Tobias was familiar with that hush, followed by the prodding elbows, and stolen glances in his direction. People were realizing he was in their midst, and who he was with.

Another, not wearing a server's apron but a shirt and dressy slacks, rushed to Tobias. "We're so sorry, sir. I don't know how he walked in here and ..."

Tobias waved his hand at him.

"I'm the manager here, sir, and if there's anything I can do to make—"

Tobias's gut twisted as he shook his head with silent rage. Another breach of security and with Savannah and Jacob by his side. He wasn't happy. He held up his finger to silence the blubbering manager.

"We don't want to lose your patronage," the man blabbered on in the background.

"You won't lose it, if you give me some peace," Tobias hissed, shaking with fury. The man scampered away without a further word.

"What just happened?" Savannah asked, looking fearful again. He closed his eyes for a brief second, hoping this hadn't frightened her off. It would not do to have her take another step backwards.

"He was a sleazy undercover reporter rat scavenging for news," Tobias replied, searching her face for her reaction. It was important to know how she felt about these things because they would happen every now and then because his guards couldn't always be next to him twenty-four-seven. Nor did he relish the idea of having them around him like a second skin.

What had happened was rare but it served only to reinforce his awareness that there was heightened interest in him now because of his love life. Ludwig had briefed him about the press and its ongoing speculation about his relationship. Now the rumors had shifted to an impending proposal and wedding and he was going to outsmart them. Unfortunately, incidents like this one would only increase over time.

"Was that man lying about who he was?" Jacob asked, staring out of the window where a small crowd had gathered.

"Unfortunately, Jacob, people do that sometimes."

"Is it because of who you are?"

"Who am I?" Tobias asked, bemused.

"A filthy rich man."

"Jacob!" Savannah cautioned.

Tobias peered closely at the boy who appeared to shrink back in his seat. He smiled. "Who told you that, buddy?"

"That's what Henry Carson said."

"Have you invited that little—" He paused, changing his choice of words, "that little boy to our party?"

Jacob nodded. "I didn't want to, but I did because you said to."

"Good boy, Jacob. Is he coming?"

"I don't know, he didn't say but everyone else is."

Tobias turned to Savannah. "Did Candace give you an update about the RSVPs?"

"Mostly everyone is coming," she replied, giving him an incredulous look. "Surprisingly, only two have declined, and they're your mastermind buddies, who are out of the country. Plus, we're still waiting to hear from the Carsons."

He wasn't surprised, most people showed up.

"Were they your security guards?"

"Yes," replied Tobias.

"Are they always around?" Jacob sounded impressed.

"All the time, buddy."

"Cool! You mean I never have to be scared again?"

"What are you scared of?" Savannah asked, turning to him.

"Nothing, no more," said Jacob. "We saw your mom!" he told Tobias, his exuberance returning.

"My mom?" Tobias turned to her in surprise. "When?" And how come Savannah hadn't mentioned anything last night?

"She came over a few days ago, when I got back from meeting Brigitte."

"You never told me."

Savannah smiled. "You only got back last night, I didn't want to talk about that." She hadn't said much, not about the meeting with Brigitte Obenchain. Even when he probed, she'd had other things to distract him with, and he'd been happy enough to let her.

"I don't know why she did that," complained Tobias. "She knew I was away."

"I thought she might."

"I'm sorry you had to deal with her alone."

"Don't be sorry," Savannah replied. "She was nice."

He snorted with laughter. "That's impossible," said Tobias, "You mentioning my mother and 'nice' in the same sentence. You don't have to lie about her, Savannah. I know what she can be like."

"She kept asking me about school, and who my friends were," Jacob told him.

"Yeah," said Tobias, feeling disgruntled. "That's exactly what my mom would do."

"Rosalee doesn't like her neither!" Jacob added.

"Jacob!" admonished Savannah. "Rosalee never said anything of the sort."

"She doesn't like her," Jacob persisted. "Your mom wanted to know if she was a cleaning lady or a cook."

"I called Rosalee later and apologized," explained Savannah.

"That's my mother all over," groaned Tobias.

"I see now why you say she's an acquired taste."

"What does that mean?" asked Jacob.

"It means," said Tobias, running his eyes over the menu, "that not everyone will like her. She takes some getting used to."

"I think I might have to get used to her," said Jacob agreeing.

"Jacob! What is it with you this morning?" Savannah sounded shocked. "Don't be so disrespectful."

"What did I say?" asked Jacob, turning red as he lowered his head, no doubt knowing from the tone of his mother's voice that he'd said something wrong.

Tobias chortled. "It's not his fault," he told Savannah. "I've learned that there's no bullshit with kids. Sorry, buddy," he said, knowing he'd committed the cardinal sin of swearing. "Children tell it as it is and they never dress things up. I like that."

"Your mother wasn't *that* bad," said Savannah.

"Now *you're* dressing it up," he said, taking her hand. "You can be honest with me."

"She could have been worse is what I mean." Savannah explained, still obviously trying to rectify the situation, and he appreciated that she did. He tugged at her hand and dropped a kiss on her lips.

"I love you," he murmured, and he didn't care who saw or heard him. "You don't have to make excuses for my mother. I know exactly what she's like." He turned to Jacob. "Knowing her, I bet she probably interrogated you."

The boy nodded his head vigorously. "And she probably interrogated Rosalee. I'll have to apologize to her when I see her. Is she coming to the party?"

"They all are. Her son and his wife and her grandson," Savannah replied.

"Diego's coming?" Jacob asked excitedly.

"Yes, he is."

"Maybe I'll apologize to her in person. Maybe," he said, "I'll embarrass my mother in front of her."

"Tobias," said Savannah. "You'll do no such thing."

"My mother thinks she's above some people. And that's not acceptable to me. I know she stopped by to look you over."

"She's a mother. I'd probably do the same if I were in her shoes."

"Not like she did," he countered. "I'd rather not let our weekend go downhill talking about my mother all day long."

"What are we doing today?" asked Jacob.

"We can do anything you like, buddy, but first we need to order some food. I was under the impression we came here to eat."

Jacob giggled.

"I was going to meet with the realtor," said Savannah.

He looked up.

*Not that business again.*

She'd hadn't mentioned anything lately and he'd believed that she might have stopped looking. "This wouldn't have anything to do with my mother, would it?"

"No."

"You're not a good liar, Savannah," he said. "As it happens, I need to visit the realtor too."

"What for?" she asked, surprised. "Is that what the reporter was talking about?"

"Who cares what he was talking about. He was digging for more information."

"But was he onto something?" she asked, probing.

"He must have found out, these rats often do, that I looked at a few properties before I went away," he replied, mesmerized by the flecks of amber in her eyes.

"Those big residential properties you mentioned before?" Savannah asked.

"That's right, but they'd also be for investment purpose, obviously," he replied. A family home was an investment. "And I'd like you both to tell me what you think of them."

# CHAPTER EIGHTEEN

She had only seen multi-million-dollar homes on TV or in magazines and had never even considered how much they cost because they were in another stratosphere. Yet this afternoon, Tobias had taken her and Jacob to see a couple that he liked.

And she'd understood for the first time—really understood— the difference between their worlds. Where she'd been fretting over apartments that cost around $2,000 a month, Tobias had shown her properties that had a lot of zeros in the number.

Homes that were a lot of money. Amounts-she-couldn't-get-her-head-around type of money. They were more like buildings than homes, so vast and sprawling that they were almost as big as Kay's entire apartment building, if not bigger. One of the properties had so many floors, she soon lost count. She even forgot what floor she was on. She felt as if she was trawling around an empty department store, it was that big.

She couldn't understand why Tobias wanted something so big. What would he do with so many bedrooms and so many bathrooms? *Wouldn't he feel lost and lonely in that big rambling building?*

And then she wondered, what with all his talk of the future, whether he had it in that calculating head of his for her and Jacob to move in. And even if they did, and added another twenty people, even then the place would still be too big.

"It's that time of night, is it?" he asked, joining her in the bathroom as she rubbed the new serum that Briony had recommended into her face and neck. Apparently, it was supposed to take years off her appearance.

"What time of night?" She looked at his reflection in the mirror. "This, you mean?" She picked up the dark bottle. "According to Briony, it's going to take years off my age."

He stood behind her, with his chest to her back and smelled her neck, inhaling the scent of her body lotion while his hands traveled lightly along her stomach. "I love you just the way you are," he said, brushing his lips along her shoulder blades. "And I wouldn't change anything about you." She shivered in anticipation as his words seduced her and tiny goosebumps popped up all over her arms.

"I think your mother might have a different opinion." His hands stilled below her navel.

"I don't care for her opinion much," he murmured. "You're all that matters." He dropped a kiss along the side of her neck, and she arched her back, pushing her shoulder blades into his chest. She moaned softly as he cupped her breast over her silky nightgown. "She may not seem like it but I promise you she's harmless, despite her mouth."

She took a hold of his forearms and held them securely around her, loving the feel of him behind her.

"Did that scare you today, the reporter?" he asked.

"I can deal with that." Because it was a part and parcel of his world, and she knew she would have to, whether she liked it or not. She turned around and put her arms around his waist and moved in closer.

"I'm sorry you had such a tough time of it while I was gone." She'd told him in detail about her meeting with Brigitte and then the conversation with his mother.

"I'm used to fighting my own battles," she whispered, sliding her arms around his neck, "but I did miss you." He brushed his lips over hers then stilled.

"I'm sorry Brigitte gave you such a hard time."

She groaned. Thinking about the whole single mom's initiative made her feel wary. But if she got pregnant, and they had a baby, she wouldn't go back to work for a while. Being with Tobias meant she never really had to work ever again but she wasn't a lady who lunched. She'd always been busy. Her whole life she'd been used to *doing* things.

She pondered what Briony had said, that this was Tobias's idea. That having her do some charitable work on the side would keep her busy. She looked at him, at the questioning gaze on his face, and wondered.

"She hates me," replied Savannah. "And I don't care. I'll find someone else to help me." She traced the outline of his lips with her tongue.

"That's the spirit," he said, moving his lips over hers and teasing her slowly with his tongue until their mouths meshed together, soft and wet. He kissed her slowly, his hands exploring underneath her nightgown and feeling her body with an urgency he often had when he returned after a business trip. "I haven't had a chance to show you how much I missed you," he said, brushing his lips over hers fleetingly then moving them away, teasing her and ratcheting up her heart rate slowly.

"I was thinking the same thing," she said, moving her hands to the waistband of his boxers.

"Jacob loved the houses," he murmured.

"Who wouldn't?" she asked, the fire around her body spreading to the far corners, making her toes curl, and her breasts heavy. She eased her fingers inside his waistband. But he stilled her hands with his.

"What did *you* think?"

"You mean after I stepped through the main entrance? Or as we drove up to them? Or as we walked around and I got lost? I thought I was in another world." She looked into his face, saw that he was listening carefully, had come to recognize when he was hanging on her every word. Knew that he tiptoed around her, that he always wanted to do the best for her.

"They were nothing like the properties I've been looking at," she said.

"I guess not. But which one do you like the most?"

Her brows knitted together. "I—I guess both of them."

"But which *one?*"

"The one with eight stories was huge."

"And the other one? The one with three townhouses that I'm thinking of combining into one?"

"Isn't it big? For just you?"

"It's not just for me, I was hoping it would be for all of us, Savannah. You, me and Jacob."

Which was what Briony had told her, and she'd come to suspect as much, and so him saying it didn't come as a complete shock. But it still left her speechless, and all she could think of was how long it would take to clean those properties.

"I can't live my life without you in it, Savannah. You and Jacob, I need you with me. I love you both, and so I would like for us all to live together, if that's something that you might perhaps want to think about. Especially since you're also looking for a place to stay."

Her skin tingled as if dandelion blowballs had brushed along it and a flush of adrenaline through her body made her a little giddy.

"I want to start in a new place, make new memories and put

the past behind me, Savannah. It *is* behind me, and has been ever since I met you, but I need to physically move to a new place, and I would very much like for you both to move with me. We'll make a home, a real home, for us, and who knows..." He paused. "Who knows what the future might hold?"

She was overcome with a rush of emotions, overwhelm and gratitude and happiness. "I would live with you anywhere, Mr. Stone," she finally said, when she had composed herself enough. "Even in a shed." *Even in a tent, in a caravan, in a one-bedroom apartment.*

He moved away a lock of her hair. "You would?"

"Without hesitation."

He looked at her curiously, the corners of his lips creeping upwards, not yet breaking out into a smile but they could, depending on her answer. "Are you easily accepting my proposal? That you'll live with me and stop looking for an apartment?"

"Yes." If that was what he wanted. His hand skated along her back and over her bottom, squeezing both cheeks, which was something she noticed he liked to do.

"You like doing that, don't you?" she asked.

"This?" He squeezed again, this time slightly harder. He liked feeling her up, more so if he'd been away. It was as if he was familiarizing himself with the feel of her body all over again. He captured her lower lips between his, then sucked it, slowly teasing her mouth with his tongue, before he kissed her deeply, their mouths crushing, firing up her body with tiny sparks of fire. "How about that," he murmured, pausing for air and staring at her as if he didn't want to let go. "You agreeing to live with me—not *temporarily* either—and without a fight."

"I don't always fight you," she said, her voice husky. But there had been something about today, about them all coming together and having brunch, about discussing the future and looking at homes together that had finally hit home. Maybe Millicent and Brigitte warning her off had made her all the more determined to hold on to what she had.

"But you don't always agree so easily, either," he whispered, his hardness pressing into her.

"I really missed you while you were away, and I've been thinking about a lot of things."

"That makes both of us," he said, stroking her shoulder. "And?"

"And being with you is better than being away from you," she said, looking at his lips.

"I came to that conclusion months ago," he said, his fingers feeling around the thin band of her panties.

"Call me careful," she murmured, "I had to be sure."

"I know. I was willing to wait, didn't want to pressure you into doing something you weren't ready for."

"I'd rather not tell Jacob yet."

"Why not?"

"Let me get used to the idea first."

"As you wish," he said, and started to pull her panties down.

"Oh, no," she said, her voice thick and raspy. "You don't get to have your way this time." She slowly tugged at his boxers and peeled them all the way down.

"What are you—" He stopped mid-sentence because he knew the answer already.

"I've been wanting to show you how much I missed you," she whispered, leaving his boxers around his ankles so that they handcuffed his legs together.

"So let me—"

"This isn't about you," she said, taking his length in her hands, and kneeling in front of him. She examined his face and caught the flash of desire burning in his eyes. "This is for me," she breathed, licking her lips, her thumb sliding over him, loving the strained voice as he groaned her name.

"I want—"

"No," she said, watching his mouth open, his eyes roll back as she stroked him slowly. "*I* want."

"Savannah," he croaked, gripping the crown of her head as her lips slowly slid over him.

# CHAPTER NINETEEN

The Fourth of July weekend came and went, and they spent it at home, finalizing the plans for the upcoming party and having a cookout on the terrace, taking another helicopter ride because he knew how much Jacob had enjoyed it that first time.

His parents had been in town but he'd managed to avoid visiting them knowing full well that his mother would be on his back. She obviously knew that Savannah had moved in, had obviously read the papers and was therefore desperate to find out what was going on with him.

He guessed she would be one of the first to arrive at the party. But the party wasn't the highlight for him. Flying to Miami the day after would be.

He could tell Savannah suspected he was up to something, but he would never make *that* kind of announcement in public. He suspected everyone thought there was a reason behind the party—there wasn't and many would be obviously disappointed.

He wasn't one for parties, as many people kept telling him, but he was looking forward to this one, to seeing everyone he knew—all the people who had contributed to his life in one way or another—in one place and at the same time. Back in the early days, it had only been through the parties Ivy had thrown that he'd managed to catch up with people. He was a workaholic, and life at the top was lonely. Apart from his regular meetings with his mastermind group, Tobias had no outlet for socializing, and now he didn't feel as if he needed anything or anyone, aside from Savannah and Jacob, but through them, his circle of friends was growing. And because he didn't trust many people, it made him cherish what he had even more. But this party wasn't only for him, it was also for the people Savannah and Jacob knew. He was even looking forward to seeing Henry Carson now that Candace had confirmed the final guest list. Jacob had excitedly told them that everyone at school wanted to play with him at recess time.

The following week slowly inched to a close and by Thursday, everything was falling into place. Deals were turning around and Sygon had just come back to him with an agreement that was favorable to both parties.

Within moments of the confirmation email from Sygon's CEO, Matthias called him.

"Sygon's back on?" was the first thing Matthias said.

"Yes," Tobias replied, smiling. It had been a long detour, going from Seattle to Houston but it had been worthwhile. His whole trip had been definitely worth it and he'd managed to meet with Becker Schwartz as well.

"Boy wonder works his magic again," Matthias remarked.

"It seemed to do the trick."

"And we'll be celebrating properly this weekend, I assume? Candace was finalizing last-minute things for your big party on the weekend. Is that a good use of her time?"

"Is she with you in Arizona?" asked Tobias, pissed off with the question.

"Of course not."

"Because it seems that news reaches you so fast, maybe I ought to ask you for any updates I might need from her."

"Did I just piss you off?" Matthias asked.

*Yes*, but Tobias wasn't about to confess so readily. "She's not organizing the party," he replied instead, forcing himself to sound cheerful. "And even if she was, that shouldn't concern anyone." Because she was his PA and he could use her as he wanted. "She's delegating at a very high level to the party planner. After all, we have a company to run."

"It's good to know that you realize that," Matthias commented.

"I've always known it," Tobias replied, massaging his temples lightly. Why did Matthias seem to take a dig at everything he did lately? "It might seem that I'm not paying attention, but if there's one thing you should know about me, if you don't already," Tobias said, "it's that I always pay attention."

A short silence followed before Matthias asked, "Anything in particular we're celebrating?" he asked. "It could have been a Fourth of July celebration but since you're having it the weekend after, I'm wondering whether there might be other motives for it."

"No," replied Tobias. "No motives, ulterior or otherwise. Just a good old-fashioned party. Having a good time with people we want to be around."

"I remember the parties you and Ivy used to have. Do you remember?" he asked, "back in the early days, in the basement of that shared apartment?" Back when he'd lived in Queens, way before he and Ivy were married. Matthias continued, ignorantly reminiscing away. "Quite a different type of affair back then, beer and a couple of bags of fries, and lots of loud music. The weed was good too."

"I wouldn't know about that," replied Tobias.

"So, no celebration," said Matthias, "and it's nothing to do with you looking at multi-million-dollar homes?"

"Nope."

"I guess I'll have to wait until the day like everyone else."

"It's an informal party," Tobias told him. "There's no announcement, I'm not resigning or anything, if that's what you're thinking."

"That's not the kind of announcement I had in mind."

"We've even got children coming."

Matthias groaned. "What?" And then he paused. "Wait. They'll be coming with their moms, won't they?" His voice turned hopeful. "Make sure you introduce me to the single moms."

"I don't know if there are any."

"You took the last one?"

Tobias smiled to himself. She wasn't going to be single any more, he hoped. He had no idea how this would go. She'd taken easily to his suggestion of moving in with him but he could never tell with Savannah.

"I'll see you on Sunday," said Matthias.

"You'll be back by then?"

"Yup. I'm flying back tomorrow night. The meetings were productive. I'll brief you on Monday."

"I won't be around," Tobias reminded him.

"That's right, you're away on vacation, but you'll still be calling in each day?"

"Yes." He would never get to have twenty-four hours uninterrupted.

"I don't want to talk about business at your party," warned Matthias.

"I don't intend to," replied Tobias. "Are you bringing anyone with you?" He was curious.

"I might. It depends on how Saturday night works out for

me." Tobias was still shaking his head when he hung up. His friend was never going to change.

Not long after his call with Matthias, Tobias's landline rang. He glanced at the number on the display. It was a foreign number and one which he recognized instantly. It was the call he'd been waiting for. It was time to get this over with.

_____

Savannah hadn't looked too happy when he'd announced that he and Jacob were eager to leave the mayhem of the apartment for a few hours. She was trying to clear away as many things as she could before the cleaning staff arrived later in the afternoon, to get the apartment ready for the party tomorrow.

"I want to give him a pep talk so that he can deal with Henry Carson," Tobias had whispered into her ear and that was how he'd been able to get out with Jacob. He wasn't so sure it was such a white lie, either. With the Carson kid and his parents accepting the party invitation, Tobias was looking forward to meeting that family.

"Hot dogs?" asked Jacob as they walked up to The Stand, a place Tobias and his friends had frequented while growing up in Queens. He'd never been to this store in Brooklyn, which had only been around for a couple of years.

"You said you were hungry." Tobias opened the door and let Jacob pass through.

"I was but only a little bit," admitted Jacob, looking around. He sniffed the air. "But now I'm starving."

The interior hadn't changed much. It was still red Formica

tables, laminated menus, red and green neon lights. It was as if time had stopped.

"Can we go to the park after?"

"We could," said Tobias, as they sat down, "but your mom didn't want us to be out for too long."

"She's getting stressed about the party, isn't she?"

"It's not stress, I don't think," Tobias told him. "She just wants everything to be perfect. I do too, but I know that everything's been taken care of. We have lots of people helping, but your mom, like most women, wants to check everything anyway and make sure."

"Is that a woman thing?" Jacob asked. "Like this is our man thing?" He nodded his head, indicating the space between the two of them.

"You could say," replied Tobias.

"What are we celebrating?"

Before he could answer, a friendly server greeted them. "Good morning, Mr. Stone." Instantly Tobias's stomach hardened.

*Not another goddam undercover reporter.*

He'd never seen the boy before, but the server obviously seemed to know him. Tobias relaxed when the boy, probably in his late teens, asked for nothing more than their order. "A large hot dog and some of that freshly squeezed pineapple juice for me, please. Jacob?"

"The same, but can I have Cajun curly fries and onion rings, too?" he asked Tobias.

"Don't ask me, buddy, tell the server," Tobias said, noting that Jacob always seemed to ask for permission to do anything. "You can have anything you want."

The server took the order and vanished.

"You wanted to know what we were celebrating," Tobias said, picking up the thread of their conversation, "Well, Jacob," he leaned forward, seizing his moment, "that depends on how you look at it." He clasped his hands together on the table. "How do you like living at the apartment?"

"It's cool," replied Jacob, putting down the menu. "I really like it and I really, really don't want to move."

"I figured you didn't, and I think your mom is getting used to the idea of us all living together in one home."

Jacob blinked rapidly. "You mean we don't have to move anymore?"

"We might have to move one more time," said Tobias. "But we'd all move together. The three of us. I was thinking it would be cool if we moved into one of those two houses I showed you last week."

"They weren't houses," said Jacob, puzzled. "They were *buildings*."

"And a building can be turned into a home."

Jacob's mouth fell open.

"I wanted to ask you something, buddy," said Tobias, waving away the server who was starting to walk towards them. "Give me ten minutes," he said, not wanting to lose this moment.

All of a sudden, his insides felt all fluttery just as they had once before, the first time he'd told Savannah he loved her. Words he wasn't sure he would ever get to say again after Ivy, and yet he had. He had known then what the consequences of saying those words might be and he'd said them anyway. And here he was again, about to ask Jacob something that would change all their lives forever.

Tobias wasn't sure how to start and when his cell phone rang, puncturing his thoughts, he quickly looked at it, saw that it was Matthias and sent it to voicemail. "I've already asked your Grandpa." He hadn't only asked, he'd won them over, and made arrangements.

Jacob blinked again. "Asked him what?"

"What I'm going to ask you now." He took a deep breath, surprised by how nervous he was. "That's why I wanted you and me to have another one of our man-to-man talks, especially since you're the man of the house, so..."

"What's a man of the house?"

Tobias swallowed. "It's been you and your mom for a long time, hasn't it, buddy? I know you've been looking after her, just as she's been looking after you and so I guess that makes you the man of the house."

Jacob smiled shyly, as if he liked this new label.

"And so," said Tobias, swallowing, "I wanted to ask you how you would feel if I married your mom."

Jacob's eyes grew round, and very large, and his smile grew even wider. "You want to marry my mommy?"

Tobias nodded, unable to speak because of the lump that seemed to be stuck in his throat. He tried to regain his composure. "I do. I would very much like to marry your mommy. But she's yours first, Jacob, and so I wanted to make sure it would be okay with you."

"What did she say?"

"I don't know," replied Tobias. "I haven't asked her yet."

"She'll say yes," the boy told him with great confidence.

"She will?"

"She said if you asked her, she would say yes."

"You've already spoken about it?" Tobias asked, surprised.

"It was a long time ago," he said, biting his lip as if he was snitching on her. "I always wanted her to marry you, and I even asked her one day." Tobias grinned.

"So I guess what I'm asking you, Jacob, is for your permission to marry your mom and to see if it would be okay for me to join your family."

"Then you would be my daddy?"

"Your daddy is still your daddy, Jacob. Nobody can take that away from him."

"But I don't want him to be my daddy."

"Hey, buddy, I get that. But I think your daddy still cares for you, in his own way, and maybe later on...well, we'll see. We'll see what your mommy has to say about that." Because later on he hoped to adopt Jacob and make it official.

"Can't I call you daddy?"

"How about we take it one step at a time, hey, buddy?"

Jacob stared at the table and nodded.

"So, would you like me to join your family, Jacob?" Tobias asked.

"Yes." The boy's eyes shone like stars.

"And do I have your permission to marry your mommy? She will always love you, Jacob, her love for you will always be as strong as ever, but love is like elastic—there's always enough to go around, even if I squeeze in."

Jacob looked at him with shining eyes, forgetting to answer, but Tobias already had his answer. "Then I can get some brothers, one day?" The child looked at him with the innocence of a six-year-old. As if getting some brothers was an item on a grocery list.

Tobias rubbed the back of his neck and pondered what sort of future lay ahead. They wanted the same thing, he and Jacob, and he knew Savannah did too, except that it would take her a little longer, while she worked her way through her maze of questions and what-ifs, to discover the same thing: they needed one another. It wasn't just love, it was a need to be together, as basic as food and shelter, not only an emotion, but something as fundamental as that.

"We could think about it. We'd have to see what your mommy has to say about that." The air turned silent while the server delivered their hot dogs. Two large greasy, tangy, oniony hot dogs and side orders of fries and onion rings. It was too early in the morning for comfort food, but it didn't matter. His appetite had suddenly doubled.

Jacob picked up a bottle of ketchup and squeezed it all over his hot dog. He put the bottle down slowly. "She likes flowers," he said, his face serious. "Pink ones."

"Pink ones?"

"If you want her to marry you, pink flowers might help," he said, putting his fingers around the hot dog and getting ketchup all over them.

"Pink flowers," Tobias asked, thinking about it carefully. "You want me to get them today? Because I wasn't going to ask her until tomorrow night, when we get to Miami. Think you can keep this a secret until then, buddy? It's really important that you do." Just as it had been important for him to find out Jacob's views, before he popped the question.

Jacob's hot dog remained an inch from his mouth. "Are we going in your private plane?"

"Yes," replied Tobias, smiling. As soon as the party was over, they were going to take off. He wasn't sure whether to ask her when they landed and were out by the pool around midnight, or the next morning. He'd have to gauge it.

"You might as well get them now," suggested Jacob.

"Sure, buddy. Any ones in particular?"

"Nah," replied Jacob. "Any pink ones will do."

# CHAPTER TWENTY-ONE

Savannah let him into the apartment, surprised to see him on a Saturday. "I thought the cleaning staff had arrived early," she said, smiling as Matthias walked in.

"Where's Tobias?"

"He's out with Jacob. He should be back in a while," she said, puzzled by his testy temperament.

"Damn," he said, wiping his hand across his brow.

"He shouldn't be long," replied Savannah. "Tobias said there was a hot dog place he'd been wanting to take him to." She was trying to make polite conversation, but Matthias's face was hard and he walked around the apartment like a territorial dog, making her uneasy. His eyes were ringed dark blackish-blue, as if he hadn't slept.

"Is something wrong?"

"It's been wrong for quite some time."

"What's happened?" she asked, fear twisting her gut.

"Quite a cozy little setup you have here, isn't it?" he asked, ignoring her question.

"Excuse me?" The tone and use of his words startled her.

"This," said Matthias, looking around the apartment. "So

homey, just like when Ivy was here. You must think you've slipped right in?"

Her thoughts fell into disarray and she wondered what had happened, and why he was here. "I don't know what you mean."

"Sweetheart," he said, his gaze slowly traveling over her and making her feel naked. She stood up straight, wishing she hadn't worn this dress with its slit going from her knee to mid-thigh. "It's beautiful, this home you've wormed your way into. And now he's looking for a bigger place, I hear?"

"You know what Tobias is like," she said slowly.

"I thought I knew what Tobias was like," he replied, creasing his forehead. "But even I don't know what's going on inside that head of his anymore."

"He shouldn't be too long," said Savannah, sensing that Matthias was worked up about something. "Can I get you something to drink?"

"A bottle of scotch," Matthias replied, then glanced out of the floor-to-ceiling windows.

"A bottle?" She laughed nervously and looked around for her cell phone, thinking it might be a good idea to call Tobias. "The party's tomorrow afternoon, Matthias."

He turned around and walked towards her, his eyes seeing the magazine she'd left lying on the coffee table. He picked it up and flicked through it, finding the four-page spread of her and Tobias with photos of them both taken recently. One with her and Tobias out walking hand in hand, and another one of the three of them at the park, with Jacob's face blurred out.

"That was taken at Brooklyn Gardens," she told him, trying to make small talk.

Matthias scrubbed his chin, staring at the images carefully. "Quite a change of scenery."

"It's a lovely place," she agreed. "It's beautiful, have you ever been?"

"I meant this," said Matthias, sweeping his hand around the light and airy apartment. "Living here, on the Upper East side. It must be a real change for you."

"I'm looking for an apartment," she said, not wanting to tell him the truth, and the way he looked, the way he spoke, put her body on alert. He was pissed about something.

"Are you?" His laugh was vicious. "You expect me to believe that you're still looking for an apartment to rent, when you're sleeping with a billionaire and he's looking for a bigger home?"

Her mouth turned desert dry, leaving her unable to speak.

"Are you, sweetheart?" he said, walking towards her. She forced herself not to shrink back. Not to let him know she was afraid. "I have a hunch that you're not looking too hard." His smile was like all of his other ones, cheesy and overdone, but this time his eyes were hard.

"I—I don't know what you mean," she replied, feeling a spray of panic wash over her. Warning signs from her days with Colt. Her body screaming that something wasn't right.

This man was pissed as hell.

"I'm sure you know exactly what I mean, sweetheart." He smiled his sickly smile again. "You're not stupid. In fact you're a very smart and very clever, almost calculating little woman. You've done very well to get him, a simple girl from North Carolina, a single mother at that, divorced, poor and broke, and with emotional baggage the size of a blue whale."

"I think you should leave," she said, summoning her strength and trying to stand tall.

"Except I'm not done talking yet. And I'm waiting for Tobias."

"You're pissed about something. Have *I* done something to upset you?" she asked, because everything about him indicated that.

"Am I pissed?" His voice boomed out loud and frightening.

"Pissed doesn't even come close." A chill iced over her and her lungs struggled to breathe. She advanced back but he stepped towards her. "Am I pissed at you, sweetheart? That's the question you need to ask."

He was standing so close to her that she could smell his breath. Hot and heavy. She took a small step back, while her heart rattled violently inside her chest. "Ever since you've come into Tobias's life, he's been the happiest, most grounded, most settled man I've known in a long time. I never thought it would be possible, not after Ivy. You never met her, did you?" he asked.

Her mouth turned dry and she swallowed. "No."

"Pity," he said.

"Why?"

"Why?" he bellowed. "He doesn't tell you much about her, does he? He doesn't talk about her too much, I'll bet. She was the love of his life, and the baby....you do know about the baby, don't you?"

"I know about Zachary," she said, narrowing her eyes, wishing he would leave. Wishing that Tobias would hurry up and come home.

"Of course you know about the baby, just like you knew about Naomi," he bellowed, freezing her to the floor. Terror engulfed her because the man before her wasn't the Matthias she knew. "You've got him by the balls. Who'd have thought it was possible? A girl like you, but you managed to do it, you managed to get your claws into the most eligible man in New York." He bared his teeth. "And you convinced him to take you on *and* the boy. Bravo," he said, his nostrils flaring. "This must be your life's achievement. What a catch after the pig you were married to."

"I think you should leave." But he wasn't listening to her. He'd closed his eyes as if he was in pain and scrubbed his forehead again.

"That stupid, stupid girl," he muttered bitterly.

"What girl?" she asked, backing away, looking around for her cell phone in sheer desperation.

"The uptight bitch," he snarled. "She's good at her job, very efficient, very conscientious, but a ditzy bitch when it comes to Tobias. Trust her to go and mess everything up."

Savannah stared at him, her breath sticking in her throat. "Who are you talking about?"

"You still don't know?" he said, surprise coating his venomous tone. "Candace, of course."

Her eyebrows drew together. "What's Candace got to do with anything?" His glaze slid to the slit of her dress, then traveled back up to her face again. She folded her arms and drew her feet together.

"It was her fault that your ex-husband found out where you lived. If she hadn't given him your address, none of that drama would have happened, you might not have rushed back from Miami and this little romance of yours might have slowly withered away. But it brought you closer, didn't it? Tobias thinking he was going to lose you and the boy. It took him back to his past all over again. And here we fucking are."

The words landed like bricks in her stomach and stayed there, hard to shift and weighing down her insides. "I'd like you to leave," she said, backing away from him but she hit the edge of the couch. "You're obviously very angry about something. I'll get Tobias to call you when he returns."

"I should have been celebrating," he said, trapping her between the couch and him. She'd been trapped like this before, with Colt, and knew that face. Knew what a man was capable of when he was this angry. She prayed that Tobias was around the corner.

"Celebrating what?" she asked, trying to look calm.

"I should have been celebrating my fucking multi-million-dollar deal with Yanling."

"Yanling?" His reply caught her off guard.

"All I had to do was to get him to sign on for another three years. Three more goddamn years with Yanling and his associates, and the deal would have been complete."

"Tobias didn't want that deal anymore."

"But he would have, given time. I was working on him but he decided, just like that," he clicked his fingers. "Didn't even wait for me to get back. He did it while I was away. He severed the deal."

"Tobias knows what he's doing," she said, "I'm sure he had his reasons."

His venomous look bore down on her, and she feared for her life. "The man can't think straight anymore. You bewitched him from the moment you turned up and you'll be the ruin of him yet. He's lost the sharp killer instinct that made him a billionaire. He's distracted. He thinks he's in love again."

She shook her head. "You don't mean what you're saying, Matthias. I can see that you're really upset but you need to calm down and speak to Tobias. Don't do or say something you'll regret."

"What I fucking regret is losing that deal that would have made me a very rich man, even richer than I am now, but your pussy got in the way." He grabbed her arm and pulled her into him. Her body tensed. She wanted to push him away. She wanted to escape, but if she struggled, she knew her reaction would only spur him on. She tried to reason instead.

"You're upset, Matthias. I understand that, but you need to calm down."

His red-veined eyes glared at her. "I should have tried harder to get you into my bed first. If I'd have gotten to you first, he would have backed off."

"You?" She sneered, then realized her mistake.

"Is my money not good enough for you?" he snarled. "Is it only billionaires you fuck?"

"Get out," she said, keeping her voice low, and wriggling her arm out of his hold. But he paid no attention.

"That's been my problem all along, living in the shadow of Tobias fucking Stone. He gets the fame, he gets the money, he gets to be king. It's bad enough that he gets all the women and the glory. Fucking boy wonder."

"He's your friend," she yelled, horrified by his words. "How can you talk about him like that?"

"Try living in someone's shadow for years and you'll see why."

"He trusted you." She said, freeing her arm and leaning as far back as she could without falling onto the couch behind her. She rubbed the skin where he'd grabbed her.

"I love him like a brother. I really do. But this deal," he balled up his hands. "This goddamn deal, all he had to do was agree to it. Except that his mind hasn't been on the business lately. It's been with you." His alcohol breath wafted into her face. "Now I want to see what's so sweet about this pussy of yours." He reached down to her dress and pulled it up roughly. She froze for one second before she sprung into life, then kicked him hard, and fell back onto the couch as she lost her balance. She heard the dress rip, then felt his hard hands between her legs. Rage fired inside her as panic gripped her.

*Not again. This could not happen again.*

"Get off!" she screamed as loudly as she could, not recognizing the frenzied scream that left her mouth. His fingers probed over her panties, clawing at her as he tried to invade her most private space. She twisted and clamped her legs together, then drove her knee into him.

"Bitch!" he yelled, and grabbed her buttock, squeezing it hard.

"Get off me! Get off!" she screamed over and over, fearing the worst.

"You excite me, Savannah," he murmured. "Dressing like this, looking all pretty and sexy. No wonder his mind isn't in the right place." His hand moved to her front, his fingers grappling with the crotch of her panties. She wriggled furiously, fighting through the panic and screaming and trying to stop her body from going into lockdown.

"Get OFF!"

And soon he was off her. As if he'd been plucked from her like a feather. In the next moment she heard a splat, loud, like a crunch, and blood spurted from Matthias's face as he fell backwards onto the coffee table.

"What the fuck?" Tobias bellowed. She sat up quickly, saw the dress ripped right up to her hips, saw Jacob's wretched face looking at her. Saw Tobias offer her his hand to pull her up.

"You bastard," raged Tobias. "You goddamn filthy bastard."

She barely had time to absorb it all when she heard Jacob's voice behind her. She turned and looked at him. Her son looked petrified and the haunted look that he'd left behind in North Carolina returned. She rushed to him as he hid behind the couch.

"Mommy," he whispered, his voice barely audible. She grabbed his hand and pulled him away and into the study around the corner.

"No, no, honey. He didn't." She hugged him close, falling to the floor as she shut the study door behind them. She heard more shouting and screaming as Jacob cowered in her arms.

"Did he hurt you, Mommy?"

"No, honey."

"But your dress is ripped."

"It's just a rip." She whispered, straining to make out what was going on in the other room.

"But, Mommy." Her son sounded scared and she hugged him even tighter.

"It's going to be okay, Jacob. It's going to be okay."

In the next moment the sound, of an almighty crash rocked through the air. "Stay here," she told him. "Don't be scared. Everything's going to be all right." She rushed out to find Matthias on the floor, the coffee table turned over and Tobias standing over him.

# CHAPTER TWENTY-TWO

He heard her screams and flew to the door.

"Get off!!" Her primal scream ripped through the air and his muscles turned to stone. He rushed to the door, saw a man on top of her, saw her arms and legs flailing. His blood boiled and his pulse race.

With one deadly hand, he yanked the man off, and threw him to the floor, his body high on adrenaline and rage.

And then he saw Matthias's face. A cannonball of rage shot through him.

*Matthias?*

He didn't stop to think beyond that, but drew back, putting his body weight into the punch that landed smack in the middle of his face. Blood gushed as Matthias stumbled backwards, knocking over the coffee table and landing on his back.

*What the fuck?*

"You broke my nose," Matthias yelped.

"You bastard," raged Tobias. "You goddamn filthy bastard." Tobias flexed his fingers, his hands fidgety, itching to break bone, rip skin, draw blood. He turned to find Savannah struggling to sit up, her dress ripped and up to her waist.

*Fuck.*

He gave her his hand and pulled her up but he couldn't move past the red fog of what he'd seen. Savannah rushed over to Jacob as he faced the man he'd regarded as his brother.

"What the fuck were you doing?" he asked, his knuckles still ready. His chest thumped and he could hear his heartbeat thrashing in his ears. From the corner of his eye, he saw Savannah scurry away.

He couldn't get rid of the image of Matthias's hands over Savannah's body. It would be burned into his memory forever.

Matthias stood up slowly, pulled out a tissue and held it to his nose. The soft and flimsy paper slowly turned blood-red.

"Give me a reason I shouldn't kill you now," growled Tobias, baring his teeth.

*Had the bastard always been after Savannah?*

He tried to recall past encounters, tried to piece together the conversations with Matthias.

"I called you earlier," Matthias said, in between wiping his nose and trying to stem the flow of blood. "You didn't answer."

So he had. When he'd been at The Stand with Jacob. "What's gotten into you?"

"You went behind my back," Matthias hissed.

"What are you talking about?"

"Yanling. You didn't sign, and you did it when I was away. Sneaky," Matthias hissed, nursing his nose. "Very sneaky."

*That was it?* "You were away in Arizona," Tobias replied, sizing up what Matthias had done. His reaction didn't make sense. Something was missing. "He wanted an answer. I called a meeting and this time senior management agreed with me. I gave him his answer."

"You were waiting until I was out of the picture?"

"You being here wouldn't have changed a thing. The

outcome would still have been the same. It was never going to happen."

"You should have talked to me first," snarled Matthias. "This is a big mistake, pulling out."

"Open your eyes and smell the goddamn coffee," Tobias yelled at him. "The deal's been off for months, you chose not to listen."

"I tried to get you to see the possibility."

"And I tried to get you to see sense."

Matthias glowered at him. "You stopped listening to me. You started listening to *her*. You lost your focus. Fucked up your direction, you're steering us into dangerous waters."

"I'm steering us through difficult times. Things are a mess in Europe and China. We can't afford to take the risk."

Mathias winced, pressing his fingers along his nose. "And to think you were a strong advocate of Yanling once."

Anger engulfed Tobias's body. Why was this man not getting it? Why was he so adamant about wanting to do business in China? Even senior management could now read the warning signs. Tobias studied the man's face, saw the ugliness and the bitter hatred that refused to hide.

"You threw it all away, and for what? For pussy," Matthias smirked. "Do you have any goddamn idea what you lost? Do you have any idea what that fucking deal might have bought us?"

"Us or you?" replied Tobias, the painful realization sinking in. "I didn't lose anything, but it sounds to me as if you cut a deal. You did, didn't you?" He'd suspected as much.

"You lost your head."

"I think you fucking lost yours," barked Tobias. There had been a reason for Matthias's simmering resentment. His small comments, his extended stay in Hong Kong, his suddenly developing friendship with Yanling. All of it had gotten him thinking.

He'd had an inkling, but he had never assumed *this*. "What was it?" Tobias asked bitterly. "A couple of hundred thousand?"

Matthias grunted "It was $1.3 million, if you must know."

Tobias sucked his breath in sharply. "You did this for $1.3 million?" Yanling had been even more desperate than he'd first thought. "I've made you a rich man many times over."

"You *screwed* me many times over."

Tobias stepped closer to him, enraged by his words. Was this what Matthias had been thinking the whole time? "You think I screwed you over? Are you fucking serious?"

Matthias grabbed a handful of tissues and held them to his nose, the blood staining his face and hands. "You were always in the limelight, always the one with attention. First, Becker, then the company, and all the time I was the one propping you up."

"Propping *me* up?" Tobias was dumbfounded. "Are you sure you've got that right? You think *you* built up Stone Enterprises?" yelled Tobias, raising his voice. "You were too busy with women and booze and fuck knows what else. You were happy for me to make all the decisions, you were happy enough for me to build up *my* company. I gave you an elevated position." Tobias jabbed his finger at him. "I didn't have to but I let you coast along on my coattails and don't you fucking forget it. You knew it, and so did Becker. You had plenty of opportunities to run your own company but you never wanted to. You never wanted to because it was too much hard work. Becker realized that about you, and that's why he put his effort into me. He often told me you had it, you had the smarts but you were too goddamn lazy."

"You've had it easy all your life, Stone, that's what *you've* never realized."

*An easy life? Him?* A dyslexic child who struggled through school? Who never had enough growing up?

"Easy? Me?" yelled Tobias, outraged. "You know everything about me, how can you say that? I worked hard, while you partied." Tobias remembered the twenty-hour days he'd put in at Becker's company, swallowing up and soaking every piece of knowledge he could. Working with his mentor had given him a thirst for learning that he'd never had, and he had taken the bull by the horns, learning everything he could, absorbing information like oxygen. "I never saw you do ten-hour days, you knew it, I knew it and Becker knew it. So if he took me under his wing, it was because he must have seen something in me that he couldn't find in you. God knows you'd already been there long enough before I showed up."

"And what a goddamn boy wonder you were. Always stealing my thunder. You were too smart, and too good-looking, and things always fell in your lap. Do you know how much I had to pay that bitch to convince her to spill your story?" For a moment, Tobias was too stunned to move, and then as the words slammed into him like flying shrapnel, he lowered his head in disbelief while rage, as deadly as poison, slowly seeped into his veins.

"She didn't want to do it," Matthias continued. "She didn't want to sell you out, wouldn't listen but everything has a price. That's what you always said, remember? Naomi Rivera had a price too. A hundred thousand."

The insides of Tobias's stomach turned to fire and ice and his body started to shake. "You were behind that?"

"You can get anyone to do anything if the price is right. She told me it killed her to betray you. She said you were good to her. Fuck," Matthias shook his head in disgust. "Even your whore fell in love with you."

It was automatic, the way Tobias's fist, like a miniature

wrecking ball, connected with Matthias's cheek. Almost like a thousand-pound weight of forged steel, it rammed into bone and Matthias fell backwards again, on top of the upturned coffee table. He struggled to stand up and then thwack! Tobias smacked into him again. He lay sprawled on the table, a trickle of blood dripping from his nose, and an ugly open mass of bruised flesh, red like pomegranate across his cheekbone. "You despicable, worthless son of a bitch," Tobias snarled.

Matthias got up slowly, dazed as he tottered around, looking like a real mess. "It hurts, doesn't it?" he managed to say. "She made a killing from it all, the money from the papers, too but it was hard to get her to do it. She had some fucked-up sense of loyalty towards you. I tried to get it through that thick head of hers that it was purely business. That she could take the wad of money she'd made and to hell with her conscience. She said she was going to take off for a while, that she couldn't bear to run into you again."

"And what did you hope to gain from it all?" Tobias asked, his insides spinning.

"To split you up, of course. To shake you and Savannah up, to shake *you* up, even. That maybe you'd back off, not wanting to drag her name through the media gutter. I couldn't stand around and not do anything. I couldn't just watch you wine and dine her like a pathetic lover on honeymoon. I had a deal to see to, and you were supposed to be running a fucking business."

"But none of this is Savannah's fault."

"She got inside your head."

Tobias too stumped to answer. His body was tense and tight, a hardened block of nerves and muscle. "You fu—" Tobias lunged forward, his whole body bursting with adrenaline.

"Stop!" Savannah yelled, pulling him back with both of her hands. "He's not worth it."

He felt her hand on his arm, then felt her fingers entwine

with his. Savannah stood by his side and all at once he was protective again, moving his body so that he was shielding her.

Matthias stared at her. "I was hoping she wouldn't trust you. I thought she might back off, after all that other stuff she'd been through. All you had to do was sign the deal." Matthias wiped his nose, with his hands which were a dirty brown shade of dried blood.

"I was *never* going to sign the deal!" Tobias yelled. "But you kept pounding on and on and on at me, even when I knew it didn't make sense. I suspected then, that you might have more at stake here but I didn't stop long enough to think it through." Matthias had been right, Tobias had been distracted, and if he had taken the time to keep a closer eye on his alleged friend, he might have been able to see earlier that something wasn't right. That Matthias's interest in doing business with Yanling had a deeper agenda.

"It wasn't even the right deal for our investors. It was the right deal for you. How greedy can you get?" asked Tobias, his voice low and steady. "Get the hell out." Matthias grabbed another handful of tissues, and moved towards the door.

Tobias watched him walk towards the door as Savannah's arm slid around his waist. He instinctively hugged her closer to him. "Clear your office out this weekend. You won't be allowed back in on Monday," Tobias warned him. "I never want to see you again." He stared at the blood on the floor, felt Savannah's hand press gently into his, heard the door close as Matthias skulked out, and still his body stayed tense.

He'd see to it that Ludwig's team made sure of it. He'd stopped his men from patrolling inside this condo, or in the hallways outside, because he'd never thought danger would come. Only close friends and family were allowed in, and he thought he'd be safe. Never in his wildest nightmares had he expected this.

Savannah wrapped her arms around his waist as she looked up at him. Her face was full of love and concern and worry. She lifted up on her tiptoes and kissed his chin. "I'm sorry," she whispered, stroking his face with her fingers. "I'm sorry he did that to you." She kissed his lips tenderly, then hugged him again, pressing her warm and soft little body against his, never letting go, and slowly, little by little, his body started to soften.

"It's nothing for you to be sorry about." But even though he tried to push this bitter wound away and pretend it didn't exist, Matthias's betrayal cut bone deep. "Did he hurt you?" he asked, wanting to know what exactly he'd done. Savannah shook her head, and even though he desperately wanted to believe her, he sensed she would say anything not to make him angry.

"I think I hurt him more."

"I'm being serious, Savannah." But he knew it would kill him to find out that Matthias had done something.

"He's ruined my dress."

"Did he *do* anything?" To the end of his days, he didn't think he would ever get that image out of his head.

"No," she said, pursing her lips together tightly. Tobias pulled away and reached down to examine the rip in her dress.

"The sonofabitch," he snarled. "Did he—"

"Tobias, no. He didn't do a thing. I swear."

"Is he gone?" They turned suddenly at the sound of Jacob's voice. Inquisitive eyes, green and bright, like shiny marbles, peered at them from the corner of the hallway.

Tobias strode up to him and lifted him easily, hugging the boy to his chest. "He's gone and he's not coming back, Jacob." The boy put his arms around Tobias's neck and clung on and Tobias's heart melted.

"You're safe now. He won't ever come back." The boy lifted his head up and stared back at him. This time Tobias saw relief in the boy's face.

"What about Mommy?"

"He didn't hurt your mommy. You should have seen him, buddy. I think I hurt him more." They looked at the almost-perfect circles of blood on the wooden floor.

"Are these for me?" asked Savannah. She picked up the bouquet of flowers that he'd dropped on the floor. His intention had been to sneak them into the apartment and hide them out of sight until tomorrow evening. They were already in a plastic bag of water, and he thought they would last until they arrived in Miami, for *that* moment. That moment he'd planned and worked out in his head.

Jacob looked at him expectantly, but Tobias shook his head, saying nothing. He slowly put him back down on the floor again. Savannah put her nose to the bouquet.

"Pink lilies and pink roses, how beautiful. I love pink anything," she said to Tobias, giving him a curious smile. "How did you know?"

"I told him," Jacob piped up.

"Thank you," she said, sniffing them again and walking towards him. "But you do know that we have a gazillion flowers arriving tomorrow morning. Just as you requested, pastel-colored roses, over two hundred bouquets." She dropped a kiss on his chin. "I thought you weren't going to go overboard with the party?"

He smiled and tried to figure out a way to fix this. The party and going to Miami and his plans were still in place, but at that moment, Tobias realized what Savannah had known all along, that there were some things in life that couldn't be controlled, that best-laid plans could get disrupted, that life didn't always work according to a plan, that shit sometimes happened when you least expected. Some moments in life *had* to be spontaneous, that was half the fun of them. And for a question as big as the one he had—asking Savannah to share the rest of her life with him— for something like that there would *never* be a moment big enough, or perfect enough.

What he realized in that instant was that *this* was his moment and it was up to him to seize it.

His heart was beginning to thump again as he stepped towards her, taking note of the look of complete surprise in her eyes.

He knew this moment would be frozen in time forever, that he would remember it for the rest of his life, and it made him savor it even more. He took her hand in his, "I've been wanting to ask you something for a long time, Savannah Page." Her eyes widened, and she stopped blinking.

He kissed her hand. "I'm in love with you, and I want you by my side for the rest of my days because I don't want to grow old without you." Her hazel eyes misted over as her fingers flew to her neck, to the rings in the necklace she always wore now.

"You and Jacob," he said, "you mean the world to me and I would like to be a part of your family, if you'll let me. Will you let me, Savannah?"

He put his free hand into his pocket and felt for the box, for he had dared not leave it unattended.

# CHAPTER TWENTY-THREE

W as he asking her what she thought he was asking her? Or was this about the baby, or the bigger home? Because she didn't want to make a massive assumption and then look foolish for getting it completely wrong.

"I said he could, Mommy," Jacob whispered. "I told him he could join our family." She watched Tobias slip his hand into his blazer pocket and pull out a box.

It was that-kind-of-sized box.

And then he got down on one knee. Her hands dropped to her chest, one over the other, as if to absorb the shock of this moment. In the background, she heard Jacob giggle, as she suddenly felt weightless, suddenly felt free and ready to fly. This was *that* moment.

"Will you marry me, Savannah?"

She felt the trembling first, and wasn't sure if it was his words that had shocked her, or if every nerve in her body now jumped for joy. She wanted to cry, and to laugh, and to fall into his arms, and yet she couldn't do a thing, and all of sudden her heart crashed and bopped inside her.

Because he'd asked her to be his wife and he was waiting for her answer. She was breathing so fast that it almost turned her dizzy and in her chaotic happiness, she dropped her flowers.

*Tobias wanted to marry her.*

He wanted to marry *her*.

She loved this man who smelled of designer cologne, who could be like a raging river one moment and as tender as the summer air the next, a man whose words uplifted her and made her believe again, a man who made her feel like she was the only goddess in the heaven he'd created for her.

Her gaze was locked with his, and time stopped, everything around her froze, but her body—her heart and chest and her breathing—it continued, like the beat of a drum, steady and loud, telling her that this was real, not the stuff of dreams.

"Savannah?" he said, staring at her with the intensity that was so much a part of him, and still she heard his words, watched him move, watched him open the box and turn it to show her. And she gasped in silence, because there was no voice inside her, because she was still frozen and in awe, and because the ring shone so brightly, the way a million shards of crystal might, all concentrated in one huge diamond that winked at her.

Hell, yes. Because he was her soulmate, and a soulmate was for life.

She lifted her gaze from the ring to his face and it was this, more than anything, that she couldn't turn away from—the face she would see last thing at night, and first thing in the morning, and for all the days they would have forever after.

"Yes," she said, nodding her head, letting her smile spread out of control, feeling the surge of joy shoot up her stomach as happiness spread around her like summer heat across a field. "Yes, yes," she said, twice, in case he hadn't heard her. And the tears fell anyway.

He slipped the ring onto her finger and then wrapped her in his soft embrace as she crumbled against him.

# CHAPTER TWENTY-FOUR

She was a vision of loveliness as she sashayed through the chattering laughter, like a Grecian goddess in her long, sleeveless floral print halter dress, a mixture of coral pink and purple chiffon. Heads turned everywhere to watch her floating gracefully among the party guests.

The apartment had been transformed. The furniture had been moved away, and the already huge living room looked gargantuan. There was enough space to accommodate everyone easily, and their guests slowly spilled out onto the terrace, enjoying the summer sun. It felt like a summer garden party even though there was no leafy, green garden outside, but the backdrop of Central Park more than sufficed, and the view from the terrace was glorious.

The upstairs floor was off limits but some people sat on the glass staircase. Jacob and his friends hadn't left the game room.

Everyone started to arrive soon after the 2:00 p.m. start time and it wasn't long before the party was in full swing and the apartment swelled with people. Most noticed her ring as soon as they walked through the door, adding a celebratory air to the already buzzing atmosphere.

Women wore summer dresses and men came in open-neck shirts and casual pants. An attendant at the door showed people through, taking their shawls and jackets, and even though Tobias had hinted at a laidback, casual affair, one that he'd tried to enforce by wearing beige slacks with a white button-up shirt, but some guests still arrived all dressed up as if they were going to the Oscars.

Tobias had told her that he wasn't going to go overboard, but the catering staff brought tray upon tray of the most stunning-looking canapes, pink champagne flowed freely, and everywhere she looked, vases full of pink flowers adorned the apartment. He must have switched things at the last minute because not a single pastel-colored rose graced the apartment, instead, pink lilies and roses adorned every corner.

*The things he did for her.*

She'd put her own flowers in their bedroom with the full intention of taking them to Miami with her tonight.

Savannah clasped her hands together, still unused to the chunky ring that rubbed against the fingers of her other hand. Happiness filled every cell inside her each time she touched it and this day felt like a hazy midsummer night's dream.

*She was engaged to Tobias.*

He'd told her that he'd never intended the party to be an engagement party, and that he had planned to propose to her in Miami, because that was where they had shared some of their happiest times. But with all that had gone on, things hadn't worked out that way and perhaps it was better to let the news seep out this way.

Most people, his mother, Lenny's mother, Julia, and a few of the other school moms had already noticed the glittering jewel on her finger for it was impossible *not* to notice.

She met and mingled easily with her guests and walked around with an air of confidence and ease that now seemed to come easily. She was a gracious hostess and happily greeted all of Tobias's friends, many of whom she was meeting for the first time.

They saw Xavier arrive, and went to greet him but he disappeared just as suddenly. Tobias then became distracted by another guest, a girl in a black jacket and jeans, and Savannah wondered who she was. Then Kay had walked in, wearing a full-length red halter neck dress and a face that was frozen with awe as soon as she stepped inside the apartment for the first time.

"Sav," she exclaimed, her jaw almost dropping as she handed Savannah a big bunch of white lilies. "Is that a Roberto Cavelli?" she asked, casting an inquisitive eye over Savannah's dress.

"A what?" Savannah asked.

And then Kay screamed. "Oh my GOD." She looked as if she'd seen a tarantula. "What is *this*?" She grabbed Savannah's hand and held it up, examining the huge diamond. "You're... you're...you're freakin' ENGAGED? Oh, Sav!" She threw her arms around Savannah and hugged her as if she wanted to squeeze the life out of her. Then, pulling apart, "Oh my god, oh my god, oh my god. Is that the big surprise? Are you pregnant?" All this while standing near the door, when other guests were arriving.

"Shush," said Savannah, partly annoyed, as she pulled her cousin away.

"What do you mean 'shush'?" Kay refused to 'shush.' "Are you?"

"What? No!" retorted Savannah.

"But you're *engaged!*"

"Tobias surprised me yesterday," she said. "It was spontaneous," which wasn't far from the truth. "We haven't really announced it."

Kay snorted. "You're freakin' kidding me. You expect people not to notice *that*?" Her high-pitched exclamations drew glances from the people around them. "That could be lethal," Kay said, staring at the ring like a green-eyed monster. "It could take someone's eye out."

"It's big, isn't it?" Savannah sighed and stole an admiring glance at the rock. "If people notice, they notice, but I don't blatantly want to announce it."

"*That* is something worth announcing."

"Hey," she felt his soft hand trace along her shoulder first, then saw Tobias lean forward and kiss Kay on both cheeks.

"So good of you to come, Kay." Her cousin's mouth opened and she remained thankfully voiceless. Her eyes were unblinking.

"I cannot believe that my brother hasn't had the decency to properly introduce us yet," said Xavier, suddenly appearing in front of Savannah. He kissed her on both cheeks. "Welcome to the family, Savannah."

"Thank you," she replied. Though it had been many months since she'd seen him, she felt as if she already knew him because Tobias had often spoken about him. Savannah looked at Xavier carefully, noticing the similarities. Xavier's eyes were blue and dark like his brother's but bigger and rounder, where Tobias's were narrower, and often cold and suspicious, and Tobias's hair was sandy brown, where his brother's was darker. Like his brother, Xavier was an obvious looker, though where Tobias oozed quiet sensuality, Xavier swaggered around with in-your-face sex appeal. It didn't take a genius to guess Kay's intentions.

"Hey, congratulations, bro," said Xavier, engulfing Tobias in a manly hug. Tobias had called his family last night to tell them that Savannah had accepted his proposal of marriage. She'd been about to call her parents to deliver the good news, but Tobias's sensual charms had distracted her.

"You kept that kinda quiet."

"You know me," Tobias replied.

"What the hell happened to your hand?"

"It got caught when I tried to move the furniture," said Tobias, covering it with his other hand. "Kay," he said, quickly taking charge of introductions, "I'd like you to meet my brother, Xavier." He turned to his brother. "This is Kay, Savannah's cousin." Kay's eyes opened wider and Savannah watched in amazement as her cousin batted her lashes shamelessly.

"Nice to meet you," he said, unaware of the electric effect he'd had on Kay. She'd suddenly lost the ability to pay attention to anyone else but Xavier.

"Where's Petra?" Savannah asked, hoping to extinguish all romantic ideas from Kay's head. She'd seen a six-foot mannequin on his arm earlier and assumed that this was the infamous and tempestuous Petra.

"She's here somewhere," replied Xavier, not even bothering to look around. "Is this the reason for this party?" Xavier asked his brother, staring at Savannah's ring.

"Believe it or not, no," Tobias replied. "I wasn't going to propose until after."

"I can believe it," Xavier said, rolling his eyes at Savannah. "He's always trying to outsmart people. It's a thing he has, in case you haven't noticed."

"Oh, I know," replied Savannah. "Tobias lives life as if it were a chess game."

"Each move is strategic, huh?" Xavier returned, winking. "But seriously, this is the best news. I knew my brother was crazy about you when Bryant Park became his favorite hangout."

Savannah smiled as Tobias nodded his head in agreement. "You can't beat Bryant Park on the weekend," he said.

"You'll make a decent man of him yet." Xavier told her.

"Won't she just?" Millicent's voice reached her ears before she saw Tobias's mother. The woman smiled at her. "Congratulations, my dear. That's some diamond you've got there."

"Savannah," a tall man with sparkling eyes greeted her warmly. "It is a pleasure to meet you at last."

"This is my dad," Tobias told her and they hugged briefly.

"We've just met Jacob, haven't we, Milly?" his father said, instantly making her feel relaxed. "I'm absolutely delighted that you accepted my son's proposal."

She smiled shyly at them, grateful that Tobias had placed his arm firmly around her waist. "This is my cousin, Kay." She told them all, while Kay flashed on the charm to full voltage.

"Time to make a hasty exit," Tobias whispered in her ear.

"Let's." She watched Millicent interrogate Kay, as Xavier looked on.

"If you'll excuse us," said Tobias, before pulling her away. They walked towards the terrace, his hands hugged the curve of her waist, unable to stop touching and teasing while moving across the soft fabric of her dress. She placed her hand over his to still it.

"We're not alone," she said, smiling up at him.

"I can't help it. You have that effect on me," he whispered close to her ear. "You've always had that effect on me, Savannah Page."

"But there's a time for everything, Mr. Stone," she said, as they headed towards the den. "And your time will come tonight."

"I can barely wait," he said and stared at the same girl she'd seen earlier, dressed in jeans, and a t-shirt, and a black leather jacket.

"Who's that?" she asked, and was more surprised when Jacob, with a mini hot dog in his hand, ran up to the girl, his face an expression of joy and surprise. Savannah watched in astonishment as the girl bent down and talked with her son.

"That," said Tobias slowly, "is Isabel Laronde. She's the one who saved Jacob."

"That's her?" Savannah murmured, and watched Jacob walk towards the game room with Isabel following.

"You said you wanted to meet her, and I finally managed to convince her to come."

"I need to speak to her." She tugged at his hand and started to head towards that direction because there was a lot she had to thank Isabel for. But another group of visitors all arriving together caught their attention. "Oh," she said, really happy to see them. "Look who's just arrived." Briony, Max and Candace hovered around the hallway. "I need to speak with Isabel first," she said.

"I'll be with you in a moment," Tobias said, leaving her. But as she walked past the kitchen, she caught sight of Rosalee talking to the catering staff. Savannah shook her head and walked over.

"Rosalee," she said, taking the woman's hand and pulling her away.

"I was talking to them!"

"You're not here to help, Rosalee. You're here to enjoy yourself." Rosalee patted her hand, smiling at her

"I *am* enjoying myself. I've done nothing but eat a bit of everything."

"And that's exactly what you should be doing," Savannah told her as they stood in the wide hallway. "Where are Eduardo and Juanita?" she asked, looking around for the rest of Rosalee's family.

"They weren't sure," explained Rosalee. "They thought they wouldn't know anyone."

"They knew me, and Jacob."

"That may be," replied Rosalee, "but they weren't sure."

Savannah understood their hesitation. "Tobias doesn't bite, Rosalee! But I understand."

"Diego is here," Rosalee said. "He went in there." She pointed towards the game room.

"Let's go see," Savannah suggested. They peered into the room full of boys gathered around different machines but the biggest draw appeared to be the gaming station. "Yes!" said Savannah, relieved. "They're fine." And Henry Carson wasn't running riot. Aside from an introductory welcome, she and the boy's parents hadn't exchanged much conversation. Savannah was glad that Julia was here. Lenny's mother was the social queen bee and Savannah saw her holding court with all the school moms outside on the terrace as they all clutched their glasses of pink champagne and exchanged animated conversation.

"Shall I get you some champagne? Or fruit juice?" Savannah asked, anxious to make Rosalee feel at home.

"Champagne would be nice."

"We have pink champagne," said Savannah, looking around for a server. "Let me get you some," she pulled away, but Rosalee took hold of her hand.

"Pink champagne, pink flowers, and you in a beautiful long dress and this beautiful ring," she said. "And you expect me to believe that this party was for no reason?"

"It's true," Savannah replied. "Tobias wasn't going to propose until we got to Miami—we're flying there straight after the party. But in the end, he just proposed on the spur of the moment."

Rosalee smiled for the longest time. "Look at you, Savannah," she said proudly. "You were a frightened, timid little thing when you first moved into Kay's apartment. You were worried about finding a job, worried about Jacob and his new school. You told me you wanted to do your own cleaning, but I could tell you were lonely and scared, and I didn't want to leave you alone."

"And you offered to babysit for me so that I could work. I'm so glad you were there to help me, Rosalee. I won't ever be able to thank you enough."

The two of them looked at one another with a deep understanding. "Let me get you that glass of champagne," Savannah said, feeling her emotions beginning to get the better of her. "Don't move."

She walked over to a server and picked up two glasses, then walked back towards Rosalee, who now appeared to be talking to Isabel. *Perfect*, thought Savannah.

"Thank you, darling." Max swiped a champagne glass out of her hand, and Briony took the other one, leaving Savannah empty-handed again.

"Jesus, hon," Briony gasped. "What the hell is that?"

"Darling," purred Max in amazement as she gawked at Savannah's ring. "Congratulations, you lying little minx! You told us this wasn't an engagement party! We haven't even brought a gift."

"Oh, hon," gushed Briony happily. "Congratulations. I hope both of you find the happiness you deserve."

"Thank you, but it's not an engagement party," Savannah insisted, happy to see them both.

"You've somehow managed to get engaged between Friday and today?" Briony asked, puzzled.

"That's kind of how it happened, yes."

"That looks like nothing less than a five-carat diamond and flawless, too, I would imagine," purred Max, lifting Savannah's hand high up as if it were a crystal glass.

"Oh, hon," said Briony. "I don't know what to say! Except maybe that I told you so." She hugged Savannah again, this time in a tight grip. "I'm so happy for you," she gushed. "I can't cry, I can't."

"I wouldn't want you to," replied Savannah, surprised by Briony's emotional outburst.

"That dress looks simply divine," Max declared, almost half-emptying her glass.

"I only bought it because it was on sale, and because *you* persuaded me to," Savannah told her.

"I've got good taste, haven't I, darling?" Max took another sip from her glass. "This is wonderful!" she cried. "What is it? Leclerc Briant Brut Rose or Laurent Perrier Cuvee Rose?"

"I have no idea," confessed Savannah.

"Are we going to get a wedding in the Hamptons?" Briony asked.

"We'll need to get started on your wedding dress," said Max, "I have ideas."

"Stop that! Both of you both," cried Savannah, hushing them. "I haven't had a moment to think about that." If only they knew what had happened yesterday. Wedding preparations where the last thing on her mind.

"Do you think Tobias might be persuaded to become a sperm donor?" Max asked. Savannah almost choked at her words.

"Has she told you yet?" Max asked.

"Told me what?" Savannah tried to look as innocent as she could.

"Let me tell you *our* news," Max said, lowering her voice and moving her head closer to Savannah, away from prying ears. "We're planning on having a baby."

Savannah opened her mouth in mock surprise.

"Or adopting one," added Briony. "We're still negotiating the finer points." She rolled her eyes at Savannah when Max wasn't looking.

"Are you really?" exclaimed Savannah. "What a surprise."

"I know," beamed Max. "I'm so excited." But Briony looked quite the opposite. Not wanting to be caught in the middle of a potential domestic dispute at her own party, Savannah looked around and at that moment, she saw Isabel Laronde walking towards her with a bottle of beer in her hand. "I'll be back," she said, "just a moment," and escaped.

"Isabel?" she said, as Isabel stopped in front of her.

"Savannah? Jacob's mom?"

Savannah nodded, and hugged her at once. "I've been wanting to meet you for a long time," she gushed. "I wanted to thank you for what you did."

"You don't have to thank me," Isabel replied, looking a little uncomfortable as she chewed her gum.

"But I do," Savannah insisted. "You saved my little boy from something that doesn't bear thinking about."

"I'd have done that for anyone. I could see it wasn't right. He didn't look happy and I could tell." She nodded, and chewed, and looked around. "This is a pretty cool place," she said. "I wasn't going to come but Mr. Stone insisted, he said it meant a lot to you to meet me. So," she said, blowing a chewing gum bubble, "here I am."

"Thank you."

Isabel shrugged. "You already said that, but it's fine, I get it. I would have done that for anyone. She looked odd, you know, and Jacob looked terrified. It was so not right. Hey!" she said loudly, when a gazelle-like woman brushed past her in a hurry. She'd knocked Isabel's arm, causing the beer to spill onto her jacket sleeve and hands.

"Sorry," Xavier said, following the gazelle. "Oh, just go then," he muttered angrily to himself and stopped. "Sorry about that," he said, grabbing a couple of napkins from the passing server and handing them to Isabel.

"She should be," Isabel muttered crossly, wiping the beer spillage from her hands and jacket.

"What's happened?" Savannah asked, although she could guess.

"I'm not going after her," he said, exhaling heavily as if he'd just lifted a heavy weight. "I've had enough of her moods." Savannah gave him a knowing stare. *That* had been Petra, and *this* had been another drama.

"This is Isabel," she said, and stopped herself from introducing her as 'the woman that saved Jacob.' "This is Xavier, Tobias's brother."

They looked at one another dubiously.

# CHAPTER TWENTY-FIVE

He couldn't believe the transformation. She had put the ugliness of yesterday behind her, and when she'd stepped out wearing that dress, and his ring, and that smile, it gave him a warm and fuzzy feeling all over.

She'd said yes.

Not that he'd ever doubted she would say anything else. But still, with Savannah Page and her million doubts and excuses, he couldn't be completely sure.

The blood had been cleaned up and all traces of Matthias's visit had been wiped clean, and now the apartment was ablaze with life and color and warmth as their guests talked and laughed, clearly enjoying themselves.

Even Henry Carson and his dour-looking parents seemed to lighten up, and Henry, now that he was here, seemed to be playing well with Jacob. Maybe it was because he wanted to be seen with the boy who was suddenly the most popular, or maybe it was because all the kids were in awe of the game room, whatever it was, Tobias didn't care. Jacob looked like the king of the castle and that was all that mattered.

In fact, Jacob had been a picture of happiness ever since Savannah had accepted Tobias's proposal.

Tobias looked around the apartment and knew that this weekend would stand out in his life as a turning point with two events that would stay with him forever. Matthias's betrayal followed by Savannah's acceptance. Life's ups and downs.

He'd been keeping an eye out for Candace as he walked around meeting his guests, and just as he and Savannah were on their way to speak to Isabel Laronde, he saw his PA arrive with Briony and Max, looking polished and exuberant, and no doubt thrilled to be here.

It was time to uninvite her. Savannah had told him what Matthias had let slip, about Candace's involvement in Colt finding her and Jacob, and there was no way she could be his PA. He never wanted to set his eyes on her again, just as he never wished to cross paths with Matthias.

Excusing himself from Savannah, he rushed to intercept her as she made her way towards the terrace and reached her before she started to work the room, as he knew she would. "Candace."

"Tobias," she said, her face brightening. "You changed the flowers—"

"A word, please," he said, beckoning her to follow him. He walked out of the apartment and into the wide-open hallway.

She looked puzzled. "What is it?" she asked, her smooth face looking up at him without a clue.

He wasted no time. "You were the one who gave Savannah's ex-husband her home address."

Candace's lipstick-coated smile slid south. "How did—" She blinked a few times, then narrowed her eyes, her smooth face wrinkling. "Did Matthias—"

"Matthias no longer works for Stone Enterprises," he said, watching her reaction carefully.

"What?" She was shocked into silence.

"It's true. I'll leave it to Matthias to tell you." He was certain the two of them would get together. "As for you," he said, looking at her squarely in the eye, "your employment is terminated immediately and you are no longer welcome in my home."

The color drained from her face, and she opened her mouth. "Tobias," she began, a mixture of hurt and shock flashing across her features. "I didn't mean to—"

"You put Savannah's and Jacob's lives at risk. You should be thankful they weren't hurt because if they had been, I would have destroyed you by now."

"But, Tobias, I never meant to—"

"Leave," he said, "and don't make a scene."

"I'm sorry," she wailed, as he walked away. But he didn't care and he didn't turn around to look at her again. He walked back into the apartment and searched the room for Savannah, then found her talking to Max and Briony. And at that moment, he caught sight of Savannah's parents standing quietly in the corner, looking a little uneasy.

He walked straight over to them. "Dale, Jean," he said, greeting them warmly. "I'm so pleased to see you." They made small talk and he thanked them for coming, knowing that he had to be careful not to give away Jean's sixtieth birthday surprise. "Was the flight all right?"

"Yes, thank you," her mother replied.

"Thank you for coming," he said to her father, the two men exchanged a knowing glance. He had arranged for them to fly up yesterday then put them up at one of New York's finest hotels, and he'd insisted on arranging a flight back for them tonight knowing that they had to go back to work tomorrow, before Dale swept his wife off for a surprise sixtieth birthday cruise two days later.

"We're so excited," said her mother. "Does she have any idea what you're about to do?"

"Actually," he said, eyeing Savannah with two more glasses of pink champagne in her hands. He was about to tell them that he hadn't thrown the party in order to propose to her, "I've already proposed, and she's accepted."

"Oh, how wonderful!" Jean cried, looking at her husband. "Isn't it the best news, Dale?"

"Mom! Dad!" They turned to find Savannah flying towards them and in the next moment, they exchanged excited greetings mixed with surprise, elation and congratulations. "I didn't know you were coming," Savannah exclaimed.

"We wanted to surprise you, Ruby Red."

"But you have 'work commitments'" she said to her father knowingly. "Don't you?"

"Your young man kindly arranged for us to come for one night. We're flying back this evening."

Savannah's face glowed with happiness when she looked at him and she didn't need to voice her thanks because he could see it so clearly in her eyes.

"You're too generous for your own good, Tobias," her father said. "And we are grateful for your generosity." He'd paid, because he wanted them here, and he didn't want to dwell on that any longer.

"Oh, my." Her mother gasped. "Would you take a look at that ring?"

"Ruby Red," said her father, staring at the huge diamond. "Well, I'll be damned. I hope you're not planning on wearing that out in the open."

"She'll be fine, sir," said Tobias, reassuring him. "Her security is always my main priority."

"I can't believe you're here," Savannah said, the excitement in her voice still evident.

"I can't believe you're engaged. Come here, dear," said her mother, overcome with emotion.

"Where's Jacob?" Her father asked, looking around.

"He's in the game room," replied Tobias, "or he was when I last checked on him."

"Let me take you there," offered Savannah.

Tobias saw a familiar figure out on the terrace. "Are you coming?" Savannah asked him.

"You go," he said. "I'll come find you." He wanted Savannah to meet the man who'd had such an impact on his life but first he needed to speak with him alone.

Becker Schwartz had made it after all. This was a surprise. Tobias had called his mentor on the phone late last night, overcome by the need to speak to him about the betrayal that had cut deep. And though he'd invited Becker to the party weeks ago, Tobias knew how busy the old man was these days, sailing the ocean and enjoying his well-earned retirement. It meant a lot to Tobias that he'd actually shown up at all.

"Becker," he said, his smile as wide as the ocean as he greeted his friend. Tobias hugged him tightly, even though it hadn't been that long since they'd last met. He took the man's arm and guided him out towards the terrace. "Thank you for coming," he said, "especially since I only spoke to you last night and you were in Santa Barbara then." He grinned.

"The benefits of owning a personal jet, as you well know." Becker replied with a knowing smile. "I had to come." He held up his glass up towards Central Park with the New York skyline in the distance. "Beautiful view, isn't it? I love this city," he said, sniffing the air with a sigh of contentment. "This place lives in my bones."

"And yet you continue to spend your life in the most exotic of places," Tobias joked. "And deservedly so."

"I have a yacht and I want to see the world, but I'll always come back home. This is all that matters, Tobias. This and roots, and having a reason for the things we do, a 'why.' We always need a 'why.'"

"I know."

"It's even more important in our business where we deal with obscene amounts of money," Becker said, "and soon it ceases to hold real value. The numbers become bigger and bigger and cease to be currency. They're just numbers. That's when greed kicks in." The old man paused for a short while, thinking. "Unless you are grounded, unless you have a 'why' behind you, it's easy to become obsessed by the numbers and to chase them the way an addict would chase their next hit. It's a shame about Matthias. I've been thinking about him ever since you told me what had happened. I had hoped he'd have calmed down a little, settled down even, or at least found his 'why,' his reason for living. Once you've achieved a certain level, it's no longer about the money. It's about the power it gives you. I can't say that I'm surprised by his motives, but I am disappointed. Badly disappointed in him, but," he sighed, and his baggy eyes looked downwards, "such is life and that was his choice. Now *you*," he said, prodding Tobias's chest with his index finger. "You seem to have found your way again, son. I can't tell you how happy that makes me. You lost it for a while back there, but that was to be expected. Any normal person who loses so much would have done what you did but it warms my heart to see you grounded and happy again. I've been watching the two of you together and it's as plain to see as anything, how happy she makes you. You'll have to introduce us."

"I will."

"And Tobias," he said, "you put the rest of that business behind you now."

"I have, I will," Tobias replied. Ugliness had no part in today for him but he knew that this whole business with Matthias and

Candace, as well as Yanling and Naomi would stay with him. The only thing that made the wound less bloody was to learn that Naomi's involvement had been forced upon her—to an extent. She could have refused, but she must have been desperate to resort to such measures.

"You'll be fine, son."

And he would, too.

"Time to make a short speech, I think," Tobias said, looking around. Only a short speech, for he knew Savannah would have a heart attack the moment he started to talk.

He looked around and saw her standing with Isabel.

"Excuse me," he said to Becker, then walked to the center of the living room and raised his voice, asking for a moment of everyone's time.

"I'd like to take a few moments to say some words," he said, looking all around him at the sea of smiling faces which were turned eagerly towards him. He couldn't help but smile as Jacob, followed by his gang, slowly traipsed out of the game room and hovered around the edges of the room. A glance at Savannah's suddenly tight and unmoving face, while she held the champagne glass frozen in her hand, prompted him to make this a quick speech.

"I will keep this short, because my fiancée wouldn't want me to take up any more of your time. I want to thank you all for coming today. Many of you have wondered why we decided to have this party. Many of you have been wondering what we were celebrating. And many of you believe this was carefully orchestrated. The truth is, I've learned that nothing can be carefully orchestrated, not really, not in the way I'm used to orchestrating my takeovers and financial moves. Savannah Page is another thing altogether." A chorus of laughter rolled around the room but Savannah looked as nervous as hell. She gripped her champagne glass as if it were a panic button.

"The truth is, Savannah has taken over my heart." A murmur fell and there was complete silence. "It's been a long time since this apartment was filled with so many people and with so much laughter, though lately I've had my fair share of laughter listening to Jacob." He smiled at the boy and Jacob smiled shyly back. "Savannah and Jacob have brought love and laughter back into my life and they've made me believe I'm worthy of it once more. So, you see, I have much to be grateful for and today is an acknowledgement of that gratitude, of appreciating what I have, and having you all, my friends and my family, and now this beautiful woman and Jacob by my side." He winced at her apologetically as all their guests turned to look at her.

Tobias continued, "The reason I wanted to throw this party was because it's been a while since I gathered together all the people who have shaped me and supported me through various points in my life. The fact is, I wasn't going to propose to Savannah just yet. That's not the reason for this party, but let's just say it happened and I'm relieved that she accepted." More laughter and cheers. "We would like to thank you all for coming, and please, continue to enjoy yourselves."

He walked over to Savannah as people clapped all around him. He grabbed her hand as the noise in the room faded into the background.

"That wasn't so bad, was it?" he asked.

"The champagne helped," she said, leading him away. People smiled and congratulated them as she led him to the far side of the terrace which was as yet relatively empty since most people were still cloistered together indoors.

"Did you really mean that?" asked Jacob, running up to them. Henry and Lenny followed.

"Which part?"

"When you said we gave you love and laughter."

"Yes, son," Tobias replied. "I really meant that." He ruffled the boy's hair when Jacob smiled in response. His friends stood silently behind him, looking on.

"Are you enjoying yourselves?" Tobias asked them. They both nodded. "And you've already met Jacob's mother?" he looked directly at Henry.

"Let them play, Tobias," Savannah said, in a voice quiet enough so that only he could hear. Tobias continued.

"We've heard lots of things about you, Henry," said Tobias as he felt Savannah's fingers digging into him gently, a warning. "And I hope that from now on, we'll only hear *good* things about you from Jacob because I don't want to hear that anyone is being mean to him." Savannah's fingers dug deeper into his hands. Henry looked petrified.

"That's enough, Tobias," Savannah whispered. "Why don't you go play, boys," she suggested, and off they ran. "You can't do that," she said, as a smattering of guests walked onto the terrace and stood in a small cluster at the other end.

"He shouldn't have said those nasty things."

"He's a child."

"He should know better."

"Shush," she said. "What if his parents hear you?" She glanced quickly over her shoulder.

"And what if they did?"

"It comes from his parents," she whispered. "You can't blame a child that young."

"You've done a great job with Jacob."

"Thank you," she said, as he curved an arm around her back and placed his hand on her waist.

"I wanted to call you up to stand beside me when I made the speech," he said, dropping a kiss on her cheek. "But I could see you didn't want me to, so I didn't ask."

She tilted her face towards him. "I will be ready," she assured, "but it will take some time. I'll get there."

"I know. And you can take all the time you need. I know all of this will take some getting used to but you've handled everything just fine so far." He splayed his fingers along her side and squeezed her gently while thinking he couldn't wait to get to Miami. Three glorious weeks away, and this time he'd need to keep a closer eye on the business now with Matthias out of the picture.

He'd need to replace him and Candace quickly. He was about to tell Savannah that he'd fired Candace, but decided she didn't need to know right now, and he didn't need to tarnish this day.

"You were saying I've done a great job with Jacob," she whispered, dropping her voice lower. "I hope that together we'll do a great job with the next one." He barely had time to acknowledge her words when she leaned her body into his and she whispered into his ear. "I stopped taking my pills as of yesterday."

His mouth fell open and a joyous surge of happiness swirled around in his chest. "You did?"

She nodded.

"Are you sure about having another baby, Savannah? It's got to be something *you* want, not something you're doing for me."

"I want your baby, Tobias."

He felt a chill, not of fear, but of something else, of excitement, and anticipation, of the kind of life he'd closed himself away from, of the possibilities that now lay ahead of him. A baby. He smiled and kissed her again, breathing in her summer scent of fresh apples and flowers.

It didn't matter that Matthias and Candace were gone. Those people were replaceable. *This* was what mattered;

Savannah, and Jacob, and more children. Something more meaningful than money and property. A legacy of love.

Together, they looked out at the New York skyline while the sound of happy chatter floated around them, mingling with the warm and balmy summer air.

Thank you for reading THE VOW, BOOKS 1-3! I hope you loved The Billionaire's Love Story as much as I loved writing it.

**I have written a bonus epilogue for Tobias, Savannah and Jacob which you can get by subscribing to my newsletter.**

While Tobias and Savannah's main story ends here, you can still get glimpses into their lives in THE BET (which is Xavier's story). It begins with Tobias and Savannah's wedding!

**He thinks he's god's gift to women. She thinks he's a sex-mad jerk. For $10k he'll prove he can win her over.**

Driving a Ferrari 488, living in Tribeca, and running businesses that spit out $$$, Xavier Stone is living the dream. He can, and often does, have any woman he wants.

Except for Isabel Laronde. That chick is something else.

And right now, she's not interested.

I've also written a short story which takes place after THE VOW. It's called THE WISH and it's not on sale at any ebook retailer. This is a gift to my existing newsletter subscribers and it is FREE. If you haven't subscribed, you can do so here: http://www.lilyzante.com/newsletter

I appreciate your help in spreading the word, including telling a friend, and I would be grateful if you could leave a review on your favorite book site.

You can read an excerpt from **THE BET** at the end of this book.

Thank you and happy reading!
Lily

## PREVIEW: THE BET

**"O**ne woman, for life. Hell, no."

Xavier had waited until Tobias was well out of earshot to state his observation. They were sitting outside on leather couches, on the rooftop terrace of The Oasis, the bar his friend owned.

Tobias was flying Luke and his team to his wedding on Kawaya, his 300-acre private island in Fiji. Luke and his staff were taking care of the drinks for the four-day wedding extravaganza.

"He's your brother. Be happy for him," Luke drawled.

"I *am* happy for him," Xavier insisted. Tobias seemed more relaxed these days, and it was all due to Savannah and Jacob. "It was about time he met someone. I could say the same about you." He glanced at his friend, but Luke kept quiet.

"Not me." Luke shook his head. "I'm too busy to be dealing with women."

Girlish laughter bubbled around the room making Xavier glance over his shoulder. Even though it was late evening and the night sky had darkened to a rich navy-blue, the soft lights from the lamps made it easy to see everyone. He raised his glass to the group of women who sat around a table scattered with jewel-colored cocktails. A couple of them acknowledged him with an interested smile.

"Know them?" he asked his friend. Luke seemed to know everyone who came here.

"Lawyers and legal eagles, celebrating an engagement. That's all you need to know."

Xavier eyed them slowly, his gaze lasering in on a woman with long wavy hair and what looked like a big and beautiful pair of breasts. His mouth watered at the sight of her hard-to-miss nipples poking through her silk dress. He flashed a smile at her, appreciating the view.

Even with the slight chill in the air—a promise, in this last week of September that fall was around the corner, it wasn't that cold because of all the heaters Luke had placed around the terrace. Or maybe the woman wasn't cold and was just excited to see him.

"Quit bugging my clientele."

"I don't see them complaining." Xavier lifted his beer bottle to his lips.

"That's because they don't complain to you."

"Bullshit." Xavier looked at his friend dubiously. "Nobody's ever complained to you about me. You're making that shit up."

On second thoughts, it was probably better not to risk anything while Tobias was around. With his wedding to Savannah a week away, his brother could sometimes get easily irritated. In fact his family, especially his parents, seemed to get annoyed when it came to Xavier and his love life. He didn't understand why. He was young. Maybe not *so* young. But twenty-seven wasn't exactly old.

Tobias was going to celebrate his thirtieth birthday the day before he got married. Talk about hitting two major milestones one after the other.

Luke's gaze drifted to the table of women before returning to him again. "Is Xavier 'The Stud' Stone in action again? Won't your girlfriend mind?"

Xavier rolled his eyes at the mention of the nickname Luke had given him many years ago. "I'm only looking." Gisele wouldn't like him ogling other women, but she wasn't here, and he wasn't about to do anything silly. He wasn't that much of a douchebag. "You all set for the wedding? All set to show off your mixologist skills?" he asked, his fingers curling around the glass bottle.

"Don't call me a mixologist. I don't need any fancy, stupid labels."

"Okay, calm down." But Xavier guessed that his cocktail-making skills behind the bar helped him pick up a lot of girls. Not that the dude needed to be behind the bar. "Think of the shit ton of publicity you're going to get from it."

"That's not why I'm doing it," Luke protested.

Xavier snorted in disbelief. "It's not as if you would have turned this opportunity down." It was *Tobias Stone's* wedding, for fuck's sake.

"Tobias doesn't want any press,"

It was true. Tobias was an intensely private person. "My brother's anal like that."

Luke leaned forward. His sleeves had been rolled up, revealing hard, tattooed forearms that had Xavier wondering if he should get a couple of tattoos himself. Chicks loved that stuff. And that, along with the handful of bars and clubs Luke owned in and around New York, made him a babe magnet. Xavier envied him a little, and for having a thriving business which didn't seem like that much hard work.

"I don't blame him. He wants no paparazzi and nothing leaked. I respect that, and I haven't told anyone outside of my team. My staff is discreet, and they won't leak anything to the press. I'm honored that Tobias asked me."

"He's asked you based on *my* recommendation."

"He's been here plenty of times without you."

Xavier scratched the side of his jaw. "When?" Tobias wasn't a party animal. "He'd rather watch the stock market than hang out in a bar."

"He's been here a few times with Savannah." Luke's eyes twinkled. He seemed to be enjoying the telling of this news. Xavier angled his head. Yeah, well, things were slightly different now that his brother had met Savannah. These days Tobias was a changed man who had gone from spending most of his time in the office to actually having a life outside it.

Another shriek of laughter bubbled across from the table behind him, forcing him to cast another look over his shoulder. He quickly scanned around the table and zeroed in on the same woman again. His gaze settled on her a moment longer than usual, until she returned the stare, and then he turned his back on her.

*Show interest, but not too much. Raise their hopes, get them excited, and then pull back.*

"His fiancée seems like a nice girl," Luke said. "And he looks happy."

"He is. He never used to go out much. I had to drag him out so he could mingle and get some pussy."

Luke slanted an eyebrow. "That was considerate of you."

"I thought so, too." Xavier leaned in, eager to know. "Are you getting any?" Luke's mouth twisted as if he was trying to formulate an appropriate reply.

"For a twenty-seven-year-old, you still talk like a teen."

"I'm being serious, dude."

"I am too. Quit the pussy talk."

*Quit the pussy talk?* It made him wonder. "Are you batting for the other side?"

"You idiot." Luke gave him one of his you're-a-shithead looks. "Some of us don't like to talk about it as much as you do."

"Where were we?" Tobias rejoined them, slipping his cell phone away.

"You were about to order a glass of whiskey," Xavier replied, then raised his hand to summon a server. He should have ordered Tobias a drink while he was taking his call.

Tobias turned to Luke. "Do you have everything under control?"

"It's all taken care of," Luke assured him. "I've met with your security guys. We arrive the morning of your birthday, and I'll be there to oversee everything. You don't have to worry about a thing."

The server placed the whiskey glass down, and Xavier slid it over to Tobias. "Here you go, bro."

Tobias dismissed it with a wave of his hand. "No thanks. I'm good."

"Since when did you give up drinking?"

Tobias gave him a hard stare. "I haven't. I don't need one now. Get me a Coke, will you?"

"Coming up." He caught the server's attention again and ordered the drink before turning to Tobias. "You need to loosen up."

"I still have work to do before we fly out. We can't all work from home in our PJs."

Luke sniggered. "What is it that you do again? I've never been able to figure it out."

Tobias grinned back at him. "Let me know when you find out, because I still can't figure it out myself."

"He drives a 488 Spider, though," Luke remarked casually. "He can't be doing too badly."

It ground on his nerves, the two of them talking about him like this. "I'm here, guys. I'm right here. And I'm doing fine." Xavier raised his bottle and waved it at the two of them for ganging up on him. Tobias and him were opposites. His brother was far too rigid, far too organized. But then, he was a billionaire running a hedge fund. People thought that because he was Tobias Stone's brother, that he was as successful, and as wealthy. He was nowhere near a billionaire, and never would be, and he'd almost made it to millionaire status a couple of times.

Sad thing was, a million was nothing in today's world. You had to have at least ten mill to get by. "Not all of us get Daddy's trust fund." This was aimed at Luke.

"I gave my old man the middle finger," Luke shot back. "And I'm building my empire with my own blood, sweat and tears. I haven't taken a cent from *Daddy*."

Tobias listened and nodded his head. He didn't need to say anything because he was a self-made billionaire who counted politicians and captains of industry as his friends. Not particularly close friends, Xavier assumed, but close enough that he could call them up if needed.

It wasn't that Xavier was jealous, but he knew he couldn't rival that. He had never been as smart, or as astute as his brother, and he was painfully aware of the fact. "Laugh all you want, but I've been creating and running businesses ever since I quit high school," he said, a little too defensively. "And I can afford the Ferrari just fine." He lifted his chin in defiance.

"To confirm," said Tobias, ignoring him and turning to Luke again. "Do you have the agenda?"

Luke nodded.

"And you've signed the agreement?"

"Yes. No talking to the press, no pictures, no exclusives for any of the papers or magazines. Understood and noted."

Xavier suppressed a breath. His brother's paranoia bordered on OCD at times. He took a swig of his drink and listened to Tobias and Luke discussing the wedding details. He felt like a third party in a business meeting for two.

He was happy for Tobias. Of course he was, and it was about time things turned around for him, especially after what had happened with Ivy. But honestly, aside from that huge life-changing event, things had always gone pretty smoothly for his brother.

Unfortunately, for himself, things weren't so easy. Business had been slow lately. He didn't have the smarts and the genius to run a hedge fund, but he'd had to find his own way.

He wasn't living off of Tobias's generosity, nor did he want to. The problem with starting and running lots of small businesses, trying and failing many times over before finding a few that worked, was that it wasn't consistent. He was always looking for new business opportunities. But when he made money, and sold a business off, or made good with the stock market, he did pretty well. Well enough to afford a Ferrari and a loft conversion in Tribeca. Well enough to easily afford thousand-dollar bottles of champagne when he needed to impress.

But things hadn't been as great ever since he and Petra had broken up. She had been his lucky mascot but ever since the split, at Tobias's party back in July, he hadn't seen her. A week later he'd heard she was doing the rounds with a quarterback from the Miami Dolphins.

Not that he'd been lonely for long. Shacking up with Gisele, a cute B-list actress, had relieved him of too much wrist action.

He looked up as a gorgeous woman swept past their table, then stopped and stepped back, placing her hand on Luke's shoulder and greeting him. Xavier eyed her butt as she talked to Luke, flirting with him like a nymph. Her hand slid down his arm, fingering his skin and tracing over his tattoos. "Come on over and say 'hi,' when you've finished, stranger." Her pomegranate red nails squeezed his friend's bicep as a parting gesture. Xavier watched her until she was out of sight, and then turned his attention back to the conversation.

"I think we're done," said Tobias, getting up and shaking hands with Luke. "See you in Kawaya."

"Thank you, for the opportunity." Luke looked chuffed as he got off from his stool then excused himself.

"Lucky son-of-a-bitch," Xavier sniped, watching Luke and the woman talking. "I bet he has everyone's number." It seemed like a waste because for all the phone numbers Luke might have had, Xavier hadn't seen him with anyone for a long time.

Tobias gave him another one of his steely looks. "You're like a walking hard-on."

"This place is full of beautiful women, what do you expect?" The brunette on that table was giving him the come on. His mind was already in the gutter, and he could see by the way she licked her lips that hers wasn't far behind.

"You haven't confirmed if your girlfriend is coming."

"Would you mind if she did?" His mother would give him a hard time, and he would have to make sure she didn't get her claws into Gisele for too long.

"I don't care if she does or not," replied Tobias icily. "But if her coming stops you from hitting on all my guests, then go for it."

"You have the wrong impression of me, bro."

"Do I?" Tobias sounded testy. "If she comes, she'd better stick to my privacy policy."

That's what he was worried about. He wasn't sure Gisele could keep her mouth shut. She was easily impressed, and a little too text-happy. Each time they went out, she'd take pictures and post them to her social media accounts before they'd even had dessert.

"If she's not on Vivian's list, she's not getting in."

Tobias and his goddamn lists. Xavier didn't envy Vivian, Tobias's new PA, the task of organizing the list of attendees. This 'small' wedding was turning out to be a security nightmare, and Xavier was still none the wiser as to what had happened to Candace, Tobias's previous PA.

He'd had her once, in the supply cupboard in The Vault, Luke's club in the basement. He'd had her up against the door with her legs wrapped around his waist, and her panties around one ankle. Maybe he shouldn't have, what with her being Tobias's PA, but the girl was a flirt, and she'd wanted it. And he had been single at the time.

It had been a simple case of supply and demand.

Maybe it was as well that she had left, or had been fired, or whatever. Even Matthias, who had been a close friend of his brother's for as long as he could remember, had left at the same time, and Xavier was still none the wiser as to what had happened to either of them.

Tobias refused to discuss it.

Xavier ventured another try, at the risk of getting shot down, as he had on the other occasions. "Are Candace and Matthias coming?"

"No." The tone of Tobias's voice warned him against probing further.

He could take the hint. He knew that if someone pissed Tobias off, his brother would cut them off and be done with them.

"You're flying with Mom and Dad, right?" Tobias asked, indicating the topic was done with.

"Yup."

Fuck, yes. Xavier's insides tanked at the thought.

Gisele *had* to come, if only to be a distraction. The seventeen-hour flight from New York to Fiji, with a stop in LA, was tough enough, and if his parents were going to be on the same flight, it was going to be Hell on Earth. On landing, they had to take a small plane or a boat from the main airport to Kawaya.

The thought of being stuck on the flight made his stomach churn. "Shame you decided to go a few days beforehand." Otherwise, they could all have traveled on Tobias's private jet, and it would have made the journey bearable.

"It's my wedding, and I'll do whatever the hell I want." Tobias was traveling a few days earlier with Savannah and Jacob. Everyone else was coming a few days later on commercial flights, all paid for by Tobias.

With it taking almost an entire day to get there, then four days on the island and a day to get back, it was going to be nearly a whole goddamn week. He had to make sure Gisele came along because, in that heat, with his parents and god knows who else, on an island that was remote; he'd go crazy unless he had something to do. And *doing* Gisele would be the best way of passing the time.

Tobias gulped down his drink and announced that he was leaving.

"Already?"

He'd been hoping to hang around The Oasis for longer and spend some increasingly rare time with his brother who he barely got to see much these days. It used to be the case that he could convince Tobias to come out every few months. Xavier used to insist on it just to get his workaholic brother out into the world of the living. But, ever since he had met and fallen in love with Savannah and her young son, Jacob, his brother no longer seemed to have much time for anyone else. Xavier missed that, a little.

"Has Savannah ordered you to be home for dinner?" The idea of domestic bliss bored the hell out of him.

"I promised Jacob I'd be home early."

Xavier's eyebrows shot north. Pretty soon Tobias Stone's household would be like *The Waltons*. Saccharine bliss.

Enough to make him want to puke. What the hell had happened to the man once dubbed New York's most eligible bachelor? Not that Tobias had ever been a player but, as Gisele had shown him on one of those stupid online celebrity websites, his brother still held strong on the list. It didn't seem to matter that Tobias Stone was getting married. But what irritated him was seeing that he was number seven. And what pissed him off even more was finding out that Luke was number four.

*Number fucking four.*

And the man didn't even seem to be interested in chicks.

As for himself, he knew why he was so far down the list. He was nowhere near as wealthy as Tobias.

He wasn't a billionaire.

*Yet.*

And if truth be told, he wasn't so sure he wanted to work that hard to become one. He was doing pretty well as he was.

# ACKNOWLEDGMENTS

I would like to thank my wonderful group of proofreaders who check my manuscript for the errors, typos and weird words and phrases which sometimes find their way into my story. These ladies give me the confidence to release each book and I am eternally grateful for their help and support:

Sherrie Brown
Marcia Chamberlain
Nancy Dormanski
April Lowe
Dena Pugh
Charlotte Rebelein
Carole Tunstall

I would also like to thank Tatiana Vila for creating my awesome covers:
**www.viladesign.net**

# ABOUT THE AUTHOR

Lily Zante lives with her husband and three children somewhere near London, England.

## Connect with Me

I love hearing from you – so please don't be shy! Email me, message me on Facebook or connect with me.

Join my Facebook reader group
Follow me on BookBub
Follow me on Amazon
Follow me on Goodreads

**| TikTok | Instagram |Facebook | Website | Twitter | Email**

amazon.com/author/lilyzante
facebook.com/LilyZanteRomanceAuthor
twitter.com/lilyzantebooks
instagram.com/authorlilyzante
goodreads.com/authorlilyzante
bookbub.com/authors/lily-zante

Made in the USA
Las Vegas, NV
26 May 2024

90386155R00288